The Frogs of War

ALSO BY ANDREW HARMAN

The Sorcerer's Appendix
The Tome Tunnel
101 Damnations
Farenheit 666
The Scrying Game
The Deity Dozen
A Midsummer Night's Gene

THE FROGS OF WAR

Andrew Harman

ORBIT

An *Orbit* Book

First published in Great Britain by Legend Books 1994
Reprinted by Orbit 1997

Copyright © Andrew Harman 1994

The moral right of the author has been asserted.

A CIP catalogue record for this book
is available from the British Library.

ISBN 1 85723 588 6

Printed and bound in Great Britain by
Mackays of Chatham PLC, Chatham, Kent

Orbit
A Division of
Little, Brown and Company (UK)
Brettenham House
Lancaster Place
London WC2E 7EN

For Mum and Dad.
   A great big 'thanks' for supplying the cerebral skirting board for smashing my mental Dinky toys against!

And a huge 'thumbs up' to John for being mad enough . . .

'Come to Daddy . . .'

It was almost as if the weather could sense that something extremely unpleasant was about to happen. Almost as if the million-volt flashes of lightning, searing earthwards through the dark curtains of pre-dawn rain, were the involuntary nervous twitches of some giant meteorological mind quivering behind the sofa after an all-night horror-movie binge. The particularly unpleasant something would happen here. It would happen soon.

A giant crash of thunder shattered the sizzling silence of the torrential rain and echoed away over the mountains.

In a room standing as naked as the day it was built, stripped of anything even remotely inflammable and metaphorically blushing without even the smallest of tapestries to hide its architectural modesty, the Thaumaturgical Physicists of Losa Llamas made final feverish preparations. In the din of the rain which cascaded down in lashing waves and the elemental tantrum the tall black-cloaked figure of Arathoostra handed a heavy-set man a piece of chalk, five candlesticks, a protractor, a slide-rule and pointed impatiently at the centre of the cold stone floor.

'C'mon, Alsos,' snapped Arathoostra. 'Hurry it up! We haven't got all night.' His grey-blue eyes flashed with eager excitement as he watched Alsos begin to measure out a series of lines and angles, fingering his lab-cloak and nervously tapping his pointy feet as he watched the shape form. Arathoostra revelled in the smug knowledge that soon they would set their collective shoulder of thaumic research hard against the barriers of ignorance and together, in one unified effort, force them back, splitting them asunder and letting in the light of intelligence. The glorious spotlight of 'military intelligence'. He was blissfully

1

unaware of that particular mutually exclusive concept.

Another torrent of rain crashed against the tiny window high in the stone wall, temporarily drowning the nerve-shredding sound of scratching chalk.

'Stop making it squeak like that!' snapped Arathoostra, kicking out at the kneeling figure of Alsos. 'You know I hate it. You're doing it on purpose, aren't you! Like you always do with your fingernails on the blackboard.'

'No . . . I,' began Alsos.

'Get on with it!' shouted Arathoostra.

Phlim brushed his long brown hair out of his eyes and rummaged in the capacious pockets of his lab-cloak, eventually pulling out five tall, tallow candles. Nervously he twisted the wicks until they were ready to light. Why it had to be *him* that lit the candles he didn't know. Silently he cursed Arathoostra as he blew several strands of hair out of his eye and attended to another wick.

To everyone's relief the sound of grating chalk on stone stopped and Alsos stood, moved away from the geometric shape, and addressed the group. He pointed to the five-cornered figure on the floor. 'My responsibility for the Pentagon has been despatched,' he said, 'It is ready.' A blast of cold blue light flashed and died outside, followed almost instantly by the type of deafening crash usually produced by several thousand tons of collapsing glacier. The eye of the storm moved in for a closer look.

Phlim edged forward and began arranging the candles at each corner of the chalk Pentagon, his hands shaking as he took out the box of matches. He prayed silently to fifteen randomly selected deities from the Thousand Fanatical Gods of Sweetly Favourable Assistance, whistled a swift psalm to soothe the soul of Aggrho the God of Petulant Misfortunes and gulped nervously as his troubled thoughts flashed back to the strings of calculations scribbled on the huge black-board upstairs. Mentally he retraced his finger as he checked, double-checked and checked again. He couldn't see any mistake. The figures were right. With a start he relived the bolt of fear as he had realised . . . too much energy in too small a space! Oh God! Any God! Is there anybody there?

He recalled silently the head-scratching months of brain-numbing calculations made by the whole team, trying desperately to disprove his theory. They looked at the size of critical matter, the inherent background decay constants, the rapid rupture coefficients and it all pointed to the same conclusion. If the ensuing implosion wasn't contained accurately by the thaumaturgic wave guides, and the sophistry coefficient fell below 4.8, the energy build-up would cause fusion of the helium nuclei resulting in instantaneous world-wide atmospheric combustion. This had all led up to Phlim's deeply scientific comment, 'Woooof! There goes the neigh-bourhood!' In the few areas which escaped utter incinera-tion,* oxygen depletion would soon take its deadly toll. He shuddered as he thought of the engulfing flames and dropped the matches. Arathoostra turned on the trembling thau-maturgist. 'Are you *still* fussing about the sophistry coeffi-cient?' he barked. 'We've been through it a hundred times. The figures are correct, the Pentagon *is* the right size. There'll be *no* problem. Trust me!' he sneered with all the trustworthiness of a viper. 'Light the candles – you're wasting time!'

Phlim grinned feebly, brushed his hair away from his eyes and struck a match. With theatrical timing so devastating that it *had* to be coincidence, three million volts of static electricity discharged directly overhead with a brain-wrenching combination of blinding blue-white light and ear-numbing thunderclap. Phlim screamed, dropping the unlit match, the hairs on the back of his neck bristling in fear and crackling electric tension. Arathoostra rolled his eyes and uttered an oath beneath his breath.

Phlim trembled as he pulled another match out of the box and attempted to light it. His hands shook violently as he

*For instance, five miles down in the Mreeyannus Trench in the Pathetic Ocean.

placed the head on the roughened strip. He closed his eyes, concentrating hard, snapping the thin shaft as he shook once again. Cursing violently he flung the tiny broken stick across the room, biting his lip and breathing fast as he pulled out another. He hated fire. Practz could stand it no longer; he gently removed the box from Phlim's quivering hands and in a moment five tallow candles spluttered in gloomy anticipation of the event to come.

Now the scene was set. The candles cast five pools of yellow, shaky light onto the cold stone floor. The group of four Thaumaturgical Physicists stood in a square surrounding the Pentagon, three waiting apprehensively for the fourth's command. Arathoostra flexed his long fingers and swam in the anticipatory throb of these last few minutes, like some cliff-diver standing cruciform atop a vast precipice certain in the knowledge that one step forward and the future would all be different, he would be committed, no turning back if the tide was out. This whole project had been his idea, his baby. Only he had any real idea what the potential outcome of this next few hours would be. That was, if the great cosmic coast-guard hadn't lied about the phase of the tides.

Arathoostra's grey-blue eyes turned a shade bluer, as they had a tendency to do when he was angry or excited. He was the driving force behind this entire experiment and it was on his tall, thin shoulders that the responsibility of starting the chant rested. He pulled the hood of his lab-cloak up and over his mat of black curly hair, preparing himself for the most momentous moments of his career to date. Alsos, Practz and Phlim pulled at their hoods and stood waiting. The room fell silent. Even the raging storm seemed to have stopped, its huge eye squinting through the tiny window in baffled meteorologic curiosity. Tension rose in the room as the mental preparation began. They knew that what they were about to attempt was dangerous. But only Arathoostra knew *how* dangerous. Only Arathoostra had any inkling of the trouble there'd be if the truth got out. Of if *they* got out. Deep down, in his heart of hearts, he knew he shouldn't be

4

doing it. Even deeper down, in his gut of guts, he knew he must.

Right now, in the few cold hours before dawn, in this locked room just below ground level with walls thick enough to withstand the largest of energy releases, here, in the opera of Arathoostra's life, the fat lady was about to sing!

Arathoostra stood with his back to the tiny window, a black-cowled silhouette reaching out towards the candle-lit Pentagon. Quietly, from deep within the recesses of the hood of his ceremonial lab-cloak, he began to moan. A cold flash of blue lit his outline and another roar of thunder drowned his unearthly utterances as the eye of the storm shifted slightly to get a better view. Arathoostra coughed with irritation as he wondered if other great thaumic scientists throughout history had suffered such elemental intrusions. Had Gren Idjmeen suffered from wind during his development of the Gravitic Acceleration Constant? Had Leweepp Hastoor struggled bravely on to grow plates of mould despite monsoons and tidal waves? Would Dhah Whynn ever have propounded his theories of a unified creationist evolution based on observing lizards and turtles if he had spent fifteen hours a day sheltering from hailstones and forked lightning? Arathoostra doubted it.

He cursed his luck and began chanting again, stronger, his irritation bolstering his confidence. A low rhythmic moan, a cross between a hum and the sound in the dentist's waiting room resonated in his nose. Alsos put his finger in his ear and joined in, holding his other arm out over the Pentagon, his barrel chest raising the volume dramatically. Phlim was last to join the rising crescendo of Alsos, Practz and Arathoostra, the pulsing incantation reverberating irregularly as Practz lost his pitching for a brief moment. They had practised this two thousand times. This was 2001.

'NAAAAAAAAA,' chanted Alsos.

'NAAAAAAAAA,' answered Practz, a fifth above.

'NAAAAAAAAA,' joined in Phlim an octave above Alsos, completing the chord.

5

'NA NAAA,' bawled Arathoostra above the chordal racket. 'Bhumm bhumm, bhumm bhumm, bhumm bhumm, bhumm bhummmmmmm,' they thrummed in unison, like boiling kettledrums before starting again. Phlim, for the two thousand and first time, found himself imagining a large hairy humanoid figure hurling a thigh-bone high into a clear primeval sky. He never had figured out why.

Outside, the storm (bored with the seeming lack of excitement) shifted uncomfortably, sending flashes of lightning down with seemingly redoubled elemental energy. The Thaumaturgical Physicists ignored it now as they immersed themselves in their work.

'NAAAAAAAA,' groaned Alsos again. The others joined in, raising the volume rapidly as the four men's moaning mingled synergistically with the whole. Growing, feeding, resonating. Without warning Arathoostra raised his hands and began to chant a counterpoint across the slow monastic rhythm. It sounded like language, it had vowels, it had consonants, it had assonance, it even sort of rhymed, but it was incomprehensible to all but the four men gathered there. It was as if a tape recording of a traditional folksong had been finely diced, tossed thoroughly in a nice olive oil and glued back together again randomly. The frail voice of Arathoostra rose and fell in pitch as he struggled to control the complex melody. His brow, hidden deep within the folds of his cowled hood, knotted with lines of deep, straining concentration. It was a frightening scene. With their black ceremonial lab-cloaks, deep cowled hoods and the strange wailing chant it would have appeared to outsiders that four rabid were-monks were having a good night out. But there wasn't a full moon and these were four Thaumaturgical Physicists approaching the conclusion of many years' hard work. Tonight would see the culmination of all that effort.

Arathoostra was swaying uncontrollably, as if he were in a deep manic trance. Practz was breathing deeply as he intoned the backing chord. A sudden spark crackled off the edge of one of the candlesticks, earthing itself at a point dead

6

centre of the Pentagon. Curiously, it was green. The intensity of the incantation rose another few vital decibels straining Arathoostra's voice with the effort of keeping up. The edges of all the candles shimmered with green sparks, like verdant iron filings on flaming wax magnets. The air began to taste of ozone. Another bolt of lightning arced overhead and a mighty rumbling echoed over the mountains. The storm, still bored by what it considered to be an appallingly substandard group of absurdly amateurish folkies, trundled forlornly away over the mountains. But this time the rumbling showed no signs of diminishing. It reverberated long, low and loud. The floor vibrated as if dozens of stone trolls were rearranging several small continents in the next room. It became difficult to hear the chanting over the combined tumultuous noise. A green spark lanced off Phlim's hooked nose, crackling onto the cold stone floor, badly singeing his eyebrows. The whiskers in Alsos' moustache crackled like a Geiger counter in a critical reactor core, as tiny green sparks darted back and forth. The chant was racing to its climax. The insides of their noses tingled as it rose to an unbearable level, Arathoostra almost screaming the last few vowels over the rumbling floor. On cue, the four wizards reached out, grabbing each other's wrists in a square around the Pentagon. A massive bolt of energy surged through their bodies as the thaumaturgic wave guide became whole, the chalk lines of the Pentagon shone with thaumic verdance, tiny green sparks fizzing around them, the rumble rising with terrifying intensity. Suddenly the floor exploded in a shower of flying stone fragments. Searing heat blasted the room, belching hot gases into the air like a red giant turning super nova after a particularly hot vindaloo. Fortunately it vanished just as swiftly. An uneasy calm settled behind it.

Something had happened. Something nasty. *It had worked!* Their hearts pounded with exertion and fear. After years of preparation the result of their efforts was before them. The four Thaumaturgical Physicists remained locked

7

in their square, their eyes firmly shut. They listened intently, each hoping to hear another's reaction before he risked opening his own eyes.

Almost as one they became aware of a new sound. It was quiet, regular and slow. It sounded like two very large clammy somethings calmly breathing; assessing their new environment. Arathoostra risked opening his cold blue eyes first and looked with disbelief at the two dark figures before them. He almost screamed with joy. The others opened their eyes with a sense of acute trepidation. Instantly, Phlim wished he hadn't.

Inches away from their faces, completely filling the space between their eight arms, rose two walls of skin. Dark green skin, covered in knobbles and pits, glistening damply. The creatures squatted on four huge legs each, their webbed feet spread nonchalantly beneath them. Huge flaps of pale yellow skin oscillated beneath each chin, marking time with each creature's breathing, as if some huge bellows were working inside them. Arathoostra broke the square, stepping back to stare proudly at the pair of creatures.

In front of them stood the fruit of their labours. The Ultimate Weapon. Ruthless, cold-hearted, thick-skinned and biodegradable. *Rana militaria*. The Frogs of War.

Arathoostra grinned at the other three, whispering in a voice harsh with exultant evil, 'Now I am become the Angel of Death!' His co-workers looked at him strangely.

Alsos shuffled uncomfortably round the giant amphibians, admiring the pillars of legs that would give them unstoppable all-terrain capability. They squatted moistly motionless except for the constant neck flapping and stared at the four men. Practz edged towards the door. This was more than he had expected. This was dangerous. He felt a sense of fear, betrayal and overwhelming stupidity all at the same time. The creatures exuded an air of immense power and almost complete disrespect for human life. Phlim was shaking again, nervously playing with his hair as he too moved towards the door. One word kept rising in his mind over and over again.

8

He had to get it, he needed a lot of it, as much as possible. Distance. Three hundred miles between him and them would be nice, he thought. Now! A brief few lines of scripture floated heavenwards to any god that happened to be listening.

As if a giant statue had come alive, one of the enormous amphibians suddenly became aware of the fact that it had human company. Its dark soulless eyes focused as its giant head moved ponderously downwards. Without warning, and far faster than anything that big should be able to move, the frog's mouth gaped suddenly open, a deadly pink blur lashed across the room and a moist sticky patch was all that remained where Alsos had been standing. The giant frog's eyes bulged into the top of its mouth, pushing, as the struggling wizard began his journey down the vast amphibian throat. Practz and Phlim were out of the door in a flash, followed fractions of a second later by Arathoostra, slamming the door on the last muffled screams that marked the end of Alsos' promising career. They stood in mortified silence in the corridor, Phlim trembling in abject terror murmuring reams of blessed gratitude in the direction of the Thousand Fanatical Gods of Sweetly Favourable Assistance.

'Th . . . th . . . this never happened, all right,' stammered Arathoostra feigning absolute terror with alarmingly consummate ease. 'We saw nothing and we heard nothing, all right?'

Phlim nodded mutely, the whites of his eyes shining with luminous panic from behind a cascade of mouse-brown hair.

'But what are we going to *do* with them?' gasped Practz.

'Leave that to me,' said Arathoostra with the reassurance of an undertaker. 'I'll think of something.'

And as he stood in the cold corridor with dawn still a few hours distant, the storm grumbling over the mountains blissfully unaware of the sight it had just missed, he did indeed think of all the things he could do with the Ultimate Weapons. A wild and evil grin slunk across his face with vulpine greed and peeked into the chicken coop of future possibilities. He rubbed his hands together feverishly, his eyes glinting with cold blue malice and his heart pounding wildly as he thrilled to a new and terrifying vice.

Arathoostra had discovered power.

Oh yes, he told himself, I'll think of something!

The first thing that Arathoostra thought to do with his pair of *Rana militaria* was to make them welcome, as one would any lethal eight-foot amphibian. He ordered a high-security holding pen to be built, together with a series of variable-terrain training arenas, all with virtual attack scenario capability. The output from several fish farms was directed straight to their pen and a team of keepers was appointed from the most trustworthy of orderlies available within the confines of Losa Llamas. He did everything within his considerable sphere of power to ensure that 'his babies', as he grotesquely thought of them, wanted for nothing.

The final few months of OG 1014* passed with alarming

*Original Gravity. A calendar system invented by Gren Idjmeen who studied the rates of acceleration of bricks dropped out of tall towers. His studies brought him to the conclusion that 'as the brick cannot change its velocity by its own volition then gravity affects time. Henceforth, when calculating the time a gravitic attractor constant must be used and all measurements of time must be compared with that at sea level, on a sunny day. Henceforth this will be known as Original Gravity.'

It has been rumoured that Gren Idjmeen, the now infamous philosopher mathematician, invented and introduced this fiendishly complicated calendar system to enable himself to avoid paying off a series of long-term debts that his research work had accrued. This rumour has gained a lot of credence in its short life owing to the fact that Idjmeen's pioneering research was carried out from a series of seven specially constructed towers of variable height connected by a fully furnished, custom built state-of-the-art observatory, brimming with essential modern scientific equipment, such as jacuzzi, en-suite massage maidens, permanently restocked bars and a sizeable expense account, sited on the southern shore of Lake Squibb, the highly desirable haunt of the chronically rich and famous. The rumours were entirely true.

Having secured a hefty grant from SERC, the Sorcerer's Eccentric Research Club, after a particularly lucky and extremely drunken evening, which enabled him to pay for the construction of the observatory in cash and still have some left over to create a sizeable pension fund and have a bit of a do, he then formulated a foolproof method to ensure he was set up for life.

Utilising his theories to show that, prior to the acceptance of OG as the uniform standard, all temporal calculations had been fundamentally flawed, he sued SERC for vicious and malicious breach of contract on the basis that 'as the grant contract rapidity, and Practz and Phlim began to see less and less of their erstwhile leader. The restraints of Professional Integrity and the ethically binding Hypocritical Oath prevented them asking him what it was that was keeping him so engrossed for so long. When they did catch fleeting glimpses of a wraith-like Arathoostra snatching books from library shelves, like some book-thirsty praying mantis, or dashing down corridors, lab-cloak tails flailing, murmuring to himself with a wild glint in his eyes, it was as if they were complete strangers: he did his best to ignore them and return to his work, his work! Alarmingly, the boundaries of Arathoostra's reading list had been flattened by the stampeding herd of information-hungry theories and ravening fact-starved possibilities that had been breeding in his feverish, seething mind. He devoured books, his tastes turning from the staple diet of thaumaturgical physics (pure and applied) alone, to the hors-d'oeuvres of parchments detailing the waterways network of the surrounding area, the mignon-morceau of seasonal temperature charts for the major mountain passes, or the exotic succulent haute cuisine of maps, charts and extensive cartographic studies oozing with succulent scraps, like relative distances between major expanses of fresh water, relative moisture contents of valleys and availability and positioning of fish farms and other aquatic breeding areas. In a matter of days Arathoostra had acquired the starved wild look that has attended driven thaumaturgists since the dawn of time. His hair grew long and wild and had a tendency to stick out at strange angles, especially at the sides where he had a habit of pulling at it nervously when he was excited, or when a new fact swam into view spawning new possibilities for his babies. The Ultimate Deterrent.

But the most worrying change was the look in his eyes. The bright, innocent cornflower-blue of the past was long gone,

was drawn up and dated using a false and outmoded calendar system that has no basis in the current system, the date and therefore the entire contract is, in the eyes of the law, a complete work of fiction'.

usurped by a sharp wildness cold enough to chill the hearts of glacial ice-flows. They roamed his sockets, like rabid lychees, spinning in power-hungry circles, snatching information from here, stealing facts from there, constantly on the move, betraying the perilously shaky footings of Arathoostra's sanity.

He was extremely close to the edge.

It wouldn't take a very big push . . .

Phlim looked from one dragon to the other in frustration, wishing that he knew what to do. The decision he made now would affect considerably his fortunes for the next few minutes. He had one of two choices to make and little or no indication as to which was right or wrong. Silently he floated a surreptitious prayer heavenwards, begging for divine assistance from Zhorroh, the far-seeing God of Jammy Timing and Narrow Scrapes. On this knife-edge of in-decision teetered the chance to sidestep disaster and race forth to a stunning victory, or equally easily lose everything in a few short seconds. One choice, two dragons. 'Decisions, decisions,' he muttered under his breath. Practz tapped his fingers in vexed irritation while he waited for the outcome of Phlim's pedestrian deliberations. It was always like this when his hand was close to the limit.

'Red dragon,' said Phlim, cringing as he expected a cry of victory from his right.

'I can see that,' chuckled Practz, grinning to himself as he picked up the tiny form, placing it in his hand and discarding the bamboo bird that he'd almost come to regard as his mascot. 'One for Mah-Jh'reen!' he yelled, sending a chill deep into Phlim's shaking heart, and chuckled quietly. The two technicians glanced up from their rows of tiles and took their turns. Phlim watched the moves, eagle-eyed, waiting for his chance. He reached out, took his tile from the very short pile of remainders and deflated in the manner that you do if you are staring at twelve unique wonders, a winning hand, and you know that the tile you have just discarded was definitely the wrong one.

'Red dragon,' grunted Phlim, spitting the words out as he threw the tile into the middle of the table.

'Again. Oh, my dear chap, that is sad,' mocked Practz as he picked up the tile, declaring, 'Mah-Jh'reen!' He pushed his tiles over to reveal the limit hand 'Saving the moon from the bottoms of thirteen green jade demons'.

'It's always the way,' muttered Phlim, 'If I'd kept that red dragon instead of the green one I would've gone Mah-Jh'reen.'

'Oh. You've got my nine characters. And my two bamboo,' whined Wat, the first technician.

'No. I was dealt them. Well, you always try for silly hands so it serves you right,' answered Gilbry, pulling a face.

'I've got nothing now, and it's all your fault.'

'You've got a plum,' said Gilbry, pointing to the single tile.

'Oh super, four measly points,' moaned Wat. 'That's really going to get me a long way . . .'

The argument stopped mid-sentence, distracted by sprinting footsteps screeching to a halt, a door bursting open, and a wet and panting figure clad in what remained of a white lab-cloak grabbing their collective attention firmly by the throat and holding it in stunned surprise. All four pairs of eyes stared at the dripping figure and came to more or less the same conclusion, at more or less the same time.

An unannounced intrusion, without knocking, probably means something unusual has happened. A technician with a sense of urgency probably means that particular unusual something is well into the realms of that which is not right. But a wet technician wearing a slashed and dripping lab-cloak and the expression and level of panic of someone who has all too recently witnessed things that people only normally see once in a lifetime, and then only briefly, probably means that this particular unusual something was not only horribly and drastically wrong, but was getting much worse. Right now. Alarmingly fast.

The technician trembled in a growing puddle of water and stared wildly about him in a frenzy of panic.

13

'What's happened?' asked Practz anxiously.

'. . . e . . .'

'Yes and . . .' he waved his hands encouragingly in an attempt to extract any information.

'. . . e . . .' repeated the terrified technician as a fish struggled for breath in his top pocket.

'Do you know you've got a fish in your pocket?' asked Phlim fiddling with his hair. 'Do you think he knows he's got a fish in his pocket?'

'. . . eg . . .'

'Does it have any "p"s in it?' asked Wat and nudged Gilbry.

'Shut up!' snapped Practz. 'This is serious!'

Wat turned faintly pink and looked at his shoes.

'Come on, you're safe now. Tell us what happened?'

The technician looked over his shoulder and twitched several times. His eyes shone with the glaze of the mortally terrified as the images of the recent past burned in his eyes. He struggled once again to speak. '. . . eg . . . eg . . . zzzz.'

'I'm sorry but I still don't understand a single syllable he's uttered,' complained Phlim. 'It's that fish, I tell you. Flapping about like that in his pocket's enough to distract anyone.'

The technician suddenly stopped twitching and stared at Practz. It was like looking into a deep, dark well that contained its very own resident hurricane. Hollow, deeply terrifying and in a state of absolute turmoil. He opened his mouth to speak, finding his voice with a high panic-ridden scream '. . . eggs! . . . eggs! . . . eggs! . . . eggs! . . . eggs! . . .' he cried, before collapsing in a wildly sobbing heap.

Practz's chair crashed to the floor behind him as he leapt to his feet and flew out of the door, yelling to Phlim to follow and for Wat and Gilbry to take care of the technician.

It was only the fact that over the past few years he had become quite attached to the human race that made him move so fast. If what he thought was happening turned out to be even partially true then there were only a few people who

14

could do anything about it. And one of them was probably already ahead of him.

Even though he was still minutes away, Practz could already hear the screams as he sprinted towards the Chamber. Human voices were twisted in the agonising yells of the mortally terrified, cries of pain echoing along the corridor to die at the same moment as the throat that issued them breathed its last breath. Deep, foundation-shaking crashes rumbled through the floor as carnage and wild destruction continued unabated. It was just like a barbarian's Christmas Party.

But as terrifying as all these sounds were, they were as nothing compared to one sound that rang high and loud over the massive cacophanous maelstrom, punctuating the chaos with a rhythmic, maniac pleasure.

While misery, fear and death stalked The Chamber, one single human voice was raised in cracked and raucous laughter. Belly-rolling, white-knuckled guffaws echoed through the thick walls whilst hyenic, cacophanous cachinnations yelped and cavorted with manic menace, revelling in the foaming froth of carnage. But this laughter held no joy, cradled no mirth. For this was laughter that had long ago divorced itself from humour, had sold the house, burned the love letters and was starting again from scratch. Leaner, meaner and suing for acrimony.

Its source: the pits of depravity that lurk in the souls of evil genius.

Its pleasure: the adrenal charge of manic mayhem.

Its joy: the thrill of utter destruction.

And its voice: that of Arathoostra. The Self-Declared Angel of Death.

He threw back his head and screamed with laughter, edged with steel, as another technician was attacked and brought down kicking and screaming. He stood on the platform just inside the reinforced steel doorway and looked out over the heaving pool before him. Across the other side

15

of The Chamber a new motion caught his eye. One of the hundreds of football-sized spheres, coated in jelly and heaped in the corner, twitched violently. Through the pearly translucent surface, Arathoostra could see the creature move. He knew what was about to happen. He had already witnessed this miraculous event nearly a hundred times today.

'Come to Daddy!' he cried with misplaced paternal encouragement, his eyes flashing with cold blue.

As if it had heard, the creature twitched again and began to claw at the translucent skin, its whole body twisting and thrashing as it tore at the barrier between itself and the outside world. Its hind legs, already webbed, pushed hard as its front legs slashed and ripped with razor-sharp claws. In a few moments the barrier was in ribbons. The egg split, the amniotic fluid that had nurtured it for the last few months spilling out over the remaining hatchlings and a new and perfectly formed *Rana militaria* swaggered arrogantly into the world. It was born with all it needed to survive in a hostile world. Claws, teeth, skin like a rhinoceros with hard pad and a very, very short temper. *Rana militaria* had outgrown its other froggy cousins long ago, both in size and development, leaving behind the pathetically bulbous tadpole stage and opting for the ability to come out fighting. Survival of the meanest.

Arathoostra screamed with joy as he watched the latest addition leap off the top of the pile of eggs, execute a neat dive into the pool, then execute a very surprised low-grade technician.

'That's my boy!' yelled Arathoostra, shaking with mirthless laughter.

Practz couldn't believe his eyes as he peered around the door-frame. It suddenly became very clear to him why he had not been allowed to visit The Chamber for the last few months. If he had known about all this . . .

It had to be stopped. Arathoostra had to be stopped. If it wasn't already too late. Heaving nauseously at the sights and

16

sounds from inside, Practz turned and ran, stopping only briefly to help Phlim up off the floor where he was kneeling, bobbing up and down, scattering prayers and invocations randomly heavenward, like some scriptural muck-spreader fertilising a field of atheism. The events behind them continued with undiminished fury and another grotesquely mauled scream flew invisibly past, pausing only to lodge in their memories for the rest of their lives.

It had been a struggle but they had finally managed it. It had taken eight burly technicians to overpower Arathoostra. He had flailed, fought and spat like a cornered tabby that has suddenly realised what the vet's pliers are for.

As the last technician fled from the cell, Practz slid back the tiny panel in the door and peered inside. A lump quickly formed in his throat as he saw the once-great figure squirming and writhing in the strait-jacket, cursing and yelling about human rights abuse.

It was hard to remain unmoved by the sight of one of the finest Thaumaturgical Physicists ever known lying dumped in a padded cell, arms restrained, brain bursting with ideas so wild, so dangerous that the cell was sound-proofed, but Arathoostra had been the victim of his own genius, as much as any of the shredded technicians. This whole messy incident had halted the research work, forcing them all to think seriously about the semantics of the words 'pure' and 'applied'. Reality had lifted the lid and dropped in some common sense. Stop and Think. It would be one of the most expensive salutary lessons ever to be learned, both in terms of contractors' bills for building a new, larger and far more secure pool for 'Arathoostra's Babies', as they had been christened, and in chewed-up staff.

As Practz stared at the madman before him, the self-proclaimed Angel of Death, he knew he stared at the past. Arathoostra had made a mistake, a very big and dangerous mistake; it would have to remain a secret. Who knew what would happen if the frogs were released? Practz shuddered.

Tomorrow he would convene a discussion group and place an order of absolute secrecy on this entire situation. He slid the panel shut and sprinted away to the amphibian chaos in The Chamber, leaving a hail of vicious abuse clattering against the door as Arathoostra strained and flailed against the strait-jacket.

In the same way that nuclear power plants, no matter how careful they are, have a slightly higher background radiation than most other areas, and churches and cathedrals have a tangible underlying holiness about them found in few but the most devoutly worshipped-at shrines . . . in that way Losa Llamas, owing to the poorly shielded, throbbing Thaumatron Generator buried deep in its heart, powering all the experiments, heating systems and mystic strip-lights, had a raised background thaumic quotient found only in a few other rare places.* The corridors of Losa Llamas were regularly doused with transient free radical peaks following times of high power demand and peak consumption. This temporarily saturated atmosphere gave rise to thaumic clumping and the formation of invisible autonomous nano-fields. The floor of the coffee lounge was littered with them.

Arch-Mage-in-Chief Phiynmn, developer of the principles involved in accelerating thaumic particles in a densely varying magikinetic field, had, in OG 1009, carried out extensive tests on the dangers of long-term exposure to low-level magical radiation and had concluded euphemistically that 'by ensuring that all males wishing to sire offspring in the next generation protect their interests with the lead-lined undergarments supplied, there is no major danger to health. So any problems you have with your kids are your own affair.'

---

* One notable place being a small and insignificant mountain region on the Rhyngill–Cranachan border high in the Talpa Mountains, where the raised background thaumic quotient caused a whole host of problems for not only the local yellowish rodents, but more for the villagers trying to earn a living, quite literally, off the back of them.

His findings were correct – as far as they went.

Unfortunately Prof. Phiynmn hadn't thought to investigate the effect of prolonged nano-field radiations on the internal phraseological structure and grammatical integrity of the common conversation. Well, you wouldn't, would you? Shame. If he had, then there would have been a lot less hassle all round.

It had taken sixteen hours of constant work, with the Thaumatron heaving out a constant twenty-three gigathaums, to clean up The Chamber and contain the frogs. It had almost beaten the combined sorcerous skills of Practz, Phlim and a host of white-clad technicians, but finally they were able to declare the situation safe.

Or so they thought.

The air in Losa Llamas that night was buzzing and crackling with super-saturated thaumic particles, whizzing and humming as they clumped into nano-fields. The host of technicians, running on adrenalin, like a pack of Ammorettan Death Lizards in at the kill, chattered and babbled about what they had just witnessed, filling the air with facts and opinions, thoughts and feelings, exaggerating deeds of heroism, spinning yarns of bravery, threads of untruth. It was a heady mixture. Odd phrases collided with nano-fields, thaumic free radicals bound to wildly spinning threads of fiction. Magic stole the conversation, kidnapping it, snatching it from the playgrounds of chit-chat, moulding it like some phraseological Fagin commanding his babble of verbal urchins. Cold grey fact became gloriously colourful rumour.

From all over Losa Llamas squadrons of invisible speculation leapt into the air, droves of hearsay buzzed through windows, tidings turned and rushed out from every downspout and conduit available, gossips of flying rumours in close formation raced eagerly to fertilise the open virgin imaginations of the populace, to set wagging the idle tongues of the world.

It would only be a matter of time before someone heard of the secrets of Losa Llamas.

'Thire, Thire!'

Dawn rose slowly and crept over the small pile of leaves in front of the large beech tree. She wriggled along on her belly, snapping a branch in a moment's incaution and startling a small bird into the sky. She froze, tautly glancing left and right for the enemy. Her chest muscles fought to silence her breathing, her ears filtering out the background buzz and rustle of the local forestry inhabitants, straining for sounds of pursuit. Nothing. No movement. It was too soon to hope she was safe.

After a few nerve-racking moments of sieving the silence, she felt confident enough to snake forward, edging warily through the undergrowth to hide behind a large, dark-green bush. Now she had the tactical advantage. From the cover of her botanical bunker she could survey the whole area, double-checking the final details of her plans. Stealth and observation were the keys to success. She had learnt that lesson well recently, having witnessed a great many operations slip, plunging from the pinnacles of near glory to be smashed on the rocks of anguished defeat below. She was very well aware that the chances of the final approach being easy were about as high as the IQ of the average perambulatory slime-mould.

Ahead of her, glimpsed through the tree cover, she could see the portly figure standing guard over the prize. Her target: the treasure. From this distance she could barely glimpse it. A tiny shining thing glinting in a heap of crispy leaves, her mind's eye observed, surveying every mark on its surface, every shining hand-worn dent. She probably knew it better than anyone, it had been hers for nine years, ever since her first birthday. She had brought it down from the mountain village of Middin eight months ago, packing it

20

safely away, carefully carrying it over miles of rough country, only to have it snatched from her grip and flung into this forest under heavy guard. Now she wanted it back. So did the other three.

Dawn, like the other 'thieves', had willingly accepted their mission to steal the treasure from under the watchful gaze of the Guardian's nose and return it to the courtyard of Castell Rhyngill, its new home. The prize of failure was high, capture meant certain death. Or worse.

This was not the first time she had carried out a mission of this nature: today was far from her maiden assault on the Guardian. She was acutely aware of the dangers, fully informed of the risks, mindful of the plethora of perils waiting for her. That was what made it so much fun! She thrilled with anticipation as she readied herself for the final dash. Momentarily her thoughts flashed back to the Talpa Mountains and the times she had played with her elder brother Firkin and his friend Hogshead. Angrily she recalled her jealousy as she had watched them play whilst she lay pathetically in bed, too weak to stand, too ill to join in. Life in the mountains, scraping an existence from the dregs of nature's larder and being taxed for the privilege, had been almost too much for her.

It was a different Dawn who watched the Guardian now. Somehow the recovery from her illness, combined with the last eight months living in Castell Rhyngill with her new friends, Courgette, the cook's daughter, and Klayth, the youngest ever king of Rhyngill, had given her an outlook on life that made fanatical religious fervour seem like a passing fad. Even a train spotter would have said she was obsessed. She positively hummed with life. She had a new pair of red ribbons tied in her long brown hair, a present from Klayth, and a new pair of calfskin boots. She felt wonderful. She wanted to scream and yell and . . .

A flash of motion off to her left brought her back to the matter in hand. The prize, she thought, I want it. She spied through the bush and glimpsed the squirrel-haired Courgette

21

gearing up for a final dash. Dawn, even though she had most of the clearing in view, still hadn't worked out where Firkin, her brother, or the King were hiding. She had a sneaking suspicion that they would try a joint attack. It was one of their favourite moves. Firkin would feign an assault, distracting Hogshead, or whoever happened to be Guardian, and at the same time Klayth would break cover, sprinting in from nowhere to snatch the treasure and make off for the courtyard. Dawn considered that to be cheating. Not in the spirit of the game. It was supposed to be one against one, not pairs.

Suddenly she saw Firkin away across the clearing, gesturing and waving, sending instructions to Klayth. Almost immediately she had an idea, the filaments of inspiration igniting in the naive vacuum of her young mind. If they can use the distraction technique, she thought, so can I. Hogshead still hadn't seen any of them, so her plan might just work. Firkin broke cover and started to run, shouting as he did so. Hogshead turned, alert and ready to guard the treasure. Dawn, snatching her golden opportunity with greedy hands, exploded from the bush at the same moment. Keeping low she sprinted across the clearing, flinging herself to a halt against the back of the beech. Firkin was weaving towards Hogshead and holding his attention brilliantly. In a moment Dawn would have it! Suddenly Courgette broke cover, her red hair flying free behind her, sprinting, her mental filaments flaring with the same idea. Dawn, timing her action to perfection, danced around the tree, ducking between Hogshead's legs, snatching the tiny shiny pebble from the leaves and ran. Firkin snarled as he saw her sprinting hard, her flying legs covering the ground easily. In an instant everyone was on her tail. She shrieked and yelped with wild excitement, cradling the pebble, *her* pebble, neatly in her hand. Ahead of her, and closing fast, was Klayth. The King had broken cover on an intercept course. She stared hard at the powerful blond-haired boy, feeling the pebble and deciding in an instant to take him on. My pebble, she told herself, I won it. Courgette, seeing it was hopeless for her to try and catch the fleeing Dawn, had stopped to watch the fun, admiring her neat move. She would remember that one.

Klayth was almost on top of her, running hard, and Dawn was in no mood for slowing down. She had reached the green sward in front of the drawbridge and showed no signs of tiring. Klayth reached out to grab her and in a single fluid motion she ducked, feinted right, side stepped left and was round him, the King's arms closing on thin air. Bewildered by the speed at which she had moved he tripped and collapsed in a long slow tumble across the grass. Courgette squealed encouragement as Dawn rattled across the drawbridge and out of sight into the courtyard. Firkin looked hot and flustered, miffed that his little sister had outsmarted him, especially in front of Klayth. The King, with an acute lack of regality, lay on the grass panting and laughing wildly as the dust settled behind Dawn. It had been a good game.

Hogshead, Courgette and Firkin strolled up to the giggling monarch, helped him up and strolled back towards the castle. There was probably enough time for another game.

As they neared the castle it appeared that they wouldn't get one, though. A small man was running across the grass towards them. Klayth groaned audibly as he set eyes on the newly appointed King's clerk, messenger and general dogsbody. Mynyn ran towards the King on tip toes, waving a white handkerchief and gesturing desperately. He looked like a ballet-dancing poodle. He had the tights, the mop of white tightly curled hair and the yapping voice, all he needed was the red ribbon in his hair and crowds would be throwing him scraps for a glimpse of his pas-de-deux.

'Thire, Thire, er, your highneth. *Thire!*' he shouted in his pathetically thin voice. 'Thire, Thire, er your highneth, Thire. Your Imperial Prethenthe ith needed, Thire.'

Firkin more than half expected Mynyn to roll over and wait for his tummy to be tickled and was a little disappointed when he remained standing expectantly, looking up at Klayth.

'Oh, what is it, Mynyn? Can't it wait?'

'Yeah,' said Firkin, barely disguising his utter lack of respect for the little man. 'Can't you see the King is busy?'

'No he'th not,' squeaked Mynyn righteously at Firkin, then, turning to the King, added, 'Thire, it'th a matter of gweat importanthe, Thire.'

'What?'

'Give him a biscuit and tell him to come back later!' grumbled Firkin.

'It'th a matter of thivil dithorder, Thire,' said Mynyn pointedly ignoring Firkin.

'Really. That th . . . serious?' asked Klayth.

'Oh yeth, Thire. It hath involved fithticuffth, your high-neth, Thire,' replied Mynyn earnestly trying to please the King.

'Oh no! Fithtic . . . fisticuffth! Again?' Klayth scowled as a hail of barely contained sniggers floated into earshot. 'Sorry,' he said, shrugging his shoulders to his three friends, 'Got to go. A King's work is never done.' He smiled wryly, and headed off towards the rambling bulk of Castell Rhyngill with Mynyn trotting in circles around him, explaining what had occurred.

'Well, that's *that* for another day!' grumbled Firkin, looking at the back of the receding monarch. 'It was the same yesterday. And the day before . . .'

'If you're going to start sulking again,' interrupted Courgette, surveying the degree of pout of Firkin's lower lip, 'then I'm off to the library.'

'Well, it's not fair, is it?' complained Firkin to Courgette's deaf ears.

'No, Firkin.'

'He's always getting called away . . .'

'Yes, Firkin.'

'It wasn't like this before . . .'

'No, Firkin.'

'Are you listening to me . . .?'

'No, Firkin. I'm off to do some reading, I saw a brilliant

24

looking encylopaedia the other day. Coming, Hogshead?' said the girl over her shoulder as she headed castlewards.

'Er, yes. No, I . . .' he faltered, torn between the two of them.

'It's all those soldiers' fault. I sometimes wish they'd stayed in Cranachan . . .' muttered Firkin, kicking irritably at a stick.

Oh no, he's off again! thought Hogshead, panic welling up inside him as visions of endless hours of Firkin's ear-numbing complaints lurched into his mind's eye.

'Courgette!' he cried. 'Wait for me!!!'

Far away from the ivy-draped, rambling rockery that was Castell Rhyngill, in one of the valleys in the foothills of the Talpa Mountains, three figures were busy. A clank of chains rattled noisily, barely masking the blasphemy of curses issuing from a tall, skinny figure as he swung his rusting pick-axe at the ground. He spat as he wiped his brow, sneering at the two huge leather-clad guards from behind eight months of beard growth. If looks could kill, the two guards would, at the very least, have been reeling on the ground suffering from extensive internal bleeding, acute major organ damage and a severely impaired long-term reproductive capability. Watching them finish yet another turkey leg each and lie back in the pleasantly warm autumn sun, he added three doses of salmonella and chronic dysentery to the list. Snydewinder always was the most generous of hosts when it came to dishing out suffering.

Burnurd scratched the back of his tightly cropped head and smiled contentedly to himself. Maffew, the other half of the team, absently winkled a few fragments of gristle out from between his back teeth with his dagger. They liked their new jobs as Executive Chain-Gang Security Specialists on the Trans-Talpino Trade Route Improvement Scheme. It was a wonderful title, thought Burnurd smugly, studying the words on the piece of parchment thoughtfully supplied by King Klayth, just in case he forgot it. One day, he told himself, he'd learn to read, then he would *really* appreciate it. A grand title for a grand job. He swelled with pride a little more as he thought of how far they'd come in the last eight months. Geographically, the Trans-Talpino Trade Route had been completely transformed into a swift, modern, sleek communication system that would rapidly enhance trade between Rhyngill and Cranachan.

Okay, so they'd only covered a total stretch of about five yards, but it was the principle of the thing that thrilled Burnurd most. It gave him a sure feeling of power that he had never experienced during his decade or more as Castle Guard. And he was helping the community on its long and rocky road to prosperity. *This* long and rocky road, he thought to himself, grinning broadly. But, more satisfying than any feeling of civic worth, far stronger than any sense of leaving a landmark for future generations, the best reason for being Executive Chain-Gang Security Specialist at this time, with this chain-gang, had to be the enormous perk.

After the twelve years of abuse, cruelty and tyrannical bossing-about which they had endured under the hooked nose and glaring eyepatch of His Eminence, the Lord Chancellor of Rhyngill, justice had finally turned its balanced smile on Burnurd and Maffew, and the calm seas of job satisfaction now lapped gently over the jagged rocks of ritual barbarism. The tides had finally turned. It was Burnurd and Maffew who could now hurl the abuse, dream up cruel schemes and be generally not a little tyrannical. Burnurd had heard that this was called something like 'karma'. He didn't believe it though, there was a lot of catching up to do after being on the receiving end of twelve years' incessant, merciless victimisation. One thing he *didn't* feel was calmer.

All this thinking, especially on a full stomach, had put Burnurd in the mood for a little post-prandial entertainment. A nice brandy, followed by a spontaneous act of malicious cruelty would be perfect. Mercilessly ripping the final few scraps of meat off the last turkey bone, he hurled it at the

26

back of the skinny labourer in a coldly calculating manner, specifically designed to proffer the maximum degree of irritation. It whistled forward, bouncing off the back of his victim's thin skull with an immensely satisfying thud. Snydewinder, the ex-Lord Chancellor of Rhyngill, turned and snarled at the two guards.

'Get on wiff yur work!' shouted Maffew.

The half-heartedness of Snydewinder's labours was not entirely due to the physical strain or the annoyance he felt at being made, for the first time, to work at something he not only detested but, crucially, knew that he personally would make no gains from. In the last eight months his attitude had changed. Hardened. Deep inside his eyes burned a fire with more bright intensity than all his previous internal fires put together. But now his urge for power had been placed on the back burner. His days of power-base building sequestered, for the moment, temporarily stored in the freezer compartment of the coldly ruthless space that was Snydewinder's mind. Right now his every waking thought was centred on one thing. One word that stood between him and freedom. Escape. He looked once again at the chains on his wrists and ankles and shook with angry frustration. How could he escape? There had to be a way! There had to be! There was no way that he could survive the winter in these mountains, with these idiots with ideas far above their station! His eye narrowed, he clenched his fists and began to breathe deeply.

In an overwhelming fit of anger he attacked the innocent earth with shattering blows from his pick-axe. Clouds of soil flew up, small stones ricocheting out from under the wild onslaught. His temper won out. Frustration was vented on the ground beneath his feet.

Burnurd looked up at the sudden increase in noise and smiled.

'It's good to see him settling down to work at last!' he said. Maffew nodded simply.

Snydewinder's one good eye burned wild with anger,

roaming its socket like a wild caged animal as he plotted, schemed and destroyed.

If an innocent being from an insignificantly obscure two-dimensional universe was suddenly peeled off its plane, shaken furiously and hurled into the realms of three dimensions, then, assuming its mind could stand it, without turning into a monolayer of gibbering jelly, the profound sense of freedom and space it would experience would be almost infinitely unimaginable. It would have to learn new words, up, down, gravity, hang-gliding. It could try new things: experience the thrill of abseiling: leap feet first into the delights of trampolining: or head-first into the ecstasy of bungee-jumping.

In her own small way, Courgette was experiencing a similar sense of profound personal daredevilry, but with a lower risk to life and limb. Her extra dimension was infinitely more fragmented, far more complex, steeped in archaisms, allusions, aphorisms, multi-faceted systems of nomenclature, the list was almost endless. Her extra dimension was *words*. Millions of them. All around her were thousands of books sitting on the parallel vertical rows of dark shelves like ancient planktonic comb-jellies on the fossilised baleen of a million-year-old whale. Manuals rubbed spines with volumes, scrolls nestled against tomes; there was row upon row of publication after publication simply oozing with kerjillions of strings of words.

Is that a real word? she thought suddenly. 'Kerjillion.' Leaping up from the table, she ran through the library, snatching a large dictionary from a shelf and riffling through its huge pages with frantic eagerness. K. . . K. . . kerf, kerfuffle, kermes. No! Not a sign of kerjillion. Had she made it up? She felt certain she had heard it before . . . kerjillions of stars whizzing by. It sounded right. She might have read it somewhere in one of the hundreds of books she had devoured since discovering the library of Castell Rhyngill.

Up until eight months ago when two fifteen-year-old boys had wandered into the kitchen,* Courgette had only had two immensely well-thumbed books to read. Since then, following the destruction of Snydewinder's tyranny and the re-population of Castell Rhyngill, she had been free to spend as much time as she liked in the library. And, her literary lips chapped from years of fictional desiccation, she had plunged headlong into the vast pool of collected stories and tales, submerging herself completely in imaginary realms, diving through shimmering emerald seas of folklore, plucking pearls of wisdom from the clams of blissful ignorance. The flower of her latent intelligence blossomed, glowing with collected facts and fictions. The colour of this flower was read, of course.

Still pondering the origin of 'kerjillion', Courgette replaced the dictionary and wandered back to her encyclopaedia, stumbling slightly over a small metal ring set into the stone floor. She sat down at the table, picking up where she had left off, staring wonderingly at a picture of a deep-purple crystal.

'Amethyst,' she said quietly to herself, rolling the word around her mouth.

'Hmm, what did you say?' asked Hogshead looking up from the bottom row of a particularly dusty stack of shelves.

'Oh. Nothing,' she mumbled, turning the page. 'Armadillo!' she squeaked.

'Where?' shouted Hogshead, standing up suddenly and banging his head on the shelf.

'Here, on page 14, silly!' smirked Courgette.

'I wish you wouldn't do that,' moaned Hogshead rubbing his head, 'I get all confused.'

'I'm sorry. I get a bit carried awww . . .' she stopped.

'What's "carried awww . . ." mean?' asked Hogshead, confused.

*Firkin and Hogshead, followed by a wandering pieman, a knight with a north country accent and a wizard with a pet tawny owl had 'invaded' Castell Rhyngill at the end of a difficult mission to rid the kingdom of its unbelievably greedy ruler. Courgette just happened to be in the right place at precisely the wrong time to become embroiled in this whole escapade.

'Sshh!' whispered Courgette. 'I can hear someone!'

'I can smell someone.'

'Me too.'

'It's probably Firkin,' whispered Hogshead with a grin.

'Don't be horrid,' sniggered Courgette. 'It doesn't sound like him.'

'What's Firkin sound like, then?'

'Oh, I don't know. More sort of big for his boo . . . ooh!' Courgette held her breath as a tall figure crept slowly out of the shadows of the library shelves. He wore a long overcoat that had definitely seen better days and large boots repaired in several places with large patches of yellowish fur. On his back was a large pack, seams grinning with the strain of holding itself together. A shapeless green-brimmed excuse for a hat squatted on the ageing intruder's head, completing the picture of chronic shabby dereliction. Except for his eyes.

Courgette stared in awestruck silence at the empty, green circles residing where any normal human being's eyes would be. This was no normal human being. This was Franck the Prospector and his cold, impenetrable stare was due to his glasses. They clung precariously to his ears with strands of wire bent into a permanently temporary frame that he had knocked up one day, long ago, to hold the two thick plates of glass that looked as if they could easily have once been the bottoms of a pair of beer bottles. Probably because they had.

Franck had spent most of his life* in the Talpa Mountains, searching for a way to get rich quickly. Had he been asked, prior to OG 1023, how this would be achieved, the answer would almost certainly been an emphatic: 'Gold!' Nobody, least of all himself, expected the source of his fortune to be countless, yellowish, furry rodents with an overwhelming urge for voluntary self-destruction.

---

*An indeterminate number of years that probably lay somewhere significantly higher than twenty-five and less than three hundred and twelve. But it was hard to be sure.

'Didn't mean to disturb you,' said Franck. 'I just came to get a book for my journey.'

'What journey?' asked Hogshead. 'Where are you going?'

'Back,' replied Franck simply. 'Up there,' he jerked his grubby thumb towards the Talpa Mountains.

'How long?' asked Courgette, wrinkling her nose.

'As long as it takes.'

'But why? There's nothing up there,' argued Hogshead, looking around and dreading the thought of visiting Middin again, let alone living there.

'Oh, yes there is!' replied Franck, his voice brightening as he tapped his inside pocket significantly. '*I've* got a map, see!'

'What for?' asked Courgette.

Franck moved closer, looking nervously around him for any signs of hidden ears. 'Won't tell no one?'

Hogshead and Courgette shook their heads, and held their breath.

'Promise?'

They nodded, turning redder.

'Diamonds!' Franck whispered, the single word conjuring images of untold facets glistening with unfathomable worth. 'I've got a map!' he repeated, grinning.

Hogshead was surprised. 'But, you've got all you need here!' he blurted, quickly snatching another breath. 'It could take years to find the diamo . . .'

'Sshh!' barked Franck, squinting over his shoulders. 'Not so loud!' He tried to resume a more conversational tone. 'What I've got here's not the same as before, is it? It's not *mine*. I didn't find it.'

'But it's comfortable, and miles warmer than Middin ever was!' said Hogshead.

'True, but it's so . . . *crowded*! There's people everywhere!'

Hogshead had to agree. Since the return of the Prisoners of War, Castell Rhyngill had been almost unbearably stuffed with people. Noisy boisterous men and screaming women, chattering and arguing all hours of the day and night.

31

'I've made up my mind,' said the Prospector. 'You don't need my stories any more, you've got more than enough here. There's two things that really makes me want to get back in the mountains, though,' confessed Franck as he pulled 'Ye Omnibusse of Faerie Tayls' off the shelf. 'I'm bored,' he said. 'There's no entrepreneurial opportunities to be had by a wrinkly like me. Mountains is where I belong,' he added, shoving the book into his protesting back-pack and headed for the door.

'. . . and?' asked Hogshead.

'What's the other thing?' quizzed Courgette, relieved to be able to breathe again.

'Eh? Oh, yeah. Baths. I hate people tellin' me to get a bath!' he grinned and closed the door.

Now that he had mentioned it, Hogshead wasn't surprised.

Oh no. Not again, thought Klayth to himself, sighing heavily as he walked towards the Public Chambers of Castell Rhyngill. Mynyn trotted in circles around him keeping up a flood of constant babbling chatter. Klayth had lost count of the number of times he had been called upon to pass judgement over matters of civil unrest. There seemed to be an almost constant flood of petty disagreements, fights and arguments coming to his attention lately. He still wasn't sure if it was his imagination but it always seemed to involve someone who had served time in Cranachan and he was sure it was getting worse every day. Today, unfortunately, was no exception.

Klayth sighed again and tuned in to the babbling summary supplied by Mynyn.

'. . . and he thayth it wath *hith* fault, Thire. But the other one reckonth that it wath all becauthe of a bad gambling debt from when they were in Cranachan, Thire, but *he* thayth that he cheated and the debt ith all lieth tho he took it to pay him back, Thire. That wath when the *other* one got angry and dethided to . . .'

'Mynyn! Shut up, will you!'

Klayth stood in the corridor outside the Public Chambers and fervently wished, yet again, that the soldiers would hurry up and readjust to normal life, get their fingers out and settle down. Having been locked in the Cranachan prison camp for twelve years had obviously been difficult for them, but King Grimzyn had assured him that they had been treated well. Eight months should have been plenty of time to get back into the swing of Castell Rhyngill, he thought in his naive way. They've got their freedom, they've got their families back, they've got jobs. Why were they being so awkward?

He squared his shoulders, adjusted his baldric, straightened his tunic and pushed open the doors to the Public Chambers. Abruptly the noise of raised voices stopped. Hassock, the haulage contractor, released Mulben, the market trader, from a full-nelson and smiled sweetly at the King. 'Your Highness, it is my unalloyed pleasure to see you!'

'Hmm, I wish I could say the same,' answered Klayth under his breath, as he slumped onto his throne.

'Sire,' pleaded Mulben rubbing his neck, struggling to catch his breath, 'I have been assaulted . . .'

'Shut up,' snapped Hassock sporting an angry oil-slick of a black eye.

'. . . my character maligned . . .'

'Shut up!' repeated the sweating bulk of the haulage contractor.

'. . . and my trustworthy name dragged through the mud of slander . . .'

'Shut up, shut up, shut up!'

'Shan't!' Mulben barked at his tormentor, childishly stamping his foot. He turned to Klayth. 'Sire, Your Exquisite Highness, I pray that in your Unfathomable Wisdom you will find the answer that evades us, the solution to our disagreement, and sort this whole shoddy matter out.'

Oh God! thought Klayth, rolling his blue eyes heavenward, they're creeping. Bad news! Bad news!! Raising a plaintive prayer to Aykhass, the Deity of Difficult Discussions, the Almighty Arbitrator and the King of Celestial Conciliation, he swallowed hard, took a deep breath and stared at the two complainants before him.

'Well,' said Klayth, wishing that he was somewhere else, anywhere else really, 'if you could just explain your dispute I may be able to see what I can do.'

The two men leapt forward, slapping each other's arms and shouting their different, and wildly opposing, sides to the story.

'THTOP! THTOP!' screamed Mynyn bouncing up and down, flapping his handkerchief in an attempt to regain some order. 'Hith Regal Highneth can only hear one argument at a time. Otherwithe it'th a thilly lot of thtuff and nonthenthe. Thee? Now, one at a time, *pleathe*.'

Mulben and Hassock paused, wiped their tunics, took a deep breath and continued almost immediately, strained notes rattling in their voices as they tried furiously to shout each other down. The noise was deafening, Hassock's bullish haulage contractor's bellows clashing with Mulben's roars, the marketeer's vocal cords rippling with muscles developed through years of volubly cataloguing his latest, never-to-be-repeated bargains. Both of them held a firm belief in trial by volume. The louder you protested your innocence, the more likely it was to be true.

Klayth was bombarded by the intense verbal barrage, his hair streaming behind him in the typhoon of tempestuous objections. All he could do was frantically wave his hands, appealing for silence. Mynyn's face was red from leaping up and down like an overwound morris man as he strove for silence.

'SHUTUP!' yelled Klayth in angry frustration, jamming the word into a split-second gap in the din. 'Stop your wagging tongues or I shall have them stopped for you. Permanently!' he added imperiously. The two men stood open mouthed as the worrying thought occurred to them, rather belatedly, that they might have gone too far.

Klayth turned to the glistening bulk of Hassock. 'Now

please, slowly and carefully explain *what*, in the name of Rhyngill, is going on. *Why* it is going on. And what you want me to *do* about it!'

'Thank you, Sire,' said the haulage contractor grinning slyly at Mulben. 'The problem, Sire,' he began nervously, 'in a nutshell is, Sire, that, well . . .' Hassock shrugged his shoulders as he gave up the struggle to find the Regalese way of saying it. 'Sire, this disreputable, slime-ridden, blighted scum of a so-called market trader is refusing to pay me all that he owes me for the delivery of goods to his stall. Sire.'

Mulben's face turned beetroot, his back arching in anger. 'I'm not paying twenty, I'm not paying fifteen, I'm not even going to pay *five* shillings for a delivery that is *far* from complete! Extortion, it is!' He bellowed, opening and closing his fists as he looked at Hassock's other eye and thought of pandas.

'It was complete when I started out . . .' shouted Hassock.

'So you say,' bellowed Mulben. 'I have only got a fraction of what we agreed . . .'

'A very *large* fraction . . .'

'Hah! So you admit it's *not* complete!' shouted Mulben sensing victory.

'Of course it isn't,' countered Hassock, his black eye glowing angrily. '*You* removed several boxes from the back of my cart as I backed up to your stall.'

'You liar! I wouldn't stoop so low . . .'

'Thyutup! THYUTUP!' yelped Mynyn desperately.

'That's the type of thing you'd do to try to extort even more money out of innocent market traders,' continued Mulben, anger surging through his veins.

'Are you suggesting that my activities are less than legal?'

'I should say so. Everyone's heard of your scams. Old Grunion was tellin' me the other day about . . .'

'Don't bring Old Grunion into this,' protested Hassock, his fists making small circling motions in the air. 'What does he know about anythin'. . .'

35

King Klayth shook his head in resignation and sighed wearily as the argument raged and boiled before him.

Mynyn yapped and leaped, ineffectually appealing for calm as the two traders argued about the whereabouts of the missing goods. Wearily Klayth slouched lower in his throne and wished fervently that this was someone else's problem. That he could sneak out, close the door behind him and leave them to it. It was times like these when he longed just to be normal. To be just Klayth. King Klayth was damned hard work.

Immediately outside the rambling expanse of lichen-and-ivy-covered masonry that was Castell Rhyngill, a forest began. At a respectful distance, it gingerly skirted the lily-covered moat and the dark green creeper curtains of the outer walls before plunging verdantly onwards across the undulatory foothills of the Talpa Mountains, eventually approaching the festering den of iniquity, crime and casual murder that lurked under the name of Fort Knumm. Here it stopped, leaving the murky backstreets of the Fort entirely to the pleasure of its less than trustworthy denizens. Rows of elders looked with scorn down their phloems at the revolting patch of sticky humanity with a shudder of acute arboreal distaste. No self-respecting shrub would be seen dead within a five-hundred-yard exclusion zone around *that* wall! Only the dregs of nature's botanical barrel lived in and around Fort Knumm. Funguses and ambulatory slime-moulds fought for limited growing space with the epiphytic tendrils of climbing spongewort and canopy ferns.*

Fort Knumm lurked black and forbidding within the Rhyngill Forest like a disused slate quarry in a national park.

Back at the smarter end of the forest, where the sun seemed to shine a little brighter and hoards of marauding squirrels set out on badger-mugging excursions a little less frequently, two figures sat in their favourite tree, dangling

---

*Generally, the nimbler slime-moulds won.

their legs over the drop below. The small, brown-haired girl's eyes were wide with delight as she listened intently to her elder brother telling her tales of incredible bravery and unlikely heroism.

'How did you find Fort Knumm?' asked Dawn eagerly.

'We followed the music,' answered Firkin casually.

'Music?' It was whispered with awe.

'The choirs were in full voice, filling the honeysuckle-scented air with heavenly sounds. It raised my spirits and seemed to give life to my heavy footsteps. I almost ran through the gate,' said Firkin dreamily, as if remembering a profound personal event.

'Oooh! What was the gate like?'

'Er, wooden. Er, with brass fittings and it swung open on silent bearings.'

'Was it guarded? Did you have to fight with big guards? I bet you did. Like when you had to fight with all those vampires. Did you?' babbled Dawn excitedly.

'I, er, yes. Well no,' floundered Firkin, trying to remember what he had told her previously.

'What then?'

'It was guarded by two, er, two . . . lions.'

'Lions! Did you fight them?'

'No.'

'Why not?'

Why not, he thought, why not, indeed! I know . . . 'Because they were made of gold.'

Dawn's mouth fell open. 'Gold!!' she whispered.

'Hey, you two,' came a voice from below.

'Real gold?' asked Dawn.

Firkin looked down to see the stocky figure of Hogshead gazing up at them. 'I've been looking everywhere for you. It's getting late. You'd better come down.'

Firkin looked around at the gathering gloom and Dawn pulled a face.

'Tell me more!' she said. 'I want to know more!'

'Tomorrow,' said Firkin with acute relief as he began to

climb down. In a moment he was standing next to Hogshead. As Dawn scrambled down the last few feet and before she could ask any more questions he shouted, 'Race you all back to the castle!' and set off sprinting.

'Last one back's a wet fish,' yelled Dawn, unable to think of a suitable insult. She sprinted after her brother.

'Oi! Wait for me!' shouted Hogshead, taking some time to accelerate. 'Come back!!'

Suitably groomed and physically, if not mentally, ready once more for the rigours of his monarchical duties, King Klayth stood momentarily outside the Public Chambers.

'Who's first today?' he asked Mynyn.

'Thire, a dithpute involving, er . . .' he glanced officiously at the parchment held in his clip-board. His face fell.

'Who?'

'Thire, I think I had better exthplain . . . Thire!'

'Never mind! Let's just get it over with.' Klayth swept into the fifteenth trivial dispute in as many days.

The sound of shouting from within suddenly ceased as the large brass rings in the huge doors rattled behind the King. Mynyn quivered in the cold corridor as he awaited the reaction. He didn't have to wait long.

'You two. *Again*!' bellowed Klayth, clapping eyes on the two wounded parties.

'Yes, Sire! It's not what you think, Sire!'

A trembling Mynyn slunk around the edge of the door and crept into his seat, head down, praying Klayth would not see him. He failed.

'What *is* all this?' snapped Klayth at Mynyn.

'Thire, I, er, well it'th like thith . . .' squirmed the clerk, agitatedly rubbing his hands.

'Sire, we have more information regarding our little, ahem, altercation yesterday,' oozed Hassock.

'I suppose that you are still blaming each other,' groaned Klayth, turning to the haulier.

'No, Sire. Far from it, Sire.'

38

'You mean, Hassock, that you are not going to deny that anything was stolen from your cart and you, Mulben, are going to say that you perpetrated this wild and reckless non-theft that didn't happen.'

The two traders scratched their heads and rolled their eyes as they considered this.

'No,' answered Mulben.

'Yes,' agreed Hassock at the same moment.

'Good,' said the King simply.

'Sire, we came to give you more information,' began Hassock again. 'The argument we had was a mix-up and, well, we're sorry for wastin' your time yesterday but, erm, it just seems so surprisin' that we thought it couldn't be true, Sire.'

'What are you *talking* about?'

'Well, Sire, all the things that I thought Mulben here had stolen, had been.'

'But I didn't steal them,' interrupted Mulben, quickly.

'They went missing on one of the higher passes on the Trans-Talpino Trade Route. How, I don't know, but it's all gone.'

Klayth sat up and, despite his irritation, started to pay attention. 'In the mountains, you say?'

'Yes, Sire. An' that's not all. It's not just me who's had stuff stolen. I've been talkin' to some of the other traders an' they reckon that every wagon comin' over the mountain in the last three days has arrived light.'

'But why? What's going on?' asked Klayth, shocked and dreading the answer.

'Don't know, Sire. But the funny thing is it all seems to be food an' the like. Almost as if someone's settin' up home out there. Although why anyone wants to live in the mountains with winter comin' on beats me.'

'Yes, well, thank you. That is most interesting. If you hear anything more about this matter I would be grateful if you could let me know and I'll forget about the waste of time yesterday,' said Klayth, already deep within a growing forest

39

of troubled thoughts. An ashen looked washed over his face as he thought of the only person he knew who was in the right place, who had the motive and capability to steal – and worse, who had the opportunity.

Hassock and Mulben bowed and scraped their way out of the Public Chambers, completely ignored by the troubled King, his thoughts hang-gliding over the Talpa Mountains.

One word troubled him more than the others – opportunity. How can *he* have the opportunity? He is under heavy guard. Watched by the combined security blanket of Burnurd and Maffew, serving time for crimes against the state. There's no way it can be him.

Is there?

'Suddenly, as if appearing from her wildest dreams, he stood silhouetted in the bedroom door. Her young, tender heart thrilled at the sight of his strong handsome body. She had kept her love burning and now, as she knew he would, he had returned for her. In a moment she was in his arms, his manly hand caressing her luscious femininity.'

Chomp.

'He pulled her slim figure closer towards him and ran his fingers through her shining auburn hair.'

Chomp.

' "Oh, my darling!" she whispered. "You came back!" '

Chomp.

' "I knew I wouldn't wait in vain. I never gave up hope." '

Chomp. Chomp.

Ch'tin sighed as he ate his midday meal. Chomp.

'He said nothing, but his muscular arms tightened their loving embrace and she melted further, surrendering to his touch.'

Chomp.

' "You will stay now, won't you?" she urged, praying for the right answer. He nodded, silently, his eyes saying more than mere words could convey.'

Chomp.

'The war was over, he could stay and devote his life to her.'
Chomp.

'The way he had always wanted to.' Chomp.

The tiny bookworm finished the final page and sniffed as he swallowed the last sentence whole. He loved a good romance. But that wasn't too bad. A bit sloppy in places, and a little heavy once or twice, but generally pretty good. He liked the heroine though, he thought, licking his mandibles. Oh, yes. Very tasty!

'Finished already?' asked Hogshead, looking down from one of the top shelves of the cavernous castle library.

'Mmmm. Good it was!' answered the tiny, green bookworm waving his antennae in appreciation.

'Cor! It doesn't take him long when he's got a hunger on,' said Courgette, her face framed between two tomes as she peered through a curtain of a bookshelf. Her face turned red with effort as she struggled towards Ch'tin, heaving a huge, thick volume onto the table, raising a small cloud of dust.

'Pudding?' asked Ch'tin hopefully.

'Ooh, no, you hungry thing. You can't have any of this, keep your greedy mandibles off!'

'Mandibles now it is. Impressive very,' he piped.

'Oh yes,' answered Courgette, investigating her fingernails in mock nonchalance. 'Dictionaries are wonderful things!'

'What there have you?' asked Ch'tin raising himself to his full three-quarters of an inch and staring through his pair of unusually large compound eyes.

'A book,' she teased.

'That I know. What subject?'

'Mineralogy. The study of rocks.' Courgette flicked through a few chapters, stopping when a picture of what looked like a fish embedded in rock caught her attention. She stared at the page, completely absorbed.

'What've you got there?' asked Hogshead, having come down from the top shelf empty handed.

'Rocks and fish!' squeaked Ch'tin.

'What?'

41

'Fossils,' said Courgette. 'Look. Ages ago when things died they got buried and left shapes in the rocks. Like moulds or something. There's shells and birds and a fish.'

'That looks a bit weird. It's got too many fins.'

'Yes. It's a coelacanth. It says here it died about a hundred million years ago.'

'I'm not surprised with all them fins. It probably couldn't swim away fast enough.'

'Smelly it will be now!' quipped Ch'tin, wrinkling something that Courgette hoped was his nose.

'Oh, don't be silly, you two. Did you find anything?' she asked Hogshead, tearing herself away from the book.

'No,' he humphed. 'I just don't understand it. They must be in here somewhere. I've looked everywhere. A library this big *must* have some magic books.'

'Are they not over there by the conjuring section?'

'No. That's silly things like party tricks and sleight of hand. Not proper magic. Not the *real* stuff!'

'If not on shelves, where they be?' thought Ch'tin out loud.

'That's what we are trying to work out. I've looked along every single inch of these dusty shelves and there's no sign of anything. Anywhere!'

'Then they not there are,' said the worm, sagely.

'Look, I just can't believe that there are no magic books in a castle this size. There's *always* magic books in castles!' Hogshead complained. 'Franck told me!'

'If not on shelves, where they be?' mumbled Courgette, looking at Ch'tin suspiciously. She had a feeling that he knew more than he was giving away. The worm examined a spot on the table where his feet should be.

'Yes, that's what I just said,' repeated Hogshead, staring accusingly at a pile of books that stubbornly refused to appear. 'There isn't a single magic book, of even passing worth, to be found on any of these shelves!'

'Not on . . . Under!' Courgette's eyes lit up as she realised why they had not found anything. 'They wouldn't just leave magic books lying around now, would they, waiting for *anyone* to pick up and use. Not on shelves, anyhow.' Ch'tin looked up at her. The worm's face distorted grotesquely as curving mandibles slithered upward, the hard pads that passed as teeth twisting into view from behind the protective green curtain of his lips. Courgette smiled back at Ch'tin, stood up and ran off into one of the darker corners.

Hogshead scratched his head as he ran the last few sentences back through his mind.

'Come on!' shouted Courgette from behind a stack of shelves. 'Give me a hand, will you!'

Hogshead picked up the tiny bookworm, pushed him into the pocket of his tunic and ran off towards the source of the cries. He turned a corner, ran between a ravine of shelves and almost tripped over the hunched figure of Courgette, struggling with something heavy at the foot of a shelf of dictionaries.

'Come on,' she said, puffing and panting as she tugged at a ring embedded in the floor, like a demented thrush wrestling a particularly stubborn worm. Hogshead stepped up, spitting into the palms of his hands. He wasn't sure why, but he'd seen some of the soldiers do it before attempting to shift difficult things, like heavy barrels, petulant donkeys or their wives' laden shopping sacks, bulging after an expensive spree at the market. Hogshead took a deep breath and heaved. Something creaked. He hoped it wasn't him. He pulled again, Courgette joining in. After a struggle the two of them managed to move the ring. A patch of floor came with it. Followed by years of accumulated dust which billowed around their ankles, tickling Courgette's nose.

'I stumbled upon it earlier,' she whispered, wrinkling her nose between deep breaths. 'I bet this is what you're after.'

Hogshead stared at the dark hole in the floor. 'A trapdoor. Of course! Not *on* the shelves.'

There was a scuffle in his tunic pocket as Ch'tin peered over into the rectangle of blackness. He smirked to himself; Courgette was learning fast.

43

'Here you are. You'll need this as well,' she said as she handed Hogshead a burning torch off the wall.

'You think of everything, don't you? Thanks,' he replied, peering down the flight of stone steps fading rapidly into the cobwebby gloom. He took a deep breath and started to lower himself into the unknown dark. The torch flickered as a cold, unseen draught rushed past into the freedom of the library. Hogshead shivered, swallowing nervously. In a moment he had disappeared below floor level into a small, natural-looking passageway that led off in a gradual downward slope. Courgette was right behind him. Hogshead relaxed a little, he always felt better when she was around. Funny, that!

Little clouds of dried powdery soil kicked up under their cautious footfalls as they crept on through the flickering torch-lit gloom. Down. The passage felt as if no one had set foot in there for centuries. Strange markings decorated the rough rock walls in incomprehensible patterns, some looking like sheets of coloured fire outlining hundreds of black circular beetles, others like leaves and coastlines, others still seeming to be random but regular and all of them were incredibly complex. The detail was amazing, the closer Hogshead looked, the more elaborate it all seemed. He felt dizzy, as if he were being drawn into the swirling devilish designs of chaos.

They carried on, Ch'tin peering out of Hogshead's tunic pocket, until the passage grew fractionally wider and a small chamber spread out before them. The passage stopped in a dead end, offering them no way out. They looked around, standing awestruck in the flickering yellow of the torchlight, their shadows dancing wildly gyrating dances on the rough walls of the passage. The chamber was lined with hundreds of shelves, bowing under the masses of magic tomes. Silky shimmering cobwebs hung like an explorer's mosquito nets, adding an air of ancient bridal mystery, obscuring the titles of the hundreds of books, standing waiting to be opened.

This was it! He'd found them. All of them. The collection

44

of magic books that he knew was bound to be in a castle this size.

Courgette hit him hard on the arm and whispered in his ear, 'Told you they'd all be down here.' She grinned disarmingly at him.

'Hmmmph. Well done!' All right, he added to himself, so maybe I had a little help. But I would have found them, no problem.

From Hogshead's tunic pocket, Ch'tin grinned a wormy grin. Magic books! he thought. My favourite!

This time, thought Firkin, I'll get him! I'll give him a run for his money.

He mounted the log again and stood weighing the wet sack in his hands. He tightened his grip, moving forward along the rough surface of the bark. King Klayth grinned broadly at his dripping opponent.

'Firkin, you're all wet!' he taunted and laughed, his voice echoing in the tiny back courtyard of Castell Rhyngill.

'It'll be your turn soon,' replied Firkin through tightly clenched teeth as he menacingly swung his dripping sack.

'Ohhh! I'm terrified,' came the sarcastic reply.

Firkin took a few shaky steps forward, looking warily down into the pool of stagnant green water. He really didn't want to end up back in *there* again. It was cold and wet and worst of all, it smelled.

He bent his knees, sidling forward, watching every move that Klayth made, muttering under his breath and cursing his earlier dose of sodden misfortune. In the distance a raven croaked and flapped noisily between two ivy-covered towers.

'You'd better be ready. This time I'm taking no prisoners,' threatened Firkin, a small green puddle forming at his feet.

Klayth stepped forward, standing tall, balancing his sack of grain casually in his right hand. With a wicked grin, he rocked the log, almost destroying the final remnants of Firkin's shaky poise.

'Stop that, you cheat!'

'Gamesmanship, dear Firkin.'

'Cheating, I'd call it,' he replied brushing his fringe of dark brown hair out of his eyes. 'You're taking advantage of me while I'm still a little on the wobbly side.'

'Of course. Do you think a real opponent wouldn't do the same? Or worse!'

'This is *supposed* to be fun!'

'It is!' grinned the King. 'I think it's great fun!'

'I'll wipe that smirk off your face when you end up in there.' Firkin pointed to the smelly pool below them.

'It is a shame that your verbal threats aren't matched by an equal array of fighting skills.'

From behind a small clump of barrels at the far side of the courtyard, a pair of dark brown eyes watched the two fighting youngsters.

Advancing slowly along the thin log, Firkin increased the depth of his swings as he wound himself up into what he hoped was a vicious sack-fighting machine. His body rocked in the opposite direction to the sodden sack as he counter-balanced the weight, watching and waiting for his chance, any chance. He needed it! Klayth bent his knees, readying himself for the tempestuous onslaught. Without warning he leapt forward, swinging hard at his opponent's chest. Firkin ducked, the sack whistling inches above his head, grunted and followed up with a glancing blow from his own sack which caused Klayth to wobble desperately and retreat a few paces.

Klayth regained his balance first, advancing while Firkin wrestled with the almost uncontrollably heavy sack. Battle fever strong in his heart the King screamed and ran forward, seemingly oblivious to the abject lack of width of the log. The watcher behind the barrels held her breath. Firkin was for it now!

'Oh Thire, there you are. Thire. I've been thearching everywhere for you, Thire . . .' shouted Mynyn, trotting round a corner of one of the smaller towers.

46

Klayth turned, his concentration broken by the unexpected intrusion. Firkin regained his balance and swung his soggy sack around in a monarch-mangling arc. The watcher gripped the barrel with knuckle-whitening tension as Firkin's sack landed with perfect accuracy square in the King's back. The blond monarch executed a beautifully graceful half somersault as he was catapulted off the log and into the green, stinking pool. Firkin shrieked in victory. The watcher thrilled as she admired Firkin's skill. In her eyes, luck never even entered into it. Klayth spluttered, spitting disgusting pond water and scraping a layer of slime out of his hair. Mynyn skipped agitatedly from foot to foot in acutely horrified embarrassment.

'That was cheating,' spluttered Klayth expectorantly, glaring soddenly at Firkin.

'Yeth,' squeaked Mynyn, 'it'th unethical to thtab your opponent in hith back!'

'Shouldn't leave it unguarded, Your Highness,' cackled Firkin wickedly.

'I shouldn't be so rudely interrupted, *should* I?' snarled Klayth, his attention snapping at Mynyn.

'Oh, Thire I . . . I didn't think, Thire!'

'I can thee . . . see that!' struggled Klayth, slapping the water in frustration. 'Give me a hand will you, Mynyn, I think I'm stuck.'

The general dogsbody closed his horror-struck mouth and ran over to help King Klayth. 'I'm tho thorry, Thire, I didn't mean to, Thire, I won't do it again, Thire.' The tiny, poodle-like servant reached down into the pool, his hand gripping Klayth's wrist as he started to pull. 'Oh, Thire, it theemth you *are* thtuck. I can't theem to move you, Thire!'

Klayth winked at Firkin who stifled a sudden chuckle. The tiny figure of Mynyn pulled harder and the King began to move. He stood up dripping and pulled back. Far too late to do anything about it, even if he could, Mynyn realised the trick.

'No, no, no!' he yelled as he arced his way forward into the green pool.

'Oh, Mynyn,' said the King as the sodden clerk's head appeared a moment later, gasping for breath. 'Next time *don't* butt in! I would still be dry were it not for your interruption!'

Klayth laughed and set off to get cleaned up, waving absently to Firkin. Mynyn sat dripping for a moment in the pool, then stood quickly and trotted after the King, sprinkling green droplets as he ran. 'But, Thire, I thaid I wath thorry,' he whined wetly. 'Thire, you're needed in the Public Chamberth again. Thire. Thire! Wait for me, Thire . . .'

The watcher carefully crept away from behind the barrels, out of sight of Firkin. She was so proud of the way he had flattened the King of Rhyngill! She skipped away in a warm glow of reflected glory. Her brother could do anything, thought Dawn, what a hero!

Firkin stood swaying and dripping on the narrow log and launched a quiverful of sulky glances after the tiny, running poodle figure. Yet again Klayth had been summoned away. Somehow, and he couldn't work out how, there was a gap forming between himself and Klayth, and he didn't like it one bit. One of the main things that Firkin didn't like was that he was gradually being squeezed out, ignored, snubbed. In his mind's eye he could see two huge doors slowly closing on a raving royal banquet inside. If he wasn't careful, he, like a skulking stray begging for scraps, would be left outside, shunned.

Miserably, feeling as wanted as a rabid, flea-infested mongrel in a poodle-parlour, he climbed off the log and trudged inside to get changed.

Things with Klayth were also far from fine. Questions and fears vied for his attention in a whirlwind of growing panic. Thirty minutes ago, after cleaning himself up, Mynyn had handed him a copy of today's newsparchment. It happened every day. Amongst Klayth's tasks was looking through the daily newsparchment to make sure nothing untoward had been included. At first, the issue he looked at today seemed

48

to contain nothing out of the ordinary. The back page had all the usual sports reports about who was going up in the tourney league and who beat whom in the archery open at the weekend. Inside were the usual small advertisements, badly printed and poorly phrased. Sheets of them vied for precious attention. If you wanted something all you had to do was look in these yellowing pages. There were sections for knife sharpening ('Make your knife slice twice as nice'): bespoke armour fitting, repair and customisation ('Give your shield a brand new feel: make your breast plate great! Drop in to Visigoth Armour Repairs – panel beating a speciality'); 24-hour horse reshoe-ing service ('Is your horse a hobbledy horse? Give your steed the feel of feet of steel! Hop in to Spam Smith's Smith's Shop – approved percheron dealer –insurance claims a speciality'). It went on and on and on. All pretty standard stuff for a normal day in Rhyngill. But it was in the actual news section that something caught Klayth's eye. In amongst reports that final preparations were well under way for the renewed annual Fayre next month in the Castle, but a few more fire-breathers would be nice, and a report that Timmy, the cat that was lost last week had been found safe and well in a barrel, was an article that leapt from the page and sent Klayth's heart straight into his hand-tooled boots. This was trouble. He was sure it was trouble. It was the sort of trouble that gave trouble a bad name. The article read:–

MOUNTAIN MONSTER TERRORISES
TRANS-TALPINE TRADERS

Reports are piling up of mysterious mountain thefts being carried out on the Trans-Talpino Trading Route. No trader is safe, it seems, from the ruthless robber who strikes swiftly and silently in the lonely mountain passes. Tension is rising with each passing day and each and every added crime.

49

'It's a mystery' said C. Q. Hassock, Trans-Talpine Haulage Contractor and recent victim of the 'mountain mugger'. 'I saw nothing and heard nothing. He, or it, must've come up behind me.' Other contractors report similar happenings. So far there have been no injuries, but how long this will remain so could be anyone's guess. The traders are demanding action to rid them of this turbulent beast. 'If this carries on, we'll have to put our prices up, an' nobody wants that,' added a spokesman for the market traders.

As Klayth read the article his eyes widened and icicles of fear crystallised in his heart, making him shiver with terror and suspicion. He put down the parchment and stared blankly at the page, unable to believe his eyes. He had a bad feeling about this. A very bad feeling. A feeling which gave 'bad' a whole new meaning, somewhere between the serious need to practise self-inflicted surgery on one's wrists, with a blunt knife, and the uncontrollable urge to scream and run away, waving one's arms in abject, gibbering hysteria. The words poked and prodded at his conscience, niggling to remind him of events he wished to forget, straining to open a chapter in his life he hoped had been firmly and irrevocably closed. The events in the mountains had all the hallmarks of a certain ex-Lord Chancellor. The more Klayth thought about this, the more the civil engineers of his memory applied the pneumatic drills of total recall to the pavement that he had conveniently swept his memories beneath. The cracks were beginning to show.

'But is it true?' demanded the voice of an irate market trader, pulling Klayth back into the reality of the Public Chambers and the angry mob before him. Countless traders, hauliers, farmers and press were crowded into the Chamber. Having read the alarming article in this morning's parchment, they too wanted some answers.

'Of course it's true,' answered Mulben forcefully from the

other side of the Public Chambers. 'Are you trying to say that I'm not trustworthy or something?'

'Oh, er, no,' answered the voice. 'I didn't mean it like that at all.' Several people sniggered.

'I always believe what I read in the parchment,' shouted a heckler, dripping with sarcasm. Several journalists shouted back answers with a less than polite flavour to them.

The cracks in Klayth's mental pavement widened, yawning open as the drills spat shards of stone. He buried his head in his hands and wished that his throne would swallow him, swiftly, quietly and preferably now.

The crowd was getting ugly* and Mynyn was leaping up and down at the front gesturing wildly, yapping and appealing for some sort of calm. His insistent yelps of desperation were entirely ignored by all but the most timid of the traders. But since they were standing at the back of the crowd, near the door, ready for a hasty exit if the scene turned even uglier, they only saw an occasionally waved hand above the heads of the rest of their colleagues. Assuming that it was someone on their side, they ignored it and kept on moaning and muttering 'Hear, hear' at appropriate intervals. This had the unfortunate knock-on effect of encouraging Mynyn to try harder. Soon he looked as if he had been welded to the end of a very large and powerful spring. The situation was in danger of getting out of hand. Mynyn was not so much pouring oil on stormy waters as throwing a match into a firework factory.

Suddenly a huge trader muscled his way forward through the restive crowd. Klayth looked up and found himself plaintively wishing that Burnurd and Maffew were still here. The huge man scowled at Klayth, opened his mouth and said, 'Sire, this mornin' I got a message wiv my delivry of groceries an' I was told that it says that it will be the last

*Of course, by the classical standards set by the likes of the theatrical stars of the day, the universally lusted after Fhulla Figha and her main co-star, the square-jawed hunk guaranteed to set female hearts a-fluttering, Rok Blurblurr, many would say the crowd could be little else but ugly.

51

delivry until the problem of all this robbry is sorted.' The crowd listened with hushed attention.

'Wha', you ain't gonna get no more stuff?' came a voice from the middle of the crowd.

'That's right,' answered the big man, 'Not 'til it's all sorted.'

The volume of rapid and heated discussion suddenly rose several decibels. The huge man waved his arms for silence. Mynyn quivered silently.

'Sire,' said the trader, 'Wiv all due respect. What the bloody 'ell is you gonna do about it? 'Scuse my Cranachanian.'

'Ooh. That'th thyocking language to be uthed in front of Hith Highneth,' yelped Mynyn indignantly.

'I, I,' started Klayth nervously. 'I do.' The crowd looked baffled. Mynyn put his head on one side quizzically. 'Er, 'scuse your Cranachanian, added Klayth as an explanation. Mynyn looked shocked. The oppressive bulk of the huge trader nodded and looked for an answer.

So did Klayth.

'Does anyone have a description of the thief?' he ventured.

'Scum of the slime pits of . . .'

'No,' interrupted the King. 'I meant what does he look like?'

An uncomfortable silence floated in the room as people 'Ummed' and 'Ahhed' ineffectually.

'So nobody has actually seen the thief?' asked Klayth.

More embarrassed grumbling silence.

'Does anyone have a clue who it might be? A gang of desperate travellers?'

Shrugging of shoulders.

'Some Cranachanians causing trouble?'

Mumbled nonsense.

'One man? Any ideas?'

Will someone, please, tell me that it *isn't* him! sobbed Klayth in the safety of his mind.

The sussuration of shyly shuffling feet.

A pneumatic drill hit something inside the King's head, shattering its surface. A dull brown duct split, pouring thick black dread into the hole.

'Hasn't anyone anything useful to say? Does nobody know who it is?' pleaded Klayth.

'Is it a riddle?' asked a voice from the back. 'This is all a game, isn't it?'

'Yeah! Who is it?' added another.

'You *know*, don't you? Hey, everybody, the King knows!'

'Tell us the answer,' yelled another.

'I don't know the answer,' answered Klayth, black dread filling his mind.

'You can guess, though,' came another voice.

'I, well, I have my suspicions.' This was too much.

'Who is it?'

'I believe I might know who is behind all of this,' said Klayth, hoping fervently that he was miles from the mark, praying that someone would shoot his theory down. The crowd's spirits rose as they clamoured for the answer.

'Who is it . . .'

' 'ang 'im by the ba . . .'

'. . . yeah . . . by the boar pit! . . .'

Klayth stood, raised his arms and appealed for peace. 'I may not be right. I want to investigate this further so I want several strong men to come with me into the mountains.' The crowd went very quiet at this point and began shuffling carefully backwards towards the door. Klayth continued.

'I think I know where to find some answers.' He pointed to the far corner of the room. 'I want volunteers to assemble in that corner . . . '

Hogshead still couldn't believe his eyes as he stared at the large yellow-paged book lying on the table in his special room. It wasn't really so much a room – more a space underneath the tiles in the castle roof that hadn't yet been filled in. He had found this place soon after moving into

53

Castell Rhyngill, quickly making it his own, disguising its tiny entrance so that it became a perfect place to hide. Courgette and Ch'tin were the only others who knew about it and they were sworn to absolute secrecy. Here he had the privacy to read, understand and learn. And now he had the book. A magic book. *His* magic book. The only limits were those of his imagination! His heart pounded with excitement as he placed the ancient book on the table. Courgette looked on nervously and sipped quietly at the cup of water that she had brought with her.

A satisfyingly usable glow appeared as Hogshead lit a small tallow candle and placed it in the jury-rigged holder perched on one of the joists. It lit the illuminated script on the yellowed and ancient tome, adding an extra degree of flickering mystery to the whole scene. The letters seemed to dance in tantalising ways urging Hogshead to start to spell. He was fascinated, almost mesmerised by the words. Words in a magic book. Courgette and Ch'tin's eyes glowed in the reflected light of the tallow candle as they watched Hogshead.

'Careful you must be. Magic like fire can burn!' said Ch'tin in his high-pitched voice. Courgette looked at the tiny bookworm with alarm.

Hogshead stared fixedly at the page.

'Do not too quick too much do. Addictive it is,' piped the worm.

'Yes. Please be careful,' whispered Courgette nervously.

Hogshead's eyes seemed to bulge as his concentration centred on the pages before him. Ch'tin would have furrowed his brow and stroked his chin in concerned curiosity, had he possessed them. To the young man sitting in the tallow lit room, all that mattered in the whole world was contained in the volume before him. Everything he needed to know to give him the capacity for brave deeds, missions of valour, head-to-head combat with monsters and demons of the imagination – the stuff of legend. Fleetingly he revelled in the glory of all the countless ways he could carry out daring

54

acts of honour, single-handedly turning back the black tides of evil: setting unrequited love back onto its true course; rescuing plaintively wailing damsels from crumbling prisons of towers; it was all there in bold characters on the page. He wasn't so keen on the cure for warts. Of course, he told himself, it would be the actual act of rescue that would give him all the satisfaction he needed, not any of the rewards offered by well-endowed, yearning maidens, fantastically grateful, and willing to show it. This book, along with many more in the depths of the library, held all the magical power he needed. And it was here at the end of his fingertips just waiting, like a groaning buffet display, to be dipped into and devoured in a frenzy of thaumic gluttony.

All he needed to know was how to get to it all.

The ASCII's* were completely indecipherable to him. It wasn't going to be as easy as he had imagined. Not like the way Franck had described it at all. The old Prospector hadn't mentioned the fact that magic was written in a different language, with different letters and, worse, no punctuation. Of course, having no punctuation made it very easy to write, but the devil's own job to understand, let alone chant properly. One of the earliest lessons in spelling is to impart the required skills of splitting your mind into unequal sections, one to concentrate on the actual casting of the thaumaturgical wave guides and the other, and some say more important part, to look ahead by four or five lines to find a convenient space in the text to insert a breathing space. Many apprentice sorcerers had been known to turn blue and faint from oxygen starvation caused by poor breath foresight, especially whilst reciting 'Werflox's Pan Dimensional Mantra in B Minor'. It was the breathing that was always the problem; if you were good at breathing you were almost certain to be good at getting results. It was for this reason, several influential scholars had noted, that many of the most

---

*All letters and characters designed and utilised by the Advanced Spell Casting and Influential Incantations Board are held under strict copyright and are known as ASCII's in magic circles.

successful sorceresses looked surprisingly like Opera Sopranos from high in the Ammoretto Mountains.

All these difficulties of breathing, reading and hyper-accurate phonetic diction could be overcome given an infinitely long time and an infinite number of lives to play within. But fortunately for Hogshead he had a tutor. He might be three-quarters of an inch high, green and view the world through a pair of compound eyes, but, due to a light snack of Appendix IIIb of Vhintz the Travelling Sorcerer's magical book one afternoon, he was now inherently magical. This gave Ch'tin an acute and remarkably detailed insight into the magical world. He had also learned a lot during the short time he had spent with the Wizard Merlot and was now in an almost ideal position to help Hogshead, to guide Hogshead, and above all to prevent Hogshead from doing anything extremely rash and unbelievably stupid.

Ch'tin was probably going to be needed very soon.

Hogshead sat motionless, apart from the occasional turning of a page. He was deeply engrossed in the ancient book before him. He looked like a cat staring into a small pond, transfixed by the shoal of fish gliding by under the smooth glassy surface. Courgette had never seen him so enthralled by anything before – well, except for a well-decorated, fresh-baked chocolate gateau. But that was different, more innocent, more naive. This was a different sort of hunger. The look on his face was more . . . she didn't like to say it, even to herself, more . . . *power* hungry.

Suddenly, the musty silence was broken as Hogshead thumped his index finger onto the page before him, stared at Ch'tin and said simply, 'That one!'

'A spell you have found,' squeaked the tiny worm. 'Good.'

'It's nothing dangerous, is it?' asked Courgette, nervously.

'Pass me that cup,' commanded Hogshead pointing at the vessel in Courgette's hand.

'But I haven't finished drinking yet.'

Hogshead pointed to a spot on the table a few inches in

56

front of him and Courgette found herself obeying. The look in his eyes made her feel uncomfortable.

'Do I need anything else?' he asked Ch'tin.

'Luck in amounts large. Levitation spell not too difficult is, though.'

Hogshead felt confident. In the last eight months he had spent many long hours gathering as much information as possible from Ch'tin about his time with Merlot, asking questions, watching Ch'tin carefully, hanging on his every disjointed phrase and absorbing it all. He was a perfect student – hungry to learn. He'd always believed in magic, secretly knowing it to be real, constantly confirming this knowledge by devouring any tale that anyone could tell him which had anything, even remotely, to do with magic. And now he had the chance, having experienced magic first hand, to begin to use it for himself. A twinge of excited nervousness raced up his spine and made him shiver.

He looked at the words on the page. It was a foreign language, the letters were the same but the order bore no relation to anything that he had ever seen before. It was a short spell. Straightforward levitation, pick an object up and put it down again. None of this somersaulting round your head business or any other fancy stuff, well, not just yet anyway. He looked at the cup and wondered if it was actually possible to raise it off the table without physically touching it. There was only one way to find out. Inside he felt sure that it *was* possible, but when it actually came right down to it, the cup looked remarkably solid and, er, stationary.

That, he promised himself, was about to change.

Hogshead concentrated on the spell on the page. He read it through, trying to figure out the correct pronunciation of the words. After a few quiet moments of preparation, he felt he was ready. He took a deep breath. Courgette watched him, still with very mixed feelings about this. She couldn't stop him until he had tried it, she knew that, and if she *tried* to stop him, he would be in a terrible mood for weeks. Part of her hoped that this silly nonsense of wanting to be a Wizard

57

would lose its charm. It scared her. But part of her, the larger part, hoped beyond all hope that it would work and that he wouldn't be disappointed. It was bad enough trying to cope with a sulking Firkin.

Suddenly a strange strangling sound started to issue from Hogshead's throat. It sounded like a chewed up tape recording of an obscure religious mantra being played backwards, at half speed, while a cat was being cheerfully throttled. It was a promising start. Ch'tin nodded wisely as the guttural, inhuman sound proceeded. Hogshead stared defiantly at the cup and continued the agonising racket. He was determined that it was going to work. Courgette edged uncertainly away from the table. Hogshead's contorted guttural wailings grew louder. Ch'tin looked on proudly. It was going well.

Abruptly there was a single knock of pottery on wood. Courgette caught her breath and watched the cup, wide-eyed. It was in exactly the same position as before, looking as defiantly solid as before, and equally as heavy as before. Had she heard that tap? It seemed impossible.

Hogshead's brow was furrowed in deep concentration as he carried on, deeply engrossed in imitating unspeakable acts of catricide. Had he heard the cup rattle? Had it been Courgette's wishful thinking?

Another tap answered all questions. The cup moved. It definitely moved. Hogshead's voice faltered as he took a breath at a difficult phonetic change and redoubled his efforts. Five kittens screeched and drew their claws down a blackboard with glee. Another tap. Then a whole series. The cup rattled and paradiddled faster and louder, although not moving from the central spot. The sound resonated noisily through the table as if an army of death-watch beetles was headbanging at an all-night rave. Courgette held her ears. It was getting painful. Ch'tin began to vibrate across the table as the amplitude of the cup's oscillations increased. The book began to move. Courgette felt as if her teeth were rattling in their sockets.

Suddenly, there was a sharp splitting sound as the internal stresses within the cup proved too much. It exploded into a thousand tiny fragments, spilling the water and washing Ch'tin off the edge of the table. After the noise of the previous few minutes, the abrupt silence seemed painful. Courgette took her hands from her ears and stared bewildered at Hogshead and the evidence of a wet patch of pottery fragments on the table. He looked pale and drained, as if a trainee vampire had used him for practice. But despite his appearance of physical exhaustion there was a look deep in his eyes that spelled victory. Knowing Hogshead, it probably spelled it with a 'k' and two 'e's.

As a levitation spell it had been an unmitigated disaster, but things had changed. He hadn't physically touched the cup. Nobody had. Somehow, using words and sounds he had actually moved it. He felt exhausted, euphoric. He wanted more. He could do it. Magic. He had done magic!

From far below the table Courgette heard a pathetic spluttering sound as Ch'tin coughed up a mouthful of water and struggled upright. She lifted him onto the table. His face, a tangle of nightmarish mandibles and bulbous eyes at the best of times, was contorted into a seething nest of frothing, snapping mouthparts.

'Purposefully that do at me, did you? Mmmmh!' he squealed, staring defiantly at Hogshead. He was annoyed. His grammar always went haywire when he was annoyed.

Hogshead stared at Ch'tin, dripping and fuming on the table, half expecting sparks to leap off the ends of his wildly gyrating antennae, and laughed. Courgette shuddered as she heard the sound. It wasn't the laughter she was used to hearing. This was different, colder, harder. Hungrier. She stared at Hogshead as he looked back at the wreckage on the table. He seemed no different from before. She shook her head in confusion. Had her ears played tricks on her, or had Hogshead's laughter really echoed?

In the King's personal chambers, behind the Conference

Room, Firkin's tongue wriggled around the corner of his mouth as he concentrated on the last few folds of the tiny parchment bird. He adjusted the beak, trimmed the flight feathers and smiled happily to himself as he admired his creation.

'Ready,' he said. 'Shall we see how it goes?'

'Mmmmm,' muttered Klayth absently, slouching vacantly on the heap of cushions in his private quarters. Next to him was his tired and soggy old bear. It watched him in glass-eyed wonder. Firkin wasn't sure whether the bear or the King looked more intelligent. Klayth hadn't said more than 'Mmmmmm' for hours, the result of the whirls of meetings, talks, inaugurations, banquets and a million other functions and duties he had to attend. Firkin could sense that the burdens of rulership were getting a bit too much, and it was going to get a lot worse . . . *unless!* A tiny spark of inspiration winked in the deep black void of despair.

Unless, he thought again, with the desperate naivety of the terminally optimistic. Yes, if I could find a way to solve his problems and make everything right, then, well, everything *would* be right! Ha! Simple!

He smiled to himself as he thought of all the ways that he could help. Then thought of all the problems and snags that would prevent him having a hope in hell of even getting anywhere near an attempt to begin to solve anything of even the slightest importance. The tiny spark winked out.

Parchment birds, he thought, that's all I seem to be good for. Oh well.

'Shall we see how well it flies?' Firkin repeated.

'Mmmmmmm,' repeated the King, black dread still oozing out between the cracks of his memory's pavement.

'. . .' said the bear in full agreement.

'Shall I tear it into little bits then stamp on it?' he asked, frustration scratching at the tinder-box of inspiration. Something inside him wasn't going to give up that easily. The spark glowed red, a gentle puff of encouragement, cup your hands, blow, *gently*, gently! The tinder wrinkled, smouldered and caught. The spark lit a door ahead. It was closing fast, Klayth shutting him out. If he could just jam his foot in the bottom corner, like those door-to-door Ghyee Yohvass Witnesses . . .

'Mmmmmm,' came the distant gloom-ridden grunt.

'. . . ?' said the bear.

The gap in the door was as wide as his leg, he hoped his boots were strong enough . . . 'Klayth, what's the matter?' said Firkin. 'Are you listening to me?'

'Mmmmmm.'

'Klayth!'

'Eh? What?' said the King, struggling to pull the wellingtons of his psyche out of the mire of self-pity.

'I said "Didn't you hear me?" I bet you haven't heard a single word I've said for the last ten minutes.'

'Oh sorry. I was, er, thinking,' replied Klayth, fishing about for the socks of self-respect that lay crumpled at the bottom of his wellies.

'Penny for them.'

'Eh?'

'A penny for your thoughts, my liege,' said Firkin scooping the floor with an over-exaggerated bow, in an attempt to lighten the mood somewhat.

'I wouldn't know where to begin.'

'Well, as Franck used to say, "Begin at the beginning and carry on until the end, then stop."'

'Hmmm. That's easier said than done,' sighed Klayth.

'Is it those thefts in the mountains?' asked Firkin sitting down, and bracing himself.

'Yes.'

Suddenly, like a trawl-net opening on the deck of a ship, tons of wet sloppy emotions spilled out, gaping for air, squirming and flipping in the alien environs of outside.

'Yes,' sniffed Klayth. 'Yes, yes. It's those thefts. And the soldiers and . . . I don't think I'm doing very well at it.'

'At what?'

'Being King!'

'Why?' asked Firkin, in great danger of being swept out over the side of the ship, or worse, staying on board to gut what he'd just dredged up.

'Just look at all the unrest. I keep having to break up squabbles and arguments all the time. All the soldiers that were in Cranachan haven't really settled into life in the castle and I don't know what to do.'

'I wouldn't even have a *clue* where to begin.'

'That's just it.' Klayth looked hard at Firkin with an expression that yearned for help. 'That's exactly it. I don't know where to begin.'

'Begin what?'

'Being King! Are you really listening?'

'Well, that's easy,' started Firkin, trying to be helpful. 'Kings, er, kings . . . well, rule!'

'Yes, and what does that mean?'

'He . . . er, tells people what to do . . . and stuff,' struggled Firkin, floundering, beginning to wish he'd just left Klayth to sulk.

'*What* does he tell them to do?' burst out Klayth. 'How does he tell them to do it? How does he know what to tell them to do? Why does he tell them to do the things that he has thought for them to do?'

'I, I, er, I know the last one,' said Firkin, his eyes crossing as he tried to decipher Klayth's questions.

'Tell me. Nobody else has.'

'Well . . . well . . . because,' began Firkin, his brain whirring to come up with a response, ' . . . because you're the King.'

It was a pathetic answer.

Klayth looked at the earnest expression on Firkin's face, which resembled the cleverest spaniel in all the world: he'd fetched the King his own slipper of a solution, and now he wanted a reward. It was too much. Klayth exploded in a flurry of laughter, his face suddenly crimson as the pressure valve blew. He rolled off the heap of cushions, shrieking, while Firkin looked on baffled.

'What did I say?' he blurted trying to contain the contagious viruses of laughter. 'What?' He never did get an answer. Within a few moments they were both helpless in the throws of a debilitating bout of acute hilarity.

Minutes later, as they eventually calmed down, their throats sore, their ribs aching, Klayth managed to struggle to say, 'The only thing that'll make everything all right, for me, is if the war had never happened. And that's impossible. Now, what about those birds you were wittering on about before?'

'Huh. I'd forgotten all about them,' came the answer.

'Ready!' taunted Klayth.

'You?'

'Yes,' answered Klayth holding his bird aloft, his left arm out in front. Firkin stood in a similar manner.

'Go!' shouted Firkin, releasing his parchment bird in a practised smooth movement. It flew straight and, for Klayth at least, irritatingly well. The King's bird shot out of his hand, flipped upside down, arced sharply to the left and rattled onto the floor.

There was a knock on the door.

'I'll show you how to make them if you like,' said Firkin, picking up his bird.

The door was politely, but firmly, struck again.

'Come,' shouted Klayth. 'Yes, I'd like that,' he said to Firkin.

'Thire, thire, have you forgotten your meeting? It hath been thceduled for thome time!' bustled Mynyn, trotting up to the King.

'Oh no! The volunteers. I completely forgot. You should have fetched me, Mynyn.'

'That ith what I am doing, Thire!'

Suddenly the door burst open again and three wildly enthusiastic youngsters bounced into the room like month-old red setters.

'Firkin, Firkin, Firkin!' shouted Hogshead excitedly, as he careered through the door followed by Courgette and Dawn.

63

'I'vedunnitI'vedunnitI've . . .' The room seemed full of waving arms and bouncing Hogsheads, Courgettes and Dawns.

Klayth slipped out to his meeting, followed by Mynyn and the gaze of Firkin.

'It didn't work quite how I thought it would but it worked and rattled and then it exploded and made a mess but we can clear that up and I want to do it again and and . . .' as Hogshead took a breath, Courgette started up, pinning Firkin's attention like a lepidopterist mounting a moth. 'It's true I was there and I saw it and it rattled I didn't touch it and he didn't touch it but it moved and it was full of water too and he made it work and . . .'

Firkin was forced deeper into the cushion he was sitting on by the barrage of words and nodding faces. He found himself thinking of four-month-old labrador puppies. 'Stop!' he shouted in self-defence, finally managing to get a word in. '*What* have you done?'

Hogshead closed his mouth and looked a little embarrassed.

'Ah. Sorry. I, er, got a little carried away. But it's so exciting 'cos it worked and I did it and I didn't touch it at all and . . .'

'You're doing it again. Slow down and tell me properly. What have you done?' Firkin knew he was bound to be told, and since Klayth had gone for the moment, it might as well be now as later.

Hogshead looked at Courgette and Dawn and giggled in a remarkably childish way. Even for him.

'Well,' he began coyly, and explained the incident with the cup. Courgette and Dawn listened enraptured, even though they knew all about it and had heard the story at least three times each.

'. . . and that's it. I worked some magic!' finished Hogshead, triumphantly.

'Magic,' said Firkin flatly. 'You can't do magic.'

'I couldn't before but I've learnt. I did it,' answered Hogshead, itching to bounce again.

'Yeah, yeah. Great,' replied Firkin moodily.

'Well I thought I'd get a better reaction from you than that!' moaned Hogshead. 'You miserable thing.'

'I've got more important things on my mind.'

'What could be more important than magic. . . !' burst out Hogshead before Dawn cut in and silenced him.

'What's wrong?' she asked her brother as the look on his face began to recall the strained evening in Middin before he disappeared. She had a bad feeling about this. A very bad feeling. So did Hogshead and Courgette.

'Well, if you'd listened instead of babbling on at me wildly you might have found out before,' said Firkin. 'It's Klayth . . .'

Hogshead coughed. 'Er, sorry, ha! Just remembered I've left an . . .'

'. . . incantation on,' finished Courgette.

'Dangerous to leave it . . .' said Hogshead as he disappeared out of the door.

'Might go horrid . . .' agreed the vanishing form of Courgette.

Firkin turned to the quivering figure of Dawn. She was trapped. Too slow to think of an excuse. She was there for the full innings.

'It's Klayth . . .' began Firkin again.

Silently, within the confines of her head, Dawn, like an urchin about to be bathed, screamed.

Quite how many volunteers Klayth expected to get was unclear but, judging by the look of mingled irritation and annoyance he now wore, it was certainly more than three. Of course, he could have ordered people to go, but Klayth felt that one volunteer was worth a hundred orders and, besides, he still wasn't entirely sure what he would find in the Talpa Mountains. The fewer people who knew the potentially horrific truth, the better. No point in making a mountain out of a molehill.

The progress of the group so far had been somewhat on the

noisy side due entirely to the complaining and argumentative natures of both Mulben and Hassock who, for reasons best known to themselves had decided to come along and see with their own eyes precisely what was going on. Hassock, being the penny-pinching haulage contractor that he was, wanted to see who or what was relocating his goods without his approval. And Mulben joined the party to keep a firm eye on Hassock whom he trusted about as far as he could spit a camel.

The third volunteer accompanying the King approached the journey's end with a feeling of trepidation and fear almost equal to Klayth's. Had they been forced to leap blindfold off a high diving-board, perform a double-back pike, three half-twists and land in a flaming barrel, it wouldn't have elicited anywhere near the surging torrents of nervous adrenalin that flooded their bodies now. As they neared the narrow gully where the chain-gang should be located, Firkin felt sick with worry and wished that he had at least brought a small bucket. The wellingtons of Klayth's psyche struggled through the rising tides of dread.

Klayth crept quietly into the gully, walking upstream in the eerie, unwanted silence. This was a chain-gang site, there should be some noise, even if it was only the gratuitous physical abuse of the slave. Klayth would have felt an awful lot better if he could have heard the sweet sound of a suffering Snydewinder. His eyes moved constantly in their royal sockets, alert to the slightest movement in the vicinity. A bend in the gully blocked their view, preventing them from seeing what lay beyond. Klayth signalled the traders to stop and Firkin to follow. Nervously the two boys crept forward and looked around the corner, a cold wet dread slipping over the rim of Klayth's wellies.

Firkin gasped and shuddered as his worst fears were realised. There, lying limply against the rock wall of the narrow gully, were the two prone bodies of Burnurd and Maffew, motionless. For Firkin the shock was almost too much, he lurched backwards round the corner and stood, eyes closed, back against the steep rock wall, shaking, wishing for that bucket again. He couldn't believe what he had just seen, it seemed impossible. It couldn't be true, everything he feared had happened. Snydewinder had obviously escaped somehow, and left Burnurd and Maffew lying in his wake. He shuddered again as the image of the two guards swam up in his mind.

Klayth, his psychic feet squelching clammily with dread, stood and stared at the crumpled bodies, unaware that he was under close scrutiny from above. Hassock, his eyes on stalks, his face drained of all colour, goggled at the two bodies. Terror and Death grinned and waved translucently at him, their arms linked, holding their scythes with evil nonchalance.

The tall, thin figure of the covert observer peered over a large rock, his straggly beard scraping a green patch of lichen, watching the young King begin his first uneasy steps forward. The watcher fingered his battered leather eyepatch nervously and shifted his position to get a better view. As he did so, his make-shift rucksack dislodged a loose stone, sending it crashing down the steep slope. Klayth turned reflexively, barely sidestepping the spinning rock as it whistled past him, colliding with the opposite side of the gully. He glimpsed the back of a strangely familiar figure sprinting over the horizon, carrying a large pack. 'Stop him!' shouted Klayth pointing desperately. 'Look up there. He's getting away!'

Firkin, ran at the bank, arms flailing windmills as he fought for grip, sprinting vertically, failing miserably. With half a dozen pitons, ten or twelve crampons, a hundred feet of rope and a pair of ice axes he might have stood a chance. He slipped back into a muddy panting heap at the foot of the incline.

A wild cackle of freedom floated into the gully.

Firkin seethed. Snydewinder had got away.

Suddenly there was a deep inhuman moan and a rattle of chains: Hassock turned, his face pale with fright. Terror and Death winked, collecting souls . . .

The bodies of the guards were moving. Coming for Hassock's soul. 'Ohhhhh,' groaned the prone black bulk.

Hassock screamed.

A huge black hand raised itself, flexing in the air, crawling onto the shoulder of its colleague.

'Eh, Maffew. Wake up, we've got visitors!'

Hassock fainted.

Sprinting away from the gully, dipping and darting through the now very familiar section of the Talpa Mountains, Snydewinder shrieked with wild delight as he recalled the look of dumbfounded surprise on the two guards' faces.

Yes, he thought, definitely dum. Dum, dum, dum!

He recalled the scene as clearly as if it were being projected in 80mm Superthaumination* onto the back of his retina. He was amazed how perfectly it had gone.

But then with a mind like mine planning it, he told himself arrogantly, could it have been any other way!

Turning sharply, he ducked behind a mossy rock, squeezed through an entrance carefully hidden with bracken and heather and stepped into a large cave.

Once out of sight of prying eyes he allowed himself the luxury of choosing a seat, ordering popcorn and settling down in the magic lantern palace of his mind to watch, and revel in, his escape. Lush red drapes swung silently open, there was a moment of numbers counting down, a brief flash of fluff in the gate, and then it began.

It had been just over a week ago that Snydewinder had begun to put his plan into action. the only thing preventing him enjoying complete freedom was the fact that two immensely heavy chains were locked around his ankles, firmly attaching him to the side of Tor Tellini, a fifteen-thousand-foot extinct volcano, somewhere in the Talpa Mountains. Many times during the last few months he had picked these locks and appraised himself of the surrounding

---

*As used in all the finest, wide-screen, magic lantern palaces.

terrain. After three or four of these little nocturnal excursions he realised that he had to have a base established nearby and that unless he took the two guards out of action, he would be rounded up again in next to no time, after which the security would be doubled at the very least. No, he needed an escape plan that would allow him freedom to establish a camp in the mountains and avoid detection by removing the guards' pursuit. Very soon he had hatched a scheme that filled his needs perfectly. All that remained was to execute it.

He swung the heavy sledgehammer down onto the rocky edge of the gully for the last time and stopped. With the sudden silence Burnurd looked up to see Snydewinder bent double, rattling the chains that held him to the rock face.

'Get back to work,' shouted Burnurd.

'. . . or I'll fump yer!' added Maffew.

'Gentlemen, please. It is with good reason that I have stopped,' said Snydewinder, the coming speech rehearsed carefully over the last few days.

'What?' asked Burnurd.

'Health and Safety of Prisoners at Work Act, OG 1023. Paragraph 32, Section C, Sub-Section f),' said Snydewinder matter-of-factly.

'Yeah. What about it?' asked Burnurd while Maffew scratched his tightly cropped head.

'I think you might be operating in breach of it. That's what.' Receiving the expected blank looks of utter incomprehension, and giving himself an internal thumbs-up, Snydewinder continued. 'Paragraph 32, Section C, Sub-Section f), states that, ahem, "All road workers, farm labourers and chain-gang personnel pressed into service for the purpose of penal servitude and correction shall be at all times contained within a manner deemed secure and non-facilitative of egress from the site in any perambulatory or vehicular manner." See?'

Maffew continued scratching his head.

'In other words,' continued Snydewinder. 'Criminals should be kept locked up safely.'

Burnurd nodded slowly. 'That's why you've got those chains,' he said, proud of this remarkable feat of cognitive reasoning.

'Ah, it is to these chains that I am addressing my concern. My dear gents, over the last few months I have come to regard you as less my jailors and more my friends.'

Maffew grinned.

'So the possibility that you would both end up in deep, deep trouble over such a trivial and easily checked item, fills me with sheer dread,' continued Snydewinder, laying it on thick.

Maffew scowled.

'What're you on about?' asked Burnurd once again.

Snydewinder rattled his chains and said, 'After all the wear and tear these have had over the last eight months don't you think that it's about time they were checked. You see, I feel as though they are not as strong as they look and if I were to, you know, slip anchor, as it were, due to metal fatigue or the like, then, well it doesn't bear thinking about for you . . .'

Burnurd hadn't thought of that.

Snydewinder continued. 'The way they test these chains is to hang heavy weights on them and see if they are strong enough. You're stronger than I am so what I was thinking was, for your own peace of mind more than anything, really, I think you should test them. It wouldn't take long and I bet you'd feel a lot happier afterwards knowing that I'm not likely to disappear, as it were.'

'I fink he's right,' whispered Maffew.

Burnurd stood up, walked over to Snydewinder's ankle, picked up the chain and tugged hard. It clanked a little but held very firm.

'It's fine,' he said, and turned to lumber away again.

'Er, I hope you don't think I'm being intrusive, or trying to tell you your job, but that doesn't really test it properly. See, there's the strength of the actual ankle clasp to check as well,' commented Snydewinder. 'If you check that then you can be certain that the chains are strong enough.'

70

Grumbling about the extra things to do, Burnurd unlocked one of the anklets and examined it closely.

'Looks fine,' he mumbled after a few minutes and made to refasten it on Snydewinder's ankle.

'Ah! But are you *sure*. There could be rust hiding deep inside or metal fatigue, or anything. The best way to try it is to give it a few good tugs yourself. Here, let me help.' He took the keys, and the anklet and casually fastened it around the guard's ankle. Burnurd tugged at the restraint, smiling happily as it didn't give an inch.

'Feels fine, very secyu . . . sickyou . . . firm,' he reported finally.

'Good. But there's still just one thing you haven't tried,' said Snydewinder pointing to the ring fixed into the rock. 'According to the Penal Servitude Security Council's 1015 Report on Stress Testing Rock Fixings, "At least twice the force normally experienced in normal use is ideal to test a rock-metal fixing of this nature." '

'So?' said Burnurd.

'So, if Maffew pulls at the same time . . .' Snydewinder bent down and began unlocking his anklet as he spoke, '. . . then I'm sure that will be a perfect test of the full system.' He held out the open anklet and waved Maffew over.

'Are you right or left footed?' enquired Snydewinder casually.

'Er . . .' replied Maffew as the anklet closed around his right ankle.

'Good,' said Snydewinder and stepped back out of reach. 'Fifty good strong tugs should be fine.' he added. 'One . . . two . . . three. That's excellent . . .'

Whether they reached fifty he didn't wait to find out. Pausing only to throw the keys into the stream he strolled jauntily out of the gully and away to freedom.

'More careful this time will you be,' repeated Ch'tin, his piping voice floating through the space under the roof.

'Of course, I will. I know what I'm doing,' answered

71

Hogshead, impatient to get on and do some more magic. He flicked quickly through the ancient book to relocate the levitation spell. He wanted to try it again and get it right. 'I've read all the introduction bit, so it'll be fine,' he added curtly.

'Humph!' replied Ch'tin sceptically.

Hogshead flicked a few more pages and stared hard at the book, lit once again by the pale glow from the tallow candle. To his right lay a small rounded pebble and on his left, at what the bookworm hoped was a safe distance, sat Ch'tin, looking on in the manner of a wise and ancient prophet teaching his star pupil. If he had been humanoid in shape he probably would be wearing a dull-grey cowled cloak of rough hessian-like material, tied around the middle with a length of rope. He would also have had both hands resting on his gnarled oak stick, walk with a limp (just for effect), have the urge to refer to Hogshead as 'my son' and have a name which rhymed with pagoda. Suddenly the scraping of parchment leaves stopped, Hogsead grinned hungrily and turned to Ch'tin.

'There it is,' he said greedily.

'What is it?' asked Ch'tin cautiously.

Hogshead read aloud, 'Levitation for inanimates. All right?' Ch'tin nodded and raised a piping prayer to Helminth, the Saviour and Protector of All Things that Slither and Wriggle. It had better be more of a success this time.

'Good!' said Hogshead enthusiastically. 'What now?'

'The instructions read.'

'Oh, I did that last time.' Hogshead's finger ran impatiently under the words. 'I don't need all this. I just want to do some magic. Now!'

'Too eager be not. To hatch before the eagle can fly he must. To learn have you whole life, my s . . . er.'

'This is important. I need . . . want to try again and make it work this time.'

'Results may good not be if rushed. Mmmmph.'

'I want to do this spell now!' Hogshead stared hard at the little worm, his eyes narrowing as he spoke.

'Very well, my s . . . er. Proceed.' Ch'tin nodded.

Hogshead grinned and suddenly felt very nervous. He looked at the pebble, small round and solid, then at the page and the words thereon. He swallowed and cleared his throat.

Well, here goes, he thought to himself and swallowed again. He raised his voice and began to strangle a kindle of innocent kittens, wailing the difficult, cut up, backwards, almost alien words. His strangulated voice strained to navigate the treacherous channels of diction. Local teen-agers passing by discovered the word 'grunge'.

'Zhunfar terrack tack ito meso ghurnlick . . .'

His larynx contorted wildly, his epiglottis thrashing like an eel on a barbecue as he fought to pronounce the words.

'. . . femtoshi thesau inshmurrin nachoszzgggh . . .'

He strained to breathe and control his voice. It seemed easier this time. Sort of . . . familiar.

'. . . hhvvvwheeezh hhhahtnkgh spligg . . .'

His voice grew stronger as he concentrated, becoming engrossed in the sound of his own voice. Somehow it seemed to him that he knew the strange words off by heart and was only using the page as a guide. Almost as if he'd done this hundreds of times before. But that was impossible. Wasn't it?

'. . . hhytjurknealish mi tressk hhvvwrshh omb.'

Hogshead glanced up from the page as he heard the sound of rock on wood. It had moved. He breathed in slowly while chanting and gave his voice a different tone. The pebble moved again. Twice. He furrowed his brow, beads of sweat blossoming with the effort. The pitch and timbre of his voice was crucial to the success of the spell. Several gentle taps on the table and he knew it was working. He closed his eyes in concentration, his voice rising in volume as he chanted with increasing confidence. The tapping grew faster, quieter and quieter until it stopped altogether. He uttered a few more phrases, realising with a shock that the last half of the spell had been cast with his eyes shut, not reading the page.

He made a mental note to ask Ch'tin about that at a later date. Right now he was bursting to know if the spell had worked properly. He hadn't heard any explosions.

He opened his eyes and looked at the table top. He gasped as he stared at the spot where the pebble had been. He wasn't quite sure what he expected to see but this wasn't it. There was a small space on the table where the stone had lain. It had vanished completely.

'It hasn't worked *again*,' he complained to Ch'tin. 'Why hasn't it worked? It should be floating above the table and I've made it vanish. Is it my pronunciation or something?' He swept his hand across the spot where the stone had been. 'Gone. It's gone. Why hasn't it worked right?'

Ch'tin looked into Hogshead's eyes and said, 'Judge too quick you do.'

'Eh? It hasn't worked. It's vanished!'

Ch'tin's antennae angled forward and pointed upwards. Hogshead's gaze followed. Then his jaw fell slack in utter amazement. There, four feet above the surface of the table, floating on a column of nothing was the pebble. It rotated slowly, making tiny little geostationary orbits around a small clump of very confused nitrogen atoms.

Hogshead stared in fascination. His face creased into a crocodile smile. He'd done it. Right this time. No mess, no mistakes. There was no going back! Hogshead the Magician! Hogshead the Sorcerer! Hogshead the Necromancer!

An overwhelming feeling of satisfaction coursed through his body as he sat, motionless in the tallow gloom, grinning wildly as he watched the tiny orbiting pebble, and began to chuckle to himself. A quiet, self-satisfied chuckle with only the slightest hint of post-thaumic enhancement reverberating hollowly around it.

Another icy blast raced through Snydewinder's cave, thrusting its cold, sharp fingers deeper into his thin, shivering body than a whole army of thermal pick-pockets. He cursed and swore at the heap of sticks lying on the cave floor and vowed next time to steal a box of matches. He had lost count of the number of times he'd tried and failed to light the pathetic attempt at a camp fire.

He crawled forward along the floor and peered out of the cave entrance to look at the weather. A north-easterly wind was blowing which would probably turn northerly before nightfall. It looked like a cold front was coming through. He cursed once again as he considered the harsh winters the Talpa Mountains could throw at unwary travellers and the warmth he had once enjoyed in the safe surroundings of Castell Rhyngill. Winter was approaching rapidly and he relished the thought of enduring it up here about as highly as spending the rest of his existence working for a living. He longed once again for power, needing it, aching for its warmly satisfying glow. He imagined Klayth, sitting at the large banqueting table having just polished off a feast fit for, well, a King, and he hated him. Jealously he wished he was back as Lord-Chancellor of Castell Rhyngill with all its associated creature comforts. Instead he was out here in the cold of a damp mountain cave with only the occasional mountain goat or stray lemming for company. This simply would not do.

I could die up here and nobody would know, he thought. I'd just be a body without a name if anyone found me, which is very unlikely in this hole. I might get eaten by something or just rot away.

He shivered again, horror shoving the accelerator and shunting out a new train of thought.

I have my freedom, he thought, I have my health and I have a fair amount of food. I think it's about time I took my life in my own hands and went and did something about it.

After packing all his stolen belongings, wrapping himself up well and hiding the pile of sticks he took his bearings and set off away from the mountains, away from Cranachan and away from Rhyngill. He lodged images of Klayth in his mind and filed them in the neural cabinet labelled 'Revenge'. Someday he would do something about that. In the future he would cancel that debt.

Dawn struggled up into the tallow gloom in the roof space a few moments behind Courgette and waited for her eyes to dark adjust. 'Hello,' said Courgette, moving carefully over the boards laid on the rafters to the table where Hogshead was standing.

'What are you doing up there?' she asked, looking at Hogshead on the table.

'You wouldn't understand. It's magic . . .' He stepped sideways and revealed the shiny pebble, still spinning in tiny little circles, four feet above the top of the table.

'You've done it! Oh, that's brilliant!' shouted Courgette.

'I did it last night and . . .'

'It's been there *all* night!' Courgette interrupted enthusiastically. 'Wow!'

'Of course,' said Hogshead, swelling with pride. 'It'll stay there as long as I want.'

'Stuck it is!' piped Ch'tin, peering out of Hogshead's pocket.

'It's *not* stuck. I like it there.'

'My pebble!' squeaked Dawn suddenly.

'What's *she* doing here?' shouted Hogshead pointing imperiously at Firkin's sister.

'What've you done to my pebble?' she whimpered.

'Stuck it is!' whistled Ch'tin again.

'It's not *stuck*.'

'Get it down,' snapped Dawn.

'Don't you like it there?' asked Hogshead.

'No!'

'I do!' answered Hogshead defiantly. 'I put it there and I like it there!'

'I want it down!'

'You can get it down, can't you?' asked Courgette, suspiciously.

'Yes. I . . .'

'Stuck it mmmmffmmfmfm!' squealed Ch'tin as Hogshead shoved him into his pocket.

'. . . can get it down. But . . .'

'Yes?' asked Courgette and Dawn.

'Well, not just yet. I don't know why you want it down, anyway. It's brilliant there. Watch.' He grabbed the pebble with both hands, picked his feet up and hung from it, rotating gently in mid-air. Courgette laughed out loud. It was a ridiculous sight.

'But can't you cast another spell to bring it down?'

'Well, I would,' answered Hogshead climbing off the table, 'but I can't read it. Some idiot's wrecked it.' He showed Courgette the spell that he'd used, then turned the page to show the opposite spell, but the writing was impossible to read. It was blurry and smudged beyond recognition, looking suspiciously as if someone had dropped a large cup of hot liquid all over it.* Dawn peered underneath Hogshead's arm, trying to see.

'What *is* she doing here?' snapped Hogshead once again. 'She's too young for magic. This room's supposed to be secret.'

'She's here because we've got a problem.'

'What?'

'It's Klayth . . .'

'No! No!' shouted Hogshead throwing his hands up in horror. 'It's bad enough with Firkin, but you as well?'

'He'll get worse if you don't listen,' commanded Courgette, sounding very like a schoolmistress chastising a stroppy select committee on education. 'They've just come back from the mountains and Klayth's fears are right.'

'What? Snydewinder's . . .'

---

* Urklid the trainee mage, whose book it had been, was without doubt the clumsiest and most foolish of trainees in the class of OG 1022. Even to the day he was ejected from the correspondence course for handing in his homework written in thaumatin ink, a substance banned from use by all but the most experienced inkanters, due to its ability to rearrange letters on the page, lie and/or spontaneously combust, he still maintained that the cup levitating above his book was not full of hot tea when it went up there. Where the tea came from and who it was for remained a mystery.

'Yes.'

'Firkin told me that Klayth doesn't want to be King,' said Dawn.

'What?' said Hogshead, his eyebrows migrating up his forehead.

'. . . and the only way he can see that happening is if the war never happened!' finished Courgette.

'The war . . . ?'

'That spell's gone to your head,' sighed Courgette. 'If the war never happened, then Klayth's father, King Khardeen, would never have left Klayth on the throne in the first place.'

Hogshead's eyebrows knitted and purled furiously, fighting to follow the thread of logic, before losing it completely in a tangled heap of temporal floss.

'That all happened twelve years ago. What are we supposed to do about it?' pleaded Hogshead, feeling a headache coming on.

'Nothing,' said Courgette.

'. . . ?' It was the best Hogshead could manage.

'How *can* we!' she snapped.

Hogshead appeared to think about this. Then gave up.

'What can we do, then?'

'Well,' said Courgette, the slightest hint of extreme pride showing around the corner of her mouth. 'I've got an idea . . .'

A cold wind blew hard from the north, oblivious of the fact that he was there. It was a wind in a hurry, it took all the shortcuts it could, cutting straight through him, plunging deep cold fingers into his body and coating his bones with a silver sheen of frost. It had been like this for hours and Snydewinder felt like a walking glacier. He would have enjoyed cursing and spitting to himself about the bleak area of the Talpa Mountains through which he was now walking but he was afraid that his saliva would freeze. Instead, his fertile mind just cursed and swore twice as much as normal. He trudged miserably on through the ice-flecked wind and wondered precisely where he was heading.

He had been moving steadily east for the last few hours and the ground had changed to a more tundra-like affair. He had seen the odd grouse flap uncontrollably out of the scrubby grass from time to time, but there was little sign of anything else. Except more scrubby grass. Behind him the Talpa Mountains looked dark against the late afternoon sun, a slight sprinkle of snow having settled on Tor Teehya's tip. This was the only thing that gave him any sense of satisfaction at the moment: they were behind him. He had escaped. Out of the frying-pan into the freezer.

He shivered violently, sneezed and pulled his collar tighter around his thin blue throat. Ahead of him lay more miles of empty treeless tundra. Miles of nothingness, acres of bleak featureless wasteland devoid of anything even remotely useful . . .

Something in the far distance caught his eye. Something unnatural. In a dip between two vast undulations stood a tall thin something with what looked like two huge arms flung wide apart. At this distance it appeared to be an emaciated scarecrow after a crash diet.

Whatever it was, he thought, it was infinitely more worthy of investigation than any of the poxy grouse that thrummed out of the undergrowth at him. He set off towards it.

*

Klayth had thought about the situation overnight and the more he considered it, the more he liked the idea. It would be difficult, lonely and he would worry until they all came back, but he could think of no other group of people he could afford the luxury of trusting more than these four.

'What are we waiting for?' said Dawn eagerly, fidgeting by the castle gate. She wanted to be off, to be away, across the moat, through the forest, over the hills into the beautiful, gleaming city of Fort Knumm, its towers scraping the sky, its streets paved with gold. Just like Firkin had told her.

'Yeah, come on. We haven't got all day!' grumbled Hogshead, his pack bulging with the magic books he intended to read on the journey. His magical skills had given him a new confidence. Hogshead the Magician was invincible. Or so he thought. He managed, by a convenient form of self-deception,* to forget about the fact that he knew only one spell, and, as testamented by the still-spinning pebble, he didn't know how to uncast it.

Courgette tugged at Firkin's arm.

'Come on. Everything's packed. Let's go!'

She wanted to get him away before he changed his mind. It was for his own good. If Firkin said, 'It's Klayth . . .' with that spaniel-eyed look again, she and Hogshead would probably end up fighting over who would throttle him first.

At the moment, Firkin was convinced that he had thought of the brilliantly simple solution. Courgette let him. She didn't care as long as it worked.

'You are sure about this, aren't you?' asked Firkin, looking at Klayth.

'Of course,' answered Klayth wearily. 'We went through all this last night. Having Snydewinder behind bars again wouldn't put an end to my problems. I need my father back. Otherwise things will become even more unbearable.'

Firkin nodded. It had been a hard decision to make. Dawn, in her well-rehearsed, innocent way, had asked the questions that he himself should have asked months ago. She had focused his mind on the real problem. The root of the problem. Courgette had been proud of her as she had stood listening by the door. How to get an experienced King onto the throne, a King who could be trusted, so that Klayth could learn to do it properly. You don't just give a young man a

---

* A psychic pastime invented and developed to extraordinary heights by the Blikni Yogis of the Meanlayla Mountains who achieved inner levels of utter self-deception deep enough to convince themselves that, merely by sitting on a large inflatable mat and bouncing up and down, everyone else in the room could fly. Co-operative flights by the Yogis, each member convincing one other member that they could fly in a complex cross-linked arrangement similar to a multi-level five-pointed star, were banned when a carpet of Yogis plunged twelve hundred feet down a ravine after their collective consciousness was shattered following a single individual's sneezing fit.

collection of highly polished, awesomely sharp surgical equipment, several vials of canabinnoid pain-killer, three yards of cotton, fifteen clients in varying degrees of health and expect him to deal with them all. Of course not. He goes through years of training, starting with broken fingers, working, via knee-caps and nose jobs, to legs, livers and lungs, until finally, after a long and intensely difficult learning curve, he can start his very own extortion racket.

Firkin shouldered his pack and adjusted the straps, took the small painting of King Khardeen that Klayth handed him and looked at it. There was a striking family resemblance, although it would be several years yet before Klayth could grow a handle-bar moustache that long.

'I wish that I could tell you where to look,' said Klayth. 'But I haven't a clue. All important information and documents from that time were destroyed by Snydewinder. I can only think that you should try Fort Knumm first and see what happens.'

'Yes, yes! Fort Knumm!' squeaked Dawn, leaping up and down.

Hogshead, standing off to one side, had a bad feeling that Dawn was shortly going to be a little surprised by the appearance of Fort Knumm.

In the distance the sound of effeminately tiny feet was growing louder.

'Let's go, Firkin,' said Courgette.

'Everybody knows that we are going on a camping trip so we've got a few weeks before we'll be missed,' said Firkin, reminding Klayth.

The feet pattered forward, a small figure waved a hand-kerchief.

Dawn tugged on Firkin's sleeve. 'Come on, let's *go*!'

'You go on, I'll catch up in a minute,' he said and watched her skip off to join Hogshead and Courgette.

'Thire, Thire . . . !' bleated a voice.

'I'm going to miss you lot,' said Klayth. 'You'd better not be gone long, otherwise you'll find me a real tyrant when you get back.' They both forced a laugh and stood in a short but very uncomfortable silence.

'Thire, your highneth, Thire . . . !' yapped Mynyn.

Firkin's throat was tight and dry. His eyes had all the moisture.

'Goodbye, Klayth. Take care.'

'Goodbye, friend Firkin. May fortune follow you.'

Firkin turned quickly away as he saw the skipping dogsbody pattering across the courtyard. He had to go now. One quip from that yapping buffoon, thought Firkin through the clenched teeth of his angry mind, and he'd wake up in hospital.

'Thire, thire . . .'

Firkin couldn't explain it, but somehow he felt that it would be more than a few weeks before he saw Klayth again. As he walked away from Castell Rhyngill, the sun still cold on that fresh autumn morning, the yapping of Mynyn ringing in his ears, he looked back only once and committed that scene to his memory. He sensed that it would look very different when he next saw it.

Standing below the tall thin something Snydewinder braced himself against the wind and thought hard. He stared at the signpost and struggled to catch a memory. He stood at a junction and was faced with three choices: Rhyngill, back the way he had come – right out. Cranachan: over the mountains to the left where a threat to remove all of his major organs one by one beginning with those used for reproduction was still waiting – not a great possibility. Or Losa Llamas: off to the right, downhill, somewhere he wasn't known and in the middle of a huge, dense forest – a real place with lots of potential.

As he set off towards Losa Llamas something nagged at the back of his mind, a rumour of something that had happened years ago, something terrible, something hushed up. Something that should never have been allowed to happen in the first place.

Not far away, in a hole in a dead tree, a gossip of rumours preened their wings as they sensed him approach. A fresh set of ears. In a short space of time the rumours would be flying once again, spreading their seeds of intrigue, steering conversations and giving work for idle tongues to wag about.

Snydewinder stood at the northern edge of the forest surrounding Losa Llamas and thought very carefully. He fidgeted uncomfortably as he pondered the possibility of plunging deep into the forest ahead, where wild beasts, muggers, assassins or worse a group of Ghyee Yohvass Witnesses could be ready to convert him. Anything could be hiding in, or behind, any of the countless trees and bushes in that dark green interior. Cautiously, he decided to edge around the outside in the hope of finding a better way in, less risky at least.

Ahead of him a flurry of excitement rippled through the gossip of rumours in the tree.

As he trudged wearily around the outside of the forest, Snydewinder considered his position and came to the easy conclusion that he hated it. Here he was sneaking around outside, in the cold, like the worst dregs of a thief of the night. If he was caught he would have no authority to call on, no threats to rain down on the heads of his captor, no subtly wicked strings of untraceable blackmail to pull in high places. In short, he was powerless. Reduced to the status of a common criminal. He knew that he was not a *common* criminal. He was an extraordinary one. It all boiled down to one thing. Power. Right now he had none. All he needed was one chance, one tiny opening and he'd be through it, into the driving seat and bashing heads together in a reign of terror worse, more deadly than anything he had ever dreamt of before, starting with anyone who had ever crossed his path.

All he needed was one tiny lever. He would do the rest.

A flurry of tiny wing-beats sounded in the dark recess of the dead tree as the rumours took to the wing. They had been sitting in that tree for years. Waiting. Nobody came to Losa Llamas anymore so there was nobody to hear them. They were reduced to sitting in the tree recounting their creeds and tales to one another. Part of a symbiotic legend. Keeping the spirit alive. Ready and waiting for their chance.

A chance called Snydewinder.

On gossamer wings, in formation, the rumours flew. Through the trees they weaved, over bushes, thrilling to feel the uprush of air on their wings. They had a mission. The years of boredom suddenly seemed but a distant memory lost in the scramble for the air. Their target lay directly ahead, just beyond the edge of the trees. A buzz of excitement accompanied their flight through the last few feet of forest then suddenly they were free, screaming through the open air, soaring towards their mission end . . .

Snydewinder grumbled to himself as he trudged through the boggy ground on the edge of the forest. No power *and* wet feet! This was getting beyond a joke.

Still in close formation, the rumours flew directly at the grumbling man. To them he seemed huge, a mouthpiece for them of enormous proportions. They homed in towards his head on an approach line just to the back of him. Their leader had the nape of his neck in its sights. Without an order given the rumours streamed themselves smoothly into a line, each slipstreaming the one in front. Snydewinder's head grew in their sights, filling their field of view as they approached. Nearer. At the last possible second the leader flipped onto its side, turning, changing course, hugging the hairy surface of the back of Snydewinder's neck. In that instant their horizon changed. Now they were flying through a jungle of tall, thin stalks on a pinkish planet, covered in dandruff. Split-second timing was needed to dodge through the stalks as they raced for their target.

Suddenly, ahead of them loomed a huge pinkish over-hanging structure, its size only glimpsed through the hairs on Snydewinder's head. With perfect timing the leader pulled away from the surface, performing a wing-over turn, plunging full speed into the dark depths of the huge hollow cavern. The others followed close behind. Without slowing the leading rumour raced down Snydewinder's earhole, boring an opening through the thin membrane of his ear-drum. The other rumours whipped through the tiny pinhole, into the dark interior. They knew their mission. Bisecting the enormous hole in the centre of the stirrup, through another membrane, into the spiral horn of the cochlea. Along the aural nerve, crash through process control and straight for the memory centres.

Picking his foot out of a particularly squelchy path, Snydewinder suddenly stopped, motionless as a frozen heron. Absently he scratched the inside of his right ear and suddenly remembered, in surprising clarity, the things that he had heard about Losa Llamas. Memories flooded back to him; the rumours had succeeded.

With the cross-matching skill of a Mendelian Geneticist Snydewinder's brain flew into a frenzy of mental activity. Within seconds his power-hungry cravings had been grafted onto the memories and knowledge of the Ultimate Weapon and had produced a hardy annual of a plan that was growing like knotweed in spring.

'The frogs. I need the Frogs of War. *Rana militaria* will be mine!'

Across the bare tundra, carried on the early autumn wind, Snydewinder's evil mind found voice as he took a deep breath and laughed out loud. He had a direction and now he had a glint in his eye that had been lost for an age. An old friend had come to visit.

'Cheers!' said Greed as he settled in front of the fire and clinked glasses with his old friend Cunning.

'Good to have you back, Greed,' smiled Ruthlessness from her armchair.

Beneath his twitching eyebrows a glint of cold calculating madness sparkled, like a Snow Queen's abacus, in Snydewinder's evil eyes. Galvanised into action he moved off in a definite direction.

Slowly, like a particularly unpleasant bubble of swamp gas, evil chuckles of wicked laughter rose through his thin body. As he warmed to the ideas streaming around his head he laughed longer and harder, his wild cries echoing on the previously advertized tundra.

Greed threw on a few more coals, stoking the fires of evil within.

The rumours projected 80mm Superthaumatron images across the widescreen of his imagination. He witnessed the mustering of the formidable froggy force; observed the march of the unstoppable amphibian army, crushing resistance beneath massed volleys of lashing ranine tongues, dissecting armoured ranks with slashing claws. And he saw himself, General Snydewinder, commanding the blitzkreiging batrachian battalions!

'Scream Hoppit! . . . and loose the Frogs of War!!'

Somehow, Snydewinder's wet feet didn't seem so bad now.

St Swindling's Day

The sound of the River Caman was almost deafening as it rushed madly by a few feet away to his right. Gallon upon gallon of water surged over submerged granite boulders in huge fluid whale-backs. Curls of white froth tipped the peaks of stationary bow waves at the front of jutting rocks, sending eddies spinning away in the rapid current. Snydewinder edged nervously along the steep dripping bank of mossy rocks, like a black spider looking for a mate. His progress was slow, his knee throbbed after being wrenched when he had slipped a few minutes ago. He swore again as another cold stream of water squirmed down his back. Everything was dripping; cold, soggy cloth clung to his skin, peeling on and off as he moved. Heaving himself up and onto a lichen-covered boulder he irritatedly swatted a branch away from his face. Suddenly his right foot slipped on a patch of moss. Reflexively he snatched at the branch and held on, scrambling with his feet. The river surged by on its wild race downstream. He slipped further towards it, the branch bending under his weight. The waves roared louder as he sagged closer, yelling torrential encouragement, jeering aquatically. Panic crossed his face, and he dropped again sharply. He looked up to see the pale-brown contrast of fresh wood against lichened bark grinning malevolently wider as the branch snapped. His feet windmilled against the slippery rock surface, desperate for any ounce of friction he could muster. Still clinging to the now useless extra burden of the branch he plummeted riverward. Rocks flew by as he fell in a green and grey blur. The breath was knocked out of him as he jarred to a shocking halt, his feet on the back of a rock inches away from the river edge. The water roared in frustration. Snydewinder roared in anger and fear and lay on his back panting hard. He flung the branch at the river. It landed in the middle of a large smooth spiral eddy, floated for a second and disappeared as the whirlpool's aquatic hands snatched it down. Like a witch's broom on a bank holiday trip to Hell, small twigs broke surface once or twice but in a moment it was gone. Snydewinder swallowed hard. That could so easily have been him and with his pack on he probably wouldn't have lasted as long as the branch. He shivered at the frigorific image of unseen currents grasping at his drowning body, tugging him down into a darkening green grave, which flashed across his mind. A man with an ounce of religious fervour would have raised a prayer to heaven at being spared such a fate. Snydewinder swore and spat.

High on the adrenalin that powered his frenetic mind he reaffirmed his hatred of the world at large in no uncertain terms as oath upon oath followed in a torrent to rival the river. Still swearing about the unfairness of it all he struggled to his feet and limped along the river bank. He detested being powerless, hated having to creep about (it sounded *so* demeaning!), abhorred using back entrances like an inconsequential sneak-thief. One last back door, one final skulking entrance, then *front*-doors would be flung open in welcome, he would be ushered in, invited to enter. Soon, he thought. Soon!

There was a tiny unused passageway that led straight into the centre of Losa Llamas. If he remembered correctly it should be half-way up the bank under a large waterfall just around this next bend in the river.

Deep in the memory centres of Snydewinder's seething brain one of the group of rumours redoubled its efforts, flashing an image into the thought-processing centre.

A half-seen recollection of an ancient map of this area showing the curves of the River Caman, the waterfall as the River Gharial emptied into it, and a passageway marked with a dotted line leading from there directly into the centre of Losa Llamas flashed unbidden into Snydewinder's consciousness. He smiled wryly as he adjusted his eyepatch.

What a brain! he thought arrogantly. Throw a problem at it and it hurls back the answer in seconds. His face creased in a grim sneer of acutely supercilious pride.

What a sucker, thought Secret Door swinging on Snydewinder's memory centres, throw him an answer and he leaps like a starving cur!

Reassured by his astounding superiority over everything around, above and below him, or so he thought, Snydewinder picked his way carefully across the treacherous rocks and dreamed of power. Power. Power!

Fort Knumm, thought Dawn as the group of four walked through Rhyngill Forest's maze of fiery autumn trees. Fort Knumm! I'm going to Fort Knumm. I'm on a venture. She kicked a few leaves about and skipped happily around a tree.

Fort Knumm!

Firkin had told her all about Fort Knumm.

'Are we there yet?' asked Dawn, for the hundred and tenth time, tugging on Firkin's sleeve.

'No. Not yet.'

'How far is it?'

'Have a guess,' sighed Firkin wearily.

'Er, "A few more miles. We're about half way there," ' answered Dawn, quoting Firkin, hoping he'd tell her she was wrong, that it was 'just over the hill', or, 'just around that corner'.

'You'll know when we're getting near,' said Hogshead, smirking. 'You'll be able to smell it!'

Firkin glared at him.

The smell! thought Dawn, dreamily. Firkin had told her all about the scent of blossom that lingered in the air all year round, the showers of pot-pourri, the incense burners . . .

'If the wind's in the right direction,' said Courgette, grinning, 'You might be able to smell it very soon!'

Firkin scowled.

'Ooh!' said Dawn excitedly, her mind's eye leaping ahead through the trees to an imagined Fort Knumm, zooming in low over the painted glory of the Fort itself, racing through the streets envisioned in minute detail. Firkin had talked for hours about its glorious golden towers rising like auric mountains from the ground; about its beautiful people whose jaw-dropping good looks were matched only by their overwhelming generosity; and about the warm scented streets upon whose pavements it was sheer delight to walk.

Firkin had the uncomfortably sticky feeling that the reality might not match up with Dawn's slightly overinflated expectations of the town to come.

Against the backdrop of the constant deafening roar of the impact of two rivers, a single black object snaked over the edge of a patch of dripping moss. Its tip somehow gripped and pulled a fraction of an inch up. Just enough to be joined by another. Working in tandem the two leather fingers hauled again, and were rewarded by the welcome appearance of a third and a fourth glistening digit. A barely audible grunt from below and the trembling of the black-gloved hand showed the effort needed for this struggle. Puffing, panting and dripping from head to foot Snydewinder scrambled squelchily up the steep wet rocks behind the rushing green curtain of the River Gharial as it tumbled into the pool below. Directly above him now was a slight lip which formed the last solid base for the millions of gallons of water before they plunged the hundred and fifty feet down to become the River Caman. All around him the rocks dripped as the moisture-laden air dropped its load on the first solid surface it touched. Salamanders scurried out of hidden nooks and crannies, disturbed by Snydewinder's hand searching for holds to pull him up. The constant rumble of the torrential deluge thundered around him deafeningly.

Was it *déjà vu* or just his remarkable imagination that made him think that he had been here before? Somehow he knew exactly where to put his hands and realised with alarming certainty that if he could manage to haul himself up onto the ledge a few feet above him, pull back the layer of undergrowth and force open the door, he would be standing in the entrance to the passage that led directly to the centre of Losa Llamas.

With one more herculean effort he pushed himself up onto the narrow ledge. Kicking wildly he somehow wriggled to safety. He lay full-length along the ledge, listening as his pulse pounded through his arteries, surged through his veins, drowning even the sounds of the crashing water. He was soaked. A mixture of condensed water, drips and the streams of sweat that were the result of his climb. He was barely fifty feet from the top of the waterfall. One slip at any point of the climb would have meant almost certain death for any muscle-bound barbarian foolhardy enough to have attempted this climb, let alone the stick-insectile physique of an ex-Lord Chancellor. He cursed as he thought of the energy he'd just expended, the struggle he'd had to get this far. Snydewinder hated the great outdoors, nature, countryside. It was always so much effort. *Up* hills, *down* hills, always fighting something. It was stubborn, ignorant, he could shout at it until he was blue in the face and it still wouldn't take an order. It wouldn't even accept bribes. He shivered as he thought of the looming danger all around him. One slip . . . Land in the torrent of the Gharial and you would be swatted to the bottom of the river and held there by the tons of rushing water. Land to the side and the Caman would swallow you and smash you against its rocky teeth until you breathed your last and your body lay in shreds. Snydewinder breathed deeply and was quite happy that he hadn't thought of those cheery options as he had climbed one hundred or so feet up what felt like the back of a greased tyrannosaurus, nobbly, slippery and extremely dangerous.

Still panting he peered behind the layer of undergrowth that lay between him and the rock face. A twinge of fear shot through his mind. Suppose it was all lies? What if he had to climb all the way down again? He shut out those thoughts and pushed at the undergrowth. It moved to one side, revealing a small wooden door which almost certainly opened onto a passage. Despite himself he thrilled with relief. It was amazing, behind that door lay the route to his future. The key to re-establishing his power base and allowing him to return to the life he was used to. All he had to do was turn the handle, open the door and walk straight into the middle of Losa Llamas. His black gauntlet grasped the cold metal ring, turned and pushed. The door remained firmly where it was. Locked. Snydewinder swore. How pathetic! he thought. A door as inaccessible as this and it was locked! As if they thought anyone fool enough to struggle all this way was going to be put off by a lock! 'Oh, it's locked, I'll just have to retrace my footsteps one hundred feet vertically down and then risk falling in the river again,' he grumbled, oozing sarcasm profusely as he pulled out his trusty set of skeleton keys and began expertly to pick the lock. Snydewinder thrilled as he felt around inside the barrel and moved the lever mechanism. A two-mortice dead-lock! It took him back to the days in Cranachan when no legal document or piece of sensitive information was safe from the prying eyes of 'Fast Fingers Fisk' as he'd have liked to have been known to close friends. His skill as a safecracker, like the lock he was now addressing, was very rusty but in a few moments the second mortice had moved, squealing ferruginous protests, and the door creaked open. He was inside slicker than an eel in vaseline, wriggling and writhing towards the dawning of a gloriously dictatorial future, with just the tiniest hint of absolute tyranny.

In the small market square, just below the neglected, crumbling skeleton of the Fort from which the town had got its name, hundreds of people bustled between the dozens of stalls set up for the celebrations.

Throughout the seething tangle of dim alleys and dull passages swarmed the dim residents and dull visitors to Fort Knumm's shady underworld.

And in the deepest, darkest part of Fort Knumm's cold heart, a slab of air smirked. It was warm, clammy, and it pulsed with excitement. A broad Cheshire cat grin leered into translucent view in one of the smokier corners of Ye Silver Spittoone, puffed out its cheeks and blew a long, flatulent raspberry at the poker-faced assassin sharpening his fourteen-inch gutting knife. The Atmosphere's tongue waved a feather of smoke under the assassin's nose, pushed its rainbow party-hat over to an even more rakish angle, exploded a small bomb of smoke tinsel, nimbic shrapnel and vapour paper trails, and vanished. Its grin lingered momentarily in the smoke. The grin of the Party Atmosphere.

It was St Swindling's Day and Fort Knumm was gearing up to have a party.

St Swindling (Retired, Excommunicated, Disowned), to give him his full title, was the patron saint of the criminal fraternity that dwelt in the pit of iniquity that was Fort Knumm. It was said that the muddy knoll upon which the Fort squatted contained the buried remains of the Saint's not inconsiderable body of wealth, built up over many years. Early on in his pre-saint days, when still inhabiting the habit of a novice, he had discovered that religious icons, holy artifacts and first print-run copies of ancient illuminated bibles (signed with dust cover intact) could fetch an extremely high price on the black market. Very soon, and without all the ceremony normally associated with it, the novice Tog B. Swindling achieved Sainthood. He was the youngest ever novice to reach this station and he knew it. Black market Sainthoods cost a lot, even in those days, but several papal rings, half a dozen silk-lined lounging vestments (extra large) and the last will and testament of four minor deities should fetch enough to recover his costs. They did. With a little left over for a bit of a do afterwards.

Having been adopted as the patron of all criminals, life for the newly appointed Saint proceeded in a satisfyingly upward direction. As did the funds in his personal fortune. Being a Saint allowed him access to artifacts that had been impossible to reach as a novice and these, naturally, commanded a far higher price. It was only when a recently 'mislaid' solid gold bust of Cardinal Sinn was offered to Dom Rhyngill, the Godfather of organised worship in the kingdom, that the Synod became suspicious. The RUC* were called in to investigate and very soon Saint Tog B. Swindling was swiftly and again unceremoniously retired, excommunicated and disowned from all religious, pious and even remotely worshipful activities for the period of his natural life. He couldn't believe his good fortune when, instead of the twenty-two years' hard labour that he was expecting, he was sentenced to fourteen Hail Marys and told not to do it again. He turned instead to a life of writing crime thrillers and died in absolute poverty. Of course, all of this was totally fictitious but the criminals of Fort Knumm believed it for the simple and carnal reason that it allowed them to let their hair down and indulge in a whole manner of mostly unsavoury activities, in public and without the interference of any officers of the law. And this year was no exception.

Already, hundreds of people had gathered in the market square and more were still arriving, packing in from the dozens of narrow alleys that opened onto the square. An air of excitement hung over the gathering crowd and fought for supremacy with other less savoury and more usually resident airs and odours. The Atmosphere in Fort Knumm was legendary, especially with its party hat on. Hawkers and Market Traders vied for business shouting, red-faced, about their latest bargains from beneath signs hastily erected for the same purpose. The overall noise level was somewhere between hubbub and cacophany. And rising.

In one of the corners a small stage had been built and a group of minstrels were valiantly bringing their set to a close. Clad entirely in green, and long beards, they struggled to be heard over the noise as they strummed mandolins, hit tambourines and blew flutes in a song about the unlawful imprisonment of mice. In a dramatic close the lead singer launched huge pink balloons from the end of his flute,

*The Religious Undercover Crime Squad.

94

watching as they bounced out over the audience, passed from hand to hand. The song reached its final cascading chord, the minstrels bowed and headed off for some well-earned liquid refreshment to the rapturous applause of a small group in the corner of the now even more crowded square.

Ikhnaton, the Assassin, his fourteen-inch gutting knife humming with sharpness, strolled across the market square, glaring at anyone in his way, and headed off to his 'Office'. In the gloomy back alley, which his immensely broad shoulders nearly filled, he almost smiled. He was happy. He liked St Swindling's Day. The celebrations themselves didn't interest him, until they became aggressive, he liked St Swindling's Day because it was very good for business. Ikhnaton's business was finding people for other people; after he found them he would lose them again. Permanently. Down holes, over cliffs, under piles of rubble that just happened to fall on the exact spot that they had been occupying. He loved his job. It gave him the two things he most loved in life, terminating other people and money. And his clients paid him very good money. In advance, of course.

Ikhnaton settled his muscular bulk down on a small chair, carefully moving a host of small but none the less highly dangerous implements to avoid severe personal injury and, fingering his high-carbon steel cutlass replete with quick-release scabbard, waited for the first customers. It was still relatively early and he was looking forward to a profitable night's bookings.

The inside of the public face of Ikhnaton's business empire was little more than a nearly empty room with a table, a chair, now struggling under the muscular bulk of its occupant, and a small filing cabinet. Three tallow candles flickered from small mountings on the wall and lit the year planners and calendars from *Mercenaries' Monthly* and *Ye Olde Assassins' Almanacke*. On the wall behind him was a yellowing scrag of parchment certifying that 'the holder of this certificate is a licensed personnel termination specialist and is available for short-term contracts in this field at the usual rates under the standard terms and conditions applicable.' Under that and in a far less legible hand were the words 'Party rates negoshible, mass exturminashns a speshlty.'

The temporary amnesty granted on St Swindling's Day meant that many more persons of a criminal persuasion were out and about than usual, which in turn led to an increase in those who came and booked the services of the biggest and best assassin in Fort Knumm. He drummed his huge, knuckle-dustered fingers on the table and waited patiently.

Four miles from the River Gharial and three miles upstream from the waterfall on the banks of the River Caman squatted the village of Losa Llamas. It lurked in a dip in the land on a sheltered curve of the river, surrounded by the dense verdance of the forest. Years ago this spot had been chosen for its inaccessibility to the casual traveller, lack of native dwellers and distance from any major population centre. The site was cleared of all vegetation. (Much to the chagrin of the variagated hypersentient knotweed, organised copses of which would disrupt the work by burying contractors' carts, hiding hand tools, stealing scythes and other more covert operations. Firmer action was called upon when a squad of contractors awoke to find themselves almost completely buried alive. Field trials of a back-pack Thaumatron, and its herbicidal efficacy against sentient botanical nuisances, were carried out, clearing the whole area in a matter of hours.)

Once cleared, the village of Losa Llamas grew. It was a pleasant development consisting of a number of ill-matched and brightly painted buildings surrounding a central lawn. The lawn was set out in black and white squares and would have been used for playing Thrash* if anyone could be

*The local equivalent of chess. Bored by the gentle nature of the tabletop game, the technicians of Losa Llamas invented Thrash. So eager were they to begin playing that no rules were agreed upon or recorded, hence each match, involving large sticks and a host of low-level spells, tends to devolve into a wild free-for-all of utter mayhem, resulting in the not infrequent loss of loose change, blood and limbs.

bothered. A pond and a small fountain had been built in the centre of the main square and had been stocked with a variety of the local fish. Unfortunately, due to an acute lack of understanding of piscine dietary requirements most of the larger fish were eaten by patrolling gangs of ugly-looking dull-grey fish with teeth, whilst the smaller fish were eaten by the diminishing numbers of the larger fish and the remaining small fish had a stay of execution until they grew large enough for the dull-grey fish to bother about. The dull-grey fish eventually turned cannibalistic and promptly nibbled themselves into premature extinction. The only survivors from the pond were a few of the indigenous type of tree-climbing fish who'd had the intelligence to suss out what was going on and head straight for the water-free environment of the forest.

On the outside this appeared to be the most newsworthy item to come out of Losa Llamas, but one of the best-kept secrets in Rhyngill's chequered history was here on the banks of the River Caman. It would probably be more accurate to say *under* the banks of the River Caman owing to the fact that the tiny pink, blue and yellow village served merely as a front entrance for the complex warren of tunnels, chambers and research centres that plunged through the ground like the results of a colony of gophers on acid. Quite what spurred the construction of a centre for study into the development and manufacture of the Ultimate Deterrent – and who the King of Rhyngill wanted to ultimately deter – had been lost in a maze of labyrinthine intrigue and subterfuge so complex that only a genius with a penchant for logic puzzles and reverse escapology would ever have an inkling of a hope of figuring it out now.

Meanwhile, deep in one of the lower southern passages of the underground and far larger part of Losa Llamas, the sound of metal grating on metal could be heard as a large disc screwed itself out of the floor. After a few minutes the grating stopped, the disc was lifted slightly and pushed to one side. Two gauntlets appeared over the lip of the hole and hauled a tall, thin black-clad figure up and into Losa Llamas. The leather of his black clothes creaked – a result of the recent soaking he had received – as Snydewinder pushed the disc back into the hole and screwed it down. He kicked dust over it, hiding it from view, then looked around the passage he stood in.

Apart from his own breathing and the creaking of his armour Snydewinder could hear no other sounds. The passageway spread off to the left and right and was hewn directly out of the soil. Some stray roots dangled above his head and wound around the large cable leading from the humming Thaumatron, supplying power to the subdued amber lights in the roof. The whole place had an air of musty misuse about it, smelling like the burrow of some giant colony of insects. He listened again to ensure no chitinous chirrups were within earshot.

Temporarily stumped for any clue regarding which way to go, he audaciously turned left. With a stick he made a tiny mark on the soft wall and headed off down the passage. His mission was nearing its end. All he had to do was find the evidence to convince those creeps back in Cranachan of the existence of the Frogs and it would only be a matter of time before he returned to his craved-for station of absolute, undiluted power.

Rubbing his gauntlets together feverishly, eager adrenalin surging beneath his skin, he walked stealthily down the passage, on toward his goal.

Deep in the memory centres of Snydewinder's seething neuronal network a single rumour was congratulated on a job well done. Secret Door grinned smugly to itself and fluttered off into the bar of a synaptic junction for a well-earned rest and an acetyl choline cocktail.

'Well can you think of anything better?' challenged Courgette as they walked on through the forest. 'From what Ch'tin's told us he sounds perfect to start with.'

Hogshead shook his head, Dawn skipped about in the

leaves dreaming of the glories of Fort Knumm. Firkin opened and closed his mouth a few times before saying, 'It's just that I can't really see how he would know.'

'We've been through that already. He travels about so much he's bound to have heard something,' said Courgette with irritating certainty.

'Do you really think so?'

'Yes. I'm *sure* he'll know something. And if he doesn't he'll probably know someone who does. Or at least someone who knows someone who'll probably know someone who does.'

'But will he know where the King is?' asked Firkin.

'There's only one way to find out. We'll ask him, shall we?' said Courgette with the tone of voice that made Firkin feel like he was a *very* naughty schoolchild who had asked, 'But, do we *have* to do homework?'

'But how are we going to find him?' asked Hogshead, eager to see him.

'He's bound to be in Fort Knumm tonight,' said Courgette confidently. 'There's no way he'd miss out on a crowd like that. St Swindling's Day is always good for business.'

'Mmmm. I 'spose so,' conceded Firkin. And the matter was settled. On entering Fort Knumm they would start looking for Vhintz the Travelling Sorcerer, purveyor of potions, ointments and oils, rectifier of chronograph dysfunction, sealer of minor faucet leakage and occasional medium. He was a very common sight at all major gatherings with his long black cloak and pointy hat, decorated with bolts of lightning, sequin moons, stars and tacky, enamelled signs of the zodiac, as he waved his arms about dramatically and urged the crowd to bring him their broken timepieces and blunted scissors. In the buzzing throng of the market square, even on St Swindling's Day, he shouldn't be too hard to find. Even though Vhintz wasn't a *real* Wizard, lacking the high-level skills that Hogshead imagined himself to possess (Hogshead believed that the ability to become a magic user was inherited, not learnt), the rotund, proto-mage, with his one imperfect spell to rub together, was desperately looking forward to meeting a kindred spirit.

The small group rounded a minor hillock, pushed through a few more trees and left the forest behind them. They stood for a moment, looking across the black muddy space at the collective mass that is Fort Knumm. Gold towers rising proudly skyward, scattering shafts of light in myriad directions; banners of coloured heraldic cloth waving in open welcome; solid gold lions standing guard over the glittering gateway to a bustling metropolis. Not a hope.

'Arghh! You lying toad!' screamed Dawn, thumping Firkin as hard as she could.

'Er . . . I, oh dear,' he struggled.

'You told me it was beautiful and glorious and, and . . .'

'Well, er,' Firkin looked pleadingly at Courgette and Hogshead for some help. Any help. None came. They smiled sweetly and listened.

'Where are the lions? I want to see the lions!' demanded Dawn.

'They must have moved them somewhere . . .'

'Where?'

'I don't know. I haven't been here for ages,' whined Firkin pathetically.

'Find them!' she shouted.

'Er . . . I can't.'

Dawn looked horrified.

'You see, Dawn, it's like this,' continued Firkin. 'About the lions and why you can't see them, er, that's because they . . .'

'They've been moved,' said Courgette, and winked. 'They've put them in a safe place. Haven't they Firkin?'

He opened and closed his mouth in sheer surprise. 'Er, yes. That's right. A very safe place.'

With Courgette, Firkin and even Hogshead nodding in agreement, Dawn grudgingly accepted the 'safe place' theory as the truth. Firkin breathed a sigh of relief and looked gratefully at Courgette.

'But . . . why is it all so dirty?' started up Dawn again.

'Oh, because it hasn't been cleaned,' answered Firkin sharply and moved off towards the gateway. Dawn followed.

'But you said that it was lovely and shiny . . .'

'Yes, well, it's rained since then.'

'How does rain make it dirty?'

Firkin shot another pleading glance over his shoulder at Hogshead and Courgette, who stood helpless with silent laughter.

'Er. Each spot of rain has a piece of dirt in it and when that falls it . . .'

Courgette and Hogshead watched as Firkin desperately tried to paint himself out of the corner that he now found himself in.

'Serves him right. Lying to his little sister!' whispered Courgette.

Hogshead nodded, stifling his giggles as they approached the other two waiting at the gate.

To apply the word 'gate' to the structure that the children now stood before is, without doubt, stretching a noun to the very limits of its definition. Decades ago it might have been apt, but not any more. The hole in Fort Knumm's outer defensive wall which could once have been closed and sealed in an instant to form an impregnable barrier against enemy invasion would now yield at the lightest of knocks. Assuming, that is, that the 'gate' could, in fact, be closed. The two giant halves, which once slid smoothly and silently on well-greased hinges to form a brass-reinforced, solid oak wall several inches thick, now leaned precariously against the stone pillars that had supported them. The hinges were unrecognisable arthritic knuckles of rust, broken and useless. Huge weeds grew where gatekeepers once stood sentinel. The massive panels of proud oak now formed high-rise accommodation for woodlice, woodworms and bracket fungus.

'What about the incense sticks and pot-pourri showers and birds and . . .' twittered Dawn, tugging at Firkin's sleeve.

'Ahh, well, er . . .'

The 'gate' represented a microcosmic reflection of the state of the rest of Fort Knumm. Once glorious, proud and honest, now shoddy, redundant and the home of thousands of unsavoury characters competing for space to live, breathe and fleece each other senseless.

It was through this portal that the group of children entered and walked up the muddy street towards the market square. Hogshead brimming with excitement; Dawn seething with acute disappointment; Firkin trying furiously to ignore the barrage of barbed questions hailing him from his sister's lashing tongue. The shops along this section were all closed up; their owners, not happy about missing out on the festivities and wary about the excessive numbers of criminals enjoying the amnesty, had moved their businesses to stalls in the square. The inactivity lent a curiously sinister air to the normally busy street. Away ahead of them the noise and clatter of a boisterous crowd could be heard. Roars of drunken laughter swam up through a boiling sea of riotous voices, breaking surface momentarily, before being pulled back into the churning, fathomless depths of revelrous abandon. Like a bottled message from a happily shipwrecked sailor, shouts of victorious joy floated on a frothy ocean of tumultuous babble. The coquettish giggles of the Fort Knumm Hand Maidens fizzed like bubbles in the heady champagne of the uproarious jollification. It was a grand party.

And above it all, winking here, grinning there, flashing a wide, toothless grin, exploding bombs of nimbic tinsel and fireworks of stratospheric extravagance, dipped and darted the Party Atmosphere.

Dawn began to fidget as she heard the racket. It sounded like fun and she wanted to be in there. Now. Firkin grabbed her collar and strained to hold her back. They were on a mission, there would be no partying. And in that decision, he was entirely unanimous. The little group rounded a corner and were hit by the full force of the Party Atmosphere. A wild almost invisible Cheshire cat grin hung in the air topped with a brightly coloured rainbow party hat at a jaunty angle, flashing on and off. It rocked to the beat of the overpowering music. Hogshead began to tap his toes as the irresistible rhythm of a conga floated through the air. Absently, Courgette tapped her hand against the side of her leg.

'All right,' said Firkin, struggling to be heard over the racket. 'Can anyone see Vhintz?'

'No. Not yet,' said Hogshead. 'But I can't see very well from here.' His shoulders began to twitch in time with his toes.

A great caterpillar of people snaked jerkily through the heaving throng and started to head their way. The Party Atmosphere launched a barrage of exploding cumulus cluster-bombs, blowing flatulent raspberries as the vapour paper trails wriggled and squirmed earthwards.

'Where do you think he'll be?' shouted Courgette, rocking back and forth.

'Up on one of the stalls at the side I would guess,' yelled Firkin, keeping full charge of himself, peering over the crowd as best he could. Behind him, Dawn's footwork was beginning to match that of the crowd. The caterpillar kicked its left legs out. Hogshead unconsciously raised his left foot. The Party Atmosphere grinned.

'Cha cha cha cha cha. CHA!' muttered Dawn to herself.

'I can see him no-where!' said Hogshead rhythmically.

'I can't see him either,' sang Courgette.

'Neither can I, CHA!' joined in Dawn, grabbing Courgette around the waist. 'I wonder why, CHA!' she sang and kicked out her right leg. The translucent conical hat atop the Party Atmosphere's grinning face bobbed in time with the music, flashing on and off.

'Oh, wow! What a rhythm,' said Hogshead as he was grabbed around the waist by Courgette. 'Let me in, let me in!'

As the caterpillar's tail snaked past, Hogshead, Courgette and Dawn increased its length by three. A translucent flashing rainbow party hat was flung high into the air.

'Wait!' yelled Firkin, shocked as they conga'd past. 'Stop! Come back. What do you think you're doing?'

The only answer he received was three simultaneous 'CHA!'s as three more right legs kicked out sideways. In another four bars they had disappeared into the throng, the latest victims of the Party Atmosphere.

After a few minutes the floor that Snydewinder walked across changed from bare dark soil to neatly laid paving slabs. The walls here had a skin of plaster and the lights were brighter. He felt as though he was approaching the centre of Losa Llamas, or at least a part given over to significantly more activity than weeding and insect control.

His back suddenly stiffened as he heard the clicking of heels on the floor. Someone was approaching. Snydewinder ducked behind a corner, peering out as the footsteps stopped. A figure in a white lab-cloak slid back a small panel in a large oak door and looked inside. Then he put the tray he had been carrying on the floor and pushed it part-way through another sliding panel. 'All right, Arathoostra. Time for lunch,' said the technician in exactly the manner with which zoo-keepers address their favourite gorilla. An almost inhuman howl of rage echoed out from behind the door in response.

'Yeah, yeah,' answered the technician wearily. 'But at least I don't think my father was a tadpole!'

Another string of snarls questioning the parentage of the technician lashed out from Arathoostra's vicious tongue.

'Listen here, you weirdo!' shouted the technician. 'I don't have to take these insults. I could just forget to come down here and then you'd be sorry. Nobody else even wants to go near you. If I didn't come you'd be forgotten about. Lunch would be a memory!'

A more subdued string of blasphemies answered.

'Yeah, well just don't forget that, huh?'

The tray disappeared suddenly as it was snatched inside.

'Hey, Arathoostra. Any messages for the kids? I'm on my way there now,' asked the technician.

A few mumbled sentences drifted incomprehensibly towards Snydewinder. Kids? he thought. What kids? There are no families here.

'OK, I'll tell 'em,' said the technician. 'See you tomorrow. Oh, and Arry,' he added through the viewing panel. 'Don't go away.'

From behind the inch-thick padded oak door a whirlwind of insults resonated wildly as Arathoostra let off steam with a volley of wrathful fulminations.

Sliding the panel shut, the technician strolled off jauntily down the passage, chuckling.

It was with an acute sense of curiosity that Snydewinder followed the technician through the warren of tunnels that was Losa Llamas. He knew a lot about Arathoostra and he had heard a lot of rumours, but never had he heard mention of a family. Children? Arathoostra?

Rarely, if ever, was Snydewinder surprised, but this piece of news came as a shock. A very welcome shock. Children were always useful if persuasion was required. He recalled with a thrill the leverage that he had gained on numerous occasions, during periods of intensely delicate negotiations, from the simple act of dropping a child's fingertip on the table. Very effective. A surge of frigorific evil tap-danced up the music-hall stairway of his spine, twirling its white stick and top hat with acutely malicious glee, accompanied by an orchestra of iniquitous violinists sawing symphonies of sin. The world was looking good.

Silently, in the shadows, a safe distance behind the technician, Snydewinder's face sneered happily from behind his black leather eyepatch. The rattle of keys brought the power-starved ex-Lord Chancellor of Rhyngill back to the tunnels of Losa Llamas. Keys? he thought.

The kids are locked up too? Weird!

The technician unfastened a series of locks, picked up a large bucket standing by the steel door and opened the huge portal.

Dark sounds bubbled out of the open archway. Low

batrachian gruntings mingled with the undulent lappings of thick water on stone.

Snydewinder's curiosity was whetted to a gleaming inquisitorial edge as, keeping low, he peered round the door-frame.

In the dark, humid interior huge shapes moved in an ocean of a pool, showing glimpses of glistening rough skin. The room smelt of damp plaster hanging in rotting curtains of detritis, leaf litter and acres of algae. It was at once nauseating and comfortingly overpowering, like a warm, damp dog blanket.

The technician stood on an overhanging pulpit with the bucket by his side. In the cavernous gloom of The Chamber, his voice sounded small as he shouted, 'Daddy sends his love.' He upturned the bucket into the pool, stood back and watched.

Daddy sends his love, thought Snydewinder, Daddy . . . Of course!

Suddenly the low, almost bovine, grunts were but a memory. The pool erupted in a thrashing frenzy of rough skin, lashing tongues and slashing claws as the creatures began to feed. In the dark it was impossible to tell the size or number of the beasts in the pool. The gloomy mystery of the scene made it all the more sinister. Half-glimpsed flashes of projectile tongues hurtled towards struggling fish, the heavy muscular tips glistening momentarily in the twilight dampness before snatching, catching and pulling the contents of the bucket into countless giant ranine oesophagi. In seconds the snack of fish was gone.

In seconds a flash of evil had come.

Stealthily, Snydewinder edged his way into the Chamber, easing the door closed behind him. The frenzy in the pool more than covered any noise he made. Silently, he crept towards the technician who was leaning on the railings, absorbed by the amphibian feeding frenzy below. He was blissfully unaware of quite how absorbed he was soon to be.

With the cold thrill of an assassin Snydewinder, in one

fluid movement, snatched the technician's ankles, lifted and tipped him over the railings. Before reflex could take control and fire some defensive movement it was too late. Struggling for a moment in the air the technician plunged, mouth open, into the thick water. The tepid liquid surged down his throat, flooding his lungs. Thrashing wildly he clawed his way desperately towards the surface. In the dark, in the flailing frenzied jungle of the slashing amphibian legs, the surface could have been anywhere. His lungs, useless with their tepid contents, ached to explode. He coughed. A silent submarine cough reflexively aimed at clearing his lungs successfully managed to exhale the final millibars of oxygen clinging to his already blueing alveoli. He watched in mortal shock as the small bubble floated momentarily and was lost in the seething water.

Suddenly a pinkish blob grabbed firmly at his ankle and tugged. He looked down through the seething murk and recognised the silhouette of a male. Gripped by this in an alien environment and out of his depth, in more ways than one, the technician conceded defeat. Almost gratefully he resigned his aquatic struggle and slipped down the throat of the frog.

Snydewinder's knuckles were white inside his gauntlets as he gripped the railings in excitement. His teeth glistened in the gloom as his lips curled back in a sneer of evil which ranked with his best.

Everything was going perfectly. He was standing in the presence of a force of awesome cold-hearted power. Nothing was more ruthless than these creatures. They had never even had any ruth to lose.

With that technician out of the way there was no one in Losa Llamas who cared what happened to Arathoostra. And Arathoostra was the key. With the mad scientist on his side and the Frogs of War at his back – quite a long way back, those tongues had a significant reach – nothing could stop him. Nothing would stand in his way!

As the waves of the technician's final struggle lapped the

sides of the pool a low power-crazed laugh bubbled up through Snydewinder's throat.

The ranks of the host of the Angel of Death had just swelled by one extremely nasty cherub.

Firkin bobbed about on tip-toes as he strained to see into the seething throng of people. The caterpillar was growing all the time as more people attached themselves to its tail, running forward and kicking first their left, then right legs. They seemed to come from all directions. Small groups of ready-formed segments rushed past Firkin shrieking wildly as they joined onto the rapidly thrashing tail accompanied by wild whistles and tropospheric fireworks from the grinning ghostly face of the Party Atmosphere, its rainbow hat flashing and belching multi-coloured smoke signals.

A few times Firkin heard Courgette whistle uncontrollably by, pulled and pushed in the frenetic mêlée, but he didn't see her or Hogshead. He began to worry about Dawn in that huge crowd. She was so small, so squashable. Suddenly a pair of hands grabbed him around the waist, sweeping him off his feet. A smell made up of stale beer, cheese and onion hit him as he turned to see what was happening. Behind him were four drunken revellers laughing raucously as they conga'd their way into the centre of the square. Firkin screamed as he was raced through the sea of people, unable to stop, the hands tightening around his waist. Out of the corner of his eye he caught a glimpse of Courgette; a blur of dancing red hair, flashing by in the opposite direction. There were columns of people either side of him. He was hurled around a sharp corner, screaming as he saw the back of someone in front approaching rapidly. A translucent flatulent raspberry rattled squelchily in his ear, generously supplied by the Party Atmosphere. Firkin was going to be crushed, he knew it. The four-man-power engine behind him surged on with undiminished vigour. The solid expanse of horizon-filling back closed in. Nearer. He straightened his arms, preparation for the unavoidable collision. His hands

108

locked about the huge waist as he whumped into the back of the man in front. He shook his head, dazed by the impact, clouds of stratospheric sparklers and fluorescent vapour trails whizzed and flashed skyward, before he was pushed and pulled deeper into the wild frenzy.

His face jammed against the kidneys of the hulk in front, Firkin was terrified. Collisions came and went with no warning, crushing the air out of his lungs; legs, ankles, heels thrashed and kicked like stampedes of frenzied bargain-hunters in the January sales. He was snatched through ever tighter angles, accelerated in arm-wrenching sprints, decelerated in crushing pile-ups and smashed in the shins by hundreds of kicking legs. He swore profusely as the Party Atmosphere zoomed around him, cackling.

Suddenly he was pushed from behind. He lurched forward, catching the heel of the man in front and tripped. He tried to pull himself up but the pressure at his back was too great. Everything turned into arms and legs, heels and fists as the cold, hard floor raced towards him, and he plunged into a sea of footwear, drowning in a foot-fetishist's heaven. Legs leapt out of nowhere in joyous kicks as he thrashed around on the floor attempting to avoid them. Flashes of light from above lanced down into the lonely and terrifying gloom of Firkin's stampeding world. He screamed. This was the worst thing that had happened to him. He was going to be stamped to death and nobody would realise until his battered body was found, bruised and flat, in the bleary light of tomorrow's hangover. What a way to go.

Before he was aware of it a hand grabbed his collar. He was pulled along the floor on his knees before he realised that this was all the help he was going to get. Terrified still, he looked up to see Courgette desperately clinging to Hogshead as he carried out his daring rescue attempt. Firkin found his feet moments before a battalion of left feet launched themselves at the spot where he had just been. Somehow Hogshead managed to pull Firkin in front of him, sandwiching him into the conga line just as they all lurched forward.

Firkin stumbled again. His head swam as he fought to remain on two feet.

The man in front pulled away from him as the caterpillar accelerated suddenly. Firkin had to run. He hoped that Hogshead could keep hold. Somehow the movement seemed faster than before. The kicking had stopped. Everyone was sprinting to keep upright. In the frenetic, tangled mêlée the front of the line had joined up to the back and as the people nearer the front accelerated to catch up so the back-markers had to run. It was a vicious circle.

The little group of youngsters suddenly found themselves in the middle of a race to stay upright in the twisting convoluted confines of the square. It was almost impossible to keep hold of the person in front as they were snatched around hairpin corners. Hogshead was sweating with the effort. The corners grew tighter, the pace faster until suddenly a sharp left turn proved too much for the exhausted group. They shot forward, spinning tangentially out into the dark. A screaming Dawn brought up the rear as the four children were flicked into the open maw of a hungry alleyway and sent crashing noisily into a heap of discarded crates and boxes.

Arathoostra's head of black curly hair flicked back as he heard the sound of the panel sliding in the door. He stared at the eye as it peered in and waited for the tray of food. It didn't come. Instead the sound of the lock being picked floated into earshot, followed by the door itself creaking open.

A tall, thin man eased himself inside, pushing the door behind him. He moved furtively, raising Arathoostra's suspicions. In the last ten years, the door had remained firmly shut.

Snydewinder squatted next to the hunched and strait-jacketed figure, his face sneering in the certain knowledge that here was the key to the relaunch of his life. Too long he had been skulking in the shadows, commanding all the respect of a spurned scabrous rodent. Well, all that was about to change.

'The kids send their love,' whispered Snydewinder, watching as the old scientist's bearded face creased into a grin.

'How are they?' he croaked.

'Well. Ready for action.'

Snydewinder turned Arathoostra round and began working at the knotted laces behind the scientist's back.

'What are you doing?' croaked Arathoostra.

'I'm helping. You're coming with me. I've got plans for you.'

'And my babies?'

'Oh yes. Yes, indeed!'

Arathoostra's eyes focused properly for the first time in years as he turned and looked at Snydewinder. His unspoken request was eloquent in its ocular simplicity. In a moment Snydewinder had herded Arathoostra out of the cell, locked the door, and was heading off towards the Chamber.

'We can't stay long,' he said as he eased the door open and manoeuvred the pathetic old man into the musty room.

With shaky footsteps, muscles atrophied from years of underuse, Arathoostra walked forward, clinging to the railing. He looked down on the roughly glistening backs of 'his babies' for the first time in longer than he could remember, and smiled proudly as the huge amphibians flopped and gurgled in the tepid pool. Memories flooded back of the night of their birth, twenty-five years ago, and the weeks of nurturing that had followed. Then the unfortunate deaths. Arathoostra deeply regretted them, such a waste, a terrible waste . . . of time. Lost opportunities. He could have spent years with his babies if it hadn't been for those idiot technicians. His eyes flashed with anger as he thought of what he might have achieved with all that time.

Well, now that time was here. Arathoostra knew his babies, knew what they were capable of . . . knew that it was never too late to teach an old frog new tricks!

Snydewinder placed a black-gauntleted hand on the old

man's shoulder, easing him gently out of the Chamber. Checking the corridor he moved quickly and headed out of Losa Llamas with the self-proclaimed Angel of Death. By the time they discovered he was gone, it would be too late.

A hyenic power-hungry cackle rattled down the small passageway towards the secret door.

Far too late.

Beware of the . . .

How long the youngsters lay in the heap of crates and boxes in the gloom of the alleyway was almost anyone's guess, but when Firkin finally gathered together the strength of will to open his eyes the alley was significantly and measurably darker. Slowly, and with growing nervous irritation, Firkin nudged Hogshead, who was sprawled across several crates and Firkin's right leg. Behind them the party was still in full swing. Hogshead twitched, grunted and shook his head wearily.

'Well, did you see him?' whispered Firkin, an edge of vexation to his voice.

'Eh?' answered Hogshead, rubbing his shins.

'Vhintz. Did you see Vhintz? Is everything sorted out?'

'Er, I, well . . .'

'So?' said Firkin meaningfully, gently massaging his crushed ribs.

'So, what?'

'So, where do we go? How do we find King Khardeen?'

In the shadows of a small doorway, a pair of ears, honed from a lifetime of snatching the tiniest item of intrigue and wringing the maximum profit from it, pricked alertly to attention.

'Well, I don't know,' said Hogshead miserably. 'I didn't see Vhintz.'

The figure in the gloom made a mental note – Vhintz, contact.

'I'm not surprised,' snarled Firkin. 'Not surprised at all, after all that dancing.'

'We were mingling,' argued Hogshead.

'That's not what I'd call it,' grumbled Firkin.

Silently, stealthily the huge black shadow slunk out of the doorway and headed towards the small group of youngsters.

'And what *would* you call it?' snapped Hogshead.

'Wasting time and endangering our entire mission,' said Firkin, sulkily folding his arms and wincing as he bashed his ribs. 'If I hadn't saved you from that mêlée . . .'

'Now, wait a minute,' interrupted Hogshead. 'Who saved who?'

The dark sinister shadow drew itself up to its full height and lurked forward.

'Whom,' corrected Courgette.

'Shutup!' snapped Firkin and Hogshead simultaneously.

'It was *me* who pulled *you* off the floor!' grumbled Hogshead.

'You! Hah.'

'Yes, me!'

'Wwwwhhhh . . . !' said Courgette, her mouth dropping open as a shadow blacker than a black cat's insides appeared. Or rather didn't.

An enormous bulk of non-light blotted out all the remaining light.

Hogshead swallowed nervously, looked up and froze.

'What does she mean "Wwwwhhhh . . ." ' groaned Firkin, his back to the looming shadow.

'Frrknnn,' said Hogshead, trying to keep his mouth still. 'Thrr's smmthnn b'hnnd yuh!'

'Hah, ha. Very funny!' muttered Firkin dripping sarcasm.

'B'hnnnd yuhh!' whimpered Hogshead through clenched teeth, eyes wide.

'That's just a pathetic attempt to make me forget about all that nonsense in the market square, taking off like that . . .'

'Mnnstrrr!' whinnied Courgette. Dawn was out of sight, buried beneath a crate, quivering.

Somehow, in the already deep darkness of the tiny alley an even deeper darkness stood. And it breathed. It stood with its legs slightly apart, hands on its hips, one arm enveloped in leather armour, the other bare, watching the struggling youngsters. As its huge chest rose and fell, the armour encasing its massive shoulders creaked ominously and

114

seemed on the verge of bursting. It was as if a small continent had been knighted and was now standing in the alley, inches away from Firkin, deep in thought. Looming. Watching and waiting, cautiously fingering the handle of the high-carbon steel cutlass which dangled nonchalantly from its quick-release scabbard. Questions rose in its mind and began to demand answers. Answers that proved suspiciously evasive. The presence didn't like suspicion. Or evasion. Suspicious things, as a rule, often proved to be dangerous things and in its line of work dangerous normally meant fatal. Suspicious things arranged by him did, anyhow.

Now that he could actually see the bodies to which the voices fitted, he was a little surprised. By the way they had been talking; of Kings and contacts and missions, he expected something a little more, well, sinister. And/or lucrative.

In his time as professional assassin, Ikhnaton had come across a great many types of person involved in Monarch Location: estranged sons/daughters/lovers/wives seeking reimbursement for years of suffering (not his scene); estranged sons/daughters/lovers/wives seeking retribution for years of suffering (Sign here!); lords/chancellors/politicians (the list is endless) seeking swift regicide for a multitude of reasons (Let's talk fees!). There were seemingly endless permutations, but they all had an air of, well, money about them. This lot felt very DIY.

There was only one way to decide what to do with this lot. He dredged the back of his head for his tried and trusted Risk Assessment Algorithm. This would tell him what to do, simply by answering a series of simple questions with a 'yes' or 'no'.

Now how did it go? . . .

1) are they dangerous? if 'yes' go to 7)
                                if 'no' go to 2)
2) are they harmless?   if 'yes' go to 5)
                                if 'no' go to 4)

3) are they alive?   if 'yes' go to 1)
                                 if 'no' go to 6)
4) are they rich?   if 'yes' go to 6)
                                 if 'no' go to 9)
5) are they decoys? if 'yes' go to 8)
                                 if 'no' go to 9)
6) Yippee! Pay Day!
7) What are you waiting for! Kill them!
8) Kill them. Then kill who sent them.
9) What the hell. Kill them anyway.

It was a system that he was immensely proud of and it only had two effective escape clauses. If the person under assessment was deemed to have sufficient capital about their person, the removal of which would set Ikhnaton up for life in a large villa on a beach in the Eastern Tepid Seas, that person would be allowed to go free on surrendering those funds. The other was if that person was female and in possession of a hard black hand-weapon known as a handbag.

Experience had shown Ikhnaton the pain that can be inflicted using such an innocent-looking device.

As this shoddy clump of cowering individuals seemed to possess neither vast sums of money, nor a handbag, there was only one course of action open to Ikhnaton.

With a deft flick of his thumb, and a brief sussuration of extremely sharp metal on scabbard, he drew his high-carbon steel cutlass and grinned.

'Any last requests?' he asked casually.

Wat picked up the bucket of fish and walked into the Chamber. The warm damp air smothered him, making him cough. He hated this smell but he only had to feed the damn things once a week. The huge amphibians splashed in anticipation, they knew it was feeding time. Wat emptied the bucket over the railings and watched with feelings of revulsion and admiration as the eight-foot frogs thrashed and devoured the treat. He shivered as he watched.

Suddenly a patch of white caught his eyes as a tattered piece of cloth floated to the surface. He swallowed nervously as he considered why it was there. Carefully, with a long pole, he managed to pull the cloth out of the water. Landing his catch he recognised the material and noticed that the name tag was still just readable.

Against a rising tide of revulsion he picked up the damp and blood-stained rag, instantly recognising it as Gilbry's.

His head started to spin as he stood and ran out of the chamber. He turned right and ran wildly down the passageway. Something was horribly wrong and he had an awful feeling it was going to get worse. He tried to tell himself that *he* was wrong, that he was being stupid, letting his wild imagination run away with him, but somehow he knew that the rag he held was a portent, a sign, a sickening symptom of an enormous and ruthless malady that was waiting to break. He could feel it leering over the walls of decency, hurling abuse, taunting, readying itself.

He turned another corner at full tilt and screeched to a halt before a door. Reluctantly he slid back the panel and peered inside, looking around the padded walls and floors and gasped in astonishment. Even though he had half expected it, he was still shocked to find it confirmed. He stared into an empty cell.

Arathoostra was gone.

TOURISM TAKES BRUNT OF CRIME WAVE RISE
People are unwilling to visit the quaint mountain kingdom of Cranachan since the wave of thefts swept . . .

The typewriter stopped in a ripping of parchment as the man tore out the page, screwed it up, and threw it into the waste parchment bin and loaded another.

Grumbling to himself about deadlines, headlines and stress he stabbed away at the keyboard.

Fewer tourists visited Cranachan in the last year than . . .

'No, no, no,' he growled, shredding another page. He rubbed his hands through his thinning greasy hair and groaned for the fiftieth time in the last five minutes. He reached into his filthy overcoat and pulled out a small flask. Snatching open the lid he drank deeply, feeling instantly better as the warming liquor scorched the back of his throat. He stared at the ceiling and waited for inspiration.

For the latest, uncountable time he cursed his misfortune and prayed for the time when he would have his break again. He recalled the glory days of his scoop. Front page headlines. Exclusive! How soon they faded.

And what did he, Turgg Inyeff, ace investigative reporter for *The Triumphant Herald*, ever get to report on now?

MIMSY THE CAT SAVED FROM TWO HOUR TREE ORDEAL!

GRANNY TREEKS IN FULL-HOUSE BINGO VICTORY!

SEAGULL MURDERED IN LAKE-SIDE BLOOD-BATH!

It was enough to make a grown man scream. How about . . .

ACE REPORTER IN EDITOR MURDER TRIAL

It would come to that if he didn't get a decent story soon. Maybe he could make something up? Or become a novelist? Or just die of frustrated boredom? A piano-shaped cloud floated by the window.

Turgg stared at the blank sheet of mocking whitish parchment and swore profusely in the dark recesses of the back of his mind. He gathered up a motley collection of writing implements and a small notepad, stood, put on his grease-stained overcoat and shuffled out onto the street. His editor would have to wait for that pathetic article.

Turgg Inyeff wanted a story. He headed for his favourite

source of loose gossip and sustenance. A little dive on the seedier side of Cranachan Town. The Gutter.

Eight stubbily-hairy fingers, hiding beneath a mass of cheap paste-crystal rings swirled in the air above the black sphere. Gold rings which would have looked quite at home in a prize bull's nostrils jiggled at the figure's earlobes, flattened against the side of her head by the tightly wound red and white spotted headscarf. She tapped her foot with irritation and stared deeper into the sphere.

'Found them yet?' whispered Wat.

The figure grunted a terse negative and peered still harder.

There was a flash, a small spark of white and a brief crackling sound, then the sphere burst into a hail of static.

'When was this thing last serviced?' snapped the figure, thumping the side of the sphere and waggling one of the tiny knobs at the bottom right corner.

'I, er,' answered Wat.

'Hmmmph. Thought so . . . "I forgot",' mocked the figure, her eyes never straying from the centre of the sphere.

'Aha! Got them,' she grunted.

Wat stared into the blizzard of static, 'Where?'

He received no answer, as the figure swirled her hands, moaning and groaning incantations, desperately trying to clear the image. In a few moments the snowstorm had settled to light intermittent hail, and a heap of four children atop a pile of crates, boxes and other rubbish swam murkily into view.

'It's a bit dark,' commented Wat.

'It's an alleyway,' she said.

'Oh,' he answered, unimpressed.

'In Fort Knumm!'

'Ah. I see. You've got a good picture there,' he answered, sheepishly. 'What are they all staring at?'

'Dunno.' Bracelets jangled as wrists were flicked and fingers flexed in adjustments. The viewpoint shifted and looked up. And up.

'Uh oh!' said Wat with a crushing sense of understatement as he stared at the tiny monochrome image of a high-carbon steel cutlass waving menacingly in the air.

The woman was up in a flash, her chair spinning away behind her as she snapped orders at Wat.

'Get the Projector ready, now! Focus on those co-ordinates. Full intensity. Tent in the market square. Do it! Now!'

Wat almost fell over himself as he rushed in three different directions at once.

We haven't much time, thought the woman, no time to lose.

'Wait, wait!' pleaded the frail figure of Arathoostra. 'I need to rest.' A cold blast of wind raced through the high bleakness of the Foh pass.

Snydewinder snarled as he looked back at the old scientist. 'We need to keep moving. Come on!'

If I'm caught in these mountains I'm as good as dead! he thought as he remembered, all too vividly, the threat hanging over his major organs. The threat issued by King Grimzyn of Cranachan.

He turned back and dragged the limp body forward and over the top of the pass. Shaking him violently Snydewinder pointed across the valley to a high plateau and a castle squatting on the edge, surrounded by a mass of slouching dwellings.

'There!' he shouted at Arathoostra through clenched teeth, a habit he really should rid himself of as it tended to render his words almost unintelligible, 'There! Do you see it! Do you?'

The icy eyes of Arathoostra focused shakily on the distant fortress.

Above the howling wind blasting through the mountain pass Snydewinder shouted, 'Cranachan. We're nearly there!'

*

'No last requests?' asked Ikhnaton once more, waving the cutlass meaningfully. 'Not even a plea for mercy? Oh! I am disappointed.'

Four pairs of terrified eyes looked out of four petrified faces, frozen immobile with shock.

Unseen by anyone in the alley, a short stocky woman wearing a floral print dress, ill-matching pinafore and a red and white spotted headscarf, stepped into view. She stood left hand on hip, right hand swirling a black crocodile handbag.

'Hey! Big boy!' growled the woman in a strange-sounding voice. 'You teasin' those poor little mites?'

Ikhnaton turned his head, flicking his thick black pony tail arrogantly over his shoulder.

'Might be,' he answered.

'Well, that's not nice, is it?' came the reply in a croaky falsetto.

'Says who?' growled Ikhnaton, his cutlass turning to face the woman. His mind whirling, deciding that these four were classified under option 5) – decoys.

'Says me, Old Ma Tini, ready for a fight anytime, anyplace, anywhere. And my friend here,' she waved her handbag and grinned, itching for a fight. She took a step forward.

'Well, I'm *not* nice, am I? Doesn't *pay* to be nice in my job.'

'And it doesn't pay to go around teasin' innocent kiddies.' She took another step forward, twirling her handbag non-chalantly round her index finger, like a knight ready with a mace. Ikhnaton's eyes rose and fell in time with the spinning weapon.

'Is that crocodile?' he asked, trying to keep a conversationally threatening tone to his voice.

'Yup! Pure Tepid Sea. Very hard wearin'. Will stand up to a *lot* of knocking about. Like a demonstration?'

'Er, I . . .' stuttered Ikhnaton, his attention fixed on the spinning black pendulum as if hypnotised, very aware of the durability of Tepid Sea Crocodile, also very aware of its tiny rasping barbs which, if contacting the skin at the correct angle by utilising the underhand wrist technique can raise a *nasty* blister on even the most battle-hardened skin. It was this, rather than the excruciating pain that could be dealt out by those clasps and hinges, that was preying on the assassin's mind. One blister from one handbag and oh! . . . the humiliation! He'd never be able to hold his head up in Ye Silver Spittoone again, his position as leader of the Skull League would be taken by Aznar, the bouncer, probably, his entry for the fifty-ninth annual Fort Knumm Cow Toppling Championship would *have* to be withdrawn, business would suffer . . . it could take years to claw his way back to the position he now held, fighting in bars, three-shilling murders, and the sniggering behind his back. 'There goes Ikhnaton, can't even defend himself against an old woman's handbag,' they'd shout, dissolving into peals of laughter, he'd seen it happen.

'It's no trouble!' reminded Old Ma Tini.

'Er, I have a *very* busy schedule. Some other time, maybe?' he grinned sheepishly, snarled at the cowering youngsters and slunk back into his office, like an extremely miffed moray eel.

Old Ma Tini chuckled to herself and strolled jauntily towards the heap of youngsters. 'Going to stay there all day, are we?' she said. 'Come on!'

Hogshead struggled out of the crates, helping Courgette and Dawn, relief flooding his body. If I'd had longer to prepare, he thought, I could have handled that. He wouldn't have stood a chance against me. Couple of spells here, lightning bolt there. Ha! No problem, would have been begging for mercy, pleading, on his knees!

'Absolutely pathetic!' snarled Firkin, glaring at Hogshead as he shouldered his pack of books. 'You've been dragging those things around for miles, wittering on about how magic's good for this and that, and how invincible you're going to be, and the first sign of trouble you sit there going "Buh buh buh buh". I don't know why I bother.'

'I was ready!' protested Hogshead. 'A few more seconds and he would have been . . . would have been . . .'

'Yes?' Firkin stood with his hands on his hips, demanding an answer.

'. . . very sorry!' finished Hogshead defiantly. 'He would!' His bottom lip trembled with impotent rage, and the after effects of being scared out of his wits.

'Stop it, you two!' shouted Courgette.

'I didn't notice you doing anything special . . .' snapped Hogshead, prodding Firkin. 'Just sat there and didn't believe me!'

'So clumsy have you to be!' piped Ch'tin staring accusingly up at Hogshead from his tunic pocket. 'Squashed could have been I!'

'Oh, don't you start,' grumbled Hogshead feeling very persecuted.

'Now, now. We can't stand about in this horrid alley all day, can we?' blustered Old Ma Tini. 'Come with me!'

She turned on her heel and marched purposefully towards the market square. The children followed.

The noise of the St Swindling's Day celebrations continued unabated, the minstrels in the corner singing, blowing, strumming and thumping seemingly anything they could lay their hands on; the crowd shouting, leaping and cavorting with revelrous and drunken abandon; the stall owners yelling, waving banners and flags, trying to remove as much of the revellers' disposable income as possible. A wildly grinning translucent face shrieked as it flew madly about, igniting clouds of exploding shrapnel and rainbow fireworks as if there were no tomorrow.*

---

* For the vast majority of the revellers, this was in fact true. The wild alcoholic and herbal excesses to which they exposed their bodies during the course of the twenty-four hours of St Swindling's Day made any form of mental coherence in the following twenty-four hours extremely unlikely, if not entirely impossible. For a few highly unlucky individuals (or deserving, depending on your point of view), whose names appeared on a parchment list in the inside pocket of a certain professional assassin, tomorrow would start with the confusing, and not entirely pleasant, period of waiting to discover if reincarnation actually exists.

Just as Firkin was about to scream his protestations concerning re-entering the dangerously narcotic Party Atmosphere, Old Ma Tini turned sharply left, lifted a heavy cloth flap and vanished inside a red and white striped tent, decorated with open palms, stars, strange animals and far-seeing eyes, nestling in the corner of the market square. Hogshead couldn't be absolutely certain but he felt sure that it shimmered ever so slightly.

Curiously, everyone in the square seemed to be ignoring the tent.

A paste-jewel-encrusted hand thrust itself through the slit of the entrance and beckoned at the foursome.

A tidal wave of heaving drunkards surged recklessly out of the mêlée, leering and belching clouds of onion stinking breath, and a millisecond later, the children stood inside the tent, looking around at the red and white interior, the four chairs and the expectant face of Old Ma Tini shuffling a pack of cards, sitting behind a large crystal sphere. With a dismissive wave of her remarkably hairy hand she gestured to them to sit down and began dealing the cards onto the table.

It was Turgg Inyeff's lucky night. As he strolled blearily towards The Gutter two figures ran out of a back alley, round a corner and headed down towards the Imperial Palace Fortress of Cranachan. It wasn't strictly the fact that two shady-looking figures were running furtively about that attracted his attention, that sort of shady furtivity was par for the course in Cranachan. What caused him to blink in disbelief, rub his eyes, look again, then raise a swift homily of thanks to Reeevrb, the Goddess of Journalistic Fortitude and Syntax, was the direction in which they were headed and the fact that the glimpsed sneer of the face behind the eyepatch sprinted into the belltowers of his memory, scrambled up the ropes, fought with the inertia, and set ringing peals and carillons of bells to send even the most steadfast of campanologists into paroxysms of orgiastic delight. This was newsworthy.

As he half-ran, half-shuffled along the alley his mind raced. Why were they heading this way? There was nothing down here except the Palace and that was impregnable. Why was that face familiar? Who was the other man? Would it warrant a front page?

The twosome turned sharply left as they neared the base of the cliff on which the Palace stood. A scruffy-looking bush nestled between two outcrops, and seemed to be receiving far more interest from the two men than he would have expected. Somehow he didn't see this pair as the types to be interested in horticulture. The taller one seemed to have lost something. He searched the bush thoroughly, grunting as he struggled to reach the ground behind the trunk, pushing himself further and further into the foliage. Curiously, the second man joined in the search and bent down to scour the ground in the same manner. It was only a full minute later that Turgg Inyeff realised they had disappeared.

He waited a few moments and then followed, searching the greenery thoroughly, feeling the rough bark of the bush's trunk and the soil around it. Then he felt wood. Smooth, correctly planed wood, the type from which doors are made. He pushed the bush to one side and opened the small door which led to a small set of steps that climbed away into the gloom.

Now this, he thought, is worth investigating. A phrase that he hadn't had cause to think for years wriggled to the forefront of his mind, clutching its ears against the cacophony of bells, four words which he never believed he would be able to use again, 'Hold the Front Page!'

In the early hours of a still, dark night in Cranachan, Turgg Inyeff, ace investigative reporter for *The Triumphant Herald*, stepped into a bush. And disappeared.

Old Ma Tini's left eye bulged hideously as she peered at the four children through the crystal sphere. Courgette and Dawn fidgeted uncomfortably on the chairs, feeling like an interesting new type of fruit fly under a microscope.

Hogshead watched every move the old woman made, fascinated by the strange hand gestures and alien words she uttered. He was sure there was magic afoot here.

Outside, the mayhem of the party continued with frantic abandon, the constant mêlée punctuated by occasional crashes and roars of intoxicated laughter.

'Who will pick first?' croaked Old Ma Tini in her strained falsetto, gesturing to the cards.

'What for?' answered Firkin barely disguising his irritation and folding his arms.

'To find what you may seek!'

'What kind of an answer is that?' snapped Firkin, the feeling of wasting valuable time galling him.

'Unoriginal, I'm afraid,' admitted Old Ma Tini, 'but it normally serves well. *Most* people co-operate and point to a card. Most people *want* to use my powers of divination, foresight, insight and other obscure jiggery-pokery. But if you *insist* on wearing out your shoes, yourselves and your tempers in a fruitless search for a sorcer . . . er, person that isn't here, then go ahead!'

Hogshead was onto the slip in a second. 'You said sorcerer,' he accused. 'How did you know?'

'It might not be true,' said Firkin too quickly, as if trying to hide a guilty secret.

'Did I say that?' said Old Ma Tini, pleased that Hogshead had picked up on her deliberate mistake so swiftly. 'I am sorry. I will keep doing that.'

'How did you know?' pressed Hogshead, eager for knowledge. 'Tell me!' His voice suddenly seemed harder.

'The gift,' answered the woman tapping the side of her head.

Dawn's ears pricked up at the thought of any presents going spare.

'I can *see* things,' she continued swirling her hands in mystically dramatic ways. 'I can see futures, and pasts, presents . . .'

'It's my birthday soon!' squeaked Dawn.

'. . . ahem! Do you mind!' chastised Old Ma Tini, glaring at a suddenly red-faced Dawn. 'Not *that* sort of present. I mean events, happenings, signs, portents . . .'

'How?' interrupted Hogshead.

'It's in the cards. Cards that can offer predictions. It was through these cards I saw you in the alley,' she lied. 'They gave me clues, offered me information, told me to investigate . . . I don't know where I'd be without my Pwarroh Cards!'

'Can they help us?' asked Hogshead. Firkin tutted noisily.

'Choose a card and you shall see!'

Hogshead's stubby hand flashed out and pointed. 'That one!'

Firkin groaned, muttering something about 'being unbelievably gullible'.

The surprisingly masculine, ring-encrusted hand of the fortune-teller turned over the card. It showed a small colourful picture of a long and winding road. Hogshead pointed again. A card showing a long wooden staff, a pointed hat, beard and cloak was revealed. He pointed once more. Two human legs sticking out of the mouth of an eight-foot frog. Old Ma Tini's face drained of all its colour as she stared at the card.

'Ha. Mistake. That shouldn't be here,' she gabbled, ripping the card in two and throwing it onto the floor. 'Ch . . . choose again.'

There was little choice. Only one card remained. It was revealed to show a flock of things that looked more or less like mountain goats, bleating plaintively on a mountainside.

Hogshead stared at the old woman. 'What does all that lot mean?'

'Pwarroh Cards offer clues, not answers. The message needs interpretation,' she said struggling to pull herself together after the shock of seeing the frog card. Could these things really work?

'The first one . . .' began Old Ma Tini.

'The first one is easy,' interrupted Hogshead, certain

127

he had the answer. 'It's a road, so Vhintz is just down the road.'

'How do you know it's Vhintz?' asked Courgette.

'Easy,' said Hogshead before the old woman could open her mouth. 'The second card, the staff, the hat . . . bound to be a sorcerer.'

'And the frog and the goats?' scorned Firkin.

'Er . . . I . . . animals . . .' pondered Hogshead. 'Got it!' he cried, clicking his fingers. 'Vhintz is just down the road in a pet shop! Come on!'

'It could be nothing to do with Vhintz,' complained Firkin. 'It could just as easily mean "Just down the road is a fancy dress shop, owned by a frog, that sells goats!" '

'You're being silly . . .'

'Or there's a man in a pub called the Frog and Goat, who's in disguise, who mends roads in his spare time, who can *tell* us where Vhintz is . . .'

'No, I'm right . . .' protested Hogshead.

'You're all wrong,' croaked Old Ma Tini, finally getting a word in. 'For one thing, they aren't goats and the frog has got *nothing* to do with it.' She couldn't reveal the truth. Not yet!

'What are they, then?' asked Firkin.

'Llamas,' answered Courgette smugly. 'Their necks are too long for goats and they don't have horns. Also their feet are too . . .'

'We get the idea!' snapped Firkin. She could be *so* irritating at times!

'The card of the herd of llamas,' said Old Ma Tini, her voice resonating meaningfully.

'What?' asked Hogshead.

'Loads o' llamas,' croaked the old woman.

'What?'

'Losa Llamas!'

'What?'

'Do I have to spell it out!' barked the old woman. 'The message of the Pwarroh cards is clear. Follow the road and

128

you will find Vhintz in a place called Losa Llamas.' She threw a map at them. 'It's clearly marked, you can't miss it. Now get out, I'm getting a migraine!'

As the children left the red and white tent, turned a swift right and headed away from the still raving party, Old Ma Tini leapt out of her chair, pulling her headscarf, pinafore and wig off. Grumbled complaints about the itchiness of wigs floated out from beneath a furious head-scratching session. A voice disconnected from anything in the tent floated into earshot.

'Well, darling. Should I turn it off?'

'Yes,' snapped the figure in the tent, its voice suddenly an octave lower, the falsetto dropped. 'And less of the "darling"! How do women cope with all this underwear . . . ?'

'I'll show you, if you like, honey.'

'Wat! No, cut that out! Wat . . . !'

In a moment the red and white tent, jammed into the corner of the market square, shimmered a few times. And vanished.

As Snydewinder led Arathoostra up the seemingly. endless flight of dark stone steps into the Palace Fortress of Cranachan his mind seethed and bubbled with a mixture of greed, desperation and abject terror. Returning to this secret entrance after fourteen years stirred bad memories. Fragments of his past floated towards him as if through a cauldron of thin soup, turning over before him, pale in the gloom, unseasoned, jostling with the lentils of remorse, boiled emotionally dry, except for regret and loss. Try as he might he couldn't blot out the recurring vision of his earlier glorious successes in the Palace. He sneered almost wistfully in the passage as he recalled the days when he had been known as Fisk and was the Chief of Cranachanian Internal Affairs. His glory days when he had power. The days before the lemmings . . .

Snydewinder snarled as he recalled the events. It had all

seemed so easy. Always eager to impress King Grimzyn, Fisk had spotted an immense source of income that was set to line the Rhyngill pocket. A source of income that Fisk was sure should have been Cranachanian.

Its source, the lemming-skin trade.

Fisk discovered that the lemmings lived and bred in the Cranachanian region of the Talpa Mountains until the last few minutes of their lives when they carelessly flung themselves off the cliff which marked the border with Rhyngill. This discovery had led to a dispute over import/export agreements, attempts to move the border involving heavy earth-moving equipment and eventually war. Even though the hugely powerful Army of Cranachan was overwhelmingly victorious, Fisk's problems had only just begun. Cranachan was saddled with the bill for feeding three thousand prisoners of war and, to make matters worse, the expected income from the lemming skins mysteriously dried up, as the following year saw a horrendous drop in sales. Fisk was blamed and banished from Cranachan under pain of death, or non-anaesthetised internal organ examination and removal, should he ever return.

Why the sales had dropped he never found out.

That had been the turning point in his life. His scheme had been so close to working. He would have been incredibly powerful by now. Exalted, rich, a success!

In the gloomy passage he spat and cursed under his breath. Anger rose, whetting his appetite to redress the balance in his favour. The ancient Thaumaturgical Physicist struggling up the steps behind him was the key. Snydewinder knew he was taking a huge risk, but he could see no other way. He had to have Khah Nij on his side . . .

Shutting all thoughts of the past away and concentrating firmly on the present, Snydewinder listened at the door at the top of the passage. Through that door lay entry into the Palace. He had reached the point of no return . . .

In one of the thousands of halls and corridors that run through the Imperial Palace Fortress of Cranachan a tapestry twitched, a small blast of cold night air entered and two men appeared. They looked furtively about, then crept and hobbled stealthily towards an unarranged and unexpected meeting.

Despite the highly comprehensive nature of the stock of books held in the library of Castell Rhyngill; against all the expected laws dictating the manner and system utilised for the recording of history; regardless of the wealth of information inscribed on the pages of the countless books, tomes and ledgers lurking in the dark coolness of the shelves, there was nothing to be found about Losa Llamas.

Llamas. Yes. If one so desired, information regarding their habitat, geographical distribution, disease states, parasitic infections and sexual orientations could easily be obtained. There were volumes on the use of llama wool in clothing, furniture manufacture, cuddly toy production; graphic 'How-to' guides illustrating what pleasure could be obtained from llama breeding (and not just for the llamas themselves); facts and figures about llamas were legion.

But Losa Llamas . . . not a sausage.

For Firkin, Hogshead, Courgette and Dawn, this was a great shame. It has been said, on numerous occasions and normally by the most optimistically challenged of individuals, that ignorance is bliss. When that ignorance is regarding several hundred facts, historical events, creations and extremely dangerous security systems, the sudden and probably terminal facing of which could so easily have been avoided by *not* walking through a particular door, only then, looking back from a whirlpool of panic, or sprinting madly, the jaws of destruction ripping and snapping at your heels, can ignorance be perceived of as, if not truly blissful, then at least restful.

Not only did Firkin et al. know nothing of the fact that since OG 1014 the Thaumaturgical Physicists' 'defensive' research had produced such varied creations as the acid-hurling pitcher plants, five types of temperature-sensitive

131

bindweed and angstolotls (lizard-like amphibians that released the panic-inducing pheromones of fear); they were also rapturously unconscious of the fact that word-based research into the realms of prosody, phonetics and sophistry had turned up a vast amount of useful, and extremely animate, finds; but, their chronically enraptured state of nescience blinded them totally to the fact that not only have these, and many other larger and nastier things, existed, but that they were following a map that would lead them shortly to the forest of Losa Llamas. Where a great many of them still lurked . . .

'Straight on,' said Firkin folding the map away. 'Just follow this path.'

'That's easy,' said Hogshead, looking ahead at the wide, curving path. 'It's almost a road, anyway.'

A few minutes later, as they stared at the impenetrably thick wall of overgrowth that blocked their path, Hogshead hated the way that always seemed to happen. At times like this he felt sure that he could look up on a cloudless day and whisper, to no one in particular, 'What a wonderful day!' and almost before his words would be out he'd be shivering under a ten-foot snow-drift. He'd have to try to learn to keep his mouth shut when things seemed to be going well.

Out of the dense forest ahead, a small ageing signpost leaned and tried to warn them:

Go back. Danger!! Beware of the . . .

The message ended in a streak of yellowing white, stuck to it an almost unrecognisably battered brush, its bristles twisted into grotesque shapes, and a rusting tin leaking a pool of hardened paint lay below the sign. Hogshead thought that it looked like several large centipedes had sprinted through the paint, chasing the signwriter away, but it was hard to tell for sure. Courgette shivered and Dawn looked around nervously.

Firkin swallowed hard and whispered, 'Look, I'm not sure what's happened here, but it was obviously a long time ago. It could be a trick. Old Ma Tini would have told us if it was dangerous.' Silently he added, *Wouldn't she?*

He swallowed again, putting on as brave a face as he could muster, 'Come on then. Straight on.'

'Through *there*!' complained Hogshead. 'You're joking!'

Firkin pulled the map out of his pocket and stared at it, Hogshead peering over his shoulder.

'See? Straight on,' he confirmed, folding up the map and walking purposefully forward, arming himself with a big stick and grim determination. He might be terrified, the eels of nervousness writhing in the pit of his stomach feeding off the butterflies of apprehension, but he mustn't let the others see. He was the leader, after all.

After a few minutes thrashing at the overgrowth, cursing as brambles snatched at him, sweating and looking less than pristine, he had revealed a tiny track leading straight into the centre of the forest.

'Here it is,' he said triumphantly and set off again, plunging into the undergrowth.

The path snaked around tree roots, across boggy patches, through dense copses, theirs being the first human feet to pass that way in years, and all the time Hogshead fell further behind as he tried to avoid the springing branches that Dawn let whip back at him, which whacked him on various sensitive parts of his anatomy. He was berated several times by Ch'tin after branches thudded only inches above or below his tunic pocket.

As they rounded a tree and crossed a small stream Courgette stopped and put her head on one side, listening.

'What can you hear?' asked Dawn.

'I'm not sure,' she whispered.

In the distance something sounded as if it were attempting to remove its own tonsils by furiously barking. It howled, screamed, then barked again.

Dawn could hear it too. She shuddered.

'Do you think it knows we're here?' she mouthed, wishing she knew sign language.

A roar echoed noisily through the forest followed by the disturbed squawking of several flocks of large birds. Dawn grabbed Courgette's hand, stifling a squeak of terror as a blood-curdling shriek rattled and rolled through the trees.

'Probably,' answered Courgette.

'What is it?' asked Firkin.

A strangled howl sounded from a point behind a bush, a lot closer than the shriek.

'Nearer,' answered Courgette helpfully.

'What are we going to do?' whispered Dawn clutching at Courgette's hand, panic levels rising.

Her question was almost drowned out by the sudden crash of foliage, the snapping and ripping of branches and deep harsh breathing that sounded behind them. As one they turned to face it, preparing themselves to face whatever evil horror had made all that noise.

'What's making all that racket?' shrieked Hogshead, panting furiously from sprinting to catch them, twigs sticking out of his hair, trees still waving from his dramatic appearance.

Firkin stared past Hogshead in horror. How do I explain *that*? he thought. He smiled what he hoped would be a reassuringly warm and friendly smile. He failed.

'Wwwhhh?' said Courgette staring past Hogshead.

'You all right?' asked Hogshead, his lungs still straining. He didn't get an answer. 'Why are you going "Wwwhhh" again?'

'As a *purely* hypothetical question,' began Firkin, staring over Hogshead's shoulder, grimacing in attempted reassurance. '. . . as an exercise into the world of the imagination. Erm, *if* there was, standing behind you, right now . . . I did say *if* didn't I? . . . Imaginary, of course . . . something about ten feet long, three feet high, uglier than Ch'tin, squatting on a million legs, with huge eyes and long whippy antennae . . . erm. What would you do about it?'

134

Hogshead thought about this. 'Does it have teeth?'

Firkin glanced over his shoulder. 'Theoretically, no. Just great big slicing things that could have your leg off in seconds . . . er, *if* it was there, of course.'

'Does it look angry?'

'*If* it was stood three feet behind you, then yes it looks . . . would look *very* angry.'

'That's easy,' said Hogshead. 'I'd turn around and cast a spell of infinite shrinkage on it.'

'And what would that do?'

'Make it grow smaller and smaller until it disappeared.'

'Good. *If* that situation arose, in reality, just supposing it did. Could you actually cast a spell of ultimate shrinkage . . . ?'

'Infinite shrinkage,' corrected Hogshead.

'Infinite, then. Could you . . . ?'

'Oh no!' said Hogshead cheerfully, enjoying Firkin's game, glad that, at last, he was taking some sort of an interest in magic. 'That's far too hard.'

Inside, Firkin screamed. Hope threw a large suitcase on the bed and began rapidly hurling in underwear, socks, shirts . . .

'What could you actually do?' asked Firkin. 'Right now? *If* that situation arose.'

'Scream and run,' Hogshead suggested.

Oh dear, thought Firkin. . . . trousers, shoes, cardigans . . .

A sound like bone scraping on brick floated out from three feet behind Hogshead as the creature licked its 'lips' in anticipation.

Reflexively, Hogshead turned around and instantly wished he hadn't. A creature, not unlike that which Firkin had described, except that he'd far overestimated the number of legs, opened and closed its huge mouth in a slowly malevolent cycle, showing off its complex arrangement of glistening mandibles to devastating effect. In that instant Hogshead also noticed that Firkin had been wrong about two

135

other things, namely one, it *did* have teeth, several different types, from the array of pin-sharp dentition carpeting its 'tongue' to the eight-inch regiment of fangs standing to eagerly glistening carnivorous attention, and two, it was *far* from hypothetical.

'GROWL. GROWL,' growled the creature over a cascade of paint-splattered footfalls as it edged forward.

'Nice boy. Nice boy,' whimpered Hogshead pathetically, backing away, his palms outstretched.

'SNARL,' it suggested, rattling forward another few paces.

'AAAAAAHHHHH!' replied Hogshead as, true to his word, he screamed, turned and ran, knees and elbows thrashing wildly as he propelled himself rapidly through the trees. The other three were nowhere in sight.

'GROWL. BARK. SNARL. ROAR,' yelled the creature in a terrifying fusillade of shocking onomatopoeia. It lurched forward, its legs rattling like a carrier bag of crabs.

Ahead, Dawn screamed.

'SCREAM. SCREAM,' noised the onomatopede, hurtling through the forest's green blur, hard on Hogshead's heels.

Tree roots snaked and snatched under his feet, branches whipped at his face as he plunged on, the onomatopede closing at every step. Beads of perspiration turned to torrents in a matter of seconds, racing down his brow in a screen of stinging sweat, obscuring his vision, clouding his sight. Suddenly, without warning, like the greatest of magic lantern heroines on the last reel, his ankle struck a root. In a second the onomatopede was on him. He screamed as the enmandibled mouth closed in, surging towards him, salivating expectantly. It was the last thing he saw.

'SCREAM. GURGLE. RIP. SNAP.' The sounds of death by dismemberment carried through the forest to the horrified, and suddenly terribly guilty ears of Firkin, Courgette and Dawn.

'YELL. SQUELCH. SCREAM.'

It was too much for Firkin. Stick in hand, yelling wildly he ran back across a small stream to do something heroic before it was too late.

'HOWL. BARK. GURGLE.'

He leapt up the bank, rounded a tree, stick raised and stopped dead in his tracks. Hogshead lay on his back, eyes closed, unconscious from a blow to his head. Apart from that he seemed to be intact. The gallons of blood and mass of severed limbs that the appalling sounds of frenzied carnage had led Firkin to expect, were non-existent. The onomatopede stood a few feet away and suddenly looked like a dog baying at the moon as it held its head high and yelled at the top of its voice.

'SQUELCH. SCREAM. SQUEAL.' Its jaws lashed from side to side as it enacted the scene in its head. Firkin threw his stick at the creature, hitting it squarely on the head. It turned and looked up at the wild expression on Firkin's face.

'WHIMPER,' it said, followed by 'YELP,' as Firkin caught it on the side of the head with a big stone. The creature rattled away a short distance and stood staring at him through its dark glistening eyes. An occasional 'WHIMPER' or 'MOAN' floated into earshot but otherwise the onomatopede was quiet. It wasn't used to being hit.

Firkin turned his attention to the body of Hogshead. He was more than slightly relieved to find, on closer examination, that there was only a small amount of blood and that was from a small scratch on the back of his hand. Firkin shook him and slapped his face but to no avail. Courgette and Dawn crossed nervously over the stream and gingerly peeped around the tree. The onomatopede glared at them from the bushes. Eventually, Courgette threw several hand-fuls of icy water across Hogshead's face.

'No! Let me go, I don't want to be eaten . . .' shouted Hogshead as he came round, sitting up with a start. He looked around bewildered. 'I must have been having a bad dream,' he explained limply.

'WHINE,' said the creature.

'There look! Behind you!' shouted Hogshead spotting it, pointing hysterically. 'That was eating me. I dreamt it was eating me. Get away . . .'

'Bad dream that was far from!' squeaked a piping voice in extreme irritation as Ch'tin struggled angrily out of Hogshead's pocket. 'More careful should be you. Squashed was almost I!' His antennae waved and flailed, replacing the wagging finger anyone else would have accompanied the tirade with. It was a sign of how annoyed Ch'tin was, Hogshead noticed the bookworm's word order had not only gone out of the window but was heading down the street at a rapid rate of knots.

'It's all right,' Courgette soothed Hogshead tenderly.

'Far from all right it is! Protection will need I soon,' ranted Ch'tin.

'I don't understand it,' said Firkin glaring at the onomatopede in the bushes. 'If we ignore it, it goes away.'

'It's almost as if it was just trying to scare us off. Like a guard dog or something,' said Courgette.

'But it attacked me!' protested Hogshead.

'Vouch for that in no uncertain terms can I,' agreed Ch'tin with righteous vehemence.

'Yeah, we all heard it,' said Firkin guiltily.

'So where are the blood and guts? You weren't really attacked, were you? It just sounded like it. It was trying to scare us off!' announced Courgette. 'It's harmless. I think.'

But why was it trying to scare us off? thought Firkin, scowling suspiciously. What's in Losa Llamas that's worth *that* much protection?

'It doesn't look harmless,' grumbled Hogshead. 'I hope you're right.' Ch'tin nodded.

'It stands to reason,' said Courgette. 'If it was as dangerous as it looks you'd be spread thinly all over the forest by now.'

Ch'tin swallowed hard. Hogshead suddenly shuddered, heaved and turned the colour of a week-dead squid. Courgette's clearmindedness was sometimes a definite downer.

Far away, in a room in Losa Llamas, a stocky man stared intently into a spherical crystal viewer. Trees rushed by as the focal point of the sphere raced through the forest. He was worried. Arathoostra had been missing for days now and there was still no sign of him.

A tiny fish-eyed insect shot out of the trees at the far side of the forest, banked sharply and headed back towards Losa Llamas. The image in the sphere swerved sharply over the edge of the tundra and plunged back into the trees. Practz wished he had been allowed to create another Sneeke.

He'd been back from Fort Knumm for two days, and he felt sure he should have found Arathoostra. As the Sneeke raced through the forest Practz's hope dipped another few points. Closing his eyes in deep concentration he carefully steered the insect to check on the four youngsters' progress.

Crawling on his hands and knees through darkness blacker than the soul of Cranachan's ex-Chief of Internal Affairs, Turgg Inyeff edged his way up the seemingly endless flight of misshapen stone stairs. He could sense a good story here. He could smell it. His chance at front page headlines again. Back in the limelight.

With pangs of hatred and sorrow he remembered his last major scoop. Well, his *only* major scoop. What a stir he had created fourteen years ago when he had blown the cover on the Lemming Skin Scandal. Exposed it for the occultist, black-magic, money-spinning, suicide-inducing fraud it really was. He was so close to a string of world exclusive offers from other parchments. So close to becoming a hut-hold name.

Too close, it would seem. Bowing to pressure from his editor he went ahead and named names, involved the involved, dished out the dirt and made it stick. The only problem was, it stuck to him. Suddenly Turgg Inyeff was pronounced 'traitor', 'slanderer', 'scum-of-the-earth'. He held his head high. He had arrived. He had become a journalist! But the world exclusive offers dried up. He was suddenly an unemployable journalist.

What he had done wrong he never worked out. His only

thoughts were that he had trodden too heavily on too many toes and they had kicked back. Whose toes they were, and why they had kicked back, he had still to find out. This time he would be a lot more careful.

The feet ahead of him stopped and a series of noises (translated perfectly by his whirling imagination into a few conspiratorial whispers and a wary exit from a small, little-used door into a large corridor) floated back towards him. He waited for silence and followed.

The corridor was in darkness, but the silver-blue moon-light provided a few patches of brightness amongst the purple velvet shadows. Straining, he heard the tap of a footstep away to his left. Removing his shoes and wincing at the cold floor, Turgg padded silently along behind his newsworthy quarry, his passport to the front page.

He crept down the tapestry-lined corridors, peering round a corner just as a door eased itself shut on the right. With notebook in hand and pencil tip freshly licked, he positioned himself outside the door and listened.

Words floated from under the door to be snatched and scrawled down in Turgg Inyeff's spidery handwriting. As he wrote, his eyebrows raised in response to the tale of horror escaping into the corridor. He couldn't believe his ears. His readers would love it.

This was it! This was *it*!

Feeling not a little confused and sorry for itself the onomato-pede rattled off into the undergrowth as silently as a ten-foot-long creature with a toughened exoskeleton and several hundred legs could. As Courgette ensured that Hogshead was feeling fine, an occasional 'WHIMPER' or 'SNIFF' could be heard through the waving foliage. Dawn, despite the fact that she had been scared out of her wits and utterly convinced that the last thing she would see was the inside of the onomatopede's digestive system, was surprised to find herself actually feeling sorry for the creature. Such was the power of woebegone onomatopoeia on a naive and impressionable mind.

140

Firkin, despite his apprehension regarding the mystery of Losa Llamas, felt very pleased with himself. Single-handedly he had fought off the raging terror of the monster and saved Hogshead from its slavering jaws. This, he thought proudly, is what *real* men should be doing. He felt sure that Klayth would be most impressed when he heard about this upon their return to Castell Rhyngill. He might even have one of the motley clad collection of minstrels immortalise Firkin's brave deed in song. Daydreaming, he could almost hear the nasal chant of three or four minstrels, standing in the gallery, fingers in ears, singing 'If you go down to the woods today . . .'

Given a clean bill of health by Courgette, Hogshead stood up stiffly and rubbed the back of his head. Ch'tin, having aired his frustration and anger at being tossed about so violently, and been fed a few chapters of a slushy romance, had disappeared into Hogshead's tunic pocket for a brief nap.

'So,' Hogshead said, groaning. 'Which way now?'

Courgette shrugged. 'Firkin's got the map.'

'You'd better go in disguise . . .' sang the minstrels to Firkin.

'Which way now?' repeated Hogshead prodding Firkin in the ribs.

'Today's the day that Firkin wields his b-i-i-i-g stick.' The minstrels stopped, the audience erupted in rapturous applause, calling for the hero, calling his name . . .

'Firkin! Oi! Firkin, you clot. Where's the map?' shouted Hogshead.

'Eh? What?' The banqueting hall faded to green and dissolved into a forest. 'Oh, it's you,' said Firkin dazedly.

'Who did you expect?'

'I'll tell you some other time. What do you want?'

'Which way now?' asked Courgette as Hogshead grumbled impatiently.

'Follow the path. Come on.'

They fell back into order and set off once again. Firkin,

feeling invincible, set a tough pace, hacking away at the tangles of branches with great gusto.

Ahead of them, two hypersensitive ears wriggled in anticipation as they sensed the foursome's approaching footsteps.

The path was still furiously overgrown, wriggling and changing directions seemingly by the yard, but surprisingly only once or twice did they stray off it and end up teetering vertiginously on the edge of a high ravine, staring nauseously at the thin ribbon of a small river far below.

After two hours of struggling and hacking through the endless undergrowth Firkin called for a rest. The creature whose ears had detected their presence earlier spat on its tiny paws and leapt across a large gap between two trees. It swung underneath the branch, somersaulting fluidly over to another bough, thrilling to itself as it tracked the youngsters to their rest stop, watching as they sat down on a few rocks in a small clearing and nibbled some biscuits. Rubbing its tiny paws and flexing its ears with excitement, it wrapped its long prehensile tail around the branch upon which it was perched, anchoring itself safely. Two ochre-black marsupial eyes stared unblinkingly at the rocks in the clearing as it concentrated on the task in hand. It had its orders, a long time had passed since the last occasion the creature had been given the chance to carry them out. Hanging by its tail, its forelimbs and ears moving in mystical patterns, its thought waves flashed across the small clearing, penetrating deep into each of the four rocks, stirring something hidden within. The small brown marsupial-like quadruped willed the rocks to do what their name suggests. Rock.

Unknown to the four youngsters they were in the presence of another of Losa Llamas' unrecorded, top-secret lines of defence. Above them dangled a gerund. One of the spin-off branches of research the Thaumaturgical Physicists came up with after studying verbal-noun interbreeding crosses was the ability to tap into the nounal root of an object and will it, albeit temporarily, to behave as a highly active verb. They managed to give this, like the onomatopede, a physical moiety to enable it to function autonomously.

So had been created the gerund. A creature that proved to be almost the ultimate impenetrable defence. In itself it was entirely harmless, it didn't even have sharp teeth, since it thrived on a diet entirely of soft fruit. But when faced with an armoured force of stunningly beweaponed soldiers or mercenaries, the gerund came into its own. The more weapons the attackers carried, the more danger they were in. If a gerund turned its marsupial gaze upon an axe it started axing. Hammers began hammering. Knives began knifing. Swords began swording. For the Thaumaturgical Physicists all things were fair in love and war and that included massaging the rules of grammar to suit their own purpose. Thus the gerund was able to use natural objects as potentially lethal weapons. For example, lichens growing innocently on the sides of trees could be turned into million-kilowatt bolts of lichening, blinding opponents and scorching flesh.

The gerund had only one defect. Unfortunately, for some inexplicable reason which no one could fathom or eradicate, the gerund had an insatiable desire for the one soft fruit that didn't grow in the forests around Losa Llamas. A gerund would do anything for a banana.

Dawn squeaked in sudden surprise as the rock she was sitting on moved three inches to the left. She leapt off, scowling as if it had suddenly turned red hot and stared accusingly at the lump of granite. She was sure it had moved. Hadn't it? She thumped Firkin. 'Stop it!' she grumbled and sat back down.

'Ow! What's that for?' asked Firkin.

'You know very well,' she said haughtily and took another bite of biscuit.

Above them the gerund swung gently as it chittered happily to itself.

Suddenly Dawn dropped her biscuit and clung tightly onto the rock as it skipped jauntily six inches to the left, then four inches forward and then pirouetted gracefully on the spot, drilling its way several inches into the forest floor. Before Firkin had a chance to do anything about it his rock joined in, hopping about uncontrollably followed swiftly by Hogshead's and Courgette's. In seconds it sounded as if a stone troll's advanced sumo class was in full swing, as several hundredweight of metamorphic rocks cavorted, sprang and gambolled with joyous seismic abandon.

The dangling gerund chuckled with acute marsupial mirth, its tiny chest heaving with laughter as its long fluffy ears squirmed and cast more crackling thought waves at the victims below.

Dawn squealed desperately as something cold and clammy touched her clinging white knuckles. A cold green carpet slithered animatedly over the contours of her hand, spreading from a patch on the rock, its nounal root stirred by the powerful fields of gerundive magic flashing around the clearing. The gerund squealed with delight as large green patches of mycelia snaked up Dawn's arm and grabbed at her ankles. Hogshead's rock frisked and bounded like a newborn lamb, full of the joys of springing.

The mould was up to Dawn's shoulder and covered her legs like a blanket, sticking her to the rock as if with sentient biological gaffa tape. Claustrophobic fear gripped her as she screamed desperately.

The gerund kicked its hind legs merrily against the underneath of the branch, setting itself swinging as it chattered to itself, fertilising the fields of magic.

Courgette's rock suddenly skipped unexpectedly high, bucked violently, dislodging her grip and sending her flying, arms and legs flailing. The gerund turned its deadly gaze towards her. Time for the coup-de-grâce, it thought, or should that be coup-de-lichen?

In the next second a spear of blue flame lanced out of the sky, torching a small shrubbery. Horrified, her heart pounding louder than the seismic cacophony of the gleefully bounding rocks, Courgette looked at the smouldering patch of ground where the lichening bolt had struck. The gerund

144

squeaked, the lichen responded and another bolt of electro-static epiphytes leapt earthwards, lancing cold-blue fire inches away from Courgette. She dashed for cover, dodging the leaping rocks, huddling under the tree as yet another flash of static-charged symbionts seared the ground. What could she do? Where was this coming from? A fourth bolt of lichening lanced earthwards, heading straight for the top of her head. The million-kilowatt mycelial discharge struck, laying a smouldering shag-pile carpet of carbonised waste over everything it hit. A blinding flash. A muted explosion. A scream.

Despite the chaotic capering of Hogshead's granite mount, he looked up long enough to see Courgette enveloped in an explosion, a flash and a cloud of blue-white smoke. 'No, no, no!' he yelled, half-leaping, half-falling off the rock. He landed in a rolling tuck, dodged the cavorting cromlechs and ran towards the tree and the growing pall of smoke. Dreading the worst he plunged into the acrid cloud. A huge bough from the tree lay smouldering on the ground, crackling. He searched for Courgette, his throat clenching tight as he spotted the pile of blackened ash, staring silently at what he took to be Courgette's makeshift funeral pyre.

An eerie calm settled heavily on the clearing.

'Everything suddenly stopped,' said Firkin in the un-natural silence, standing behind him swathed in the dying wisps of smoke.

Hogshead stared at the pile of smouldering ash and said, 'Courgette.' His bottom lip trembled.

There was a sudden flurry of activity in Hogshead's pocket as Ch'tin wriggled upwards ready to tear him off another strip for disturbing his period of sleep. His antennae wriggled in fury, looking to Firkin as if they were somehow rolling their sleeves up ready for action. Firkin reached out and snatched the bookworm.

'Hogshmmffmfm!' squeaked Ch'tin as Firkin clamped his hand across the worm's mouth.

Hogshead's mind was running in overdrive, vehemently

denying what his eyes were repeatedly telling him they had just seen. He could hear Courgette whispering to him. Snatches of conversation floating into the earshot of his mind.

'. . . don't be frightened . . . everything's all right now. Don't worry . . . it's all so peaceful here . . .'

A tear rolled down Hogshead's cheek turning grey from the dirt on his face. Courgette's gentle voice floated back.

'. . . there, there. I'm your friend . . . Those nasty rocks have stopped . . . you've got lovely fur . . .'

His mind was playing tricks on him, shock making nonsense of her words, madness waited at the edge of his mind, drumming its long fingers patiently on the doorpost. It was getting too much for him.

'Courgette!' he blubbed.

'Yes?' came the distant reply.

'Why did it have to happen to you?' he asked, suddenly convinced that the meeting with Old Ma Tini had perhaps taught him something about communicating with those who had . . .

'Eh? Who did you expect?' she said walking around the tree carrying a small furry marsupial, which was grinning wildly as it devoured a banana.

'But . . .' said Hogshead speechless.

'Thank goodness you're all right,' said Firkin with a huge sigh of relief. A muffled yelping could just be heard. 'Shutup, Ch'tin!' growled Firkin.

'I nearly wasn't,' she said. 'If this little thing hadn't jumped off the branch and made me look up I probably would have been under it. Isn't it cute!' She stroked the gerund gently, completely unaware of its awesome power.

'But I thought . . .' said Hogshead, looking from Courgette to the ashes.

'Oh,' she said simply, blushed slightly and suddenly found something interesting to look at on the ground.

Hogshead wiped his face. 'Smoke really irritates my eyes,' he said unconvincingly. 'Always makes my eyes water. Allergic reaction or something.'

The muffled cries could be heard again.

'Look, be quiet,' whispered Firkin removing his hand from Ch'tin's mouth.

'Me not making noise. Where sister is, noise is!' piped Ch'tin smugly.

'Dawn!' cried Firkin, suddenly remembering his little sister.

As if in reply the muffled gruntings came again. Firkin turned round and saw a rock covered in mould squirming vigorously. He ran over to it and began clawing at the now immobile green strands. In a moment Dawn's head appeared crowning a pear-shaped mass of green mould. She was livid.

'Bleaurgh! That stuff tastes horrid. Get me out!' she shouted wriggling furiously.

'Are you all right?' asked Firkin.

'Yes. Just get me *out*.' She spat out a few strands of mycelium and squirmed impatiently.

Courgette kissed Hogshead gently on the cheek, then ran to help free Dawn. The gerund strolled casually away into the undergrowth, licking its lips to remove the last traces of banana.

Unknown to any of them they were being watched. A tiny insectlike creature fitted with a fish-eye lens hovered momentarily and then landed gently on a leaf. With a deft movement it arranged the specially adapted antennae and pointed them towards Losa Llamas. After sending a brief series of high-pitched pips and squeaks as a test tone the Sneeke settled down to watch.

The stocky figure in dark robes rubbed his hands together happily as the image came through from the Sneeke. With a huge sense of satisfaction he watched the fish-eye image of the youngsters as they freed Dawn from the pile of mould. Practz smiled to himself. It was all going perfectly.

Well, it would be if he knew for certain where Arathoostra had disappeared to.

*

For Snydewinder, the loudest sound in the midnight stillness of the corridor outside the private quarters of the Right Horrible Khah Nij was the tense throbbing of his nervously pulsing heart. His seething mind knew he was about to take the biggest risk of his life and was flooding his tall thin body with the chemical messengers to communicate this fact. Adrenalin surged through even the tiniest of arteries readying him for the time to come. Externally, only the slightest betrayal of the inner turmoil showed. A regularly pulsing vein pounded at his temple beneath a skin shining with perspiration.

With the odds stacked well and truly against him, but holding the most powerful of ace cards, he eased open the door and entered the darkened room. Pools of argent moonlight illuminated carefully arranged battle scenarios and sparkled on the extensive collection of axes, swords and daggers hanging menacingly on the walls. Reminding Arathoostra of the need for absolute silence with a graphic hand gesture indicating what would happen to him if they were discovered, Snydewinder crept into the Head of Security and War's sleeping quarters. A large wooden bed squatted on a plinth below a painting of a young, nubile, and remarkably scantily clad woman chained to a rock. Somehow she managed to look scared, imperilled and astoundingly lusty at the same time. Despite his fear Snydewinder made a mental note to look up the artist and discover where the model was now.

A muffled groan brought him back to his senses as the larger of the two figures in the bed rolled over, pulling the covers with it. Another groan followed as a slender hand reached across and tugged irritably at the covers, snatching them back. Before either figure could wake up Snydewinder lunged forward, clasping his hand across the bearded mouth of his victim and holding a wicked looking stiletto to his throat. Arathoostra followed suit on the other side of the bed, rather more warily.

'Don't move!' barked Snydewinder in a harsh whisper. 'Make a sound and you lose your tonsils! Is that clear?'

'. . . clear?'

The supine figure of Khah Nij nodded to his unknown assailants.

'Listen carefully to what I have to say,' continued Snydewinder, 'and we'll both come out of this a lot better off.'

'. . . better off.'

Snydewinder looked quizzically across at the shadowy figure of Arathoostra as he sneered at the terrified girl.

'I've come to offer you the best deal of your life,' whispered Snydewinder, keeping his face hidden.

'. . . your life,' repeated Arathoostra.

'Hang on, hang on,' said Snydewinder addressing Arathoostra with mounting anger. 'When I told you to do as I do I didn't mean everything. Leave the talking to me!'

The Thaumaturgical Physicist grinned sheepishly in the dark.

Snydewinder waved his knife meaningfully as he returned his attention to Khah Nij. 'Are you ready to listen?'

He felt the Head of Security and War nod, almost casually.

'I can offer you *the* most effective fighting machine ever to be developed. All-terrain capability, moats a piece of cake. Fully enclosed arrow-proof armour. Autonomous insurgence capability. Utterly ruthless, cold-blooded, merciless *and* they don't need wages!' whispered Snydewinder. 'Interested?'

Khah Nij shook his head.

'What?' barked Snydewinder releasing his hand from Khah Nij's mouth.

'We've *got* war-elephants,' he answered nonchalantly.

'What I'm offering you can *eat* war-elephants for breakfast!'

'We've tried artillery-rhinos as well. I'm not interested.'

'Artillery-rhinos! You lie there and compare *that* cannon fodder to what I'm offering you!' snarled Snydewinder.

Khah Nij thought carefully as something stirred in his memory. Arathoostra poked and prodded the Head of War's

concubine in a threateningly exploratory manner. It had
been a long time since he'd been in female company.
Especially one so, well, undressed! His mind and the tip of
his knife blade wandered.

'Armadillo personnel carriers?' asked Khah Nij.

'Oh dear, oh dear,' mocked Snydewinder. 'You're living
in the past! This is the eleventh century. We can do *far* better
than those sluggish creatures! What I can offer you is like
nothing currently employed in battle. Take these off my
hands and you'll be the envy of all enemies!'

'What are you offering?' asked Khah Nij wearily.

'The *Ultimate* Deterrent!' whispered Snydewinder.

'Oh yes. And what, precisely *is* that?'

'*Rana militaria*. The Frogs of War!'

'Oh come on. They're a myth. A militarist's pipe dream.'

'Wrong! They are alive and well and living in . . . Ahh, but
that would be telling.' He just managed to stop himself. 'Tell
him, Arathoostra!'

'Arathoostra?' echoed Khah Nij, stiffening beneath
Snydewinder's grip, his eyes widening in surprise, his mind
rubbing its hands in anticipation.

'Eh?' replied the scientist, trying to pull his gaze away
from a firm and perfectly formed expanse of exquisitely
feminine thigh and the forest of delights beyond.

'Tell him about your babies,' prompted Snydewinder's
harsh whisper.

'My babies!' echoed Arathoostra. 'My beautiful babies.
They keep them locked up. Out of sight. They need to be
free.' His gaze focused into the distance as he thought about
them.

'Is this true?' asked Khah Nij eagerly, his interest
thoroughly whetted.

'Believe it,' confirmed Snydewinder. 'Just say the word
and you can have them. The most powerful weapons ever.
You can have them all. In return for a few, ahem, favours,'
whispered Snydewinder, his face still hidden in the darkness.

'What favours?'

150

'I will take you to the Frogs *if* you see to it that all the charges against me are dropped and I am reinstated to my old job, *with* an index-linked salary increase back-dated for the past fourteen years, full pension rights and thirty days' holiday per year.'

'What job?'

Snydewinder moved forward into a shaft of moonlight.

'You!' gasped Khah Nij, the familiarity of the voice suddenly explained. 'Your old job?' he mused. '. . . and if I refuse?'

'Has senility taken you so quickly or have you forgotten my blade at your throat. Refuse and you will die here and now and I will sell my secret elsewhere.'

'I seem to have little choice,' muttered Khah Nij.

'Correct,' gloated Snydewinder.

'I will have to discuss your proposal with the King,' said Khah Nij turning over the prospect in his agile mind.

'Do so. But ensure the correct decision is made. Otherwise, our next meeting will see you, your precious King and the whole of Cranachan trampled beneath the rampaging ranine claws of *my* amphibian army! I will be in touch . . .' and with that the vice grip, the knife, Arathoostra and Snydewinder vanished silently into the night.

As Khah Nij absently comforted his stressed-out concubine and replayed the conversation in his mind a shambling figure scribbled a few more notes in his notebook, picked up his shoes, unfolded himself from behind the door and crept out into the corridor.

With immense difficulty Turgg Inyeff contained his excitement. He had to print what he had just heard. The public had a right to know!

Hold the front page! his mind screamed as he sprinted down the corridor on his tip-toed stocking feet, coat-tails waving, heading for the tapestry and the way out.

Through the dense undergrowth in the forest around Losa Llamas something cold and green slithered. It had done so for countless centuries, changing course slightly once in a while, but always ending up in the same gut-wrenching one-hundred-and-fifty-foot drop over the end of a cliff. This was the River Gharial. It was ancient. Its opacity denied any insight into its hidden depths, its smooth silent surface merely hinting at its unfathomableness, warning any innocent bystander that it was not a river to be crossed. This was a river that would not tolerate the invasive inconvenience of fords, stepping stones or weirs. In its aquatically reticent way it somehow made blindingly obvious the fact that to get to the other side you had to go round. Or risk the consequences.

It was up to the edge of this river, and a tree spanning it, that the group of four youngsters walked.

The tree lay a scant few inches above the slow, oily veneer of the river, and a few of the smaller branches dipped into the water causing chevron ripples in the still, green surface. At this side of the river a huge mass of gnarled and tangled roots was exposed to the elements pointing skyward like a headstone for the dead tree. It was fairly obvious that few other people had travelled this way in the past: although the branches had been broken off to allow an easy crossing, the bark still looked surprisingly untrodden. Firkin was excited. This appeared to offer a perfect way over the river. His only concern was that it might not be strong enough to support their weight. Courgette didn't relish the prospect of walking across such a makeshift bridge.

'It's all right,' said Firkin. 'Trees like this last for years.'

'And how long do you think it's been there?' asked Courgette.

'Well . . . years. But it looks safe. I'll show you,' answered Firkin leaping onto the huge horizontal trunk. It flexed slightly but held firm. He stamped on the wood and listened to the sound it made (he had once seen his father do this to check out roof beams back in Middin). A good, firm, woody sound resonated through the tree as Firkin jumped up and down on it.

About a quarter of a mile downstream the vibrations from the dull thuds of Firkin's explorations caressed a slumbering body. The compressions and rarefactions triggered nerves set in a lateral line close to the surface of the dark scaly skin.

'See. It's fine,' shouted Firkin jumping back onto the bank.

Courgette still looked warily at the trunk. 'Isn't there any other way?' she asked.

Firkin pulled out the map and showed her. No bridges were marked, and at Firkin's estimate they were at the ideal place to cross the river since Losa Llamas lay only a few miles away through the forest on the other side. Courgette shrugged.

'Look, it'll be easy to cross,' said Hogshead, trying to convince himself as well. 'If you just forget about the fact that it's a tree and pretend it's a path or something, you'll be fine.' He finished on what he hoped was an encouraging smile.

'I want to go over the tree,' said Dawn, with a little of her youthful enthusiasm creeping back. She had hardly said a word since her experience with the mould.

'That's it, then. It's settled,' said Firkin. 'I'll go first and check for any weak bits.'

He leapt up onto the trunk and started to walk slowly forward. With most of his weight on his left foot he stamped ahead with his right, checking the quality of the wood.

Surrounded by a dark-green frame of ancient scales and hidden beneath a hemisphere of bone, an eye twitched in the last moments of slumber. It swivelled restlessly in its socket as the regular sound waves travelled from the heel of Firkin's foot, along the length of the tree, down the branches dipping into the water and on downstream to stimulate the lateral line of nerve endings arranged sensitively for this very purpose. Silently, like a moss-encrusted clam, the eye opened. A midnight-green pupil stared out of a mud-brown iris and, with its partner on the other side of the giant head, surveyed the dense green soup of the River Gharial.

Firkin flicked a section of loose bark off the trunk and into the river. A few small mites dashed for cover, even they had more than enough sense to make sure they didn't end up in the river. He was a quarter of the way across and so far the tree had sagged only marginally closer to the slick surface beneath. Still tapping, he moved forward.

Slow thoughts trundled through the saurian brain of the creature on the riverbed as it flexed its massive paddle-like front limbs, stirring up clouds of silt. Above it a small patch of bark floated by. With the terrible arrogant slowness of all cold-blooded killers the creature raised its giant head and flexed its solid neck muscles. Silt streamed off it in dark brown clouds, revealing the highly protective array of olive-green scales covering the entirety of the leviathan body.

The tree trunk creaked and flexed as Firkin approached the middle of its span. The underside was now just touching the surface of the river, allowing an oily wave to build up against it. Firkin tapped and moved slowly and warily as the sound of cracking lignin fibres became more frequent. The reassuring solidity of the trunk was being replaced by an altogether more unnerving springiness.

A cloud of silt erupted as the river nydd launched itself from its resting place. With shocking speed its four paddled limbs propelled it upstream towards the trunk of the fallen tree. The sensors on the beast's sides and those in pits set just below its eyes homed in on the vibrations as it surged easily through the greasy water. It created no ripples as it heaved upstream towards its intended prey, although if an expert were consulted his eye could possibly have picked up a bulge in the surface as the river nydd displaced tons of water in its attack run. Experts on river nydds, however, were few and far between, often ending a lifetime of promising studies as their subject's light afternoon snack.

Just feet below the surface, but still invisible, the monster raced silently forward.

Firkin turned round as he reached the middle of the river. He called back to the watching group, reassuring them more than he reassured himself. The opaque water unnerved him more than he would care to admit. 'See – it's easy. I'm heavier than you, Courgette, and it's fine. You'll be all right. It's perfectly safe . . .'

Firkin's face creased into a wry grin as he watched Courgette and Hogshead's reaction. They stood, white-faced, pointing at a spot in the river directly behind him. He knew very well that Hogshead hadn't forgiven him for the incident with the onomatopede. And here it was, as he expected; they were trying to get their own back. He had to admit, though, they were doing well, the look of abject terror resident in their eyes, the trembling knees, the pointing arms, the way they'd both managed to let the colour drain from their faces; it was all very convincing. Just a little too obvious, though. The next thing they'd be shouting, 'Behind you.' It was just *too* pantomimic, *too* humdrum am-dram.

'Behind you!' shouted Hogshead.

'It's horrible!' squealed Dawn. Clever, he thought, they've even got her involved. When did they dream *this* up?

'Ho, ho. Very funny!' shouted Firkin.

'Oh! No it isn't!' shouted Courgette.

Wheel out the cliches, thought Firkin. 'Oh, yes it is!' he answered laughing.

'Turn round!' yelled Hogshead.

'Run away!' added Courgette.

Suddenly, a single drop of cold river water fell onto the nape of his neck and dribbled icily down his back.

Wow! thought Firkin, how did they do *that*! They've done well. Just for a second then I *really* felt like there was something huge and wet standing behind me, in the river.

A cold blast of foetid air stroked his hair and almost made him gag.

They couldn't have done *that*, could they?

The threesome on the bank were still pointing in terror.

Suddenly feeling *very* uncomfortable, Firkin turned around. He stared at a wall of olive-green scales rising twelve

155

feet vertically from the water; the enormous neck of the river nydd nonchalantly treading water with effortless ease. He looked up into two midnight-green pupils and a massive saurian maw crammed full with four rows of dental death, yellowing beneath a thick crust of plaque, exercised by the most powerful pair of jaw muscles for miles. There was little these teeth couldn't shatter and destroy in seconds. That included the life expectancy of even the most ardent of blind optimists.

Firkin felt sure its scaly lips twitched in a slight saurian smirk. The river nydd's casually arrogant demeanour almost led him to expect it to fold its front flippers onto the tree, smile sweetly at him and engage him in conversation regarding the state of the economy or the appallingly bad press large reptiles get these days; how it prevented any young damsels approaching within a mile in case they were knocked flat by the ubiquitously halitotic breath possessed by all thirty-foot water dragons; how it sent young bucks of knights out on brave deeds to rid the world of lecherous leviathans who can hypnotise women of the court for unspeakable acts of . . . well, it's unspeakable.

Firkin wasn't so lucky.

His knees trembled helplessly as, without warning, the flippers surged against the current and the neck snapped downwards. He began to run sideways but the five-foot-long head turned in a scything sweep, the cold clammy breath of countless deaths suffocating him as the jaws closed in a bone-crushing movement. He tried to scream but his ribs collapsed in a second, sending blood fountaining through his throat as his lungs were shredded. His arms thrashed in grotesque uselessness as nerves were cut and muscles torn from bones. In a moment his heart was pulped. Life left him.

The momentum of the river nydd carried it on in an arc over the trunk, landing upstream in a collision with the water that shattered the surface into a million droplets. The massive tail came down and struck the trunk in the middle, snapping it like matchwood and sending the two halves to a watery end. A tidal wave surged across the river as the nydd plunged below the surface and disappeared.

In a few seconds the oily surface of the River Gharial closed over and silence flooded back into the scene. The two halves of the tree drifted downstream, soon lost to sight. Hogshead, Courgette and Dawn stood in devastated silence, unable to believe what they had just seen.

As if in answer, a fragment of leather drifted silently to the surface and floated by. The recognition of the ripped remains of one of Firkin's boots was testament to the truth.

He was gone.

A Degree of Thaumatronics

The light from the crystal sphere shone on the bushy eyebrows of the stocky man as he scrutinised the apparent states of Hogshead, Courgette and Dawn. Everything had gone perfectly. By the time he arrived, if his calculations were correct, they should be ready for anything. In a moment he had checked his perihelion tables and apogee correction constants, rechecked that the Gren Idjmeen Factors had been added and made one final adjustment to the chronoperatic field flux parameter indices.

He was ready.

Time to go.

'Keep yer 'orrible 'eads down!' yelled Captain Barak of the Cranachan Imperial Stealth Troopers as he stood, hands clasped behind his back, and watched his men training. They squirmed through shallow pools of muddy water, struggled under acres of netting, scrambled up siege towers and over battlements to finally storm their own castle at the end of a major exercise. His short squat body swelled with pride as he looked at his men. His men! Twelve short months ago he wouldn't even have believed it possible that he would be allowed to remain in the Imperial Palace of Cranachan, let alone be in charge of a crack team of undercover police. He thought back to how nearly his retirement had become permanent and found that he was shaking as he recalled the moment when he had upended the saddlebags (which should have contained all the end products arising from all illegally imported livestock brackets rodent close brackets) in front of the mustered forces of King Grimzyn, his commander the Right Horrible Khah Nij, the Scribe for Trade and Industry, the Lord Chancellor and the Chief of Internal Affairs. The

158

repercussions of that incident had rumbled on long after the ashes in the saddlebags had settled down, resulting ultimately in war with the Kingdom of Rhyngill, the capture of three thousand strong and extremely hungry Prisoners of War and the banishment of Fisk, the Chief of Internal Affairs, to Rhyngill. Barak's retirement from his position as the then Vice Captain of the Imperial Palace Guards (F Division) had been demanded, and he had been enjoying tending his petunias when a letter had arrived summoning him to an immediate audience with the Right Horrible Khah Nij, Head of Security and War, in his private quarters in the Imperial Palace Fortress.

His eyes clouded over as he thought back to that meeting, whilst in front of him his men continued to swarm unseen up the training siege towers.

It had been almost exactly a year ago that he had shown his letter to the guards on the gate and been led up to Khah Nij's private quarters. He could still recall it clearly; shaking nervously as the guard had knocked on the heavily fortified door; almost collapsing as an angry bark had issued from deep within commanding him to enter and state his business. Timidly, Barak had eased himself through the massive door to stand quaking inside the room.

'Y . . . You wanted to see me, sir,' whispered Barak through a throat thick with nervousness.

Khah Nij looked up from a table of soldiers arrayed in full battle positions. 'Ahh, Barak!' he yelled. 'Come in!' He moved two battalions forward in a pincer movement and leaned back in his chair. Barak edged nervously forward under the watchful gaze of the Head of Security and War and the painted heads of history's greatest generals lining the walls. 'Drink?' snapped Khah Nij in the growing silence – it sounded more like an order.

'Er . . . y . . . yes, sir,' stammered Barak nervously.

'Good,' murmured Khah Nij as he opened a large wooden cabinet and withdrew an ancient-looking bottle. He poured two large measures into two very rounded glasses, handed

159

one to Barak and sniffed appreciatively. 'General Khoh Gnyak's favourite spirit,' he said swirling the rich brown liquid gently in the glass. 'Made to his own recipe and matured in oak casks. There hasn't been any more made since the end of the Khoh Gnyak Wars. Damn shame, don't you think?'

Barak nodded his nervous agreement as Khah Nij strutted back to his chair and sat down. He moved two more battalions forward, took another large slurp and looked at Barak. 'Enjoying tending your petunias are you?' he suddenly asked.

'Well . . . er . . . yes, sir. It's most rewarding.'

'Not as good as men, though, eh?'

'I . . . er . . .' Barak was utterly lost. This was most definitely not the Khah Nij he was used to.

'Not as rewarding as drilling a team of crack men, eh? The thrill of command?'

'Now that you come to mention it, sir I . . .'

'Good!' interrupted Khah Nij. 'That's settled then!' he barked and gulped a vast measure of Khoh Gnyak. Barak ran through the conversation again in his mind, shook his head and took another swig. The Head of Security and War annihilated three hundred troops with a flick of his wrist.

'Sir, I . . . er,' mumbled Barak.

'Still here?' said Khah Nij looking up. 'What is it?'

'What's settled, sir?'

'Eh? No one told you?'

Barak shook his head.

'Got a new job for you! Excellent prospects. Ideal for a man like you, eh?'

Barak gasped. 'But I'm retired. Have you forgotten the Lemming Skin Fiasco?'

'Ooh, no. Best laugh I've had in ages.'

Barak scratched his head. '. . . ?' he added.

'. . . and a job well done,' continued Khah Nij. 'Militarily perfect. Orders carried out to the letter. No escalation of a potentially sticky situation. In and out in one movement.

160

Lovely. Wasn't your fault the orders were useless. Fisk always was a prat!'

And so with Fisk banished to Rhyngill under pain of major surgery if he returned, Barak was made Captain of the Cranachan Imperial Stealth Troopers. An elite band of men, highly trained, highly fit, to what purpose Barak remained utterly clueless.

A stocky figure wearing a long, dark cloak stood observing the sobbing children with a look of satisfaction, and not a little cringing discomfort. It *was* a terrible sound. He could see Hogshead trying to comfort Courgette and Dawn. The two girls hugged him tightly, burying their faces in his neck. Under virtually any other circumstance he would have found the experience immensely delightful. Now it was hell.

The watcher stepped forward and revealed himself. Normally Hogshead would have challenged the man, or at the very least been marginally curious as to who he was, why he was here, where everyone else was, et cetera. Now it just didn't seem to matter. Hogshead raised his head, stared momentarily at the stranger, sighed a miserably lachrymose sigh and returned his gaze to a small clump of harmless moss on a twig.

'Greetings,' said the figure, sounding too cheerful. 'My name is Practz. May I be of assistance?'

Courgette sniffed, wetly.

'May I help?' he enquired again. 'You seem a little distressed. I heard a lot of splashing and . . .'

Dawn glared at him momentarily then wiped her nose noisily on her sleeve.

'May I do anything for you?'

'Yes,' answered Hogshead staring through red-rimmed eyes, 'Go away.'

Practz adopted what he hoped was a hurt expression. The type of face a small puppy would make when, after fetching a newsparchment all the way to its master and delivering it to his waiting hand, its reward is an item of large and extremely hard footwear ricocheting off the back of its head following its master's horrified discovery that the newsparchment in question is entirely unreadable owing to its having been immersed, for several minutes, in several gallons of warm, slimy, doggy dribble.

'I only offered to help,' said Practz, briefly considering whimpering for effect, but rejecting the idea on the grounds that it was terribly undignified.

'Well, we don't want any. Go away,' repeated Hogshead.

Practz shuffled uncomfortably for a moment and tried a different tack, 'Whither are you headed?'

'None of your business!' snapped Hogshead as Dawn wiped a nostril.

'May I hazard that as you are near the river, a crossing is required,' the statement held a questioning tone.

'Hazard away!' grumbled Hogshead as Dawn wiped her other nostril, equally volubly.

'May I help you to the other side?' asked Practz, barely hiding his expression of utter distaste. 'Do you want to cross?'

'We couldn't, even if we wanted to,' said Hogshead finally, wishing Dawn had used a handkerchief instead of his shoulder.

'In that case I shall continue on my way to Losa Llamas,' said Practz waving the carrot of information that he knew would make them sit up and . . .

The youngsters looked up. They had seen no one in what felt like a lifetime and now here was someone heading the same way as themselves.

'But how?' asked Hogshead. 'The bridge is gone. Do you know another way?' He suddenly realised that their map was probably several miles downstream by now.

'There are many ways to bake an Ammorettan Death Lizard,' answered Practz, enigmatically tapping the side of his nose.

'But, we want to cross the river,' said Hogshead, missing the point entirely.

'I'm not hungry,' whimpered Dawn.

Uninvited, the black-robed figure squatted cross-legged on the ground in front of them, fiddled about inside several capacious pockets lurking within his cloak and took out a small black book, an abacus, several charts and a tiny transparent rectangular box that hummed and fizzed like a handful of grilling beetles. Watched by three utterly baffled faces, he checked the angle of the sun above the horizon and marked this off on one of the charts.

'What're you doing? What's that got to do with bridges?' asked Hogshead as Practz flicked a few beads on the abacus, wrote more figures down and adjusted a host of runic dials and talismanic parameters on the crackling box.

'Watch and learn,' the stranger replied, flicking the abacus once more. After a couple of minutes of complex-looking calculations, measurements and recalculations, paying particular attention to the current SMPTE* reading, he stopped, folded the charts up, repocketed the book, held the

---

* Over the millennia that Gods and all manner of Deities have been rattling throughout the cosmos, championing mortals in their crusading conquests, altering history a smidgeon if some fortuitous love-match didn't come to fruition, or just generally messing things up for those of us with a less than zero chance of achieving immortality, they have always had a problem with time.

Temporal anomalies can really be a pain in a minor God's bottom if something happens to go wrong. One tiny little timing error can cause all manner of paracosmic poo to hit the great celestial fan. And the bigger the fan, the further it flies.

It was following the incident with G'dnshh, the cannibalistic Herring God, when, after an argument, at the dawn of time, with its piscine rival, Ploik, the hyperfertile Plankton God, concerning who could stock the Pathetic Ocean fastest, G'dnshh cheated. Using a close-proximity time loop to enable its offspring to reach sexual maturity before looping back, fully grown, to three minutes after they were first born, G'dnshh hoped to win the bet. Unfortunately, being that early in creation, time hadn't settled down and the resulting few temporal hiccups threw the calculations adrift. G'dnshh's offspring arrived three minutes before they were actually born and, being cannibalistic, almost nibbled themselves into oblivion in a matter of seconds.

From then on, all time, as perceived by the Gods, was subject to SMPTE. The System of Metaphysical and Paracosmic Temporal Encoding was a series of sequential runic digits recorded along the edge of the tape machine of time, allowing simple and accurate location anywhere within a given timespan, and allowing hyperaccurate editing. If it was required.

transparent box carefully in his hand and pulled his cowl over his head.

'What're you *doing*?' repeated Hogshead. 'Stop it.' Practz sat motionless and appeared to have gone to sleep. A slow mantra-like moaning floated out from under the cowl as Practz began expertly warping the currents of time with the chronoperatic expertise of a Ninth Aeon Deja-Moi Master using a small, crackling pocket Thaumatron.

Hogshead shook his head as the air seemed to wobble for a moment.

Practz's incantations slowed down, as if some paracosmic finger was rubbing on the rim of the tape-reel of time, the drop in pitch making it sound like the tuneless grumblings of some beastly bass, with acute laryngitis. In a state of utter bewilderment the youngsters gaped as, unexpectedly, everything seemed to stop for a moment, then the pitch raised again, slowly at first, then faster and faster until it became the garbled squeaking of a panicking mouse on speed. With a lungful of helium.

They saw Practz stand up and run backwards out of the clearing as if pulled on invisible strings. The pace of the images increased. Snatches of conversation that Courgette recalled shot backwards out of her mind. Flashing images of dimly remembered events flew out of Hogshead's past into a hazy and uncertain future. The sands of Dawn's time ran uphill as the temporal tape machine rewound.

The pace of the reversing images slowed gradually, shuffled backwards and forwards a couple of times, locating the SMPTE code on the edge of the tape, then started inexorably forward.

Practz was nowhere in sight.

Stretching across the River Gharial was a large tree which gave the impression of having been there for years. A dense feeling of acute *déjà vu* raced across the minds of Hogshead, Courgette and Dawn.

'It's all right,' said Firkin. 'Trees like this last for years.'

'And how long do you think it's been there?' asked

Courgette, shocked and horrified to see Firkin again, the words ringing with mocking familiarity in her mind.

'Well . . . years. But it looks safe. I'll show you.' And once again Firkin leapt easily onto the makeshift bridge that spanned the oil-slick surface of the River Gharial.

Courgette wanted to scream out and yell and warn him. The all too recent image of the horrific events to come still fresh in her . . . was it a memory? Premonition? Foretelling? Internally she was waving her arms in frantic desperation, calling his name, begging him to turn round, to come back. But all she could do was watch helplessly as Firkin tapped the tree experimentally with his foot. She stood cocooned in an awful frustration; trapped in the strait-jacket of the past; the thick golden syrup of inevitability. Watching as Firkin's tapping foot summoned his destroyer as surely as if he had booked a court room, assembled the jury and sent a subpoena.

'See. It's fine,' shouted Firkin jumping back onto the bank.

'Isn't there any other way?' Courgette heard herself ask and stared pleadingly at the map, feeling her shoulders shrug in resignation.

'Look, it'll be easy to cross,' said Hogshead almost sweating with the effort of trying to change the words, trying to warn Firkin. 'If you just forget about the fact that it's a tree and pretend it's a path or something, you'll be fine.' He finished with a pathetic grimace.

'I want to go over the tree,' said Dawn meaning the exact opposite. Hating herself for allowing herself to say the same ridiculous thing. The floodlights of twenty-twenty hindsight flashed suddenly on, glaring down on her, an imagined audience of specially selected guests roared with hysterical laughter as she and they looked back at how she had behaved, witnessing it all as if through some candid chimera.

'That's it, then. It's settled,' said Firkin. 'I'll go first and check for any weak bits.'

No! yelled Courgette silently, her face betraying none of the boiling anguish within.

165

A quarter of a mile downstream the river nydd had already begun its dash upsteam. Firkin walked and tapped his way gingerly across the river. Hogshead, Courgette and Dawn, in the roles already established by themselves in the past, watched helplessly as Firkin set himself up perfectly for an early, and final, bath. Just feet below the surface, but still invisible through the murky water, the river nydd raced silently foward.

Firkin turned around as he reached the middle of the river. He called back to the watching group. 'See – it's easy. I'm heavier than you, Courgette, and it's fine. You'll be all right. It's perfectly safe . . .'

'Go on!' whispered a ghostly figure in a black cloak, half-seen standing next to her. Suddenly freed from the fly-paper restrictions of the past tense, released from the syrup of history, she ran.

Firkin's face creased in a wry grin as he watched Hogshead's reaction. He was standing, white-faced, pointing at a spot in the river directly behind him.

'Behind you!' shouted Hogshead.

'Behind *you*!' answered Firkin, pointing. 'Look out!' Courgette was sprinting towards Hogshead, screaming at the top of her voice, whirling a huge stick around her head, red tresses flying loose in a torrent of waving hair that seemed to match her mood perfectly. She flashed by him, leaping onto the tree, squealing like an Amazon with a vendetta.

A cold blast of foetid air stroked Firkin's hair. He turned, suddenly feeling *very* uncomfortable. His mind registered terror, followed by teeth, then lots of teeth, then 'Aaaaaargh!'

'Move! MOVE!' yelled Courgette, flailing the branch wildly around her head, making 'whooshing' noises as it hacked through the air. Firkin stared helplessly, unsure who looked the most dangerous – Courgette or the massive alien creature nonchalantly treading water as it sized him up for lunch.

He broke and ran sideways as the river nydd's neck snapped downwards and the five-foot-long head turned in a scything sweep.

'Get away from him, you bitch!' yelled Courgette as she smashed the branch across the back of its head, ducked underneath and launched herself at Firkin's racing ankles. She grabbed him, plunging into the murky green river, snatching him from the jaws and glimpsing thousands of olive-green scales as they surged past. Somehow, she grabbed the tree and hung on desperately to it, holding herself and Firkin against the river current, dangling in the water like streamers of clinging kelp. Her shoulder-socket creaked with the effort as Firkin turned and twisted, struggling to reach the tree.

Upstream, the river nydd turned and silently dived.

In a frenzy of pushing limbs and panicked movements Courgette somehow managed to heave Firkin out and onto the tree. She clung on panting heavily.

Through the green murk a pair of slender, kicking legs floated into the river nydd's view. Flipper-lickin' good! It powered forward, accelerating . . .

How he found the energy he would never know but Firkin grabbed Courgette by the shoulders and heaved her up onto the tree. Suddenly, either side of them, two enormous towers of teeth erupted from the water, biting deep into the flesh of the tree where a split second earlier Courgette had been. She screamed as one of the thousand razor teeth gashed her shoulder. Gallons of river water and saurian saliva poured down the inside of the river nydd's maw as it thrashed about below. Seizing this chance firmly by the scruff of the neck, and arm-wrestling it into an early submission, they ran blindly back to the bank, water spraying in all directions as the huge creature roared in open-mouthed frustration, the tree holding its jaws open. Firkin and Courgette flew off the end of the tree and collapsed in a dripping, panting heap on the bank. Blood oozed from Courgette's shoulder as she hugged the ground, shouting wildly as she panted.

The river nydd wrenched its teeth out of the wood and, knowing a lost lunch when it saw one, slunk away to nurse its battered reptilian pride. The only signs that the terrifying ordeal had ever occurred were the hundreds of deeply gouged tooth marks in the tree trunk, a spot of blood and two shaking youngsters on the bank.

Firkin sat up and hugged his knees. He stared speechless at Courgette, shocked by the way she had handled the situation.

'Did you read *that* in the library?' he asked panting and dripping.

'No. I, er, something inside me just clicked, I guess,' she answered, wiping her sodden hair out of her eyes and staring up at Hogshead.

'Are you all right?' asked Dawn as Hogshead looked after Courgette.

'I think so,' Firkin said. 'How I didn't see anything that big, I don't know. I couldn't move . . .'

Practz stepped out from behind a small shrub, pointed to the tree across the river and grinned like a cheap side-show conjuror. 'Tan-naah!' he sang, failing to sound much like the fanfare it was supposed to be. 'Baked Ammorettan Death Lizard!'

'What?' said Hogshead staring at the stocky Thaumaturgical Physicist as if he were eight days short of a fortnight.

'I'm not hungry,' whimpered Dawn.

'No, no!' said Practz, sounding very pleased with himself. 'No . . . many ways to bake one . . . remember?'

'Who in Rhyngill is he?' asked Firkin in soggy bewilderment.

'I've read about some ways to help someone across a river,' said Courgette. 'But *that* has to be *the* most ridiculous . . .'

'You *do* remember! Excellent!' said Practz, quickly interrupting what sounded like it was going to be a long and vicious insulting session. 'Well, come on, let's get you all inside before you catch your death of cold,' he added, in a voice that sounded as comfortingly familiar as everyone's favourite sofa.

Before Courgette could lash his eardrums any more he tapped his finger on the side of the pocket Thaumatron, uttered a few strange-sounding words and suddenly they were inside Losa Llamas.

The shock of the change of scene took the wind out of Courgette's fury. She stood, hands on hips and smouldered angrily, as Practz said, 'Now let's have a look at that shoulder of yours. *Then* I'll tell you all you need to know.' He moved Courgette closer to the roaring open fire and pulled a little red box off a nearby shelf.

The atmosphere within the Conference Room of Cranachan was tinged with alarm and disbelief.

'Are you sure it was him?' demanded King Grimzyn, his voice echoing coldly.

'I am, Sire,' replied Khah Nij almost apologetically.

'Well, call the guards out and get rid of him!' yelled Gudgeon, the Scribe for Trade and Industry. 'Have we all forgotten what he did or what we said *we'd* do to him if he even thought about setting foot inside our borders?'

'Let's not be too hasty,' said Khah Nij holding his hands up and appealing for calm.

'Too hasty? You seem to have changed your tune,' growled Gudgeon from under his heavy eyebrows. 'Get the guards out. Rid us of this slimy little nuisance once and for all time!' he shouted, thumping the table for effect.

'Fisk's words rang true in my mind,' said Khah Nij. 'He knew things that only people who have seen the Frogs would know. And what about Arathoostra?'

'An imposter!' shouted Gudgeon. 'Fisk always was a devious little charlatan . . .'

'But what if he's telling the truth? What if he does have access to the Frogs . . . Shouldn't we find out?' urged Khah Nij. 'Can we afford to take that chance?'

'Is the Right Horrible Khah Nij scared?' snarled Gudgeon.

'I am merely urging that we check out all the facts before we make a decision we may come to regret.'

'Hah! Sounds like an excuse to me. You've lost your nerve!'

'If there was the slightest chance of ridding ourselves permanently of that reprehensible little worm I would be one of the first to . . . to . . .'

'Scream and run?' interrupted Gudgeon, laughing raucously.

'Gentlemen! Please!' shouted King Grimzyn attempting to keep order. 'Frundle, what do you think?'

'I hate to admit it . . . but he's right,' replied the Lord Chancellor, stroking the side of his long nose. '*If* he is telling the truth then we cannot afford to risk losing such a weapon. Its loss would render us harmless to an aggressor armed with it. We would be like moths attempting to beat up an army of artillery-rhinos.'

'Do I take it we are going to accede to his demands?' spluttered Gudgeon in disbelief. 'Are you going to advocate giving in?'

'Until we have determined Fisk's ability to deliver the goods we will go along with his demands,' confirmed Frundle, looking over his half-moon glasses. 'It is a relatively small price to pay to acquire a weapon of such outstanding calibre.'

'An excellent decision, gentlemen,' said Fisk closing a small panel in the wall and walking across the Conference Room. Gudgeon stared in horror at the face from the past. Its sharply hooked nose, evil sneer and power-hungry grin, topped by a black leather eyepatch and wildly piercing eye struck at his heart, causing it to skip a beat. 'I notice there was some resistance to my generous offer,' said Fisk staring pointedly at Gudgeon. 'Why so suspicious, old friend?' sneered Fisk. 'Have the years only increased your cynicism?'

Gudgeon wiped his brow, 'How did you know that . . . I, er, someone must act as Devil's advocate,' he smiled limply as he realised that Fisk had been listening to their deliberations from behind the concealed panel.

'You may dispense with that role now that we will be working together again.'

Gudgeon scowled.

'There are certain items I will need in order to facilitate the easy and safe delivery of "the goods" as you so euphemistically called them, Frundle,' said Fisk calmly. He had won.

He reached inside his leather armour and produced a roll of parchment. 'I have made a list,' he said throwing it onto the table in front of King Grimzyn.

As Fisk stormed arrogantly out of the Conference Room followed by the dishevelled figure of Arathoostra, a tall man added a few more notes to his book. Excitement flooded his body as he turned quietly and crawled away down the secret passage hidden behind a panel in the wall.

As Practz carefully attended to Courgette's shoulder the four youngsters looked around the room they now found themselves in. Apart from the austere fireplace containing the large roaring fire the rest of the room was an untidy jungle of shelves and display cases. In one corner a large grey fish with far too many fins for its own good lazily flapped in a large tank. It was watched hungrily by two cold eyes mounted above a long toothed beak which crowned the body of a peculiarly leathery looking bird. A tiny mammal-like reptile shuffled about in a cage on another shelf, which was filled with books. Above that was a series of blue and gold masks decorated in strange patterns, with dog gods and giant beetles. A crystal ball and a pair of gypsy earrings were sitting on a cupboard next to a red and white spotted headscarf. The whole place was a jungle of peculiar objects and strange devices. It was almost as if an incompetent team of bungling removal men had been responsible for relocating the entire contents of a large municipal museum. With surprise, Practz noticed Courgette's fascination with the fish.

The warm fire and change of scenery had begun to work their own special charm and allowed the youngsters to relax. Courgette's curiosity was beginning to take control again.

'Where did you get that?' she asked pointing to the large fish.

171

'Fishing expedition off the island of Khoo Stoh in the Eastern Tepid Seas,' answered Practz, watching her expression carefully. Her eyes narrowed as she searched carefully through her memory. Something about that fish looked remarkably familiar.

'But that's impossible,' she said as she thought of the huge book in the library back in Rhyngill, full of pictures of animals and rocks.

'It wasn't too bad. Big hook, large net and a devil of a long wait but once it was hooked I just had to haul it in. I'm sure you don't want to hear about my fishing trips,' he said dismissively, stifling Courgette's next question. 'How are we all feeling now? Better?'

Four heads nodded in reply.

'Now, what were you all doing in the forest?' he asked.

'We were coming here,' answered Firkin, the least shaken of the four. The least confused. 'We are looking for someone.'

'Anyone I know?' asked Practz, already knowing the answer.

'Vhintz, the Travelling Sorcerer,' answered Firkin straightforwardly. '*Do* you know him?'

'Oh yes. In fact I can take you to him if you would like. I expect it'll be a relief to find him after your long and dangerous journey from Fort Knumm.'

Bells of alarm rang in Courgette's head as the campanologists of caution leapt into action. Nobody had mentioned Fort Knumm. And that red and white spotted headscarf looked strangely familiar. Had anyone else felt strange by the river? She was scared to admit it. There was something very odd going on here. Suddenly the leathery-looking bird squawked and dropped off its perch. It flew in a shallow glide across the room and landed on the back of Practz's chair, its sharp claws scraping on the wood as it settled down. Hardly batting an eyelid the thaumaturgist reached inside his cloak and threw the pterodactyl a small dried fish. Its toothed beak snatched the offering expertly

172

from the air and crunched it down eagerly. Practz smiled and scratched the ancient reptile's belly.

Courgette stared suspiciously at the stocky man. In the short time she had known him she had formed an opinion of him. There were many qualities he had which Courgette felt they would find useful. However, trustworthiness wasn't one of them. There were too many things that didn't make sense, too many question-marks, too many enigmas. And one of them was now digesting a fish.

Her mind raced searching for a jigsaw to fit the pieces into. She knew what she had seen at the river the *first* time. Hogshead and Dawn *must* have seen it too. Why did Firkin seem oblivious to it all? What's going on?

'Well, let's see if Vhintz can give you the answers,' said Practz, shocking Courgette out of her racing thoughts. The statement had been addressed to Firkin but could she be sure of anything here? Could she be absolutely certain that the mysterious stocky figure hadn't been listening in to her thoughts?

Firkin and Hogshead leapt eagerly to their feet and headed for the door, their spirits rising rapidly. They were about to meet Vhintz, the Travelling Sorcerer. The man who would be able to tell them the whereabouts of the absent King Khardeen. Their journey was almost over, their quest for information nearly ended. Klayth would soon be returned to his state of princedom. Everything would be wonderful!

Her mind seething with wary and suspicious thoughts Courgette followed them out of Practz's room to a meeting with Vhintz. How could she trust a man who kept pterodactyls and had a pet fish that had been extinct for eighty million years?

The sheer thrill of a scoop in the making had shot through Turgg Inyeff's heart as he had preyed on and devoured every word that floated into earshot through the secret wooden panel. He had strained to hear clearly as his hand scribbled rapidly across the tiny, trusty notepad. He had listened in rapt attention as the drama had unfolded, from the first protesting, muffled struggles of The Right Horrible Khah Nij, War Lord of Cranachan, as he had been set upon in his bed; the threats; the demands; the introduction of Arathoostra, Chief Scientist and self-proclaimed Angel of Death, and the tale of his role in the scientific work at Losa Llamas; and finally the conference he had just overheard, and now crept quietly away from.

Turgg Inyeff had heard more than enough to get his scoop. He glanced at the page before him and knew without a shred of doubt that he was on to something big. He was about to get only his second-ever front page story. Bubbling with excitement he crept away from the door, through the dark and cobwebby tunnel and headed back for the passageway out of the Imperial Palace Fortress.

'Yes?' snapped the voice in response to the second barrage of knocks on his door. 'Yes, what do you want?'

'You've got visitors. Open up,' answered Practz, apparently talking to the door.

'Visitors? Me?'

'Yes. Are you going to let them in? They've come a long way.'

A bolt rattled in a clip as it was drawn back and the door to Vhintz's room creaked open.

'I'll not be able to get any scissors back till a week next Thursday, but I can do shoes by Friday,' he said as the door opened. 'Anythin' more fiddly an' you'll 'ave to wait a bit longer. I've got exams comin' up soon. What d'you want?'

'Hello. We were wondering if you could help us,' said Firkin nervously.

'What sort of 'elp?' asked the face that seemed to be more beard than human.

'Can we come in and talk about it?' asked Firkin. 'We think you can help.'

Grumbling almost incessantly, the little man pulled the

creaking door all the way open and the group trudged into the dark interior. They looked around the room in a matter of seconds. Firkin was bursting with questions, Hogshead sniffing the air, *feeling* magic all around him. Vhintz shuffled agedly around the room and sat back down. There was very little in the manner of personal possessions, everything was packed into a small battered rucksack and a tastelessly decorated cloak with many bulging pockets. Everything, that is, except for a large leather-bound book which sat on the end of his bed. Hogshead stared in disbelief. The book. The book that contained the answers, the tools to enable them to fulfil their mission. In there, towards the back was appendix iiib. Well, most of it was missing now, but it *had* contained appendix iiib, before a certain three-quarter-inch bookworm, not a million miles from his right-hand tunic pocket, had succumbed to the cravings of hunger one afternoon. Hogshead rummaged about in his pocket and withdrew a small parchmentback book. Vhintz watched in utter confusion as Hogshead opened the cover and began talking to the inside flyleaf.

'What's he doin' there? Has he gone loopy?' asked Vhintz warily.

'Oh, no. He's fine,' answered Firkin.

'What's he talkin' to a book for, then?'

'Sshhh,' said Courgette, putting her fingers to her lips. 'You'll wake him too quick, then he'll be grumpy.' Gentle piping snores floated out of the book.

'Who'll be grumpy? What are you on about . . . ?' Vhintz stopped in mid-sentence as a tiny green bookworm stretched and looked about blearily.

Vhintz strained to see into the book, his face reflecting the hundreds of questions he wanted to ask but his mouth–brain interface crashed under the load, leaving him staring open-mouthed as the creature in the centre of the book smacked what passed, in the worm world, for lips.

'What the hell is it?' shrieked Vhintz, finally finding the words.

'An old friend of yours,' answered Hogshead cheerfully.

'Mine? It . . . It's looking at me. Stop it looking at me. I hate *things* looking at me.'

Ch'tin closed his eyes.

This simple action caused an earthquake of terror to race through the discs of Vhintz's spine. He stared accusingly at Hogshead. 'Did you do that? It's a trick, isn't it? You're working it with your hand.'

Ch'tin shook his head.

'It can read my mind. I've heard of things like this. I'm doomed. Ruined. It's going to suck my brain dry and I'll end up as a lettuce for the rest of my life . . .'

'Cabbage,' corrected Courgette.

'See?' squirmed Vhintz uncomfortably, staring pleadingly at Practz. 'It's started. Turn it off. Close the lid. Squash it . . .'

'The only thing this little chap will suck dry is a particularly slushy romance,' said Practz. 'It's a bookworm.'

'Why me wake up did you?' piped Ch'tin drowsily, looking at Hogshead. Vhintz jumped and stared even more fearfully at the tiny green creature, doubting Practz's words of reassurance.

Hogshead pointed to the book on the Sorcerer's bed and said, 'Is that it?'

'It is,' answered Ch'tin and licked his mandibles hungrily.

'Oh no,' said Vhintz waving his hands possessively, 'You can't 'ave that. No way. That's mine.'

'Breakfast!' squeaked Ch'tin.

'We don't want all of it,' said Hogshead carefully, 'Just the use of one spell.'

'Yourself speak for!' admonished Ch'tin eying the book with greedy helminthine eyes.

'A spell?' asked Vhintz warily, flashing a questioning look at Practz. 'Any one in particular, or just one at random perhaps.'

'No, we want a very specific spell.'

'Which one, specifically?' asked Vhintz from under heavy curious eyebrows.

176

'Er, well, if I could just have a look . . .' said Firkin reaching out.

'No!' shouted Vhintz moving rapidly across the room, slapping Firkin's hand and snatching the book up. Vhintz scowled at them, clutching the book to his chest.

'Well, could you tell us what spells are in there?' asked Firkin rubbing his smarting hand.

'No, you tell me what it is you want and I'll tell you if I can do it!' said Vhintz.

'Oh. We were hoping you might be able to tell us which spell we need,' said Firkin, feeling a little embarrassed.

'Look, I fix shoes, an' sharpen scissors. I don't read minds. What do you want?' Vhintz asked impatiently. In the shadows by the door, Practz grinned quietly. It was going much as he had expected it to.

'Well it's like this . . .' began Firkin taking a deep breath and recounting the facts that King Klayth had sent them on a mission (it sounded better that way) to find his father, King Khardeen, and put him back on the throne.

'Sounds easy enough,' said Vhintz a few minutes later. 'Why do you want my help?'

'We've got a bit of a problem. We don't know where to look. The last thing we know is that he disappeared just before the war with Cranachan. But we don't know where he went, or anything.'

'So why are you asking me?' said Vhintz.

'Your book,' pleaded Firkin feeling very frustrated with all this dancing around the subject. 'Doesn't it have any spells in that can find people, or something?'

'What, like a location spell, or some such thing?' asked Vhintz. Hogshead and Firkin nodded wildly at the same time.

'In here . . . ?' said Vhintz tapping the book.

The four youngsters nodded. Behind them, Practz grinned.

'You want me to tell you if there is a location spell in this book. In my book?' muttered Vhintz, looking pleadingly at Practz.

'Yes please. If it's not too much trouble,' smiled Courgette sweetly.

'Er, I . . .' muttered Vhintz, fingering the collar of his tunic. Courgette smiled even wider, urging him on.

'Ahem. If there *is* a location spell in here, what do you want me to do about it?' asked Vhintz, dreading the answer.

'Use it to find King Khardeen,' answered Firkin.

Vhintz opened his mouth to say something, closed it, looked at Practz who appeared to be examining his fingernails, opened his mouth again, swallowed and ended looking at the floor.

'Why me?' he asked himself.

'Because you're a Sorcerer,' answered Hogshead expectantly.

'Oh,' said Vhintz, his shoulders sagging, making him look suddenly very old. A thick blanket of silence fell in the room as the youngsters looked at Vhintz and waited for an answer.

'You *are* a Sorcerer, aren't you?' asked Hogshead, suspiciously. Vhintz looked up and shot Hogshead a look of utter shame, inadequacy and uselessness. A look born from years of carrying a book thrust on him by his grandfather, a book that he had utterly failed to comprehend one word of, let alone cast a spell from. It was a look that lanced straight into Hogshead's heart.

Suddenly that look made both him and Firkin realise that all their efforts so far had been wasted. They had hung a whole idea on the fact that Vhintz was a Sorcerer who had an old leather-bound book of spells, and that one of those spells would be useful in finding King Khardeen and returning him to the throne that he had left nearly fourteen years ago. All that might be true, but the success of their whole mission hinged precariously on the fact that Vhintz would be able to *cast* that spell.

Somehow all four of them had whipped each other up to believe that out there, in a book, was the answer. They had faced dangers, walked miles and collected a huge number of blisters and all for nothing, a dead end, the reddest of herrings. Hogshead suddenly felt like a missionary who had trekked miles across arid wastelands, fought dangerous animals and hiked up huge mountains to the very Welcome Mat of the Gates of Heaven only to discover that God had packed up and gone to live in a seaside resort selling small animals made out of sea-shells. They had reached the end of the road only to find a no-parking sign.

The feeling of desperate hopelessness spread through the foursome like a plague. Vhintz shrugged his shoulders uselessly.

'Er, I could reheel your shoes before you set off back if you like?' he suggested, pathetically.

It was only with an immense struggle that Firkin prevented himself from hurling himself to the floor, kicking and pounding his fists on the floorboards and screaming. That, and the thought of looking very, very stupid.

Gradually he became aware of someone behind him straining furiously to keep himself from laughing. It wasn't so much that he heard anything, it was more that he felt an electric wave of ridicule lap gently at the back of his neck. He turned slowly and looked accusingly at the source of this feeling. It emanated from a man standing with both hands across his mouth and his face gleaming beetroot red. His eyes were screwed shut as he quivered silently. One more ounce of stimulation and he would explode. Firkin turned fully round, his face crimson with anger. Pathetic, impotent, paper-bag-tearing anger. Practz opened his eyes. Bad move. The final straw. He exploded in an enormous earsplitting belly laugh and collapsed helplessly on the floor. Firkin yelled as he watched the stocky man deriving so much pleasure from his misfortune.

'Shutupshutupshutup!' he screamed, stamping his foot childishly.

'Stopitstopitstopit!' roared Practz, thumping the floor and holding his ribs as if they were attempting to make a long-planned bid for freedom.

Vhintz spluttered as the wave of contagious guffaws

crashed over him. As the embarrassed tension dissolved in the torrents of uncontrollable mirth, the mood lifted and Hogshead, Courgette and Dawn sniggered, spluttered and exploded into a peal of raucous belly laughter. In a few moments all but Firkin were helplessly hysterical at the pathetic situation they found themselves in. They had successfully tracked down a sorcerer who couldn't cast spells!

'I'm sorry. I shouldn't laugh,' croaked Practz from the floor and creased up again.

'Quite right,' grumbled Firkin.

'I wanted you to find out for yourselves,' he spluttered, red-faced.

'Find out what? That we've got it all wrong. That we're stupid,' shouted Firkin.

Practz struggled to control himself. 'No. Find out that Vhintz wasn't right for you. Oh, my ribs. Look, come back to my room and I'll explain it all. I bet you're all starving. After something to eat I'll tell all. It's actually nothing to laugh about at all. It was just your face. I'm sorry.' He ushered them out into the corridor and off back to his room before he burst out into another fit of laughter.

'I thought you said he was going to *give* us these amphibians!' snarled King Grimzyn, looking at the piece of parchment Fisk had left with them. 'It would seem that a major military operation is required!'

Khah Nij looked down the list with a growing feeling of mistrust. Had he been the victim of an elaborate con? This list seemed to include everything needed for a military coup. If Fisk was attempting to recruit and equip his own private fighting force, it was a particularly hard-nosed way of going about it. Khah Nij found it hard to believe that Fisk would be able to carry out such a scheme. Although, if the mysterious figure that claimed to be Arathoostra turned out not to be . . . then who was it? And what hold did he have over Fisk? He shuddered. Listen to yourself! he thought angrily: Carry on thinking like that and you'll end up as a paranoid wreck!

You are dealing with Fisk and some mad ex-scientist who has been locked away for the last how-many-years. If you assume the truth then you stand to gain a weapon of utterly awesome power. And if it's all lies then you've got a damn good excuse to dispose of Fisk, permanently!

Having not quite settled that inner doubt, Khah Nij relaxed a little but clung on to the acute and overwhelming feeling of utter mistrust he held for Fisk. Watch him! he told himself. Watch him!

Now why does he want a highly trained team of crack troops?

The evidence that half of the children's hunger had been satisfied was spread all around Practz's firelit room. Food-streaked plates were stacked precariously on the tables, a pile of large sticky buns had somehow managed to diminish, in minutes, to a few scattered crumbs and currants, and cores, peel and pips from several varieties of fruit were all that remained of the large bowlful that had stood on the once-groaning table.

Courgette's voice broke the silence, eager for the cooling wine of fact to douse the leaping flames of the questions burning in her mind.

'Look, why don't you tell us what's going on here,' she said firmly. 'You can't tell me that something weird didn't happen at the river. Was that your doing? And what about these extinct pets of yours,' she said staring into the ancient piscine eyes of the dull grey fish. 'Coelacanths don't live in the Eastern Tepid Seas anymore. They all died eighty million years ago . . .'

'I see you know your history . . .'

'. . . and pterodactyls haven't flown for longer than that,' she added, staring accusingly at the naked pink excuse for a bird.

Practz stroked his chin and looked admiringly at Courgette.

'What's going on?' asked Firkin with a note of bewildered

181

confusion. 'I don't understand any of this. Dead animals as pets. What is all this?'

'I see I had better explain,' said Practz as he saw Courgette's gaze smouldering angrily from underneath her fiery red eyebrows. The orange firelight flickered on his face, casting a leaping black shadow on the wall as if a devil with St Vitus' Dance was peering over his shoulder. 'I'm sorry about the cloak and dagger dramatics, but . . . I had to be sure.'

'Sure about what?' she demanded. 'We are listening.'

Practz took a deep breath and began, 'I am a Ninth Aeon Deja-Moi Master. I am also one of several Thaumaturgical Physicists working here in Losa Llamas.'

'Working?' interrupted Hogshead, his ears pricking up again as he heard the magic word – Thaumaturgical. 'What on? What's Deja-Moi?'

'You have experienced the powers of Deja-Moi by the river. My, er, little demonstration. You have seen how I can change events that have already occurred.'

'What changes?' snapped Firkin, glaring at Practz. 'That *thing* just crept up behind me. You weren't even there!'

'You mean you don't remember?' asked Courgette, staring unbelievingly at Firkin.

'Of course I remember. That was a pretty amazing manoeuvre!' he replied appreciatively. 'I wasn't sure who was more scary for a moment, you or it,' he added, recalling Courgette's furious expression.

Hogshead had seen that face. His knees went weak again just thinking about her. And it wasn't fear this time.

Courgette shook her head, looking at the earnest expression of Firkin and the smug see-I-told-you-so grin of Practz. 'You don't remember the first time?' she asked nervously, not really sure if she wanted to hear the answer from Firkin.

'First time?'

'*First* time,' confirmed Hogshead, sensing that something momentous had happened, his Thaumaphilic tendencies rising.

'Then, that wasn't the first time?' struggled Firkin.

182

'No,' chorused Courgette, Hogshead and Dawn. Practz shook his head.

'. . .?' replied Firkin.

Courgette rounded on Practz, her eyebrows twitching like an irate squirrel's. 'Explain!'

'It's the rules,' began Practz. 'Something's got to happen before you can correct it.'

'Correct what?' pleaded Firkin, feeling very left out.

'How?' snapped Hogshead.

'Deja-Moi,' answered the Thaumaturgical Physicist with the tone of voice that normally precedes a bout of highly immodest nail polishing. 'You've heard of *déjà-vu*,' he began to explain, 'that uncertain feeling you get when you feel as if you've been in a certain situation before? Well, Deja-Moi is the ability to go and visit it. In common parlance – a second chance.'

'You can rewrite history?' asked Hogshead, in grave danger of tripping over his jaw.

'Not really. Just tweak it a bit. If you go back to the nearest destiny node and give it a bit of a kick, so to speak, then a different present will carry on in its place. A bit like pruning a rose bush. The past is only the present that happened a little while ago, after all.'

Hogshead's eyes squirmed around inside his head as he tried to fathom that one out.

'So that's where the coelacanth and the pterodactyl came from?' said Courgette.

'A little failing of mine, I'm afraid. Hate extinction, don't you? I'd keep more but I haven't got the space, and the cleaners might get a bit miffed. Gives the palaeontologists something to think about. It'd all be too easy if the fossil record carried on in a straight line.' He looked at the little mammal-like reptile in the cage and smiled, 'This chap was just one of an insignificant little group called the therapsids until I tried to reintroduce some of them in sub-tropical rainforest a hundred million years after they first died out. Well, I mean he's so cute it seems much a shame . . .'

183

Courgette watched as the creature munched the head off a large emerald dragonfly. 'Anyway, it appears that his cousins' fossils are causing a bit of a stir now. They've been dug up in the wrong place in the fossil record, so he's been christened *Chronoperates paradoxus*. The time wanderer.'

'Does that mean that you are a Sorcerer?' asked Hogshead.

'In a manner of speaking, yes. As I said before, I am one of a few remaining Thaumaturgical Physicists. We studied the effects that magic can have on matter, space and time. Losa Llamas was set up to provide us with a safe haven for research, away from interference from the Natural Rights Society and the like.'

'Who are they?' asked Hogshead.

'A bunch of utter crackpots who believe that people like us shouldn't mess with forces we don't understand. We kept getting trouble from them before we set up the defences. Bomb scares, raids to release our lab animals, that sort of thing. So we set up a whole series of things to scare intruders off. You've met some of them. The onomatopede and the gerund.'

'What? How do you know what happened in the forest?' asked Hogshead.

'I thought you'd have a few questions! Watch,' he replied and brought a crystal sphere down onto the table. He moaned a few well-used words and stared at the dark globe.

The youngters looked on expectantly.

'I can't see anything,' said Dawn glaring at the enormous nose of her distorted reflection.

'Ahem, yes,' said Practz with embarrassment. 'The wave guides are getting a bit old in this one. It takes a while to warm up.'

As he spoke the black began to fade and a tiny pin-sharp monochromatic image of a river running through a dense forest appeared in the centre of the globe. The image began to move. It fell away as the point of view rose into the air and headed off towards the Talpa Mountains, controlled from far below by Phlim as he carried out orders from Practz.

'Is that the river where . . .' asked Hogshead.

'Yes . . .' interrupted Practz before Firkin started asking difficult questions again. Trying to explain to someone that they have to be terminated prematurely, no matter how good the reason, wasn't an easy thing. He'd heard of a God who'd had to explain a similar thing to his Son, it took nearly thirty years to convince him that public crucifixion was a great idea. '. . . and just here is the place where you met the gerund and the rocks,' commentated Practz as the Sneeke's eye view raced over the tree tops. Dawn glared as she remembered the clinging lively green mould.

'Look, there it is!' he said as a small marsupial-like animal flashed across the sphere. Courgette felt sick as she remembered stroking it.

'Cute little chap,' said Practz. 'Do anything for a banana.'

Firkin was tired of the evasive conversation. 'Why are you telling us this? What has this got to do with us?' he asked.

'Oh, nothing really,' said Practz ironically, turning his attention away from the tiny image. His mood darkened as he wondered what Phlim and the Sneeke would find. He continued, 'Except that in three days' time all that you see around you will be dead and gone. And it will only be a matter of time before everything else in the world, all that you hold dear, everything you know and things you have only heard hinted about, are defiled and destroyed.'

Practz's voice had a black edge to it. An edge of sadness, an edge of total shame and guilt. 'A secret that has remained here unknown, hidden for years, is about to be unleashed on the world. It can only end in misery, death, absolute havoc wreaked by the corruption of absolute power.'

Hogshead looked amazed. 'You are talking in the future. How do you know?'

'Five days ago Arathoostra, the leader of the team that created the Ultimate Deterrent, disappeared.'

The youngsters looked blank. Hogshead found himself thinking of the meeting with Old Ma Tini and the hastily hidden card.

'He cannot have disappeared on his own. We had him locked up for being, er, for his own safety. Someone from outside has helped him. Someone I think you know. If I'm right, and I pray that I'm not, you four may be the only chance we all stand to survive the next three days.'

If that's the case, he thought, looking at them standing before him, we are in big, big trouble.

In one of the lower chambers in Losa Llamas, Phlim stared at a small crystal sphere. He muttered a few words to himself, brushed his hair out of his eyes and smiled as the image in the sphere banked to the left and raced towards the Talpa Mountains. It plunged on over the tundra, over the mountains until, after a few minutes' furious flight it slowed to less of a blur and swooped down over the sprawling mass of buildings perched on the windswept plateau. He murmured a few more commands and watched as the Sneeke obeyed, swooping in closer to Cranachan. He wasn't entirely sure what it was he searched for. Practz had asked him to 'look in Cranachan for anything unusual or suspicious that might relate to the disappearance of Arathoostra.'

It was a good job he'd added those last eight words. From what Phlim could see *everything* in Cranachan was unusual or suspicious. As he flew over the Imperial Palace Fortress he saw a small squad of men trying to push each other off a set of hastily erected siege towers while another group squirmed through gallons of water covered in acres of netting. There were other military looking manoeuvres going on that made no sense whatsoever to Phlim, involving large grey animals with horns and archery turrets strapped to their backs.

In the town which squatted at the base of the Palace things were no less unusual. Phlim watched in horror as a figure flung himself off the bridge that crossed into the walled town. He spread his arms, arced into a headfirst dive, and plummeted into the gorge, racing groundwards until inches away from a certain messy collision, when he reversed

186

direction and hurtled upwards again. It was only then that Phlim noticed the elastic thread attached to the madman's leg. Shaking his head he steered the Sneeke into the town and continued his search.

He practised his low-level Sneeke flying, zooming through the narrow streets, swerving round sharp corners, avoiding all manner of obstacles, keeping a constant low murmur of instructions flowing. He raced along a major market street and almost missed it. Snapping a series of rapid commands out to the Sneeke he swerved a full three-sixty turn and hovered over a small table of parchments. There below him had to be what he was looking for. He stared at the tiny image of the top of the newsparchment seller's head and looked at the headline on *The Triumphant Herald*. Across the front page was emblazoned:–

ARMOURED AMPHIBIANS AMAZE ALL

Fisk's Froggy Find Forms Fearsome Fighting Force?

EXCLUSIVE!!!!

Only a few hundred yards from the tiny hovering Sneeke, in the courtyard beneath the training siege towers, Captain Barak of the Cranachan Imperial Stealth Troopers rummaged apprehensively through his rucksack and saddlebags. He checked through his belongings, ticking off the items mentally . . . survival rations, one box, ten days – check . . . exposure suit, one-off, military standard down to minus thirteen – check . . . emergency flares, three boxes, visible for two hundred leagues on a clear night – check . . . clay explosives, four boxes, fifteen charges per box – check . . . five-denier ladies' black tights, three boxes, five pairs per box – check. All the essential items of warfare were there, especially the tights. Barak always carried them for the times when bribery or seduction were required. At least, that's what he told anyone who asked.

Around him his faithful band of twenty men made final checks on their supplies and weapons. Kholin, 'The Barbarian', carefully checked his trusty hammer, Miolinir, his winged helm glistening in the sun. Ahhrny, the six-and-a-half foot axe-wielding maniac, known to his friends as 'The Ex-Terminator', caressed and polished the gleaming three-foot blade of the weapon of his trade. Schmorgg Gashbord, the blond, seven-foot Arian warrior, sat cross-legged on the ground, polishing his six-foot rectangular shield, his club, Splatter, lying innocently next to him. These three made up Barak's heavy artillery. At a respectful distance from them the other sixteen swordsmen, mercenaries and army rejects checked on a small herd of horses and a variety of instruments of torture and death, under the watchful eye of Barak's second in command, Troop. Soon they would set off on their first real mission. Khah Nij had said so.

Where they were going, what they were going to do when they got there, how many people would be lost on the enemy's side and what the successful outcome of the entire mission should be was all a complete mystery to Barak. He had told his men it was all on a 'need to know' basis. When pressed to give an answer to 'What the hell that means', he had explained that at this time he didn't think they needed to know.

However, he had a feeling that he was about to find out. Three people were approaching across the courtyard, heading straight for him. He recognised instantly the close-cropped head on the squat figure of Khah Nij stomping towards him in front of two other men. The figure bringing up the rear looked frail, old and almost paper-thin – a few days of heavy feeding had done little to improve the effect that years of neglect had wreaked on Arathoostra's body. Barak's gaze flicked curiously to the figure in the middle. As he saw the tall, thin, black-clad figure sneering at the back of Khah Nij's head a shiver of abject terror froze the very core of his being. Fisk! He could hardly believe his eyes. After all this time, with the threat of death still hanging over his head, or so Barak thought, Fisk was the last person he expected to see alive in Cranachan. Especially standing next to Khah Nij. Questions seethed inside his brain, demanding answers. Answers that would have to wait.

'The men are all present and correct, Sah!' shouted Barak, slickly saluting the Head of Security and War.

'Excellent,' replied Khah Nij, returning the salute. Fisk sneered over his shoulder. Barak attempted to ignore him. He turned and walked towards his men flanking Khah Nij.

'Sir, what's *he* doing here?' he whispered, flicking a thumb behind him.

'You'd better get used to it. He's coming with us.'

'What?'

'You heard. He's made us an offer we couldn't refuse.' Khah Nij's voice lowered as he snarled, 'Watch him like an Ammorettan Death Lizard. If he so much as steps even a hairsbreadth out of line, you have my strictest orders to remove any part of his anatomy you think fit.'

'Any recommendations, Sir?' whispered Barak conspiratorially.

'I leave it to your imagination but . . . I don't want there to be any risk of him ever siring any offspring. Do I make myself clear!'

Barak smiled wickedly and mentally sharpened a few large knives. 'Oh yes, Sir. Very clear!'

'Very well, Captain Barak. You will receive a full briefing nearer the time. But now,' he added in a voice that all could hear, 'gather your men, it's time to begin.'

Barak thrilled as he heard the words and gave the order. In a few moments, without ceremony or announcement, fanfare or crowds of waving admirers, the small band of men that made up the Cranachan Imperial Stealth Troopers, accompanied by Khah Nij, Fisk and Arathoostra, rode out of a minor exit, into the mountains and away towards Losa Llamas.

Courgette could tell it was bad news. She tugged nervously at her leather bracelet as she watched Phlim fiddling with his hair explaining something to Practz. She stared as the stocky man's shoulders sank and the lines in his forehead deepened. Phlim stood, apologised and left the room as Practz's head sank into his waiting hands.

'Bad news?' asked Courgette.

'I was right,' answered Practz. 'It is as I feared.' He looked pale.

'Right about what?'

By way of an answer Practz murmured a few instructions to the crystal sphere and re-tuned it to the images flooding from the Sneeke. 'I think this may answer your questions.'

The sphere showed the inside of a wild grey snowstorm as it retuned. Gradually flickers of mountains showed through the visual white noise, clearing to offer more detail, resolving into a group of twenty-four men on horses. They rode in loose formation, those at the back on percherons struggling under the weight of the riders and the mass of weapons they carried. Firkin gulped as he saw a three-foot axe blade flash in the cold sunlight. The point of view swooped low over the group showing graphically the stack of weapons each rider carried. The youngsters watched with a mixture of fear and confusion. The spectacle of twenty-four riders in full battle readiness on the way to who-knows-where was thrilling and frightening, but as far as they could see it had nothing to do with them. The Sneeke passed over the front of the column, banked left and headed back over them. The youngsters swayed as the image moved before them.

'You remember I told you of Arathoostra,' said Practz, breaking the fascinated silence. 'Well, there he is. On the second horse.'

Hogshead smiled. 'You've found him. Marvellous. Every-thing's all right then . . .' His voice faded to nothing as a hooked nose, a sly sneer, and a black leather eyepatch

190

appeared from behind Arathoostra. His smiled dropped like several tons of bricks.

'What? Why?' spluttered Firkin stunned to see that face again.

'I was right,' murmured Practz. 'You do know of him?'

'Where is he?' demanded Firkin. 'He needs to be caught.'

'Impossible, I fear,' said Practz. 'Look at the company he keeps now. He rides with Cranachanian support.'

Courgette's mind flashed back to the torture chamber in Rhyngill where, as Snydewinder, he had arrested them and attempted to have *them* put to death for being Cranachanian spies. Anger surged hot inside her. 'Where is he heading?' she asked, her voice quivering with emotion. 'What poor people's lives is he about to destroy now?'

Practz took a breath. 'He is crossing the Talpa Mountains. He is on his way here.'

A flurry of questions took to the air, swarming around Practz's head like moths to a midsummer candle. What, in Rhyngill is he doing . . . ? Why is he headed this way . . . ? Where did he get . . . ? How long before . . . ? Their questioning wings flapped wildly for answers. As did the inquisitors.

'He is coming for the Ultimate Deterrent,' said Practz, with the voice of a prophet of doom. 'He means to take them for his own evil purposes.'

'Them?' chorused Firkin and Hogshead.

'Them. We developed them. We didn't know what we were doing. In the wrong hands there will be no stopping them.'

As he spoke the lines on his forehead grew deeper and he fiddled with the tuner on the side of the globe. The image changed to the inside of a dark hall-like chamber. Giant amphibians flopped in aimless malevolence within the confines of a dark green pool. Enormous scythe-like claws protruded from glistening flippers. Teeth lined the edges of their giant mouths. Somehow, even though the image was a matter of a couple of inches across, a sense of the brooding ruthless power came through.

'Uurgh,' said Dawn. 'What are they? They're horrid.'

'The Frogs of War. *Rana militaria*,' whispered Practz.

'He's after them?' asked Firkin.

'I'm sure of it. He has Arathoostra, he is heading this way.'

'You've got to stop him,' cried Firkin.

'How? Our defences will not cope. They were not designed to withstand an army, and Arathoostra knows our secrets. We need . . .'

'There's got to be something you can do,' pleaded Firkin interrupting Practz.

'You're a Sorcerer,' said Hogshead. 'You must have some spells to defend yourselves.'

'We do. But that isn't the answer. If we defend ourselves then they will bring bigger weapons to attack. Even if we destroy this wave we will never be safe. The more we defend the higher the value they will give the frogs. Fighting is useless! What we've got to do is . . .'

'So you're just going to let the Cranachanians walk in and take whatever they want! Oh, great! What kind of a strategy is that? The ostrich manoeuvre!' snapped Firkin, his face red with impotent anger.

'What does that mean?' asked Dawn and was promptly ignored.

'Hold on,' said Courgette. 'Am I being stupid here or did I miss something? You have invented, made, conjured up, whatever you like to call it, the most powerful defensive force in the history of warfare, right?'

Practz nodded, almost embarrassed.

'So powerful that the Cranachanians are prepared to risk lives in battle to come and get it?'

'Yes. But . . .'

'If it's so amazingly brilliant as a defensive force then why can't you use it against them?' asked Courgette.

Practz's face dropped in panic. If anything he went paler than he was before. 'No!!' he yelled 'We dare not risk it. They are Arathoostra's babies. They obey him. There's no telling what would happen. It would be certain suicide. No!!

The only way is to stop the Cranachanians *before* they get here. What we've got to do . . .'

'We're doomed! Doomed!' shrieked Hogshead.

'But you can do that . . .' said Dawn quietly. 'Like you did with Firkin.'

A look of relief washed over Practz's face. 'That's what I've been trying to . . .'

'Of course!' shouted Hogshead. 'Why don't you do that?'

Courgette's brow was furrowed in lines of deep thought. Practz watched fascinated as she drew imaginary lines on the table and looped them back on themselves. Her eyes were tight closed. She looked up slowly and fixed the stocky figure with a fiery gaze. 'I don't understand this. I can't believe that you haven't thought of waiting until they have invaded so that you can see how they will attack, then, using your Deja-Moi and having ambushes set up all over the place when they come.'

Practz was obviously impressed. 'If we could do that we would. But it's far too risky. As I said before, an event has got to happen *before* it can be affected by a Deja-Moi field. It's the rules. When the Cranachanians arrive, the first thing they will do, is attack and destroy the Thaumatron. Arathoostra will have explained all this to them. Without it we are completely helpless.'

'So that means afterwards is too late! You won't get a second chance,' said Firkin.

Practz nodded slowly.

'Are you beginning to see why we need your help yet?' asked Practz. 'Come on, I want to show you something. It might be a little clearer then.'

With their heads spinning like windmills in a hurricane, and trying desperately to absorb some of the information they had just been given, the youngsters followed Practz out of his room and down hundreds of yards of narrow echoing passageways.

Even before the massive reinforced doors slid open to reveal the cavernous interior of the Thaumatron Bay, the children could feel rather than hear the throbbing resonance of highly charged thaumic particles accelerating in a magi-kinetic field. The air itself had a tense aura and tiny sparks cascaded off people as they moved. They walked across an enormous floor made from open-weave strips of metal which unnervingly allowed the space below to be seen.

The Thaumatron filled most of the cavern and looked like a mass of bent and twisted sections of a bridge's substructure. It throbbed and pulsed as power surged through it.

Practz strained to make himself heard, shouting to the youngsters over the humming rumble as they stared in awestruck silence.

'The Thaumatron,' he shouted. 'Set up years ago to power all the experiments and tests we carry out here. It can produce twenty-five gigathaums if we need it. Mostly it runs at ten to twelve. If we lost it we'd be completely helpless, utterly defenceless.'

'How does it work?' shouted Hogshead above the deafening hum.

'Rather like a magical ring. Only bigger. Some natural substances have magical fields associated with them and some can be induced. If you arrange them in the right order and supply a small amount of elemental energy to them a positive feedback mechanism can be established and you've got yourself a Thaumatron. Of course, there's a little bit more to it than that. Damping rods, excessive thaumic particle absorbers and the like, you know, to avoid meltdown, but that's it, really. Simple.'

Hogshead was enthralled. Courgette hated the noise, Dawn stuck her fingers in her ears and pulled a face.

'If the Cranachanians get their hands on this we won't be able to stop them. That's why we need you. Somewhere in your past was a time, an incident, a chance encounter, a question that, if it had been asked differently would have prevented all this. A destiny node that needs a damn good kicking.'

'What?' cried Firkin, 'are you saying this is all our fault?'

'No!' shouted Practz above the hum. 'What I meant is that you hold the key. You are the link with the past that we need.'

'One of us? But how? What did we do?' shrieked Courgette, events beginning to congeal into the porridge of vague sense.

'It could be anything,' answered Practz. 'Turning left instead of right. Or just being in the place you were due to be a bit earlier. Or later. All we've got to do is find out where or what you did, what event triggered all of this . . . and tweak it!'

'Oh, is that all! It's impossible!' complained Firkin.

'No not quite. Just very improbable. The only *real* snag about all this, though, is that we've only got three days to find out how your past links with Fisk. Come on.'

Three days to find the trace of an atom of a needle in a million haystacks. Yeah. No problem!

Quietly, Dawn tugged on Firkin's sleeve and whispered, 'Who's Fisk?'

Firkin shrugged, 'Haven't a clue!'

'Aren't you cold?' asked Barak, looking at the huge bare arms and massive chest of Schmorgg Gashbord as the Stealth Troopers rode through the heights of the Foh Pass. The wind whistled from the north bringing blasts of sleet and hail. Winter, sensing the possibility of a good punch-up, was approaching rapidly.

The giant Arian threw back his blond head and laughed into the blasting wind, 'I vass born on an ice-floe in der Angstarktik midvhinter. My mudder vass on a mission.'

'Luxury!' shouted Kholin the Barbarian. 'My mother gave birth to me in a cave in the middle of the Ammoretto Mountains, surrounded by five hundred death lizards.'

'Easy!' joined in Ahhrny. 'My mudder died three vheeks before I vhas born. I had to do it all myself. I vhass fighting vhalrusses by der time I could crawl, und hunting polar bears as soon as I could vhalk!'

All three of the giant warriors looked wistfully into the distance as if recalling a time gone by.

'. . . and if you tell der kids today,' said Schmorgg, 'dey don't believe you!'

Raucous laughter echoed through the mountain pass as the Stealth Troopers disappeared over the horizon, out of sight of the Imperial Palace Fortress of Cranachan. It was downhill all the way to Losa Llamas.

'Is all this really happening?' asked Firkin. The youngsters were alone, Practz having left them to 'Sort something out'. Quite what he was sorting out he didn't make clear. Courgette wasn't entirely sure that it was Practz who should be doing the sorting out.

'Yes, it's real,' she said. 'My shoulder keeps reminding me!' A dark stain of dried blood showed on her tunic.

'Is it all right?' asked Hogshead.

'I'll survive. If any of us survive, that is!' she replied.

'Oh, come on. You don't believe all of this do you?' grumbled Firkin. 'We are wasting time here. We're no nearer to finding King Khardeen, or have you forgotten about that?'

Hogshead glared at Firkin for shouting at Courgette.

'I haven't forgotten,' she replied calmly. '. . . and yes, I do believe it. Can you explain this?' she added, waving a red and white spotted headscarf and a pair of large gold earrings which she picked up off a nearby shelf.

Firkin and Hogshead looked blankly at her. Dawn recognised them immediately.

'Give us a clue,' said Hogshead.

'Fort Knumm,' said Courgette.

'I know. I know,' whispered Dawn excitedly.

The two boys still stared blankly.

'Old Ma Tini,' said Courgette sarcastically.

'Oh. I remember,' said Hogshead. 'But what are you doing with them?'

'You saw me pick them up! Do I have to spell it out?'

196

Dawn nodded smugly.

'Practz *is* Old Ma Tini!'

'Oh. Come on,' protested Firkin.

Courgette nearly jumped down his throat. 'Where did you get the map from? How come we ended up here, in Losa Llamas? How did Practz know we had come from Fort Knumm? Nobody told him! And have you ever seen a woman with such hairy arms and five-o'clock shadow?'

'Okay, okay. So he dresses up like a fortune-teller from time to time, so what?'

'Why?' asked Courgette quickly. 'Why has he gone to all this trouble to make sure we get here?' Firkin shrugged. 'I'll tell you,' continued Courgette, now in full swing. 'There *is* a link between our past and the Cranachanians. All we've got to do is find it.'

All four of them looked at each other.

'How?' asked Hogshead after a few minutes of deep, dark silence. Firkin and Dawn shrugged their shoulders and looked at Courgette.

'Why me? Why are you asking me?' she protested.

'You seem to have figured it all out so far,' answered Hogshead and smiled pathetically.

'Pah!' she grunted, folding her arms. Silence fell as Courgette came to terms with her first experience of democracy in action. Promotion of the mouthiest.

'All right!' she said, worn down by the expectant silence. 'What do we know so far?' It seemed that reading all those detective novels in the library of Castell Rhyngill had paid off.

'Let's look at this sensibly . . .'

'Are you sure this'll work?' asked Firkin as he stood nervously inside a shakily drawn chalk Pentagon.

'Well, I've never actually tried a non-self Deja-Moi Field over such a long time span but it should be fine,' answered Practz with a reassuring smile.

'You mean you're not coming?' said Hogshead, catching Firkin's nervousness with both hands.

'Oh no, no. I must stay here in case anything goes . . . er, changes,' his reassuring smile wrinkled and collapsed, like a red giant to a black hole.

'I'll go,' said Courgette enthusiastically.

'You can't. It would be too dangerous for you,' said Practz firmly.

'Typical. I never get to do anything exciting,' grumbled Courgette. 'It's just 'cos I'm a girl, isn't it?'

'No. It's your shoulder. Let it heal.'

'Bah!' Her eyebrows wriggled into an angry 'v'.

Suddenly the door burst open and another Thaumaturgical Physicist ran in panting heavily.

'Everything's set with the Thaumatron. It's running sweet as a nut today,' said Phlim. 'Just don't go above twenty-one gigathaums. She might not take it.'

'Sounds fine,' said Practz as he checked the blue-shift temporality tables against the Gren Idjmeen constant. 'Should only need twenty, tops.' Inside, he crossed his fingers, threw several pounds of salt over his shoulder and hurled a small fortune of lucky coins into a hundred different fountains and wells.

Firkin looked nervously at Hogshead and wondered what travelling backwards fourteen years would feel like. His stomach knotted and writhed with apprehension. The plan they had come up with had seemed like such a good idea when Courgette had explained it, but now . . . actually faced with going through with it all, he was less certain. He wished get-out clauses had been invented.

A low drone hummed through the room, throbbing with power. Practz satisfied himself that his figures, corrections and total SMPTE displacement co-efficients were correct, turned to Phlim and said in a voice aching to sound nonchalant, 'Okay. Fire me up!'

Phlim nodded in reply, brushed his hair from his eyes, and made a complex series of hand motions before a small opening in the wall. He checked the positions of everyone in the room then made one final flicking movement before diving to the floor. The thought crossed Firkin's mind that he didn't find Phlim very encouraging. A blinding flash of blue light filled the room as a lightning bolt of pure thaumic energy shot from the opening, plunging into the base of Practz's spine. It hovered there, crackling and spitting like a barbecuing cobra as it connected Practz to the wall. Fifteen gigathaums.

'WOOOOOOHHEEEEEHHH!' shouted Practz, vibrating wildly. Cascades of sky-blue sparks discharged from every point on his body, his cloak billowing around him, his hair, wild at the best of times, now thrashed and twisted like a hydra in a hurricane. The whites of his eyes turned blue, glowing with sapphire sparkles. His feet were a quarter of an inch clear of the floor. It was a terrifying spectacle, almost as if every particle in his body was possessed of a charge opposite to any other particle and was trying to get as far away as possible. It was the type of thing that you might see if you shorted the fifteen-million-kilowatt output of a large power station through an angry Persian-blue cat. In a rain storm.

'OHHHWOOOOW!' crackled Practz getting high on his power trip and throbbing noisily. He brushed back his spitting hair, sending waves of sparks zapping roofward, held out his arms in front of him and cracked his fingers explosively. It was as if an insane conductor had stepped into the electric atmosphere of a world premier performance.

Curiously, that wasn't too far from the truth.

Still floating a quarter of an inch above the floor, Practz struggled to bring his sapphire eyes into focus on Firkin and Hogshead. The spitting translucent blue snake of thaumic energy bucked and snatched wildly as it continued to plunge fifteen gigathaums into the small of his back. Slowly, shakily, as if moving against massive resistance, Practz pointed to the edge of the chalk Pentagon. An audible crack signalled that contact had been made, the chalk lines igniting with blue fire. Hogshead squeaked. Firkin watched every move. He felt his hair begin to move of its own volition. Practz began to recite curious words. Seventeen gigathaums. Hogshead strained to hear them above the constant hum and the fusillades of crackles and sparks that punctuated every motion. As Practz moaned, the hum grew in intensity, the gap between him and the floor widening. Eighteen point five gigs. The throbbing was becoming unbearable. Practz's voice rose in scratchy semitones, climbing the catatonic scale, as his chanting rose.

Twenty point eight gigathaums.

The boys were shrouded in a swarm of blue thaumic mosquitoes, obscured from view but still very, very present, in the present. Phlim looked across the series of glowing runic dials, checked the thaumostat reading and cringed. As he watched, the gold dial of the thaumostat turned red, then black, then for a single heart-stopping moment all the lights went out. Phlim stared in terror at the thaumostat.

Twenty one point five gigs.

Hurry up, hurry up! he thought close to panic. She'll not take much more!

Twenty two point two gigathaums.

Practz's eyes sparkled as he stared at the two boys, then clapped his hands in a crash of sparks and they were gone.

Phlim made a series of gestures and the thaumic serpent disappeared. The silence pushed at the inside of their ears, almost worse than the chaos a moment earlier. Small crackles discharged from Practz as he sank to his knees panting with exhaustion.

Phlim looked guiltily at the thaumostat and the series of runic dials and wondered if everything would be all right. Had it been his imagination or was there a wild twitch in the chronoperatic flux field density a millisecond before the boys vanished? Was that a coil burning out? If it was, it wouldn't really matter. Or would it?

The exact moment it actually started to happen was surprisingly difficult to pinpoint. Practz chanted, floating and crackling in front of them as the humming rose, shaking the whole fabric of everything around them. Then it sort of stopped rising. The scene before them seemed to be somehow distant. Not quite there. Only after a few moments was it possible to tell that something had happened. Practz's incantations still sounded like gobbledegook, or was it koogedelbbog? Suddenly Practz stopped chanting. Then stopped glowing. Phlim sprinted backwards out of the room and everything began to stream away from them as they were pulled through a tunnel-visioned view of reversed events. It felt like they were falling, increasing speed, pulling away from all they knew. The rapidly reversing babble of snatched memories was now a high-pitched stream of sonic snatches, as if a bat with a speech defect were talking down a long-distance telephone line. Firkin was scared. It seemed to go on for ever. Further and further back through the register of time. Unfolding, revealing. Exposing memories he would rather have forgotten, peeling back layers of time to reveal scenes he had hoped to deny. Skeletons in cupboards sprouting flesh and walking again. It was a disorienting, mad, back-of-taxi dash through the back streets of half-forgotten memories and dense forests of past experiences.

Then suddenly, with a jolt, as if the taxi had hit a solid stone wall, it stopped. A table top hit him square in the face, he glimpsed light, parchments then . . . blackout.

Metamorphosis

'Givuss anothr dubble,' slurred the man pushing the glass across the bar and rummaging in his grease-stained rain-cloak pocket for a few more shillings. The barmaid smiled becomingly as she poured another double whisky, handed him a full glass and accepted the handful of small coins.

'Keep the cha . . . hic . . . nge, luv,' he drawled, stood precariously, and staggered over to a far corner of his favourite watering-hole. He spent a lot of time in here listening to the alcohol-soaked interior of The Gutter. One day, reasoned Turgg Inyeff, somebody was bound to let something slip. Some vital piece of information, leading him to the scoop he so desperately wanted, would fall out of the mouth of some drunken businessman or member of the Cranachan Internal Police in a single unguarded moment. And he was going to be there. Waiting. Ears open. Ready.

It was not going to happen tonight, though. There was no one of interest within earshot. It was always the way on Tuesdays. The place was packed out with young men after anything available in a skirt, old men whose interests in anything available in skirts had long since been replaced by the contents of a bottle, and young ladies keeping anything they may have available buried safe and deep within the folds of their aforementioned skirts. Unless the right man came along, of course.

This suited Turgg perfectly tonight. He had a lot on his mind, as well as the dozen or so double whiskies sloshing merrily throughout his forty-proof bloodstream. He was trying to place a fragment of a story into the mystery that stubbornly refused to unfold. He took another swig and looked at his little black notebook. Underneath the date, OG 1025, he had scribbled lists of words. His brow furrowed as he tried to distil some sense from the scrawled writing. It had made sense when he had written it. Now most of it was just a stack of garbled rubbish.

Only a matter of hours ago he had seen Fisk enter the wooden shack that passed as Rosch Mh'tonnay's office. He had heard snatches of conversations involving hiring civil engineers for some job over Rhyngill way and Fisk had left. What did it mean? Why would the Chief of Cranachan Internal Affairs be approaching the best Civil Engineer in Cranachan for a job on the border?

His gut feelings told him it had something to do with his story. Somehow it would tie in with the whole lemming thing. But how? What was Fisk up to?

Whatever it was, Turgg Inyeff had his suspicions it wasn't entirely ethical.

Draining his glass with one gulp he stood and swayed out of The Gutter and away back to his hut. One day he'd crack this story. He'd get his scoop. One day.

Fourteen years into the uncertain future and a few days' ride from the dingy back-streets that Turgg Inyeff staggered drunkenly through. Practz stood in an ozone-smelling room rubbing his chin thoughtfully. He scrutinised the lines of the chalk Pentagon and checked the tallow candles. He didn't like it. He had never expected to see their expressions change quite so drastically. Over the last few minutes his mind had focused in on the after-image of the faces of Firkin and Hogshead. He struggled to come up with a theory to explain why they had disappeared with their faces so distorted in terror. Shock, he would have expected, it isn't every day that you suddenly find yourself about to be hurled fourteen years into the past, but the look of terror . . . He had a bad feeling.

Courgette picked up on Practz's expression and her mind began to race. Images of disaster flashed across her mind, feelings of doom and gloom hung like palls of smoke above the dying embers of a funeral pyre. She could stand no more.

'What's wrong?' she asked.

'Eh, er, oh nothing, nothing at all,' replied Practz pathetically attempting to lie through his teeth.

'So why the gloomy expression?' she pressed. 'What have you done?'

'It wasn't me, I . . . er.' He looked up from the chalk marks and stared at Courgette. 'When I was casting the spell did anything odd happen?'

'Hah! Where do you want me to begin? Sparks. Noise. Light. Firkin and Hogshead disappearing. Nothing odd. Oh no!' answered Courgette.

Practz looked about for Phlim but he had vanished.

'Did anything look like it shouldn't have happened?' asked Practz. 'Lights going dim or the like?'

Courgette's eyes narrowed suspiciously. 'Yes. Why?'

'Well, I didn't like the look on their faces before they completely vanished and if there was a drop in power to the Deja-Moi field then . . .' Practz shrugged feebly.

'What! Will they be all right?' shouted Courgette.

'I'm not sure they'll exactly be in mortal danger where they are. Just depends what aspect of the field was affected.' Practz was stroking his chin, thinking hard and mumbling to himself, '. . . but if there's a fault with the Thaumatron causing Deja-Moi density changes then . . .' muttered the Thaumaturgical Physicist to himself as he thought out loud, '. . . or if a time coil's blown . . . or a destiny valve fused . . . or the thaumostat's melted . . .'

'Then what?' demanded Courgette.

'Eh? Oh. Yes. Let's check the Thaumatron's all right first, shall we? Before we jump to any conclusions,' said Practz quickly, smiling weakly as he hurried out of the bare room, cloak tails waving, and rushed up to the Thaumatron Bay.

Firkin groaned and rolled over. His head pulsed with a deep throbbing which rattled around his skull like a heavily booted marching band, sprinting through a cavern, rattling kettledrums and snares and blasting panting lungs through heavy tubas and trombones. He closed his eyes. The floor began to spin. Dimly he recalled how he came to have the headache. Light, parchments, then . . . blackout.

At the end of a wild tugging back through time, he and Hogshead had materialised out of the blue, quivered momentarily four feet above the floor, screamed, then crashed onto a table and passed out. He was sure it had been light then.

Now night's thick duvet lay snugly over the underblanket of darkness, illuminating the whole scene with fewer photons than would normally be found eight hundred fathoms down in the Pathetic Ocean.

How long had they lain there?

Hogshead grunted and wrestled with the overwhelming desire to keep his eyes firmly shut. He lost.

As the last of the tuba-players sprinted through Firkin's head a shimmering sense of urgency strolled up to a small stage, picked up a large conical device, put it to his mouth and yelled, 'Yoo-Hoo! Firkin! This is your 1025 alarm call.'

He groaned.

'Are you going to lie there another three days,' snapped Urgency.

How long? thought Firkin, starting to feel nervous.

'Well all right, three hours. But it *feels* like three days when you've been waiting around with nothing to do. There's only so many ways you can twiddle your thumbs, you know,' complained Urgency. 'Well, are you going to get up off your backside and do something? You haven't got much time.'

How much time? thought Firkin, beginning to fidget.

'Never enough! Never enough. Tempus fugit, an' all that. C'mon! Chop chop! Shake a leg.'

All right, all right! thought Firkin, give me a couple of minutes.

'Couple of minutes! Might not have that long. Might not have a couple of seconds! C'mon, move. Needs must when the devil drives, and stuff!' ranted Urgency, hopping from foot to foot. 'Do you want to get caught in here? Fat lot of good that'll do you. Do you want to? Hmmm?'

Hogshead groaned as Firkin poked him and hauled himself up the side of the table to stand precariously upright. The darkness was almost complete. Firkin tapped about slowly on the table, rustling through heaps of parchments, searching for some form of light.

'Wasting time. Wasting time!' snapped Urgency. 'C'mon, faster, faster! *Carpe diem!*'

Between three empty glasses and a half-eaten pie, Firkin found a candle. After cringing silently, then wiping his hands to remove the cold, congealed gravy he managed to light the wick, wincing as the light hit the back of his dark-adjusted eyes. Hogshead groaned once more and sat up with a struggle.

'I'll keep watch. Look-out. Yell if anyone comes,' prattled Urgency. 'Quick now. Little time. Faster, faster, faster, faster . . .' and vanished through the wall leaving Firkin to look around.

As he had gathered from his brief tentative tactile search, the room was a mess. The feeble light from the candle struggled to make an impression on the all-pervading darkness, striving to illuminate sepia mountain-ranges of parchment strewn across every flat surface, heaps of books thrown onto tables, countless screwed-up irrelevances of hastily scribbled notes flung onto the floor, spilling out over the top of the waste parchment bin, jostling for space amongst the empty bottles on the ash-strewn floorboards. If one's dwelling place is supposed to represent the state of one's mind, then the owner of this place must be convinced he was a sewer rat. Mad. Utterly barking mad.

As Firkin struggled through the wasteland of parchment fragments, the light of the candle glowing pathetically into the gloom like an extremely tired electric eel squirming through a centuries-old shipwreck, caked in mud, festooned with waving kelp fronds, he came upon the one attempt at order in the whole disaster area.

A large blackboard stood propped in one dark corner, covered in hundreds of yellowing parchment pages, each with a few words scribbled upon them, names, facts, opinions, rumours, each with a large thumb-tack harpooning it in place. A tracery of chalk lines linked some of the pinned parchments, marking trains of thought, looking like a certifiable tarantula's first attempt at lace-making.

One fragment had a huge number of lines coming and going to it. A name. Four letters. F-I-S-K.

Lines linked it to the Cranachanian Council, attached it to words like 'extortion', and 'blackmail?', bound it to characters with shady backgrounds, purveyors of dodgy deeds, and worse. But one thing Firkin kept coming back to: no matter which of the hundreds of chalk trails he followed, irrespective of how many other names, facts or guesses the path wound through, Fisk's name was always linked to one other thing.

Lemmings.

There was data on lemming migration patterns, border disputes between Rhyngill and Cranachan, sales figures for last year OG 1024, projected sales figures for OG 1025. The list seemed almost endless.

Firkin stood fascinated. Could this be what they had come back for? Was *this* what Courgette had in mind?

Phlim brushed his long brown hair out of his eyes with his hand, continued the movement and stood scratching his head thoughtfully. He checked the runic dials against the wiggly line on the parchment power trace and tutted audibly. He read the thaumic flux densitometer, the para-cosmic alignment vector, the thaumostat and the quasi-constant magi-kinetic accelerometer quotient. It was all perfect. Everything was as it should be. Now. The Thaumatron was running splendidly, now that it wasn't under any load. Why there had been a sudden, acute, and almost total drop in the chronoperatic flux-field density at twenty one point five gigathaums he really hadn't a clue. He hoped it wasn't a destiny valve. It was a hell of a job to change a destiny valve.*

He'd checked all the external parameters. Now he would have to look a little deeper. Grumbling to himself as he thought about what could possibly have gone wrong, he put on his lab-cloak, pulled a small key off a large hook, walked across the Thaumatron Bay, unlocked a small door and withdrew a larger, far more elaborate key. He walked back across the chamber with this, unlocked another door and peered inside. On a pedestal, surrounded by sheets of lead, stood a small black box. This was a box of nano-sprites,

---

*Destiny valves are made from highly leaded glass to attempt to contain the inevitability field and the uncertainty aura** within. This not only makes them very heavy and therefore difficult to replace, but containment of the field and aura within is never one hundred per cent. Leakage gives the technician changing the valve the overwhelming feeling that he will be attempting to change this valve for a period only three weeks short of eternity. And then it's uncertain whether it will work.

**Whilst designing the destiny valve, Arch-Mage Xhroedyngrh described the study of uncertainty aura as follows: 'The major problem about thaumaturgical physics is that magical particles are so small, and my eyesight is so bad, that it is impossible to tell if a thaumic event has actually occurred, or not. We need to observe single finite thaumic events at a scale that everyone can see, and link this directly to microscopic thaumic decay.'

He went on to propose placing a cat in a sealed box, with a single thaumic particle, a nano-sprite, a hammer and a vial of cyanide. If the particle decays, the nano-sprite detects it, swings the hammer, breaks the vial, releasing the gas and killing the cat. The observer has no way of knowing if the thaumic particle has decayed until the box is opened. Xhroedyngrh suggested that the cat would find itself in an indeterminate state between life and death, uncertain of its future until the box was opened, thus providing an ideal way of observing single magical partical decay without straining your eyes.

As grand a theory as this was, in practice it failed utterly. Xhroedyngrh reckoned without the catricidal tendencies of nano-sprites who, far from being impartial observers, vowed in the instant the box was sealed, to dispose of the cat in the most inventive way possible. The most common were the poison (46 per cent), taunting the cat until it had a heart attack (23 per cent), clubbing to death with a hammer (15 per cent), repeated collisions with the inside of the box (12 per cent) (although whether this was due to the nano-sprite or simply the unfortunate usage of claustrophobic cats was unclear), others (4 per cent).

In a later update of the destiny valve, the uncertainty aura was created using a particularly malicious strain of nano-sprites, contained in a box with a timer set to break a vial to release poison to kill the nano-sprite. The sense of uncertainty as to the time of impending death was magnified and utilised to devastating effect in the destiny valve.

microscopic relatives of naiads and nixes, their cousins were sylphs, their uncles were dryads but these were smaller and almost infinitely more technically advanced. While naiads cavorted in the gentle flow of rivers, nano-sprites surfed in the heady currents of power. While nixes frolicked in babbling forest brooks, nano-sprites romped in the torrents of surging multi-gigathaum flux fields. Comparing a nano-sprite to a dryad would be like comparing a nineteenth generation, sixteen bit, four-fold oversampling, interactive, parallel-processing pocket workstation to a bag of counting sticks.

Nano-sprites were the diagnostic tools of Thaumaturgical Physics, they could control and re-order matter at the micro-quantum level, recharging tired electrons, charming strange quarks and unsticking incorrectly attached gluons.

It was with immense care that Phlim closed down the protective field around the box and stepped closer to the black container. He inserted a small syringe-like device into the opening in the top and pulled back the plunger. He bent his ear closer to the device, listening for a minute tinitic buzz. After a few moments he withdrew the syringe, re-activated the protective field, replaced the keys and finally moved over to a small port on the Thaumatron. Inside the syringe- like device he could see a tiny spot of fuzzy glowing light. Pushing the plunger home he watched as the light from the nano-sprite disappeared into the vast mass of the Thaumatron.

The nano-sprite shot out into the surging thaumic flux and zapped away to find the fault, identify it, make it safe and adjust all the necessary parameters to ensure trouble free running in the future. Exactly the way gremlins don't.

Alcohol surged queasily through the befuddled neurons of Turgg Inyeff's brain as he swayed and tottered home through the dark and dingy back-streets of Cranachan Town. It has been said that if an infinite number of Purfidian Mandrills was given an infinite number of Bugherd* tiles, then, given an infinite length of time they would come up with the complete works of the D'vanouin bard Sheik Xp'heer. This randomly haphazard approach to problem solving was currently being applied inside Turgg's inebriated mind. He was feverishly attempting to cross-match the Cranachan Civil Engineer, Rosch Mh'tonnay, to Fisk. His mental fingers scrabbled at the edge of this fragment of rough-hewn jigsaw, turning it round, turning it over, attempting to force it into the murky overall picture. He'd seen the meeting. What was it all about?

Almost home, he stopped and leaned against a wall; fumbling in his rain-cloak pocket he withdrew a large hip-flask and took a satisfying draught of the rough whisky inside. His lip curled happily as the liquor burned the back of his throat making him cough.

Suddenly, ahead of him, something caught his eye. With the killer instinct of a starving reporter desperate for a story, faster than the blink of an eye, he was standing alert, notebook at the ready, pencil-tip licked, ready for his story.

The pale firefly glow of a tallow candle danced away from the window and moved on into the deep gloom of the hut. Suspicion rose. Burglars, thought Turgg Inyeff. Catch 'em in the act and it should be a good story. Might even get a reward from whoever lives there.

He watched the dancing candle for a few more seconds.

---

* Bugherd. A game of word-making. It is played on a board by arranging tiles to form sequences of letters for points. Different letters possess different score values depending on the difficulty of use. Extra points can be gained by tactical positioning of obscenities across the 'Double swear score' bonus space. The ruder, the better.

The game's name derives from the word 'bugherd' which, in D'vanouin slang means 'the act of taking one's goatherding habits above and beyond the call of duty by attempting to sire offspring using the goats of one's own flock.' When placed across a 'Triple swear score', 'bugherd' is worth five hundred and fifty-three points. The fact that this makes 'bugherd' itself worth one hundred and eighty-four point three points, has mystified Bugherd players for centuries. Hence the phrase, 'Well, bugherd if I know!'

Wait a minute? he thought suspiciously, looking around at the familiar alley.

Oh no! He was on the move, surging and swaying towards the door. *I* live there!

'Firkin?' asked Hogshead in a stage whisper. 'Do you hear what I . . .?'

The question hung for a moment in the air, a graceful gossamer suspicion, hanging like a lacewing before a herd of stampeding war-elephants as . . .

Hinges screamed, timbers groaned and nails screeched in stressed protest as the door to the room was hurled open with the force of an exceedingly dischuffed typhoon, revealing a profusely swearing man filling the door-frame, clutching a notebook and hip-flask, wearing an almost transparently greasy rain-cloak and an expression of outrage that would strip paint.

'Uh-oh!' squeaked Hogshead.

Firkin turned and ran.

Straight into a chair. He tumbled noisily over it, dropping the candle, watching it fly, spit and die, plunging them into utter darkness. A darkness filled by the roar of the owner of the hut. If decibels were light, they'd be blind, their optic nerves fried into overload.

Firkin felt a frantic tug on his shoulder. A hand snatching at his tunic, feverish, fearful, as Hogshead ran past. In a moment he was upright, peering into the blackness, his shin throbbing painfully. Hogshead pulled him to the left, whispering, 'Door!'

Suddenly, Firkin remembered seeing a door. A way out. Behind, the heavy bootfalls and angry yells surged out of the gloom. 'I'll get you! Come 'ere, you little b . . . !' followed by a rain of blasphemies as Turgg crashed over the chair, sending shock waves resonating through the floor.

Hogshead, miscalculating the distance with consummate ease, smashed into the wall, letting out a shriek of surprise through a crushed nose. Firkin, desperately patting the wall, seeking the door he knew was there, felt Turgg snap to attention as he heard Hogshead's collision. A crash of splintering wood sounded as the irate journalist flung the broken chair away to one side and stamped forward. 'I know where you are! There's no way out!'

Wrong again! thought Firkin as suddenly his hand grabbed the round wood of a door handle. Turning, twisting and pulling Hogshead through, he shut it behind him and ran out of the hut. Crashing into the back of Hogshead.

'Come on, move!' snapped Firkin in the dark. 'Out of the way. If we're caught . . . !'

By way of an answer Hogshead handed him a brush, three filthy dusters and a tin of polish.

Firkin's heart sank . . . a broom cupboard!

The plasma snake of pure thaumic energy writhed and spat at Practz's spine, pouring its energy into every molecule. The room crackled and sparked with alarming electric tension as he strained at the cosmic reins and steered the horses of time. His face sparkled with perspiration and the wildly discharging sparks emphasised the worried expression inhabiting his face. Apart from the pyrotechnics, the flashing ice-blue power surges and the overwhelming hum of the Thaumatron, little seemed to be happening. It had been an inordinately long time that Practz had been casting and apart from a pool of tallow below one of the candles there was still nothing to show for all his thaumic effort. Courgette fidgeted anxiously with her leather bracelet as she stared at the ominously empty chalk Pentagon and waited. Phlim stared at the runic dial on the wall. It showed a power sink of twenty point eight thaums. If they didn't get contact soon then . . .

Phlim's thoughts flashed to the nano-sprite in the Thaumatron. Had it worked? Had it found the problem? That was the only snag with nano-sprites, they did a great job but you never knew when they'd done it, or indeed what they'd done. Was there a problem with the temporal location matrix amplifier? If there was, Practz might never find them. He could be searching until the Cranachanians broke down the doors.

Suddenly Practz yelled with shocked relief and pointed to the centre of the Pentagon. A pair of shimmering shapes glowed in magical translucence above the chalk markings. The shapes grew as if they were being drawn from an immense distance. Clouds of icy vapour billowed from the pentagon obscuring the images. Phlim worked hard at the control wall, checking carefully the reading on the thaumic flux densitometer. This was the most critical part of the manoeuvre. One slip now and God knows what would end up in the pentagon. A flash of ice-blue light sparked through the room, crackling off the candlesticks. The smoke cleared a little allowing a glimpse of whatever was approaching the Pentagon.

Practz closed his eyes concentrating on the spell. If my concentration is broken for one second . . . he thought.

Oops, he thought a second later, if I've just thought that then I must have broken concentration to think it. Oh No, there goes another second of lapsed concentration! Stop it! Concentrate! Blue sparks careered off his finger tips, plunging into the clouds and growing shapes. Phlim's brow furrowed as the runic dials read a twenty-four point eight gigathaum power drain. She wasn't built for this! he thought in a surge of panic.

Suddenly, Practz's voice screamed out, the power consumption shot up to twenty-five gigs and a blinding blue flash issued from the centre of the Pentagon. Two solid figures materialised four feet above the floor, squealed and plunged into the swathes of blue smoke. The plasma snake of pure thaumic energy crackled and disappeared. Practz fell to the floor vanishing into the blue pea-souper. Dawn and Courgette coughed and spluttered.

After the deafening furore of the last few minutes the girls' coughs sounded small and fragile. Phlim murmured a few incantations and a small opening appeared in the ceiling. It hummed gently as the blue smoke was drawn through its slatted grille. Gradually the plumes of smoke cleared, revealing the scene by the Pentagon. Practz staggered shakily to his feet rubbing his head with a mixture of pain, confusion and concern at the state of the two figures lying motionless on the cold stone floor. He walked towards the two boys.

At the sound of the steps Firkin turned, panic in his eyes, brandishing a brush as if it were a sword ready to remove all-comers' heads. Hogshead hid behind a grubby yellow duster.

'Get back! I know how to use this!' snarled Firkin, not recognising Practz.

'It's all right, you're back,' said Courgette, kicking Dawn's shin, to stifle her spluttering giggles at the boy's reactions.

'I, I . . . oh!' stuttered Firkin, looking around blearily, suffering from the combined effects of utter confusion, bewilderment and met-lag.*

Phlim disappeared into the corridor and sprinted off to the Thaumatron Bay. He had a horrible feeling it wasn't a hundred per cent right yet.

Having lit the tallow candle and scoured the broom cupboard with mounting disbelief, Turgg Inyeff (soon-to-be-famous-investigative-reporter) scratched his head and stared accusingly at a bottle in his hand. He had seen those intruders, he told himself, two of them. He had chased them, the throbbing in his bruised shins from falling over the chair proved that. He'd been certain that they had hidden in the broom cupboard, there was nowhere else to go. They were there. As real as I am, weren't they? So where were they now? He glared at the bottle again. The drink! he thought. No, it can't be! Alcoholically induced hallucinatory robbers! No, no! They're supposed to be pink pachyderms or nothing.

Suddenly, he came to a decision. There were only two ways to clear this up. He stared once again at the bottle in his hand. I don't need this stuff, he thought. I can live without it. I *could* give it a rest for a while and see what happens . . .

* A phrase coined by Prof. Phiynmn following his first temporal displacement jaunt. Metapsychic time-lag, frequently shortened to met-lag, refers to the feelings of nausea, tiredness and utter exhaustion felt after a long-haul thaumic transfer.

With a deft flick of his wrist he cracked open the bottle and began pouring the contents away, down his gullet. Grinning madly as the liquor burnt at the back of his throat, he staggered wildly around yelling, 'Orlright, I'm re . . . hic . . . ady. Cummn getme!'

Firkin's head was spinning. He wasn't entirely sure whether it was due to the after-effects of the Deja-Moi field, the met-lag or the strain of answering the incessant barrage of questions being hurled at him.

As the inquiries had probed and prodded for what seemed far longer than it probably had been, several themes and items kept cropping up. These, in no particular order of importance, were the Cranachan Council Officers, Fisk, Khah Nij, Frundle and Gudgeon, lemmings, where lemmings live, where they die and what happens to their skins afterwards, Snydewinder and the Rhyngill–Cranachan border. Somewhere in that heap of information was a time, or an event, which linked Firkin, Hogshead, Courgette and Dawn to the Thaumaturgical Physicists of Losa Llamas and protecting their guilty secret from the Cranachanians.

'But where?' moaned Courgette, pleading with Practz. 'We've been through it a hundred times. What have we got to do with it?'

'I still don't know,' he reluctantly admitted. 'I only know that you *do* have something to do with it. I saw it in one of my local field prescient spheres.'

'Oh, great,' sulked Hogshead, wringing the grubby yellow duster with anxious frustration. 'We've got just over two days before the Cranachanians smash the doors in and destroy everything and we have got the job of trying to stop them because he saw us in a crystal ball! . . .'

'Prescient sphere!' protested Practz.

'. . . and we *still* don't know what in Rhyngill we're after!' continued Hogshead desperately. 'We're doomed, I tell you. Doomed!'

The room fell eerily quiet after Hogshead's outburst.

Everyone was feeling the strain of the mounting pressure. Suddenly Practz leapt up from his chair, ran across the room and began searching the shelves. 'Of course,' he shouted. 'Why didn't I think of it before? It's obvious!' He moved the cage containing the small mammal-like reptile, which sulked as it was woken and promptly chewed the head off a nearby praying mantis. Practz scoured the shelves. 'It's here somewhere. It must be.'

'What's he looking for?' mouthed Firkin.

Courgette shrugged and looked equally baffled. Hogshead's finger made a small circling motion level with his temple. Dawn smirked. 'Hah! Here it is,' cried Practz eventually as he pulled a large book down off the top shelf, coughing as he blew the years of accumulated dust off it. 'Now let me see,' he mumbled absently as he thumbed through the large book. '1033, 1028, 1012, oops too far.' He flicked back a few pages, '1025, here we are. Now, er j, k, l. Legend, legislation, lemming. Got it!' He looked baffled as he read the entry in the almanac.

'What's it say?' demanded Courgette.

'Lemming. Small migratory rodent desired for its soft yellowish fur. See also "Two-and-a-half-minute war".'

Practz instantly began flicking the pages to 'T'.

'Aha! Two-and-a-half-minute war, (slang). Name given to bloodless border skirmish between Rhyngill and Cranachan. Believed to have its roots in dispute over lemming-skin ownership rights. Victors: Cranachanians. See also "The August Strategy" and "The Gin Ether Convention" . . . Oh!'

'Lemmings?' said Firkin, his voice dripping with incredulity. 'They had a *war* over lemmings?'

'Makes a change from religion,' mused Practz tapping his chin.

Hogshead's brow scrunched up into line upon line of earnest concentration as he racked his brain for what he was sure would be a vital piece of information.

'Remember Snydewinder?' asked Hogshead suddenly, his

eyes brightening like a scientist on the verge of a discovery. 'Where did he come from?'

'Castell Rhyngill,' said Dawn, eager to appear intelligent.

'No, no, no. Before that,' pressed Hogshead.

Dawn pulled a face.

'Oh no! Of course – it's been staring at us all the time,' said Firkin, realising what Hogshead meant, remembering the awful events in Rhyngill, eight short months ago.

'What?' demanded Practz. 'Tell us!'

Firkin turned and stared at Practz with a face of stone. 'Fisk and Snydewinder are the same person. He was a Cranachanian spy. After the war in OG 1028 he arrived in Rhyngill and began manipulating King Klayth for Cranachanian gains.'

'So what?' said Practz mystified by this apparently un-related revelation.

'*After* the war!' urged Firkin. 'Don't you see? That's the link. It's up to us to stop the war ever happening!' His words sounded like a death sentence.

'And right now we've got two and a half days left!' said Practz gloomily.

'I think we need a plan,' said Courgette. 'Anybody got any brilliant ideas?'

Whipped down from the high north, a light flurry of snow gambolled and frolicked through the crevasses and preci-pices that made up the Talpa Mountains. It frisked over a sharp rocky pinnacle and rolled with gay abandon down the steep, snow-covered scree fields of Tor Teehya, without a care in the world. It plunged on, whirling and swirling round the massive giant base of Tor Telleeny, through the Foh Pass and abruptly stopped dead, its icy nose pressed against solid black, like a frozen fly to a tinted windscreen. The bare grey granite of the cold mountains was suddenly gone, replaced by the smooth black leather gauntlet of Barak, clutching his horse's reins and carefully guiding it over the rough mountain path. The progress was slow here, the utmost care being required to prevent a misplaced footfall tipping any of the Stealth Troopers into the fathomless canyon inches away to their left.

Schmorgg Gashbord brought up the rear of the team, grumbling to himself at the speed of progress. Being seven foot two and having been brought up with the Cliff Diving Troopers of Thkk he was not scared of heights. Spending his second birthday kite-hunting puffins solo had soon cured him of any vestigial vertigo he may have had.

Unfortunately, Captain Barak and his second in command, Vice-Captain Troop had not benefited from any of these confidence-enhancing experiences and so were now clutching desperately at the sheer rock face on their right, pathetically grateful for its solid presence. Through eyes blinkered from the gaping chasm away to their left Barak peered ahead. In a few yards he could see that the path widened. Then, he thought, there's nothing between us and Losa Llamas. Except a few blisters from the riding.

The tension in the room was rising and tempers were beginning to feel the strain as Practz and Phlim attempted to forge some sort of a plan out of the ideas flying about.

'I can't see anything wrong with trying to break into Cranachan and kill King Grimzyn before the war starts,' said Firkin defiantly. 'It worked last time.'

'No it didn't,' shouted Courgette. 'I don't remember the state funeral of King Klayth. Do you?'

'Well, that was different . . .'

'Anyway, you haven't got an army or enough . . .'

'Look, why can't we have a more peaceful way?' asked Courgette plaintively.

'Like banners and demonstrations and stuff,' mocked Firkin. 'Oh yes, I can just imagine it. Wearing purple, green and white sashes, strutting about in little circles waving placards saying "Cranachanians go home" or . . .'

'No,' interrupted Courgette angrily. 'What's wrong with "Fights for Women"?'

Firkin looked shocked.

'But I meant something more covert,' continued Courgette. 'Something like intercepting information and messages, orders telling the troops what to do or . . .'

'How?'

'Well, they use pigeons. We could use mist nets to catch them.'

'We'd have to have huge nets to catch *all* the pigeons. Too risky,' said Firkin.

'I like it,' said Practz. 'Suitably devious. But it's too impractical.'

'We could put little plates of breadcrumbs out and sneak up behind them when they start eating and hit them over the head and . . .' said Dawn. Firkin glared at her. Somehow his expression told her to 'shut up and stop being so stupid. If you can't think of anything useful then don't say a word. Sometimes you are *so* embarrassing!'

She stared defiantly back at him, her eyes burning into the nape of his neck as he turned away, as if to say, 'Well you're not doing so well yourself. Kill the King! Invade! Yeah sure, you and whose army? Think of something useful, something possible, you berk!'

'We need to stop the messages earlier. *Before* they're sent,' said Courgette.

'What? – like steal Grimzyn's quill so he can't write?' said Hogshead.

'Cut his hand off!' said Firkin angrily.

Dawn tutted and shook her head.

'No!' said Courgette forcefully. 'Anyone can write a message and pass it off as the King's, can't they? What makes it special? How does anyone know that a message telling you to do something is *really* sent by the King?'

Practz looked at Courgette, he had a feeling she was on to something.

'Signature?' suggested Hogshead.

'More special than that,' she answered. 'An item of which there is only one. Used on every letter, every document.'

Practz waited for the answer. She had it. He could see it in her eyes.

'I haven't a clue,' moaned Firkin. 'But I suspect that you are about to tell us!'

'A seal!' said Courgette firmly.

'What's the King want with an aquatic mammal?' asked Phlim and instantly wished he hadn't.

'Seal. As in sign, seal and deliver,' said Courgette triumphantly.

'Brilliant!' enthused Practz. 'We'd not only stop them sending messages to themselves but we could send false information. Perfect!'

'I thought it was *stand* and deliver,' mused Firkin.

Hogshead raised his hand slowly and said, 'I hate to put a damper on the proceedings but what's it look like?'

'Black and shiny, about six feet long, streamlined for a sub-aquatic life and . . . ow!' said Phlim, receiving a swift thump from Practz.

'It'll be a ring, I expect,' said Practz remarkably calmly. 'He'll wear it all the time.'

'So how are we going to get it off his finger, assuming that we even get that close?' sighed Hogshead. 'This is getting worse,' he added under his breath.

'When he's asleep,' suggested Dawn.

'When he's in the bath,' said Courgette.

'We could hack his finger off,' suggested Firkin helpfully.

'. . . and how would whoever stole it manage to escape? It wouldn't take him long to discover the theft,' added Hogshead, thinking of the annoyance displayed by Turgg Inyeff. And they were only looking, that time.

Something hard to catch, thought Hogshead. A mouse . . . no. Liable to get stamped on, might cause too much fuss . . . a ring . . . something to carry a ring . . . an animal that carries things . . . donkey . . . no . . . elephant . . . be serious! Something you would expect to find in a castle . . . how about . . .? Yes!

'We could accuse him of theft and hack his whole hand off,' said Firkin.

'No!' said Hogshead after a few minutes. 'What about birds? Practz, could you do that? Could you send us back as birds? We'd be in disguise and we could escape easily.'

'I don't see why not.' He looked at Phlim for confirmation. 'I'd have to modulate the chrono-morphogenic field but that shouldn't present too many snags. It would be fine.' Phlim hoped the destiny valve could stand it.

'That's settled, then,' said Courgette. 'Let's go!'

A few minutes later, fourteen years previously and four feet above the floor of the private chambers of King Grimzyn, a thin wisp of icy-blue fog seeped into appearance as if an invisible private eye was exhaling a lungful of tobacco smoke from beneath a transparent panama hat while holding the room under observation. A couple of drags later two boys appeared, hovered momentarily, then collapsed as the fingers of gravity found a hold and tugged. As the pall of blue fog began to dissipate a squidgy rustling and popping noise announced the disappearance of the boys and their instant replacement by undistinguished-looking pigeons as the secondary chrono-morphogenic field slipped into action. Firkin stood on his disturbingly spindly-looking legs and peered around at the room. Having eyes on the sides of his head pulled everything in at the edges like a fish-eye lens. It made him feel as if his head were about to explode.

It was a large and well-furnished room featuring an enormously squat four-poster bed, several large chests containing ceremonial clothes, and four pairs of large arched windows offering unparalleled views of the main courtyard and distant mountains equipped to furnish the casual travel-ler with all manner of winter pursuits including skiing, bobsleighing and penguin hunting. Two sturdy wooden desks stood strewn with parchments, documents and maps. There were two doors in the room, a heavily armoured one that led out into the corridor and away into the rest of the

221

palace, and another that led to the place of King's ablutions. A small room with all the paraphernalia required for maintaining a suitably regal head and body while all about you were losing theirs. Gentle wafts of steam floated out of this room as the King wallowed in his monthly bath. King Grimzyn was regarded as something of an eccentric when it came to personal grooming, he was known to partake of the pleasures of the tub once a month whether he needed it or not.

'That you, Fisk?' snapped a voice hollowly as the King heard the baggy thump of two boys dropping four feet onto solid tiles. The King often held his monthly meetings whilst in the bath. He found it helped him think. He was expecting his Chief of Internal Affairs at any moment to discuss the final expenses that would be incurred in the ensuing war with Rhyngill and what plans had been made to offset said expense against the massive profits to be reaped from monopolising the entire lemming-skin trade. He was expecting a two-season turnaround and substantial profits in the third. Wars were expensive things, but then so were fur coats! He had looked long and hard at the receipts and costings from several of the most recent wars and military incursions with a view to trimming costs. He compared the expenditure on weapons, artillery, information gathering, soldiers' wages, replacement of weaponry, artillery, etc. and was stunned by what he found. The single largest expense in any given military operation was catering. As soon as an army pitched camp anywhere overnight, a stand-up buffet was frowned upon, and a full sit-down job for a force of six whole platoons, three battalions, eighteen squadrons of horse guards . . . well it's surprising how soon it all mounts up.

'Fisk, that you? Stop dithering about and get in here. You're late!' boomed the voice of the King.

Firkin the pigeon shuffled his wings and walked off along the floor. He took one wobbly avian step forward, squawked with surprise and almost fell over. As he moved his leg his neck shot forward in a strange pecking gesture. He put his claw down shakily and looked around in bewildered confusion. He tried again, picking his claw up and slowly moving it in front of him. Just as slowly but very forcefully his head and neck reached forward. It was as if the tendons controlling his legs and his neck were wired together somehow so that every foot motion was matched with a similar head motion. He trilled a soft trill of annoyance as he realised that unfortunately that was the way pigeons were made. Hogshead tried to walk and also discovered the cruel trick of nature. No wonder pigeons always looked so miserable.

'Fisk, what are you doing out there, man?'

Trilling and cooing with extreme irritation as he tried to keep focus on anything whilst walking, Firkin made his way to the nearest mountainous desk. He stood on the floor of the chamber and looked up at the unscalable skyscraper of drawers, handles and cupboards before him. There was only one way up.

'Fisk!'

Nervously he unfolded his wings. He surveyed the double expanse of grey feathers and felt a definite twinge of pride as they spread easily at his command. The reach of his new flight surfaces was far more than his arms had ever had and when he wasn't thinking they dropped and touched the floor. He knew how to fly of course, he had watched many birds flit past him during his time as a human. It must be easy, just flap your arms about the place. If a bird could do it, Firkin felt sure he could also manage it. Up, down, up, down, no problem. Strangely enough, now it came to the business of actually taking off he realised that he hadn't a clue.

'Fisk? Can I hear pigeons?' shouted King Grimzyn splashing gently.

Hogshead looked about nervously and gestured at Firkin to hurry up. Firkin thrust his wings down in a huge experimental powerstroke and stirred up a tiny cloud of dust. His newly clawed feet lifted onto their sharply hooked toes,

223

but otherwise he didn't move. He tried again, this time starting the stroke from higher. With his elbows almost touching and his chest feeling as if it was about to explode he pushed down hard. His wings sliced through the air, slapped the floor hard, reflexively surged upwards, clapping at the top of the stroke and pushed again. Slowly, in the least ergometrically stylish flight since the demise of the pterodactyl, Firkin staggered into the air. His wings clapped at the top of each stroke and feathers flew wildly. It was more of an effort than he had anticipated, he felt certain he would get cramp soon. After a few frantic flaps with the aerobatic grace of a jellyfish he began to pant furiously, he looked down and saw that he was only a matter of inches above the floor. He gritted his beak, crossed his claws and pushed harder. Somehow, more by grim determination than sleek aerodynamic streamlining and with all the aerial panache of an old grey dishcloth, Firkin clawed and flapped his way skyward. Miraculously, and with utter disregard for the rudimentary knowledge of pitch control, yaw correction, lift/drag co-efficients and muscular power-to-weight ratios, he landed finally in an unceremonious panting heap of feathers on top of the King's writing desk

Far down the corridor, outside the highly armoured door, a pair of extremely pointed, steel toe-capped boots marched with purposeful strides towards the King's chambers.

Hogshead looked up at the immobile form of Firkin and cooed and trilled a series of helpful encouragements. Firkin's claws answered with a rude gesture as he struggled upright and began to look over the desk. Bottles of ink seemingly of all colours stood in neat rows next to a quill set, containing the blades and snippers needed to turn a humble feather into an instrument of exquisite communication. Firkin shuddered as he saw the blades. A pile of blotting pads stood in the corner and hundreds of bent bits of metal wire nestled in a small pot. On the right of the desk stood a tall wax candle in red and a large taper to melt it. Firkin searched carefully around the sealing-wax, he searched the whole desk top.

Desk planners, jotters, blotters, everything a desk should have was there. Everything that is except a royal seal. No matter where he looked there was no sign of it.

The click of metal-tipped soles against stone tiles grew louder. Time was running out. Urgency winked in the corner of Firkin's eye as if to say, 'Remember me?'

Firkin strutted gingerly over to the edge of the desk, keeping careful note of the proximity of his tail feathers to the flames from the candles behind him, and peered over. Directly below him was a drawer. With a struggle he lay down on the desk top, stretched one leg gingerly out over the edge and scrambled, in an extremely awkward and grossly unnatural position, to find the handle. Slowly, with much avian cursing he eased the drawer open. Hogshead billed and cooed encouragement from below as the expanse of wood slid painfully slowly out. Firkin looked inside and his heart fluttered with excitement. There in the middle of the drawer, flung with the nonchalant contempt of extreme familiarity, lay a highly embossed gold ring. The seal of the King of Cranachan glistered goldly. Wasting no time, Firkin hopped into the drawer, his claws closing around the ring. He had it! Squawking happily at Hogshead he launched himself at one of the windows. Once through there they could easily soar away to safety. He landed on the huge stone sill and watched as Hogshead struggled artlessly into the air, flailing inelegantly to join him on the sill. Panting in a very uncharacteristically non-pigeon-like way the pair stared with horror at the window. A quarter of an inch of vitrified silicates stood between them and freedom. And it was locked. They could clearly see their way out, they could dimly hear the outside world, but they could not reach it. So close and yet . . .

Hogshead began pecking at the shiny transparent surface in claustrophobic panic. Firkin scratched impotently at the huge metal handle holding the window shut. They had to get out. So much hung on it.

Suddenly the door burst open and the tall, thin black-clad figure of Fisk, the Chief of Cranachan Internal Affairs, strode into the chamber. He froze as he saw a pair of pigeons.

Pigeons! he thought gasping back the shock. I hate pigeons!

Firkin and Hogshead shuddered involuntarily as they saw the figure from the past. They had to escape and fast. Firkin clawed frantically at the stubbornly immobile handle, desperate to move it, unable to shift it.

'Fisk! What're you playing at!' bellowed the King from his bathroom.

'I, er. Sire, do you know there are two pigeons in your quarters?' said Fisk in bewilderment.

'What?' cried the King, followed by several large wallowing splashes as he hauled himself from the Imperial Tub.

Hogshead butted the window-pane desperately.

Accompanied by the pattering of water on stone tiles King Grimzyn appeared in the bathroom doorway, wearing a large bathtowel and a look of extreme irritation. Firkin clutched the seal in his claw and pecked at the handle.

'The seal!' yelled the King. 'The damn thing's got the seal! Stop it!'

Fisk leaped forward across the room as the two birds launched themselves unceremoniously airwards. The black-clad man, eager to impress the King stifled his fear of pigeons, channelling it into hate, grabbing at Firkin with a large black gauntlet, clipping his wing, sending him spinning onto the far desk, knocking pots of ink in all directions. The King yelled with anger, snatched a pillow off the bed and ran at Hogshead, trying to swat him to the floor. In a second Firkin was airborne again, spraying spots of ink in all directions, flapping inelegantly out of Fisk's reach. Carrying the seal and being unused to flight, the effort was beginning to tell. Firkin's flight muscles felt tight, seconds away from cramp, almost as if he was using the butterfly stroke to outswim a ravenous killer whale, whilst fully clothed. In a sea of syrup. His time in the air was becoming extremely limited. Time was flying infinitely more successfully than he was.

Hogshead was also in trouble. The King swung his pillow as Hogshead raced for a corner. He turned, banking sharply, and disappeared in a flurry of feathers beneath a several-hundred-pound soft white meteor. The King shrieked victoriously and ran to the grounded bird. Firkin's concentration faltered, Fisk leapt and swiped with his gauntlet, catching his tail feathers, putting him into a sharp spiral dive. The black and white tiles of the floor spun hypnotically as Firkin plummeted earthwards, reeling in an uncontrolled descent, whirling in a giddying stomach-wrenching spiral. Flapping ineptly, he knew he had lost control.

King Grimzyn tugged the stifling pillow off Hogshead and ran backwards in shock as a dagger of a beak lashed out, pecking at his bare toes. Fisk turned quickly, snatching Firkin from the floor, tightening his grip around his wings. Hogshead pecked and snatched bravely, losing dozens of feathers in the mêlée, attacking the King's feet and keeping him, literally, on his toes. Suddenly, without warning, Hogshead was plunged into darkness, pinned to the ground, flattened under the weight of the King's bathtowel. He flapped and cursed but the wet towel proved too big and heavy, pinning his wings to the cold stone floor. They were caught. Firkin struggled in Fisk's vice-like grip, but he had both his wings in a ring of leather gauntlet leaving only one of his legs free. The now-naked King picked up the seal from the spot where Firkin had crashed and calmly put it back in the drawer. Firkin fumed, struggling wildly and pathetically as he watched the King close the drawer and stuff Hogshead into a pillowcase. Fisk stared hard at Firkin and sneered at the bird in his hands. As the looming, and hated, face approached him Firkin's temper rose, snapping as forces within him took hold, urging him into action, driving him to kick out against the sneering face of his aggressor. His spindly leg fell short of the mark but the reflex head jerk snatched his beak forward in a slashing deadly arc. The stabbing weapon attached to the front of his head lashed forward at the face of Fisk. It surprised Firkin quite how fast

227

he had moved but in a split second, the hard, head-butt he expected ended in a soft squidgy, messy collision as his beak pecked deep into Fisk's right eye. Fisk reflexively hurled Firkin away, screaming in anger and agony, clutching at his useless eyesocket, yelling and writhing in grotesque blind agony. Firkin hit the far wall and, still stunned, was quickly and expertly bundled into a pillowcase too.

Fisk screamed with rage and sprinted blindly out of the King's chambers, blood smearing his cheek, as two guards snatched the supposed-pigeons out of the room, dragging them down the corridors, round corners, down stairs and into the belly of the Imperial Palace Fortress of Cranachan. In the dark, bouncing interior of their makeshift prison Firkin, still dizzy and only just beginning to be allowed the luxury of aching all over, trembled apprehensively as he wondered what the future would hold now. Incarceration he would imagine, or the inside of a pie!

Oh no, he thought. Not again!

In Cranachanian social circles 'upwardly mobile' meant exactly that. The higher up the social ladder one climbed, be it in terms of wealth, power, corruptive influence or just straightforward blackmail and murder, then the correspondingly higher the position that one was allowed to occupy on 'The Hill'. The Imperial Palace Fortress stood regally impregnable above the whole of Cranachan, and below the escarpment, arranged in order of respectability, spread the rest of the town, the least respectable infesting the furthest outreaches of the whole seething mass.

In one of the dwellings of the *nouveau riche*, i.e. within a hundred yards of the escarpment or spitting distance whichever was nearer, the final preparations were in progress for a very special party. Under the watchful gaze of a portly man with slicked-back black hair, calmly stroking a large white long-haired rat, penultimate checks were being made. Squadrons of even larger men in sharp suits, fitted with bulging padded shoulders, ensured that everyone on the guestlist was who they said they were, and that everyone who was 'good for business' would attend. An invitation to a party at Khar Pahcheeno's house was an invitation to be kept, at all costs.

Tonight's party was very important to him and no expense had been spared. An internationally renowned quartet had been booked to play in his specially built marble auditorium. He had ordered a sit-down buffet for thirty-three of the most eminent civilian citizens in Cranachan, featuring the usual plethora of dips, quiches, salads and savoury snacks as well as the more exotic delicacies of barbecued Ammorettan Death Lizard, puff adder pancakes, dragon-eel delight and, as a special treat for his daughter, a pot of Lemming Mousse, imported especially from Rhyngill. It was an extravagance, he knew, but for his daughter Mhar-Rheanna's fifth birthday, it was worth it. After all, why make bags and bags of money from grossly illegal extortion rackets, dubious arms deals and drugs rings if you can't spend it on someone you love?

And he knew Mhar-Rheanna would love it.

He'd told her to.

Firkin and Hogshead sat miserably in a cage and stared about them. How long they had been there was almost impossible to tell. More alarmingly, so was how long they would remain there. Contact with Practz in Losa Llamas, fourteen years in the future, was impossible. All they could do was wait. But what if they were too late? What if the Stealth Troopers had invaded Losa Llamas and destroyed the Thaumatron? What then? Firkin's back ached, his head still throbbed and his claws were battered beyond any manicurist's skills. He cooed in pathetic misery as he looked around again. The bare prison they had been flung into was only one of dozens that lined the walls of this room. A small trough hung on the front of the bare wire cage and was filled with dried seed, some of which had begun to germinate. A wire door was latched from the outside and impossible to open. Around them, in other cages, other pigeons scuffled about in subdued, miserable silence. Hogshead rubbed his bruised and battered wing and nursed a broken claw.

Beyond the cages, out on the edge of earshot the disembodied voices of people moving backwards and forwards in busy ways floated out through an open door. Despite his bruises, Firkin's curiosity was piqued as he broodily wondered at their business. Through a hole in the wall pigeons landed bearing messages in little tubes attached to their legs and left with replies or orders.

'Here's another message from Rosch Mh'tonnay,' said one of the orderlies whose job it was to untube the message and pass it on to the relevant party. 'He says he's nearing the half-way mark. But the villagers are getting restless.'

'What's 'e doin', anyway?' asked another voice floating ethereally out through the door to the main Cranachan Communications Centre.

'Dunno really,' answered the first one. 'Summat to do wi' lemmin's.'

Suddenly Firkin was alert, sitting bolt upright and nudging Hogshead to listen.

'What's that got to do wi' diggin' half a mountain away?' asked the second voice.

'Well, they jump off 'em, don't they?'

'I thought they grew on trees,' said the second voice.

'What do?'

'Lemins.'

'Oh no! You're thinkin' o' lemins. Not *lemmin's*.'

'Oh yeah!'

Firkin's thoughts flashed to the valley high in the mountains where he had grown up and to Franck who had told both him and Hogshead about the way he had discovered lemmings. How he had turned from failed gold-prospector to successful fur-trader almost overnight. And for the first time Firkin realised that he had never found out how Franck had gone from the heights of success to the depths of destitute existence. He made a quick calculation.

OG 1025. Right about now Franck would be just about getting ready for the third lemming season.

Suddenly the cages above him were rattled and bashed as a black gauntlet was dragged across the doors.

'Aauwwk!' yelled the man behind the gauntlet. 'Auwwwk!' he squealed as he bashed the cages harder. Birds flapped and fidgeted nervously as the scratched and damaged face of Fisk sneered into their cages. His right eye was covered in a hastily prepared eyepatch, a temporary fore-runner to the studded black-leather device that he would have made for him. If he had his way all the pigeons would have been destroyed. Now! His eyesocket stung wickedly as he stomped about noisily.

'AAAUUWWWKKK!' he yelled again and stormed into the small communications room.

'A message!' he snapped. 'Take it down!'

'Sir!' answered the first voice with surprising efficiency.

'To Secret Agent V. Langschweinn, Rhyngill . . .'

Firkin's lower beak dropped as he heard that name. Vlad! The pale blue face shot into his mind and smiled a pointed smile. What has he got to do with . . .

'Require current update on Rhyngill troop movements. Stop. Urgent. Stop. Reports of lemmings massing early in mountains. Stop. Must move fast. Stop. Fisk.'

Firkin could not believe his ears. That message could mean only one thing. The war was only hours away, days at the absolute maximum. The war they had to stop. And they were powerless to prevent it. Completely and utterly powerless.

Firkin stared accusingly at the cage front and the bare metal floor beneath his clawed feet. If his wingtips had possessed hands he would have been rattling the bars, white-knuckled, as he yelled for release. Instead he sat cooing pathetically. He had failed miserably. There seemed to be no hope. He squatted on the cold wire floor and wished and wished that the ground would open up and swallow him.

As Fisk swept past the wall of cages out of the Communi-cations Centre, shrieking and swearing with his usual degree of fanatical madness and evil panache, two battered pigeons, one splatted with ink and the other with a broken claw and a bruised wing, quietly and mysteriously vanished fourteen years into the future.

From his high saddle on his trusty war-horse Khah Nij peered across miles of scrubby tundra into the distance. Behind lay the snow-lashed peaks of the Talpa Mountains; ahead, just creeping over the horizon, lay the edge of the forest of Losa Llamas. Tonight, at the end of another hard day's ride, the Cranachan Imperial Stealth Troopers would break out their tents, light their fires, raise their flasks and make camp outside the forest ready for tomorrow's final push and certain victory. If their prize was a fiftieth as effective as Arathoostra and Fisk would have him believe, then, by nightfall tomorrow, ultimate power would certainly be his. The power to rule, to terrorise, to dictate! The power to treat borders as the ephemeral, arbitrarily devised divisions they were, the power to ride roughshod across any defence thrown shakily before him. Above all, the power to conquer! . . .

If, however, the truth happened not to live up to the heady power-soaked predictions he had been whipped up to expect, then the satisfaction of removing all of Fisk's vital organs, one by one, in public, would also be his. Either way, the next couple of days were lining up to be a lot of fun.

Whistling tunelessly to himself as his hulking muscle-bound steed strolled nonchalantly across the grouse-ridden tundra, he considered idly, given the choice, purely on a hypothetical basis, which of Fisk's many and varied organs would he derive the most pleasure in removing first.

Far away, buried deep beneath the Forest of Losa Llamas, out of sight and earshot of the mass of approaching Stealth Troopers, a Ninth Aeon Deja-Moi Master fizzed, crackled and vibrated riotously as twenty-two point six gigathaums of magical energy throbbed and surged through his body. The chalk Pentagon on the floor glowed with ultramarine flashes and cerulean scintillations, ice-blue clouds once again exploded from an invisible point as two figures flashed into existence, materialising four feet above the cold stone and collapsing in a heap on the floor. One was splatted liberally with ink and the other nursed a broken fingernail and a bruised arm.

Firkin was up and talking almost immediately, utterly unaware that he was, as he had been as a pigeon, totally naked. He had questions, he had answers and he had vast tracts of seemingly impassable wastelands of problems to cross. And there was so little time! Not even for met-lag.

Dawn squeaked an embarrassed giggle and Courgette turned very pink as both she and Hogshead realised, at the same time, that Hogshead was also naked. He flushed, folding his knees in front of one another to hide himself.

Desperately, almost without taking a breath Firkin plunged into a whistle-stop summary of the goings-on he had just experienced, albeit fourteen years ago. Phlim handed Hogshead his lab-cloak and passed Firkin a towel.

Courgette, Dawn and Practz nodded as they listened intently. In a matter of moments everyone was up to date with everyone else.

'. . . but what can we do about it all?' asked Firkin desperately. 'Very soon they'll be at war over the lemmings and we've got to stop it!'

'Yes, but how?' asked Hogshead.

'I don't know! I feel so stupid. If only we had the seal,' shouted Firkin.

'Calm down,' soothed Courgette. 'Shouting is getting us nowhere. We must try to think.'

'I've been thinking for the past fourteen years and I still haven't come up with anything,' said Firkin feebly.

'Any ideas, Practz?' asked Courgette.

'Well, the only thing that I can think of is that people only normally actually come to blows and fight for one or more of three things: revenge, love or greed. I can't see that the first

233

two apply in this case so it must be greed. Are lemmings worth much?'

'Their skins seem to have been, fourteen years ago,' said Firkin.

'Valuable enough to go to war for possession over?'

'But that's silly!' said Dawn, and was promptly ignored by the head-scratching, worried-faced group of brain-storming thinkers struggling with a problem that seemed to have an answer about as soluble as an average walrus.

Suddenly, and extremely unfortunately for any passing warm-blooded sea-dwelling mammals with tusks, Practz seemed to have found the nitric acid of an idea that just might work. 'That's it, then,' he said. 'It's all down to money again. The easiest way to stop this for good would be to remove any value the skins have.'

'Eh, like damage them, or paint them blue, or something?' said Firkin. 'That would be impossible.'

'Flood the markets with cheap imports,' said Courgette helpfully.

'Where from?' said Hogshead. 'They only grow in the Talpa Mountains.'

'How can we get people not to buy them?' asked Practz.

'Tell everyone they're dangerous,' piped up Dawn.

'Oh yeah, like they bite you if you're not careful! Don't be daft!' snapped Firkin.

'No wait a minute!' said Courgette. 'That's not as daft as it seems. It might just work . . .'

The four men in sharply cut evening suits strolled nonchalantly up to the huge white door of Khar Pahcheeno's Mansion, their instrument cases held tightly across their chests. The black goatee beard and long flowing hair of the leader shook as he tugged at the handle, ringing the bell to announce their arrival. From deep inside, the sound of footsteps could be heard as one of *The Undertaker's* staff marched towards the door and eased it open. He stared imposingly at the four musicians, barking, 'Yeah. Whaddah y'want?'

'Er, hi there,' stuttered the lead fiddle player, glimpsing a flurry of activity past the large man's shoulderpads. 'I'm Nhyjje. We're the band.'

'Go round a da back way,' grunted Fhet Ucheeni from inside the doorway, his slick hair glistening in the lowering evening light. 'You need a da sound check, eh?'

'Nah, 's all right,' sniffed Nhyjje, 'the boys an' me've jus' come back off tour. Full 'ouse t'night?'

'Mansion. 'Ees not a da howze. 'Ees mansion!' glowered Fhet Ucheeni, the pin-stripes on his suit glinting with alarmingly menacing sharpness.

'Whoa yeh. Wha'ever y'say, mate,' muttered Nhyjje, backing away and heading off around the back under the watchful and deeply mistrusting gaze of the thug at the door.

A small gate led through a tiny arch and opened into the back garden. The cellist whistled appreciatively as he saw the expanse of bushes arranged around the edge of a tightly cropped green lawn sporting small stone cherubs and over thirty chairs, five tables groaning under a mass of food and a gleaming marble bandstand at the far end.

'Keep it down will y', Lhoodvigg,' barked Nhyjje as he saw the angry glares lanced at the cellist from the seemingly endless rows of catering staff lurking by the mansion.

'Sorry, boss,' Lhoodvigg answered nervously, fumbling with the tips of his wing-collar shirt. 'It is impressive, though.'

'Jus' be a bit more careful. We don' wanna do nowt to upset 'is nibs t'night. It's a special day,' reminded Nhyjje stroking his beard. 'If this gig goes all right, we could be playin' 'ere more offen.'

'I hope there'll be some of that grub for us,' muttered Vhulfgang salivating hungrily as he stared longingly at the groaning tables laden with food. 'My glissando goes all to pot if I'm hungry.'

'Your glissando's never out of the pot,' muttered Lhoodvigg in a whisper calculated to irritate the crumhorn player as much as possible. It did.

'You've some need to talk!' countered Vhulfgang. 'Since when have you got the vibrato right on that final arpeggio in Queazx's "Erotic Symphony in B minor", eh? Come on, tell me once. Last Tuesday it was all over the place. Sounded like you were playin' a sea-sick cat with the screamin' abdabs. An' then there was that time when . . .'

Vhulfgang's voice faded away as he closed the door to the dressing-room in the back of the bandstand and they unpacked their instruments and began to tune up.

Throughout the mansion the whirlwind demon of preparation whipped its frantic way, arranging, sorting and re-arranging in readiness for the party to come.

Courgette looked pleadingly at Practz and begged to be allowed to go with Firkin and Hogshead.

'I'm sorry, but your shoulder isn't healed yet. It would be too dangerous,' he said as soothingly as possible.

'But I'll go mad here waiting to find out if they succeed. I need to be there in the thick of it. Let me go,' she protested.

'No. You can help here. We'll need all the hands we can get. It's going to get busy enough right here, don't you worry.'

'It's all right, Courgette, the two of us will be enough,' said Hogshead. 'Any more and we'll be spotted.'

'Can we go?' pressed Firkin. 'We are just wasting time,' he added and stepped into the Pentagon. Hogshead joined him. Phlim, grateful that there was not going to be any fancy secondary chrono-morphogenic fields to mess with, readied the Thaumatron, checked the runic dials, the talismanic charts, the thaumostat, and began to flick his wrists and arms in strange ways, summoning the power, stirring the soul of the big generator. The hum in the room began to grow.

Suddenly the door burst open and a panting technician ran in, a wild look in his eye.

'They've broken through! The Cranachanians are in the forest. Don't panic! Don't panic!' He scuttled around in a few little circles then fled the room almost as quickly as he had entered, echoes of 'They're coming. Don't panic. Don't panic!' fading slowly.

Practz looked like a four-year-old who has been told that Christmas has been cancelled. 'They'll be here by nightfall,' he said simply. 'You have eight hours at the most. If the Cranachanians destroy the Thaumatron there is nothing I can do to help you.' Somehow, the flat calm of his voice made the situation feel even more dangerous. 'It's out of my hands. It's up to you. Good luck.'

Dawn looked at her brother with the same expression she would use if her pet fish had just gulped its last gillful of water.

Phlim made the necessary digital motions and the fifteen gigathaum beam shot from the wall into the base of Practz's spine. The room hummed with electric magical tension as the power rose and sparks crackled off Practz into oblivion. His eyebrows looked like frozen caterpillars as a sheen of sparks rippled across them. His hair and cloak billowed uncontrollably, lashing forward and back as if driven by a hurricane force. The air in the room tasted thick and metallic. Phlim ramped the thaums up rapidly and was soon reading off twenty point eight gigs as Practz adopted his now-familiar position, floating a quarter of an inch above the floor. Then Practz flexed his fingers, barked a final command and Firkin and Hogshead disappeared in a flare of silver-white light and plumes of ice-blue smoke. An emptiness filled the room as all their thoughts and wishes followed across the trackless temporal wastes.

Their thoughts had a common theme.

The end had begun.

Tempus Fugit

Even though they were prepared for it, the shock of appearing four feet above the ground and fourteen years in the past was still immense. They quivered momentarily before gravity caught up with them and the current time flow settled around them. One thing that was constant in all this chronoperatic time-wandering: no matter what year it happened to be, the ground was as hard as ever.

How much time they would actually have to put into operation the plans that they had dreamed up fourteen years into a still-mysterious future in Losa Llamas they really hadn't a clue. The constant threat of something at either end of that fourteen-year span going wrong, preventing them escaping, trapping them here in this past, unable to return to the time they had left, waiting to get back to a future they had vanished from only moments before, hung over them like a mocking evil demon, dogging their steps, fighting to distract their every thought. They had to do what they could in the time available. And that meant now.

Hogshead was grumbling to himself as he rubbed his back.

At that moment a shabby figure dressed in an extremely greasy-looking rain-cloak shuffled down the alley towards them staring wildly at a small notebook, like a monk with an illustrated copy of *Fornication for Fun*. Even in the gloom of the alley his eyes shone with the light of a man hungry for more. Without looking he unlocked the door to his hut and disappeared inside. A moment later a yellow tallow candle spluttered into life and cast its excuse for light around the room.

Perfect timing. Perfect placing. Practz had got it right. Their target was before them, all they had to do was make him believe everything they were about to tell him. A straightforward and immensely simple task? Had Turgg Inyeff happened to have the trust of a new-born spaniel and the gullibility of a particularly stupid guppy, then it would have been. He didn't; it wasn't.

Blissfully unaware of the rows of pitchforks working furiously to empty the carts of doom and stack barnfuls of odds against him, Firkin stood, rubbed his bruised backside, knocked on the door and awaited the reply.

'Go away, I'm busy,' came the barked reply from inside.

This was not the answer Firkin wanted to hear. He was here for a reason, he had things to do, definite things, vital things. And he was damn well going to do them. He liked the future the way it had turned out; it could be better, it could be a lot worse. Right now, fourteen years away, he knew that the future was teetering on the edge of an inconceivably deep abyss of disaster, and somehow he had to do something about it. Gritting his teeth, he pushed the door open and walked into the grim and unfathomably untidy interior. Hogshead, still grumbling under his breath, followed.

'I said, I'm busy! Get out!' barked Turgg Inyeff, rolling his sleeves up in preparation for Firkin's forcible ejection.

'Wait! Wait!' protested Firkin waving his hands desperately. 'Surely you're not too busy to pass up the scoop of the decade!' He aimed straight for what he hoped a desperate down-at-heel journalist longed to hear.

Sure enough, Turgg's ears picked up. 'Scoop?' he echoed.

'Scoop. Front page stuff. A story that goes right to the top. Scandal on the hill,' he winked and jerked a thumb towards the Palace Fortress.

Turgg was nervously rubbing his hands, almost salivating with anticipatory excitement. 'Tell me more!' he snarled with the expression of a starving hyena being offered a freshly butchered sirloin steak.

'I happen to know that your interest lies in the direction of the skins of certain mountain-dwelling rodents,' said Firkin secretively. Turgg nodded. Half-suspicious, half-eager, open and listening.

239

'I've got some information that shows there's more to them than meets the eye,' he said and shut up.

'What d'you mean?' asked Turgg. 'What information?'

'Information that will affect everyone. Information that has been the victim of a cover-up,' lied Firkin through his teeth. 'I want the truth to be known. I want it out in the open!'

Hogshead nodded conspiratorially throughout this, catching Turgg Inyeff's eye, reinforcing the web of tangled lies which Firkin was spinning with arachnid ease.

'If I tell you now,' whispered Firkin, suggesting the information would be better not overheard by 'other ears'. 'If I give you the whole story, the whole scam, everything . . . how soon can it be in the *Herald*?'

'Well, I've got to write the story . . .' pondered the journalist.

'We'll dictate it,' snapped Firkin.

'. . . and it'll need editing . . .'

'How soon?' barked Firkin.

'. . . and my editor needs to clear it . . .'

'How soon?'

'Tomorrow morning.'

'First thing?'

'First thing. Now *tell* me,' said Turgg, sensing something hot.

'Front page?' asked Hogshead. Firkin glared at him.

'Have you ever heard of a phenomenon known as residual thaumic quotient?' asked Firkin looking mysterious.

'. . . Fee . . . nom . . . nomenmenon known as . . . what did you say it was called? Residual what?' asked Turgg looking up from the chewed pencil scribbling words across his notebook.

'Residual thaumic quotient! Look, just listen will you? We'll do the dictation later, all right?' Turgg nodded. Firkin glanced at Hogshead who stepped forward and continued hurriedly. 'Every living thing, no matter how big or small, has a piece of magic inside it that gives it its identity, makes it

240

what it is. Gives it its character. The part that allows birds to fly and stops squids trying, that makes plants photosynthesise during the day, that guides the cosmic pin to prick holes in the canopy of night. Magic's everywhere. Most of the time you don't know about it, you don't need to, it's just there in the background greasing the cogs, and smoothing the operation of life's busy machinery.'

Firkin stared in utter disbelief. Hogshead was laying it on a bit thick and was it his imagination or did Hogshead's voice have a strange echo to it? If Turgg Inyeff believed all this guff he'd be amazed.

Hogshead was still talking. '. . . when an individual dies, all the magic it contained is released and returns to the atmosphere to be recycled into other individuals. That's known as the thaumic cycle. It has been working perfectly since centuries before the dawn of time, ensuring the great cosmic cistern of absolute continuity never runs out of magic. Perfectly, that is, until very recently, relatively speaking, and a very short distance away from here. Something has gone terribly wrong . . .'

Turgg's curiosity stamped on the accelerator of interest, changed up a gear, opened the sun-roof and felt the swirling wind of intrigue blast through its hair.

'Sometimes some of the magic is left in the remains of the dead individual, a fraction of the magic that made that creature what it was. Something we sorcerers call the residual thaumic quotient.'

Firkin raised an eyebrow as he heard Hogshead's self-proclaimed title echo in the tiny hut. Suddenly, a pair of blue flashing lights appeared in the rear-view mirror of Turgg's curiosity as the highway patrol of caution shot out of a sideroad acting on a twinge of suspicion. 'Very nice, but what's it got to do with me?' queried the journalist, narrowing his eyes, sieving every sentence for the catch as warily as he would when faced with any randomly selected pair of Ghyee Yohvass Witnesses.

'Lemmings,' said Hogshead simply.

Turgg Inyeff sat bolt upright, took a swig from his flask and listened intently. Hogshead had said one of the words that held an almost fatal fascination for Turgg's insatiable desire for 'That Scoop'. Lemmings!* The blue lights faded and turned off as he pulled his thoughts back to the matter in hand, shifted up a gear and gunned towards the dangling carrot of International Front-Page Scoopdom.

Hogshead was talking again, 'Lemmings live in a valley with a high background thaumic quotient. As a result, they have an abnormally high residual thaumic quotient even after curing. Under virtually any other circumstance this would hardly matter, but with lemmings . . .'

'What? What about lemmings' residual thingummy?' pleaded Turgg, the image of the sensuously seductive maiden still glistening in his mind.

'It's having strange effects,' lied Firkin once again.

'Tell me. Tell me,' begged Turgg.

'Front page tomorrow.'

'Yes, yes, please!' implored the desperate journalist.

'There have been widespread reports recently of certain, peculiar and unexplained happenings linked to the wearing of lemming-skin during periods of full moons,' said Hogshead.

Turgg was spell-bound. For the first time in his life, listening to Hogshead's reverberative voice, Firkin wondered if that wasn't literally true. Was Hogshead using magic?

'What sort of happenings?' asked Turgg, desperate for the story. Hogshead had him. No need for frog-marching him to the brink of belief, he was following, ready, a sheep hungry for the green and pleasant pastures of top-flight journalism.

'Lemming-skin wallets leaping out of handbags and pockets, lemming-skin garters falling down, lemming-skin

* The others were murder, serial killer and, his favourite, sex! Especially when the latter was used in conjunction with words like 'kinky' or 'scandal' or uttered sensuously by a seductively becoming maiden staring longingly into his eyes, her moist, pouting lips whispering in the warm silver of a summer moonlight, 'Here, now, and all for you darling! . . .'

242

stoles jumping from bare shoulders,' said Hogshead, laying the mystery on thick.

Turgg slouched back in his chair, the magic of Hogshead's words shattered suddenly. 'Oh, come on! Is that all? I thought you had a *story*, not a blinkin' fairy-tale! Get out!' The mouthful of journalistic pasture tasted bland to Turgg's jaded, world-weary palate. No freshly crushed herbs of real political intrigue to liven it up; no marinade of murders; no fields of newly harvested serial killers; and above all, none of that essential ingredient without which *no* front page story can survive – the journalistic jalapeno peppers of sex!

'Wait, there's more,' said Firkin desperately, sensing the loss of the conversation, feeling the future slipping away, smelling the breath of the mocking demon of failure squatting on his shoulder.

'You've got five seconds,' grunted Turgg, unwilling to abandon a lemming story just yet.

'Unexplained suicides!' blurted Firkin, with a sudden flash of desperate inspiration. 'People wearing lemming-skin coats leaping off cliffs, tall buildings, bridges . . .'

'. . . happens all the time . . .' confirmed Hogshead.

'. . . er, for no apparent reason . . .' agreed Firkin, nodding feverishly, his head a blur.

'How come I ain't 'eard o' this?' asked Turgg suspiciously, the dash of intrigue working.

Firkin glanced quickly at Hogshead, then launched bravely on, 'Because, er, it's a . . .' he looked pleadingly at Hogshead.

'. . . it's a cover-up. Yeah! Of course, it's a cover-up, like you said, Firkin,' spluttered Hogshead.

Firkin wiped his brow. 'A cover-up because lemming-skin is new here and they want it to take off.'

Turgg Inyeff stared at the two boys as they pathetically embellished their story.

'. . . it happens at full moon . . .'

'. . . believe me, it's true . . .'

The longer the reporter remained silent, the more Firkin and Hogshead over-egged their fabricated pudding of lies.

'. . . stopped it being used in the Angstarktik . . .'

'. . . should be banned . . .'

Gullibility watched with horror as three and a half dozen more preposterous eggs of implausibility were hurled into the dessert of attempted deceit.

'Keep your ears open. It's all true . . .'

'. . . every word . . .'

'. . . cross my heart and . . .'

Suddenly gullibility heaved: it was far too much to swallow. It heaved again, clutching its hands to its mouth, standing shakily and sprinting off for the toilet. As it slammed the door in Turgg's mind, so the impenetrable steel shutters of disbelief and annoyance were drawn down, closing his mind to everything the two boys could say. Their time was well and truly up.

'Well, I'll certainly look out for falling wallets and countless plummeting bodies clad in yellowish fur coats. Thanks for tellin' me, I'll bear it in mind. I don't think.' Turgg stood up and in no uncertain terms showed them the door. 'Now, if you don't mind, I'm very busy. Goodnight.'

With a firm and very definite grip he hurled them onto the street.

Suicidal jackets, he thought. Why me? Why do I always get the raving nutters!

At almost the very same moment, deep inside the rambling mass that was Castell Rhyngill, a large, black rodent's eye gleamed with excitement. This eye belonged to one of the resident pack of black rats that lived in the castle kitchen. It didn't know why it was excited, merely that it was. This rat, along with the rest of the pack, had picked up on something in the atmosphere of the castle. Something almost tangible, a physical change in the mood.

Normally life in Castell Rhyngill in OG 1025 was, from the rat's point of view, pretty mundane. As the sun rose and people started to move about, so it was a good idea to stay hidden in corners, waiting patiently for a clear chance to dash

244

out and grab a carelessly dropped piece of food, or a crumb. But as the day ended and the castle began to sleep, so came the time when the rats held dominion. While there was no one to see them they had free run of the castle kitchen, and they took full advantage of it. Raiding the grain stores, hoovering up the day's crumbs from the kitchen floor, sampling the delights of the fruit cupboard. Nothing was safe. But they were also smart, and thus the perfect parasite. The rats never took too much to become a real nuisance and they protected the kitchen supplies from other, more harmful things, like packs of itinerant rats that carried all sorts of nasty diseases. *They*, the outsiders, deserved the name of vermin. The black rats in the castle kitchen were clean, healthy and above all happy.

Happy, that is, until a few days previously. Something had changed. The sun had gone down, in its normal way, and the rats waited patiently for the kitchen to clear. And they waited. And they waited.

Streams of people flooded into the kitchen, setting to work, incessantly cooking, repeatedly roasting. It didn't stop all night. Voices were subdued, people only talking if they had to. There was an edge to the activity, a nervous, desperate edge. This nervous excitement weaved and seeped its way throughout the whole of the castle, whipping itself up like a frenzied disembodied demon on a narcotics binge of excitement. No one was immune to its fever. Even the resident pack of rats in the kitchen twitched a little more nervously than usual.

But they didn't know why. Even if it were possible to explain it to them properly, the reasons for the mood in the castle would be way beyond the understanding of even the most logically perceptive rats.

The people of Castell Rhyngill were readying themselves for an immense act of violence. Their first in twenty-two years. They were preparing to go to war.

The rats would have been able to understand the violence aspect – a healthy rat is in no way averse to a cracking fight to protect its territory, or a tasty lump of reeking, blue cheese, against a pack of itinerant vermin. That is good, wholesome, old-fashioned instinct.

But war was a whole different kettle of mackerel. The concept of prearranged, premeditated violence at a given site and a given time was incomprehensible enough, but this lot were spending days beforehand running about making sandwiches for the journey! That, presumably, was what intelligence was all about.

Days ago it had started, and now the preparations were almost complete. The arms in the armoury had been cleaned, polished and sharpened; the footsoldiers' battle armour had been burnished, greased and, in some cases, let out a few inches around the middle; the war poets and artists had been re-commissioned to record the earnestly hoped for victory. And Brumas, the eighty-eight-year-old Commander-in-Chief of Culinary Supplies, Protector of the Fork of Fortune and one of the War Lords of Rhyngill, had received his all new, fully armoured, battle Bath chair.

By tonight everything would be ready.

Tomorrow was a big day.

'Why is it my fault?' protested Hogshead miserably.

'What were you trying to prove?' complained Firkin not waiting for an answer. 'That magic can solve all our problems.'

'It was working.'

'So how come he threw us out, eh?'

'It stopped working,' confessed Hogshead to his feet. 'But it *wasn't* my fault!'

'Whose fault was it, then?'

'I didn't have enough time to learn it all. The last three lines . . . I, er . . .'

'Yes?' snarled Firkin.

'I, er . . . forgot them.'

'Forgot them! Well, thanks to you and your memory, we're stuck.'

246

'Magic will work, you'll see,' said Hogshead, and he thrust his hands miserably into his tunic pockets.

Aimless, disheartened and utterly unsure of what to do next or where to do it the two youngsters wandered lost and alone through the stunningly dingy alleys of Cranachan's backside. Having paid little attention to the direction of their wanderings, Hogshead was suddenly surprised when a few idly floating notes of music strolled casually up to the doors of his brooding mind and invited themselves in for a drink. He shook his head as if waking from the sort of daydream to which teenage boys are particularly prone, and looked for their source, pricking up his ears as a few more notes floated over a nearby wall and into earshot. It sounded as if a string quartet was playing chamber music to a small group of gently snoozing people. Hogshead peeped through a crack in the crumbling wall and stared open-mouthed at the scene within. A lush lawn spread away from view, sporting life-size stone cherubs and ending in a small raised dais upon which the quartet sawed and blew merrily at their instruments under the protection of a large marble bandstand. The violinist stood for his solo, flicked his untidy mane of hair back out of his eyes, thrust his fiddle underneath his black goatee beard and launched into a screaming string of high octave demi-semi-quavers and searing forced harmonics. Most of the audience nodded their heads blearily in the numb haze of a hard evening's merry-making.

All, that is, except one. Beyond the rows of chair backs supporting lemming-skin coats and smartly dressed, dazed revellers, a little black-haired girl, sporting a large red ribbon on the top of her head and wearing a pink party dress sat on a chair, swinging her legs and fidgeting with boredom.

Suddenly, from deep within the subconscious murk of Hogshead's brain a tentacle of spontaneity slithered past his hypothalamus and squirmed into his action centre. He had just had an amazing idea. Without waiting for Firkin he scrambled up and over the wall, dropping quietly down into a border of low ornamental bushes that in a few years would prove to be a topiarist's delight. Firkin had no choice and in a state of panic followed, shocked by Hogshead's act of apparent madness.

'What are you playing at?' whispered Firkin as he settled down next to Hogshead. 'Have you gone mad?'

'Trust me. I know that I'm doing,' his friend whispered as he set off crawling quietly across the neatly cut lawn. Firkin was not old enough to know that when *anyone* says those particular words, the only sensible course of action is to run away terribly fast. He simply nodded. The wild violinist sawed away, completely engrossed in his music, wringing a searing high- octave solo from the ancient instrument. The audience nodded in dazed appreciation.

In a few nerve-racking moments Hogshead had reached the back of the audience and began to pull one of the lemming-skin coats off the chair back. It fell silently on to the damp grass, its owner snoozing gently on. In a flash Hogshead had bundled it up, dashing back into the border as the last cadence of music crashed a perfect fifth and the audience offered an inebriated ripple of groggy applause.

Hogshead stopped only briefly in the bushes, just long enough to don the coat and pick up a large rock. Firkin's eyes were wide with bewildered terror.

'What in Rhyngill do you think you're playing at?' he whispered angrily as Hogshead dashed past him. 'You'll get us caught. We shouldn't *be* here . . .'

Hogshead held his hand up, silencing Firkin. 'No time to explain,' he whispered. 'If I don't go and do it now I never will . . .'

'Do what?' croaked Firkin.

'You'll see,' he whispered. 'Just make sure everyone sees *everything*. It'll be front page news tomorrow.' He disappeared into the bushes and, keeping low, the sound of his progress masked by a jaunty little three-four number from the quartet, headed off towards the bandstand, leaving an utterly exasperated Firkin.

Hogshead trotted carefully and quietly through the thick

bushes, dashing unseen around the back of the large marble canopy that housed the quartet. At the far end, a ladder leaned nonchalantly against it, allowing access to the roof. Perfect! he thought. He took a deep breath, broke cover, sprinting the couple of feet from the bushes and quietly started to climb. In a moment he was stepping carefully onto the roof, clutching the rock. Part of his mind raced back into his memory, dredging for knowledge. Part wondered what he was doing up here. And part ran screaming into the banquet of good fortune, snapping wishbones from freshly roasted chickens, extinguishing acres of birthday candles in one breath and raising frothing glasses of bubbly to toast all the spirits of excellent fortuity.

From the far side of the garden Firkin held his breath as he saw Hogshead straighten up and walk towards the edge of the bandstand roof. The quartet played away obliviously, the audience snoozed, Hogshead trembled. He stood facing the border of bushes, dressed in a long lemming-skin coat, hoping he could remember everything he needed to. Especially the last three lines.

Firkin's face turned pale as he watched Hogshead stand right on the edge and look over. What was he doing? He'd kill himself if he fell from there. Or someone else if he happened to land on them. Was that the violinist, or was someone strangling a cat?

Under his breath Hogshead started to moan and squeal a low backwards mantra as he clutched the large stone and began to incant a spell. Suddenly, the little black-haired girl looked up and yelled. The music stopped and some of the audience rippled with automatic applause before another woman screamed, drawing their alcohol-sodden attention upward to the rotund figure teetering dramatically on the edge of the bandstand roof. Another ripple of applause started before it was realised that this was not part of the stage show.

Hogshead looked round, realised the time was absolutely right, placed the back of his hand melodramatically against his forehead and shouted, 'It's no use! I can't take any more!'

The whole of the audience stared in horror at the suicidal figure.

'I've struggled too long and too hard,' continued Hogshead. Firkin watched in shocked silence. 'Something is in my blood tonight. Pulling me, pulling me . . .'

The audience shouted protests and words of encouragement as they realised he was serious.

'Come down. It can't be that bad,' cried one.

'You'll regret it!' shouted another.

'Can't take any more what?' wondered another.

Fhet Ucheeni, the large slick-haired doorman, dashed inside to tell his master of the situation. Hogshead looked down at the sheer drop between his toes and hoped he could leap far enough to reach the bushes. 'It's pulling me!' he cried again, taking a faltering step nearer to the edge. Beneath his breath he was murmuring strings of backward-sounding words. 'Zhunfar terrack tack ito . . .' He stared at the rock hidden from the audience's view within the folds of his stolen lemming-skin coat. '. . . meso ghurnlick femtoshi . . .'

'My coat!' screamed a large woman at the back of the crowd. 'He's got my coat!'

'Sounds like he's got a cat as well!'

'It's pulling me . . .' shouted Hogshead edging nearer. 'I can't fight it. I can't go on . . . !'

Khar Pahcheeno rushed out of the mansion, grabbed his little daughter and stood looking at the bandstand roof.

'Come down-a from there,' he shouted uselessly.

A wave of cold clammy vertigo swooned over Hogshead as he shouted, 'I can't go on . . .' and without warning, still apparently muttering to himself, leaped off the roof in a defiant gesture of suicide. Firkin rubbed his eyes and stared in disbelief. Hogshead, clutching the rock, arced earthward towards the bushes, frantically reciting the mantra. '. . . mi tressk hhvvwrshh omb.' The ground surged towards him, black and unforgiving. Two women fainted as the barrel-like

250

figure of Hogshead hurtled towards such a wasteful end, flashing out of sight as he plunged inevitably groundward.

In the final few fractions of seconds before he hit the cold hard ground a thought flashed across his mind. Was that the way the last line goes? You had better have remembered it properly. Otherwise . . .

The last thing he saw before slamming his eyes shut and trusting to forces almost beyond his control was a large expanse of solidly black earth accelerating towards him. Surging faster and faster and . . .

Khah Nij watched as Kholin the Barbarian thrust his machete through another of the million verdant curtains of dense undergrowth that infested the forest of Losa Llamas. He turned to the frail and wild-looking ex-Thaumaturgical Physicist and barked a question at him. 'How much longer do we have to keep slashing through this repellent jungle?'

'Er, till we get there, sir,' Arathoostra answered, staring longingly towards their, still as yet unseen, destination.

'And how much longer will that be?'

'As long as it takes,' came the distant reply.

Khah Nij fumed. Getting a straight answer out of Arathoostra was like trying to knit eels.

'Are you sure we can trust him?' snarled Khah Nij at Fisk, jerking a thumb in Arathoostra's direction.

'Assuredly, sir,' oozed Fisk, rubbing his hands greedily. 'I have seen the prize that awaits us. I have witnessed their awesome power. I have . . .'

'Yes, yes. I've heard all that guff before,' interrupted the Head of Security and War, his temper seething fractions of an inch below the surface. 'What I want to know is, how long before we get there?'

Captain Barak's ears pricked up as he overheard what sounded like the makings of a good argument. According to Barak, any argument that involved Fisk being in the wrong against a superior force was undoubtedly a good argument. Especially if that force was a very angry Khah Nij. Barak had seen what an irate Khah Nij could do to various parts of the human anatomy. It wasn't a pretty sight.

'We'll be there befōre nightfall, sir,' answered Fisk.

'We'd better be. If I have to spend a night in this gnat-infested, flea-ridden jungle I shall hold *you* personally responsible,' snarled Khaj Nij, his teeth inches away from Fisk's ear. 'Is that entirely clear?' he added.

'Yes, sir. Astoundingly so.' Fisk swallowed nervously and decided against informing the Head of War that they were trekking through a multi-micro-climate sub-tropical forest and not, as he so simplistically referred to it, a jungle.

They were the type of horror-stricken screams, laced with shock and dripping with outraged revulsion, that no self respecting, soon-to-be-famous reporter could possibly ignore. The moment Turgg Inyeff heard them he knew he had to be there. In a flash all the nagging doubts, filling his head with restlessly disturbed thoughts, making him wander the streets like a dispossessed wraith looking for the answers, vanished. Like the strapping barmaid that inhabited The Gutter forcibly ejecting a host of drunken revellers at closing time, Turgg's mind swept questions and suspicions, such as 'What if they're right about the lemmings?' and 'How can I prove that they're wrong?' and 'Assuming they're right, how stupid will I feel when I read about it?' into the distant, clutter-filled recesses of his dirty mind.

He stood quite still for a moment, getting a bearing on the screams, then removed his black notebook from the grease-stained excuse for a rain-cloak he lurked within, licked the tip of his pencil, flipped open the notebook like a tax inspector about to detail a particularly juicy evasion and sprinted desperately towards the hoard of scoop-worthy screams.

In the back garden of Khar Pahcheeno's mansion, Firkin was up and running, unable to believe what he had just witnessed. The vision of a plummeting Hogshead flashed through his mind over and over again as he dashed through the forest border of ornamental bushes and raced towards the spot where he imagined Hogshead had landed. He hated to think what he might see, his friend's body twisted and distorted in a pool of blood, limbs wrested and mangled in grotesque mockeries of their former selves . . . He choked back the sickening thoughts and raced on. Rounding a bush, he suddenly stopped dead in his tracks, confronted by a sight that shocked him into silence. His jaw swung limply open as he stared at a scene for which nothing could have prepared him.

There, floating unsupported a scant two feet above the ground was a large soily rock making tiny little circles in the air. Draped across it, clinging on desperately, was an incredibly relieved-looking Hogshead. As Firkin appeared he rolled off and lay on the ground whimpering with shock and relief. A large brown smudge stained his stomach where the rock had been.

Hogshead suddenly grinned, 'I did it!'

'Did what? H . . . how?' said Firkin staring alternately at Hogshead and the gently rotating lump of rock.

Sprinting footsteps sounded behind the bush as the audience ran up, eager to witness the gory scene they expected to see. Hogshead gestured sharply at the floating rock, 'Hide that. Don't let them see it or it won't work!'

'What won't work? H . . . how?' stuttered a bewildered Firkin.

'Hide it!'

Limply Firkin stepped sideways and stood in front of the igneous satellite just as the first of the onlookers appeared through the bushes. Suddenly, Hogshead began to groan loudly, writhing in affected confusion, feigned pain and sham suffering as the crowd gathered.

'Is he all right?' asked a large woman festooned with jewels.

'I . . . I'm, er,' said Firkin staring wide-eyed at Hogshead and desperate for some sort of explanation.

'Where am I?' groaned Hogshead.

'You're safe now,' said the woman.

'Where's the cat?' shouted a voice.

'No! Stop pulling!' screamed Hogshead struggling to divest himself of the supposedly possessed coat.

'He's mad!' said one of the men.

'It was the coat!' yelled Hogshead, rolling his eyes for effect. 'It made me do it! Beware of the lemmings!'

'What's a-going on a-here?' demanded a voice as the crowd parted allowing a small squat man through. 'Eh? Whatsa da matter?' snapped Khar Pahcheeno. Firkin saw a brief wink and a grin flash across Hogshead's face and in that moment he realised why the corpulent figure writhing on the ground before him had hurled himself from the bandstand roof. He suddenly recalled the desperate string of wild fabrications they had flung at Turgg Inyeff.

'Why did you do it, son?' said the fleshy, jewel-encrusted woman, her forehead wrinkling in over-acted concern.

'Lemm . . . lemmmmm . . . lemmings!' screamed Hogshead, managing to produce a glob of frothy saliva at the corner of his mouth.

'What about a-da lemmings, eh?' pressed Kha Pahcheeno.

'They mm . . . mm . . . made me do it! They pulled me. Pulled me!' Hogshead thrashed a little more for effect.

'What's he talking about?'

'I didn't believe it myself,' began Firkin stepping in to offer a falsehood of corroborative evidence. 'Like you, I didn't want to comprehend. I dismissed what I now know to be the truth as a pack of wild lies. Until now. Once that coat glimpsed the moon it was too late. He had no choice but to follow . . .'

The group of people listened enraptured as Firkin explained all about residual thaumic quotients, using an impressively comprehensive list of utterly fictitious events worldwide. They pleaded for information, begging for ever more extravagant and gory tales. All the while, at key moments or phrases, Hogshead would moan, writhe or dribble. It was a stunning double act.

254

As the claims grew wilder and the crowd quieter, a figure lurked into the garden. Furtively glancing and licking the tip of his pencil, the embryonic investigative reporter approached the back of the crowd. This event was witnessed only by Firkin, through a tiny momentary gap in the crowd. Having practised spinning tales to Dawn and become expert at side-stepping difficult questions he steered his fictitious series of fantastic claims to a close.

'Is there anything we can do to help?' asked the jewel-festooned woman, knitting her eyebrows into cardigans of concern.

Firkin adopted a pleading expression and stared straight at her. 'Please, please *don't* tell anyone about this. Don't, whatever you do, tell the press. Keep quiet about it. It never happened all right?'

Hogshead moaned and thrashed about on the ground, rolling his eyes with terror. The audience's resolve was shattered.

The large woman blustered haughtily. 'This is an outrage! A danger to life. It is preposterous to think that we must keep quiet about it!'

'Please, you mustn't tell a soul,' pleaded Firkin as Hogshead groaned again. 'Above all, *don't* tell the press.'

'It would be criminal not to. I'm off to *The Triumphant Herald* offices right now!' shouted the woman.

'No need for that, madam,' said Turgg Inyeff, licking his pencil once again. 'Just tell me. I work for the *Herald*.'

In a flash, as the crowd clamoured to get their stories and their names in tomorrow's newsparchment, Firkin and Hogshead were out of the garden and away down the alley, leaving the coat and a rock spinning gently two feet above the ground. What the partygoers would make of that when they found it was anybody's guess.

Turgg Inyeff's pencil sped across the tiny notebook as it recorded the acutely enhanced versions of the tales Firkin had told. Unwittingly, this small group of people were writing the end of the lemming-skin trade, composing the headlines of its downfall, enscribing its economic epitaph, unknowingly sacrificing it to save the world from disaster fourteen years into the undiscovered country of their future.

The next day the sun rose over the Talpa Mountains, climbed effortlessly into the sky, rubbed its eyes, blinked once or twice, and peered down on Castell Rhyngill with mounting stellar curiosity. Something strange was happening. Must be, there was far too much activity for this time of the morning. The sun had been coming up here for, oooh centuries I suppose, and one of the things that it had come to expect, nay rely on, regular as clockwork was the stunning *lack* of visible activity in and around Castell Rhyngill until way after it was thirty degrees above the horizon. But this morning was definitely different. The air buzzed with excitement as people ran about their daily business and bent their backs to some mysterious task or other. The sun, baffled by the atypical flurry of activity millions of miles below, filed the phenomenon under 'curious human foibles' and continued placidly beaming, casting untold zillions of lumens into the vast and trackless wastes of unexplored space. It was not her concern, so why bother about it, and besides it takes about four and a half days, give or take a bit, for the light to travel back to her anyway, so it was all pretty much academic by now.

Down on the ground, it was as if a giant stick had been poked into an enormous ants' nest and wiggled angrily about. But this was Castell Rhyngill, the ants were people rushing to complete their tasks before the deadline, and the big stick, standing approximately six feet tall, wearing a large and immensely weather-beaten greatcoat with matching hat, peered out from behind a tatty, greying beard and an ophthalmologist's nightmare of a pair of bottle-green glasses. This stick went by the name of Franck Middin.

Right now he was amazed at the flurry and buzz of frenetic activity around him. He never would have believed anyone if they had told him he could have this much effect. Is this what power is? he thought, or just fear?

256

It hadn't taken the War Lords of Rhyngill, under the guidance of King Khardeen, long to reach the decision to don their battle-boots, polish their baldrics and embark on the road to warfare. Within a matter of hours of hearing from Franck, the prospector and founder of The Lemming-Skin Trading Co. Ltd., about the scheme being undertaken by the Cranachanians to steal all of the lemmings from under their noses, now in OG 1025, and in the future, feelings of righteous indignation were running high. Within a few more hours the rusting hulk of the Rhyngill war machine was kicked and cajoled into action and very soon everyone in Castell Rhyngill was involved in some way in the preparations. Much to the bemusement and chagrin of the rats in the kitchen.

And the surprise of the King. Two days ago Castell Rhyngill had been trundling merrily along under Khardeen's ruthless iron fist and excessively tyrannical manner. The people loved him. He commanded them to. Nobody ever complained – well, not for very long, anyhow. Everything was lovely, there was just enough torture to go round and the next spate of tithe raising was due next month. There were bound to be a few village torchings and a ritual sacrifice or two. Life had been simple then.

But, in the space of two short days, the whole of his world had been turned on its head. He was signing chits and orders, requisitioning parchments, agreeing to plans. He was spending money! He, King Khardeen, Ruler of the Kingdom of Rhyngill, Chief of the United Clans of the Foothills, Holder of the Most Spiky Glove of Tax Extraction and the Torch of Smouldering Retribution, he was *spending* money!

It was an investment, speculating to accumulate, to secure a safe and prosperous future, he told himself on this bright and sunny morning as he stroked the handlebars of his regal moustache and signed yet another requisition parchment. 'This,' he had been assured by the clerk to the under-secretary of the vice-accountant in lieu to the Chancellor of Rhyngill, 'was the last one.'

At last, thought the King, the money is spent, the time is upon us. Let me see what I have available to lead into battle.

He strolled towards the balcony of his private quarters, past the portrait he had recently commissioned and stared into the vast castle courtyard. He twirled his moustache contentedly as he surveyed all he would lead through the gates and into battle in a matter of a few short hours.

Foot soldiers streamed into the courtyard, their armour gleaming in the morning sun and lined up under the watchful eye of their Commander in Chief, the War Lord Lappet, Holder of the Key to the Foot Spa of Honour. Archers marched nervously into view and stood to attention below the hooked nose and beady black eyes of General Bateleur, Holder of the Ceremonial Greaves of Protection, the Bolas of Courage and also War Lord of Rhyngill. Cavalrymen steered their mounts into an impressive line of equine attack capability leading up to Colonel Rachnid, decorated for bravery and sporting the Shovel and Bucket of Forward Planning, and the Stirrups, Crop and Thongs of Discipline. From all corners, soldiers flooded to assemble before their respective War Lords.

With a mixed smile of pride and smouldering righteous indignation the King of Rhyngill turned from the window, his cape of office swirling in angry folds around his large black boots, reflecting his seething mood with graphic leather menace, and went to seek out his son, Klayth. He stomped on the floor once or twice for effect.

Imagine a black screen.

There is music. Fast music that sounds like it should be accompanying typewriters or massive ribbons of parchment streaming round rollers, between screens, past blocks of letters stamping inky words onto the off-white parchment as it races by. Stamp. Stamp. A picture appears. Hundreds and hundreds of copies of the same inky words being stamped onto a racing parchment. Stamp. Stamp . . .

The picture fades to a translucence.

The music rattles and pings onwards.
The blocks of letters stamp incessantly.
Stamp. Stamp.
In the centre of the picture a whirling off-white rectangle
appears. The music clatters on. The rectangle spins. Growing larger. Racing forwards. Swirls of black fade onto the
spinning shape. The music jangles irritatingly on. The black
grows deeper, solidifying as the rectangle slows and stops
off-centre. The black forms words now. Clear bold words.
Headlines.

NO LOVE LOST FOR LEMMINGS!

The music yaps on, rising in pitch, shifting a semitone of
urgency. Another rectangle spins forward. Blurred. Black
spirals. Letters. Headline letters.

SUICIDE SUITS – YELLOW PERIL LURKS IN WARDROBE!

Another semitone shift of clattering music. Another
swirling rectangle. Another headline.

GATECRASHED PARTY – BIRTHDAY RUINED BY SENSELESS SUICIDE STUNT

The next morning these headlines were everywhere. The
streets were littered with parchment-sellers yelling and
screaming about 'suicide coats' and 'wild wallets' that were
widespread amongst the people of Cranachan. All morning
people flocked to *The Triumphant Herald* offices adding
their tales of mysterious happenings to the growing body of
'evidence' and rumour. It was one of the amazing features of
human nature that once the balloon of 'truth' was inflating
people kept it going, craving the attention of the press,
adding their meaningless hot air to the litres already straining
at the gossamer skin of credibility. The more ridiculous and

259

improbable the stories printed, the more the sales rose. Throughout the day unbelievably esoteric stories appeared as the imagination of the people was fired and stoked by even wilder reports. Surprisingly, not once was the word 'hoax' used. The four-lettered pin that could burst the balloon of frenzied fiction, sending it slashing across the sky, blasting rude raspberries of denial, before landing in a wrinkled and embarrassed heap; that pin was kept firmly pushed into a dark corner of the drawers of everyone's minds.

Firkin and Hogshead were astounded by their success. In a matter of hours the whole of Cranachan was buzzing with rumours of the lemming-skin danger. Turgg Inyeff held news conferences every fifteen minutes. He had his scoop, he was enjoying his fame. Everyone in Cranachan knew the awful truth about lemmings.

The two perpetrators of the rumours stood in the main square in Cranachan, watching the droves of people arguing about the lemming-skin items they had recently bought, demanding refunds. The traders were up in arms, vehemently denying all of the claims made against them. Sale signs appeared as demand dropped and traders, like fish in a desert puddle, fought and thrashed to snatch the oxygen of their profits before the parching sun of panic dried the market up completely.

The two boys felt immensely pleased with themselves. There was no way that anyone would consider going to war over a pile of worthless skins that nobody wanted. They had done it!

They skipped joyously up and down as euphoria and relief rained down on them, splattering teacup shapes on the ground, gathering and running downhill in trickles, in streams, in torrents of joy spilling ecstatically over the edge of kerbs. They had won. The future was surely safe. Everyone knew how stupid it would be to go to war over the right to own lemming-skin.

Everyone, that is, except the people who really mattered.

Inside the ivory tower of the Cranachan Imperial Palace

Fortress life continued unaffected. Preparations were well under way for the forthcoming engagement with Rhyngill, reports were pouring in from their spies outlining details of troop movements, recent weapons build up, morale measurements. Facts flooded in. The Cranachan Information Agency scoured the goose-fleshy expanse of naked truth, collecting snippets of intelligence from along the entire length of the route to Rhyngill. They brought back accurate terrain measurements, graduated moisture read-outs, incline assessments, viaduct structural integrity and stress-test reports. They knew where every lump, every patch of mud, every hill and every dodgy bridge was. The CIA knew everything they needed to know to ensure the smooth and accurate deployment of Cranachan personnel and artillery, thus securing an easy, and above all, *outright* victory. Compiling and sorting this mountain range of information kept the CIA staff incredibly busy in their strategic bunkers deep in the bowels of the Palace.

Too busy to read *The Triumphant Herald*.

Until it was far too late.

Suddenly, a huge brass fanfare resonated across the crowded and arguing market square as the massive panel of the main Palace drawbridge creaked and rattled open, accompanied by a fusillade of barked orders and the sudden seismic rumble of an army on the move. The abrupt percussive onset of the regular thumping of thousands of feet shattered the chaotic disputes and haggles currently flourishing in the square, drowning them in a sea of dumbstruck shock as all eyes turned to witness the advancing spectacle.

Wearing the black armour of Cranachan, and displaying the colourful Banners of Insults, the loudly vibrant Flags of Offence and the gaudy Gonfalons of Mockery, their v-shaped streamers waving like two fingers raised in the eternally offensive gesture, the army moved out. Following smartly behind the King and three other mounted men, columns of troops stomped rhythmically forward in a highly drilled display of military arrogance. Each face wore the

261

well-practised, standard military battle sneer. Each throat growled military issue growls as they marched with infallible clockwork precision and impeccable muscular exactitude. Every man stood cocooned within his own private armoury, commissioned and worn with the certain unflappable knowledge that it would plunge the enemies' life into an acutely distressing sharp and spiky hell. Short stabbing daggers nestled in scabbards next to gleaming gutting knives, throwing knives and garrottes. Maces clanked against artfully honed axe blades and the shafts of six-foot pikes, short swords nudged bulging quivers of poison-tipped armour-piercing cross-bow bolts and two-handed swords lay temporarily safely scabbarded beneath round shields.

The noise was deafening as the army approached, horns blaring under a sea of brightly coloured flags, the banner of each section. Stealth appeared not to be in their dictionary of useful military terms. Why bother when you have an army of twelve thousand, six hundred and fifty-eight men? Each carrying at least four weapons, trained in the use of six and capable of utilising three different martial arts. At the same time.

Firkin shook pathetically as the army stomped past.

What was happening? It didn't make sense.

Fourteen years into the future, guided by the tall icy-eyed figure of Arathoostra, the mostly black-clad Cranachan Imperial Stealth Troopers approached the gates of Losa Llamas. Fisk felt excitement rise within him, thrilling as they reached the end of their route march. In a matter of a few hours all the power he had ever wanted would begin to be his. The Right Horrible Khah Nij raised his gloved hand, swatted another gnat from the back of his thick neck and halted the advance. One or two of the men slapped and scratched at various parts of their heavily beweaponed bodies as the resident gnats tried to increase the tally of red weals already decorating the Troopers' skin. Silence fell as Khah Nij peered suspiciously through the small, ornately painted and woefully unreinforced gateway, frowning as his practised eyes scrutinised Losa Llamas for the first time.

Precisely what he had expected to see he would have been hard-pressed to describe but this brightly painted, well kept, picturesque village in the middle of miles of verdant forest, certainly wasn't it. He looked for any tell-tale sign, any give away, any hint that this really was in fact the centre for all High Energy Thaumaturgical research. He saw none. He looked for any sign of life, any guards, any hint of a whisper of a security force. Nothing. A small brown bird flitted across the main square, chirping gaily as it alighted on a thin branch.

'*This* is Losa Llamas? What are you playing at? Do you take me for a fool?' snarled Khah Nij at the sneering face of Fisk. 'Why have you dragged us out here, over mountains, through miles of gnat-infested forest, to look at some second-rate tourist trap?'

Barak grinned as he sensed Khah Nij readying himself for a tirade of Fisk-destroying phrases, leading in time, he hoped, to the removal of at least one major organ.

'You've got to admire their ingenuity,' said Fisk, almost spitting the words, glaring loathingly at the tweely ornamental fountain trickling gently out of the mouths of two large stone dolphins.

'What?' snapped Khah Nij. Barak's grin widened. 'If you start extolling the virtues of neo-baroque cornicework or the artisan architectural idiom, or some other such nonsense, I will personally see to it that you are . . .'

'Sir, I was merely appreciating the remarkable cover they have here,' oozed Fisk smugly.

'Cover?'

'Yes. What better way of confusing your enemy than appearing as a tiny defenceless village, devoid of all aggressive tendencies and almost apologising for its existence?'

Fisk glanced at the frowning face of Khah Nij and smirked quietly. 'You didn't think we had come to the wrong place? You didn't expect floodlights, towers and miles of razorwire fencing did you?'

Arathoostra twitched impatiently.

'Which way in? asked Khah Nij ignoring Fisk's last jibe as best he could.

'Follow me,' said Arathoostra, scrambling off his horse with immense relief. Several tens of miles' riding had taken a painful toll on a backside unused to such stressful activities.

The mass of Stealth Troopers bristled in military anticipation and stomped down the ornately tiled path towards an immensely ignorable pinkish portico entrance with stucco tiling and a pair of shell-covered flowerpots nestling either side of the door.

Arathoostra waddled to a halt. 'In there,' he said simply.

Barak barked a swift order to Kholin the Barbarian. He saluted in reply, uncovered Miolnir, his trusty hammer, and walked menacingly forward, his winged helm shining expectantly. Entering the portico he swung the hammer once or twice, thrilling as he hefted its reassuring percussive mass, building up its momentum, then . . .

In a moment, the door was matchwood, the portico entrance shattered stone and plumes of pink plaster dust; the obstacle was eradicated. The Barbarian stood blinking in the cloud, surrounded by rubble, fragments of shattered wood, a confused spider and a colony of thirty-five very miffed wood-lice, his entire body and armour smothered with dust of a particularly fetching hue.

Eagerly, twenty-four pairs of arrogantly military feet swarmed through the shattered doorway and raced down corridors, axes hefted and swords drawn and ready.

The mustering square of Castell Rhyngill was full. The army had gathered and stood waiting for the arrival of their leader, King Khardeen, to give the order to advance. The War Lords of Rhyngill perched proudly on their trusty war-horses, ribbons gleaming on their chests, rewards from earlier campaign victories.

A hum of barely stifled excitement floated over the square.

It was a time to remember. In a few short hours, memories might be all that remained.

'Smell that excitement,' said General Bateleur breathing deeply and whistling through his sharply hooked nose.

'Is that what you call it,' snapped Commander-in-Chief Lappet, scowling at the General's horse shaking its tail after fertilising the mustering square.

'Reminds me of the Wars of the Rose-Hips,' mused Bateleur. 'What a scrap that was!'

'Strategic disaster!' snapped Lappet. 'Should have attacked at dawn. Used pincer movements not head-on charge approach. Surprised more weren't killed.'

'Those were the days of glory,' reminisced Bateleur.

Days of gory, thought Colonel Rachnid.

'Men dying on my blade. Wading through lakes of blood. Fountains of arrows. The crackle of roasting flesh as the dead burnt . . . Can't wait!' finished Bateleur.

A metallic rattling echoed as something was pushed out across the cobbles of the mustering square.

'You look back through rose-coloured spectacles,' said Colonel Rachnid, his blond moustache and goatee beard freshly trimmed this morning.

'Don't need spectacles,' growled Bateleur, patting his crossbow and loosing a freshly loaded bolt with a deadly twang. 'See the whites of their eyes, then fire. Never fails.'

A tirade of insults and irate rantings floated into earshot as Brumas was wheeled out in his newly requisitioned battle Bath chair.

'Whose white thighs are on fire?' snapped Brumas waving his ear-trumpet wildly. 'Eh?'

A brief flurry of confusion sounded in the ranks of Rachnid's horseguards as a figure slumped forward and slid off his horse. Bateleur's first victim.

'He's talking about crossbows,' explained Rachnid.

'Who? Eh? Whatseonabout?' babbled Brumas peering narkily about, shaking his ear-trumpet in frustration. 'Can't 'ear a thing through this. Useless it is! Useless!'

'Stick it in your ear,' said Lappet helpfully.

'Stick it where? Whatyousay, eh? Speak up if you've got anything to say to me. Not deaf you know!'

'Said stick it up your rear!' crowed Bateleur.

'Aye, where it should be, good. Not deaf you know. Hear that bird? Eh? Do you? A nightingale that is. Nightingale. Lovely bird . . .'

Brumas's senile drivel was drowned in a sixteen-trumpet fanfare from the main tower announcing the arrival of King Khardeen. He walked his stallion forward slowly, revelling in the sight of the entire Rhyngillian Army mustered and ready for action. A tiny face at a window high above the square watched his father walk on and stop before the gathered troops.

'. . . lovely chirruping.'

Brumas received a swift kick from Bateleur and silence fell across the square as everyone stood and waited for the King's Address. He stood in his stirrups, raised his voice and sang two long notes, the second an octave higher than the first. The keenly mustered army repeated the notes in answer. The King called again and like wolves at a full-moon meeting the entire army answered.

'Hi hooooooooo!' yelled the King for the third time.

'Hi hooooooooo!' answered the army, the thrill of their mustering song coursing through their veins.

The King turned his steed towards the high horizon of the Talpa Mountains and broke into full song as he led his army of three thousand men away into battle. 'Hi ho! Hi ho! It's off to war we go . . .'

As the cloud of dust from twelve thousand, six hundred and fifty-eight men, several horses and a host of wagons of supplies settled in Cranachan, Firkin stood in bewildered and pathetic shock. It had taken the best part of half an hour for the entire might of the Cranachanian Army to file past in grim battle mood, Firkin's hope descending deeper into the pits of despair with each new column of men that appeared.

The Rhyngillian Army's chances of victory against this lot in a fair fight stood about as high as a Fort Knumm Hand Maiden's morals. They would be outnumbered, out-weaponed and outright losers. The war seemed as awfully inevitable as ever. As preventable as premature hair-loss, and as avoidable as death. Firkin and Hogshead had come so close to success, so near to victory, so almost certain of saving the future from a tyranny too awful to contemplate . . . But close wasn't good enough. Fate laughed long and hard as it slapped Firkin and Hogshead's faces with the black-leather gauntlets of utter failure.

Firkin sat on the ground and buried his head in his hands. He stared at the dirt between his feet, groaning pathetically.

'What are you doing?' asked Hogshead.

'I'm sulking,' answered Firkin.

'But why?'

'Hazard a guess!' he blubbed. 'Because that's it. All over,' groaned Firkin. 'We've failed. *I've* failed. You *can't* change history.'

'We're not trying to change history,' corrected Hogshead, attempting to encourage Firkin.

'Well, we can't change the future. There's a plan, a scheme, an order to things that goes way beyond us. We *can't* change it. Forget about everything. Forget about Dawn and Klayth and Courgette. Forget it all. We tried and we failed. That's all there is to it! Close, but *no party*!'

'Pull yourself together. You can't say that,' snapped Hogshead. 'They haven't started fighting yet.'

'It's only a matter of time.'

'How do you know? It's not set in rock, is it? It's not one hundred per cent certain, is it?' asked Hogshead, his eyes glowing with desperate terrified excitement. 'Put your hand on your heart and tell me there isn't a chance . . . ! Can you?'

Firkin looked up. 'What are you trying to say?'

'It isn't over till it's . . . er, over. We can't possibly give up now.' Hogshead grasped Firkin's shoulder, pulling him round and staring into his eyes. 'Do you want to spend the rest of your life here? Do you *want* to forget Dawn and Klayth and Courgette? To deny they ever existed?'

'Of course not . . . but . . .'

'Neither do I,' snapped Hogshead, the coals of confidence flaring up, burning bright with the fires of action. His eyes flashed, reflecting the conflagration within.

'Are you just going to sit there?' he asked.

'Have you got a plan?' asked Firkin.

'Yes,' lied Hogshead. 'Come on!'

He pulled the limp, hopeless figure of Firkin off his backside, up from the floor and sprinted after the rapidly disappearing cloud of dust.

Quite what he would do when he found it was anyone's guess.

Fourteen years into the unknown future, in the cold stone cube of a room in Losa Llamas, Practz, the Ninth Aeon Deja-Moi Master and Thaumaturgical Physicist, turned away in horror from the image in the tiny crystal sphere. The Sneeke broadcast a tiny monochromatic image of the ruined portico, splintered doorway and rampaging herd of dust footprints swarming inside. His brow wrapped in angst, he spoke urgently to Courgette.

'We have about ten minutes at the most. If Firkin and Hogshead had succeeded we would know by now. What do you think?'

'Do it,' she said decisively, her eyes sparkling below her fiery red eyebrows. 'We've got one last chance! We've got to try.' She picked up a large bunch of bananas and thrust them into her bag.

'Be careful,' said Practz as Phlim worked his spells at the Thaumatron control panel, the hum in the room increasing as Courgette and Dawn stepped nervously into the chalk Pentagon on the cold stone floor. A small moist nose twitched gently, snuffling marsupially inside the bag on Courgette's shoulder. The hum rose further, the floor began to oscillate.

Phlim shuddered as he made the complex shapes and

configurations necessary to control the wave guides of the rising tides of thaumic energy.

Practz shrieked with exhilaration as the rush of fifteen gigathaums plunged into his spine, hovering, spitting and glowing, connecting him to the very core of the Thaumatron. Through him surged the power that drove Losa Llamas – a tiny clump of neurons in the back of his seething mind huddled in a circle, their axons waving as they asked, 'but for how much longer . . .?' His hair spat expectorant sapphire sparks into the air. His eyebrows shimmered like dandruff in ultra-violet.

The yells of the attack-frenzied Cranachanians echoed and bounced down the corridors as they swarmed in, led by Arathoostra. The complex maze of the thousands of tunnels, designed to confuse, was navigated with ease. They surged unstoppably towards the Thaumatron chamber.

Sparks crackled explosively off Practz's fingertips as the power increased to eighteen gigs. He began to vibrate, slowly leaving the ground behind. Cerulean tongues lashed the floor. Nineteen point five. His beard fizzed and crackled like a neon hedgehog at overload. The lines of chalk making up the Pentagon fluoresced with stunning ultramarine brightness.

The screaming Stealth Troopers, continuing to prove the folly of Cranachanian military nomenclature, sprinted round corner after corner, plunged down corridor after corridor, turn after turn, faultlessly guided by the combined power-crazed insanity of Arathoostra and Fisk, and stopped before a giant wooden door. It was barred and bolted into the rock walls with four-foot shafts of case-hardened, high-tensile steel and made from matured oak, cross-grained, three layers thick, pinned together with more fastenings than a perverted masochist's favourite undies. Hardly pausing for breath Khah Nij barked a few terse orders and Ahhrny unshouldered his axe, stepping forward with bulging biceps and a gleamingly sharp three-foot blade. Schmorgg Gashboard, stooping in the corridor, unzipped Splatter's carrying case and stepped towards the huge wooden expanse. In a moment he was joined by Kholin and Miolnir.

With the arrogance of a man who knows he has an invincible force, The Right Horrible Khah Nij looked up at the three men, their muscles straining with acute impatience and said quietly, 'All right chaps. In your own time . . .'

Hardly had his words entered his trachea, than three instruments of percussive destruction collided with the wooden obstacle before them.

Inside, the technicians shook with terror as the Cranachanian Heavy Artillery resonantly began its assault on the door, and with each directed hit counted away their final seconds.

Twenty point four gigathaums lanced into Practz's spine as he chanted the final pentameters of chronoperatic verse and crackled with harsh azure sparks. Phlim worked the control panel expertly, timing the final thaumic surge to absolute critical perfection.

Splinters of wood filled the corridor as Ahhrny, Kholin and Schmorgg hacked at the final barrier between them and the Thaumatron. Fisk, Arathoostra and Khah Nij rubbed their hands expectantly. All three knew that in a matter of minutes they would be through. With the source of the Thaumaturgical Physicists' power destroyed they would be worthless old men incapable of preventing the Stealth Troopers snatching their goal. The Ultimate Deterrent. *Rana militaria*. The Frogs of War.

Suddenly, with a cracking, splitting sound, the door shattered beneath the Cranachanian axe, hammer and club blows and the black hoard, like stygian riot-police, surged in.

Twenty point eight gigathaums powered through the stocky figure of Practz as his voice strained to be heard above the thrumming power band. He raised his hands, floating on the hissing cobra head of power, chanted the final phrases, shrieking as the energy blasted from his fingertips across to the Pentagon, enveloping Courgette and Dawn in a blinding surge of sapphire sparks.

270

In the Thaumatron chamber three white cloaks lay crumpled where they fell, stained with the blood of their wearers. Two broad swords and one gutting knife had tasted blood. Screams of terror rang through the chamber as the technicians were rounded up, shouts of wild mayhem resonating from the throats of their assailants. Driven on by barked orders and chaotic frenzy, the heavy artillery was brought to bear on the throbbing bulk of the Thaumatron, hundreds of pounds of percussive destruction swirling, like quixotically tilting windmills, above their heads.

Three deafening metallic clangs shook the chamber as Miolnir, Splatter and Ahhrny's axe hit home, shearing the main vacuum tubes and releasing clouds of hyper-ensorcelled steam. The enormous warriors writhed grotesquely as gigathaums of residual energy discharged through their mortal bodies, shorting away off their hair, blowing Kholin's helm across the chamber, fizzing round major organs, crackling through arteries, zapping away to earth. Tongues of power lashed frenetically out from the steaming slashes and died in a single final discharge, leaving the Thaumatron steaming and fizzing like a beached electric whale, and three charred and smouldering warriors, blinking as they admired each other's interesting new hair styles.

Far below, the spitting, hissing thaumic cobra connecting Practz to the heart of the Thaumatron stopped. He fell to the ground, the plug pulled, too weak to vocalise the pain he felt. He watched in appalled guilty dismay as the glowing Courgette- and Dawn-shaped aura of sapphire sparks suddenly collapsed into a tiny centre.

And blinked out . . .

Viewed from the air it was as if a giant organism with over twenty-five thousand legs had cut its way across the barren tundra of the foothills of the Talpa Mountains. An organism with an unerring sense of direction. A straight line of broken grass, trampled bushes and muddied streams lay between Cranachan and the four horsemen at the head of the massed

271

forces of the Cranachanian Army, five battalions of pike-bearers, three platoons of cavalry, an armoured explosives division and twenty-four regiments of regular soldiers. Large cages rattled along at the back on a series of wheeled carts. This was not a journey shrouded in stealth and secrecy. It was an immensely immodest show of strength designed to make the enemy tremble in its boots. The harder the Cranachanians stamped, so the theory went, the more likely it was that the opposition would turn and run screaming in terror. Khah Nij had never tried this tactic before and was interested to see if it did work as effectively as *The Strategist's Monthly* predicted in their August issue of OG 1025. The diagrams looked very convincing.

As they approached the valley where the battle was due to take place, King Grimzyn raised his hand high for all to see, then sharply clenched his fist. The entire army halted. There had been the sound of pounding rhythmic marching, then suddenly there wasn't. That's my boys, thought the King happily. Such discipline, such order. Khah Nij opened the August copy of *The Strategist's Monthly*, flicked to the relevant page and barked a series of orders at his sergeants. Frundle and Gudgeon watched with growing admiration as they passed their orders on, the twelve-thousand-strong army split into smaller groups, spreading themselves around the Cranachanian end of the valley, lining up like crowds packing an amphitheatre, turning the valley black. All eyes were on the King. He raised his hand, clenched his fist and miraculously the entire army vanished. Quite how they managed to find sufficient cover in the scrubby tundra Frundle never did find out, but before his very eyes twelve thousand, six hundred and fifty-eight troops – and assorted hangers-on – disappeared.

King Grimzyn smiled to himself and, followed by Frundle, Gudgeon and Khah Nij, rode away behind a boulder to wait for the advancing Army of Rhyngill to show up for what was sure to be their farewell performance.

From a safe distance high above the bottom of the valley two youngsters hid behind a large rock and watched in disbelieving horror as the massed Army of Cranachan vanished before their eyes. Just under a mile now separated this huge black-clad covert menace from the slowly advancing Rhyngillian Army. Everything was stacked in the Cranachanians' favour. They were fighting on home territory. They knew all the best ways to utilise the land to its full advantage. The CIA had surveyed every inch of this terrain. They had about fifteen times the amount of weaponry and each one was either bigger, sharper, heavier or just downright more lethal than anything the slowly advancing troops could even dream of. *And* they outnumbered the Rhyngillians four to one.

It was hopeless. Surely a foregone conclusion.

But somehow the Army of Rhyngill was happy. Well, the War Lords were. They laughed long and loud as the joys of war shone and sparkled like decorations upon their collective military breast. General Bateleur preened himself proudly as he marched his archers into battle, high on his horse, his hooked nose twitching in eager anticipation. The noble Lord Lappet, Commander-in-Chief of Infantry, twitched and vibrated with the tense excitement of a chess master lining up for a championship match, his eyes gleaming as he stared at the hundreds of pawns under his command.

He had waited far too long for a good battle. After twenty-two years of dull monotonous peace he had almost forgotten the delights, the thrills and spills that were all the fun of warfare. 'What a glorious day!' shouted Bateleur. 'Ready for the history books. Ripe for sonnets!'

Brumas, rattled awake as his Bath chair jerked over a stone, shouted, 'Soddit? Sod what? Whatseonabout, eh?'

'Sonnet!' yelled Bateleur, his long fingernails curling and uncurling around his reins. 'Songs of glory. Tales of Valour! . . .'

Brumas squinted ahead, ignoring the lyrical ramblings of

the General. 'Are we there yet? Eh? How far now?' he croaked. 'Eh? Is it much further?'

'. . . Poems of epic proportions!'

'Who's got epic proportions? Not deaf, you know?'

The army marched on.

Half a mile from the site of battle King Khardeen stopped his horse and watched proudly as his army marched past him. A tear sprang to his eye as the last soldier saluted and he turned away to ride up a mountain overlooking the field of conflict. From here he could watch his War Lords lead the men into battle. In a few moments he was high on his horse overlooking the entire vista. From this position he could observe all the army's comings and goings, the tactical deployment of Lappet's foolproof strategic manoeuvres, the devastating avalanches of Bateleur's archers' arrows, the shattering of the Cranachanian morale and the forthcoming Rhyngillian victory. From this point he could ride down in a blaze of glory to claim the winning crown of victory.

Or he could just slip quietly away if things didn't happen to go so well.

Out of sight the Cranachanian Army lurked in readiness. One or two of the larger and more devoted swordsmen could be found removing the last few microns of steel from their blades to achieve the type of ultimate sharpness that you could almost hear shimmering lethally. Others were checking the location of the throwing knives in their webbing harnesses, strapped around their torsos like military stays. Others still licked the feathers on their poison-tipped, armour-piercing crossbow bolts and made sure they lined up straight. In his excitement, one unfortunate bowman licked the tip and expired silently clutching his throat. Soon everyone had unhitched their shields from their backs and had all the paraphernalia of warfare, everything required for a good battle, ready and easily to hand. Everything, that is, except an opponent. And that wasn't too far away.

The Army of Rhyngill marched into the valley and, following an order from Commander Lappet, stopped and looked around. The valley ahead appeared to be lifeless, devoid of any opposition, safe.

'Where are they? All gone home? Scared 'em off?' croaked Brumas squinting across the apparently deserted landscape.

Suddenly, a ray of sunlight flashed off a lethally sharp metal surface half-way up the side of the valley. The Rhyngillian Army fumbled into military readiness and glared at the valley sides for other clues. Each had his sword drawn and ready. The familiar logo of 'The Ploughshare Military Recycling Co Ltd' on each of the swords glinted and exuded something of a feeling of security. Most of the men here had probably been using a portion of the very metal they now held only a few weeks previously as they tended their fields. The Rhyngillian Army was as ready for action as they would ever be, standing proudly in their 'Share-Wear' ex-agricultural boots. The adrenalin excitement rose, the tense hand of nervous energy gripping their throats as they waited for the order to attack. They wouldn't have much longer to wait before they glimpsed their enemy.

A fretful ripple of timorous nerves ruffled through the Rhyngillian Army as ahead of them a single, and apparently unarmed, Cranachanian footsoldier stepped casually out from behind a solitary juniper bush. He stood for a few moments feeling the admiring and envious glances of the Rhyngillians as they scrutinised his black armour, before slowly and significantly removing all of the weapons he had secreted about his person and launching into a complex series of gestures and facial grimaces conducted in the international mimic language of war as laid down by the Gin Ether Convention. (Terribly dry, awfully hard to swallow and gives you a splitting headache for the following three days.)

Whilst the entire collection of Rhyngillian troops, King Khardeen and Firkin and Hogshead watched in absolute incomprehension, the single footsoldier gestured to himself and held up four fingers, gestured to the Rhyngillians and held up one. Then he pointed to the pile of gleamingly lethal military hardware on the ground before him, held up eight fingers, then pointed to the Rhyngillians, clutched his sides and roared with laughter as, right on cue, the hidden Cranachanian Army gradually revealed itself. A black wave swept silently across the valley sides as they stood and held their weapons aloft. Sparkles of sunlight gleamed off the surgically sharp surfaces. The single footsoldier waved goodbye to the nervously trembling Rhyngillian Army. Somehow the meaning of the mimic gestures became horribly and transparently apparent.

The Army of Rhyngill was pathetically outnumbered four to one and each Cranachanian soldier carried eight times the weaponry, each part of which would probably be eight times sharper. They trembled worriedly in their 'Share-Wear' boots as the valley sides continued to turn from green to black.

Little moved inside the cavernous chamber. Wafts of smoke drifted in aimless translucency as the occasional tongue of sapphire flame lashed from the dying bulk of the Thaumatron. Steam fumed pathetically from the ruined vacuum tubes, gradually condensing to form slowly growing puddles of coolant. Splinters of wood covered the floor, fragments of the door – one quarter of which still hung precariously on one hinge, rocking gently. Away in the distant corridors that led down towards Losa Llamas' guilty secret the heavy military footfalls of the Cranachanian Stealth Troopers rattled ominously.

Ahead of them sprinted the desperate feet of Practz, Phlim, and five white-cloaked, white-faced technicians. Practz half ran and half fell as he headed for the pool. He hadn't recovered from the last spell, the power had been severed too soon and now the Thaumatron was destroyed he was virtually helpless. An old man devoid of all but the most rudimentary spells. Over the years he, like many of the other residents of Losa Llamas, had come to rely on the constant source of energy available at the flick of a spell. His own inherent magic centres had withered, atrophying back to almost nothing, to the unused organs they were derived from. Now he was virtually useless. Magically unfit.

He shook his head and tried to rid his thoughts of the two girls. Such a waste, he mused, oozing with remorse, they'd had their whole lives ahead of them, so much to offer, so much to live for. He stumbled round a corner, almost falling, he had sunk a lot of thaums into the spell and it would take him a long time to recover. He tried not to think of how long it would take Courgette, Dawn and the Gerund to recover if they hadn't completed the transfer . . . If they recovered at all . . .

The seven men rounded a corner in the corridor, plunged wildly down a flight of stone steps, round another corner and dashed through the door into the Chamber of frogs. They plunged into the dark musty interior, slamming the door behind them, starting at the low gurgling sounds that filtered into their conciousness. No matter how often Practz came here, and that had been a great many times over the years, he never managed to rid himself of the visions he had seen all those years ago.

The broken, bleeding torso of a technician flashed unbidden into his mind, spinning through the air, disappearing below the surface of the frothing, surging green water and into a frenzy of teeth. Over in the far corner another football-sized egg was slashed to ribbons, spilling amniotic fluid over the pile of unhatched, writhing eggs, and another frog swaggered into the world . . .

Phlim barred and bolted the heavy steel door, piling as much as he could find against it.

A hand reached up through the murky green surface, in Practz's nightmare vision re-running through his mind, its fingers grasping for help, opening and closing, stretching, then disappearing, snatched from below, the surface closing over it.

The five technicians passed Phlim as much debris as they could find. Secretly they all knew that this was merely postponing the inevitable, but it was a reflex action that had to be done. It made them feel better and it just might give them enough time. But for what . . .

A huge green head surged from the choppy water, knobbly, streaked with blood and slime. Its dark amphibian eyes focused rigidly on his, glistening as mucus reflected light, holding his rapt attention in beautiful deadly fascination. Its mouth opened. Teeth. Row upon row of dental death. Shining slippery saliva. A gulp. A motion. Sticky tongue lashing towards him. Closer. Deadly. Too close. The tongue of death lashed closer . . .

'No!' screamed Practz writhing on the floor. The images in his head too real. 'It must not happen!'

There's nothing to stop it now, mocked a voice in his head. It's inevitable.

No! his mind screamed. There must be a chance. There has to be a chance.

Not a hope! scorned the voice of Doom.

You don't know that. You can't be certain! screamed the voice of Hope.

You are doomed! DOOMED!

It's impossible to *know* that. Is it the inescapable truth? . . . answered Doom.

Well? Is it? squealed Hope, grabbing Doom by the lapels and shaking, demanding an answer. Is it inescapable?

. . . repeated Doom, swallowing hard, a guilty, shifty expression flashing across his face.

You can't say it? You can't! cried Hope.

There *was* still a microscopic hint of a possibility of a chance that somehow . . .

Shut up! yelled Doom.

An absurd image of a tiny white leveret being hauled kicking from a large black cylindrical item of headgear plunged curiously into view.

Hope, her hands white-knuckled around Doom's lapels, turned and fluttering her eyelids in the most ephemeral of winks, smiled and disappeared to beat Doom up a bit.

Firkin and Hogshead peered helplessly over the boulder they were hiding behind and stared at the two armies sizing each other up in the valley below. The Cranachanians had all the advantages. The result, it seemed, was a foregone conclusion. As the Rhyngillian Army moved slowly forward everything seemed lost. Firkin and Hogshead had failed. Twice.

In a little over fourteen years' time the Cranachanians would finally have in their possession the most powerful weapon ever created, the Ultimate Deterrent. There would be no stopping them. The battle, having been lost by the Rhyngillian Army, would be the last aspect of Rhyngill that King Khardeen would see as he slipped quietly away to a secret rendezvous with his Queen, leaving Klayth to begin his life on the throne of the Kingdom of Rhyngill.

The two youngsters felt incredibly small, utterly useless and, worse, completely alone. They were now destined to spend the rest of their lives fourteen years in the past, weighed down by the knowledge that both their missions had utterly failed.

Below them, watched through an almost dreamlike state of disconnectedness, the Army of Cranachan waved their weapons significantly at the Army of Rhyngill, and began to advance.

It was surely all over . . .

Suddenly, four feet above Firkin's head a flash of blue light sparked on and off as two figures materialised. They quivered momentarily, then dropped in a heap onto Firkin and Hogshead, sending a cloud of dust into the air. In a flash a hand wrenched open a small shoulder-bag, a voice shouted 'Go on!' and a small brown blur flashed through Firkin's and Hogshead's fields of vision.

'What the . . . ? How on . . . ? Oooh! Get off,' spluttered Hogshead from beneath Courgette.

Firkin removed himself from underneath Dawn's backside and watched awestruck as the small, brown marsupial sprinted eagerly towards the Cranachanian Army, puffs of dust springing from its heels. Suddenly he felt a trickle of hope begin to dribble into the wells of optimism.

Courgette struggled off Hogshead, her brow wrinkling as she fought the queasy feelings of met-lag, and said urgently, 'They've broken in . . .' Hogshead didn't hear a word. He just stared at her.

'We nearly didn't make it,' she continued, her face hardening to anger. 'There's no way back now if we fail.'

'The Thaumatron . . . ?' asked Firkin.

'Almost certainly destroyed.' Her forehead furrowed with emotion. Hogshead swooned. She was angry – very angry. He liked her when she was angry.

'Destroyed . . .' repeated Firkin. 'So it's down to us, then.'

'No,' said Courgette, pointing at the rapidly diminishing tiny brown spot. 'Him!'

The four youngsters looked over the boulder and watched the magical brown bullet speeding straight for the Cranachanians' heart. In a moment the gerund was too far away to see and a period of desperate waiting filled them as it disappeared over a rise. Nothing appeared to be happening.

The black mass of the Cranachanian Army surged relentlessly down the valley walls holding tight formation, brandishing their weapons dangerously.

Still nothing happened.

The Army of Rhyngill marched nervously forward.

Suddenly they stopped. Something was happening to the well-drilled Cranachanian onslaught. Curiously, the ranks were breaking up. Discipline was falling apart. Straight lines of troops began to wriggle. Rectangular fields of armoured personnel squirmed. Random patterns came and went. Order rapidly became a thing of the past. Shouts of terror and surprise rang out from amongst the growing military chaos. The gerund dashed between the legs of the Cranachanian Army, a small brown blur, turning this way and that, riding a bow-wave of surprise, leaving a wake of gerundive magic and with it a trail of furious pandemonium. It chuckled and chirruped gleefully, running through the army, dishing out disorder, creating chaos and releasing masses of entropy in a frenzy of destruction. A whole army! Its first whole army!

In its wake strange, unearthly things began to happen. It took a moment or two to take effect and no one linked the innocently speeding brown marsupial to the cataclysmic wave of chaos that followed. Scabbards twitched and squirmed as the swords within were infused with the gerundive magic. Knives began to move in knifely wicked ways, daggers wriggled wildly with the urge to dag and collections of arrows began to quiver. The inanimate became animate.

Order broke down as the Cranachanian weapons, so lovingly sharpened, turned on the soldiers. Other objects leapt into action as the magic snatched and caught hold of the verbal roots of their very being, shaking them unmercifully to life. Soldiers' shins received repeated poundings as their boots succumbed to the gerundive flux. The webbing belts that held the soldiers' weapons turned from full olive to a shiny sticky sheen of silver, each complete with its own resident spider. Waves of shock careered through the ranks as six-foot pikes metamorphosed, before their bearers very eyes, into the thirty-three-pound aquatic equivalent, snapping and squirming in frenzied anger. Gauntlets were no protection against the jaws and teeth of an angry pike. Hysteria blossomed as the buglers' horns turned from innocent brass instruments into sharply pointed keratin spikes the like of which any self-respecting artillery-rhino would be proud to have at the end of its snout. The horns, as if perched atop invisible pachyderms, bucked and thrusted, charging the Cranachanian Army, herding them, collecting any strays. Suddenly the flags, held so proudly aloft, turned from highly decorated expanses of cloth fluttering gloriously in the breeze into rectangular lumps of solid stone. Flagstones. The flag-bearers screamed, hardly audible above the raucous cacophony, leaping sideways to avoid the plummeting stoneware.

The youngsters watched the scene unfold in absolute amazement as the gerund single-pawedly turned the entire Cranachanian Army into a gibbering mass of sobbing, spluttering madmen. Dashing wildly about as their weapons, up till now regarded as inanimate friends, turned into livid, living adversaries; dodging pike, horns and repeatedly plummeting pavements.

Their amazement was nothing compared to that of the Rhyngillian Army. They stood rooted to the spot, totally bewildered by the spectacle before their eyes. The Cranachanians, herded by the horns, bumbled about in utter confusion, coalescing into one lump as the webbing belt of one man contacted that of another. The spiders wasted no time in spinning yards of binding thread, securing the army, preventing their escape.

Across the valley, the Army of Rhyngill stood bewilderedly unsure whether to run or stay. Was this magic on their side? Or would they be next?

In a rare act of intelligence, and probably because he was far enough away so that it wasn't as frightening, King Khardeen spurred his horse into action, surging down the hill into the valley to claim victory. A cry went up as the Rhyngillians saw their leader galloping towards them. They strode forward together.

The gerund ran out from the Cranachanian Army and bolted up the valley wall to the waiting foursome. It hurtled towards them full of the youthful excitement of a labrador puppy in a toilet-roll factory, skidded to a four-legged halt, spun round a few times and leapt into Courgette's lap, panting. She tipped out the contents of the bag and watched as the tiny brown marsupial dived gleefully into the pile of bananas.

King Grimzyn, safe with Khah Nij, Frundle and Gudgeon behind a large boulder, shook with rage as he watched his unbeatably superior fighting force writhing in a heap on the ground, guarded by flying horns. It was a very large heap. Suddenly four of the horns turned and shot off towards the group of strays cowering behind the boulder.

As the Army of Rhyngill tentatively approached the pile of black-armoured men, writhing helplessly in a sheen of silk webbing they noticed a strange sound. At first they had thought it to be the effect of such an ignominious defeat. The sound of grief-stricken prisoners sobbing with shame. But as they neared the sound became unmistakable. Hysterically uncontrollable laughter. The gerundive flux had finally reached the armour-piercing crossbow bolts, the feathers of which were now wreaking havoc amongst the more sensitive parts of human anatomy.

Commander Lappet scratched his head. The entire Army of Cranachan was helpless. Snapping the suspenders of disbelief in a moment, he amazedly accepted this writhing mass of soldiers as a fact and, still bewildered and highly confused, set about barking orders for their arrest and transport back to their home city.

Somehow, he thought, we've won Cranachan.

The pounding drum-roll of furiously sprinting feet announced that the Cranachan Stealth Troopers had found the door to the Chamber of frogs moments after the last lump of detritus had been rammed home by Phlim. A few tentative shoulder charges rattled against the steel door, followed by a brief mumbled conversation and then the voice of Arathoostra.

'Open the door,' he shouted shakily. 'It'll save a lot of hassle.'

'Never!' shouted Phlim defiantly. 'You'll never get in here.'

'The Thaumatron is gone . . . You don't stand a chance,' came the hoarse threat, the door giving it a harsh, metallic edge.

'There is always a chance!' shouted Practz.

'You always were a foolish optimist,' taunted

Arathoostra. 'Stay there if you wish, but we're coming in . . . and we will crush any resistance.'

Almost before Arathoostra's words had faded, three blows resonated clangorously in the Chamber as the heavy artillery was brought to bear.

Time was running out. Ahhrny's axe chopped and bit deafeningly, while Miolnir and Splatter struck with cracking reports. Incessantly they pounded away. Bulges forming in the door, sections of plaster falling in avalanches around the rattling frame. Behind the five technicians the frogs flopped and surged in the tepid water, curious about the noise, wondering about food. The axes thumped on. Yells of encouragement floated muffled through the rapidly buckling door. It was only a matter of time . . .

It was an incredible sight. Over fifteen thousand troops ready to march. Only on closer examination would it be clear that there were two different uniforms being worn. Two different expressions on their faces. Three thousand grins of relief surrounded the clump of over twelve thousand grimaces of defeat worn by the captured Cranachanians. They stood, still bound but upright, ready for the shameful return journey to the Palace. Before them stood the mounted figures of King Khardeen and the War Lords of Rhyngill, with Brumas as usual at the rear. Khardeen twirled his handlebar moustache with an immense feeling of relief and satisfaction. In front of them slouched the captured heads of the Army of Cranachan. Frundle, Gudgeon and a very upset Khah Nij stood either side of their King, guarded by the hovering, ominous horns and five swordsmen each, just in case.

Khardeen rubbed his hands with glee as he looked forward to the public humiliation of the four Cranachanian leaders before him and the traditional banishment from the kingdom on pain of slow disembowelment. He was also delighted at the thought of having an extra twelve thousand troops to play with. Such a lot of marching up and down could be done with twelve thousand troops . . .

With a flick of his imperious wrist King Khardeen, Ruler of the twin Kingdoms of Rhyngill *and* Cranachan gave the order to march to *his* Imperial Palace Fortress, in his newly acquired Kingdom.

In the small corridor outside the frog chamber, Captain Barak raised his hand and stopped the percussive barrage on the steel door. The three warriors had made progress, but it was far too slow for the eagerly impatient Khah Nij. Everyone wanted to get in there – now!

As the dust settled Barak barked a few orders and a small wiry man ran towards the door. He knelt, adjusted his cap, fumbled in the pack on his shoulder and slowly withdrew what looked like a handful of red-brown mud. He moulded and massaged it carefully in his hands, each movement made with the utmost care, gently, cautiously, and above all never too quickly. The little man broke off a small section of the clay and worked it into one of the joints of the door, then repeated this all around the frame. Rummaging once again in his pack, he extracted a coil of thin wire and cut it into several lengths. These he pushed gently, but firmly, into the clay, leading them off around the corner. There he pulled a box out of another pack, connected the wires to the terminals, raised the plunger and declared himself ready to detonate the clay explosive.

Inside the chamber, the sudden silence was almost worse than the deafening, skull-crushing cacophony. In the quiet they could think. They could get scared. Behind them lurked the deadly amphibian force which sooner or later was bound to get hungry. Before them Cranachanians. Trapped. Caught between a frog and a hard place.

Practz searched for an answer.

'Four . . .'

The Stealth Troopers backed away from the door.

'Three . . .'

Was this it? thought Practz, would they actually succeed?

'Two . . .'

Panic at the thought of losing rose, swirling inside him.

'One . . .'

The end of the countdown, the end of the future. Time had finally run out . . .

Dybnah, the thin explosives expert, shoved the plunger home.

The sudden increase in pressure was astounding. Practz's ears felt as though they had been crushed. Then the sound hit. Two pounds of clay explosive detonated in an enclosed space. A thundering, tumultuous roar erupted into being and raced through the Chamber yelling into everyone's ears, shouting with cupped hands clamped to the side of their heads. The steel door flew in, spinning end over end, crashing into the far wall, bouncing off and coming to rest with an immense splash. Fragments of stone shrapnel blasted from the walls like an angry hailstorm, colliding with anything in their path. A wave of masonry shards and plaster dust followed in a dense choking blanket, damping the sound, covering everything like a carpet of grey frost.

Practz coughed violently, gasping for breath as he peered through the swirling clouds. The wall gaped open as if in welcome. There was nothing to stop them now.

Silence fell under a blanket of rubble.

Suddenly, still watching from the rim of the valley, the youngsters noticed something happening. It started in the very heart of the crowd of men that was the Army of Cranachan. There was a vague blurriness about the centre of the group, as if a splash of moisture had landed on a water-colour painting. Or as if millions of tiny somethings were struggling to escape from a single central point, flexing their temporal legs and beating their periodic wings as they took to the air. A nebulous dark-grey cloud shimmered and buzzed as it spread, expanding like a spherical genie from the tiny spout of a recently rubbed invisible lamp. But this was expanding in four dimensions, stretching from the closest proximity of the immediate to the far pale horizon of the infinite future. Close to the epicentre little happened, but as the sphere grew, enclosing greater and greater volumes, differences could be glimpsed through the droning haze, alterations between inside and outside. Corrections between before and after. Little things like the amount of stubble on a soldier's chin, or the sharpness of his sword were gradually superseded by more important changes like the actual positioning of people or the height of weeds on the valley floor. Hogshead watched in a state of sheer bafflement as a large thistle that had been trampled by the approaching army was suddenly surrounded by the dark-grey curtain, covered in darkly droning particles and repaired in an instant to spring once again into its full spiky glory, repaired by the shimmering edge of the growing sphere of time flies as they swarmed forward from the centre, blurred and ran past in a flurry of thrashing wings.

With a yell he suddenly realised what was happening. They had won! They had succeeded. They were witnessing time rewriting itself before their very eyes, altering the ages, fixing the future, eradicating the errors of the eras to come. They were watching from a present in which the Cranachanians had won, but there, beyond the thrashing wings of time flies, approaching like a buzzing wall of gunmetal-grey heat haze was another present where the Army of Rhyngill were the victors. A present they had created. A present that was unwrapping itself before their awestruck gazes. Through the shimmering wall of the time-event horizon they could see objects being rearranged, shifted by the time flies. Placed where they should be *now* according to the rules of cause and effect in *this* present. Continuity errors were being eradicated with the correcting fluid and clipboard of inevitability. It surged unstoppably up the valley towards them. Erasing, altering, correcting.

A terrifying thought, like a bolt of naked lightning strutting on the great cosmic catwalk, flashed into Hogshead's mind. Suddenly he realised that he was one of a small group of the most serious continuity errors within five hundred miles. He, like Courgette, Firkin and Dawn, was a temporal anomaly that would have to be replaced. Re-positioned. Relocated. Removed.

When the outer edge of that swarming wall of humming translucence hit them what would happen? Where would they go?

In a few short minutes he would find out.

Practz rubbed his neck as he picked himself out of the rubble. Small rocks and fragments of stone still fell from the remains of the doorway, motes of debris floating in the air. His throat was coated with dust. He tried to swallow, gagged and coughed violently, the sound eerily muffled in the aftermath of the explosion, vying for attention above a nagging buzzing in his ears, like a narked hornet in a cathedral organ-pipe.

There was hardly a sound, apart from the distant irritated humming of . . . of what? Or was it his ears? Behind him the water lapped thickly against the sides of the pool. He looked around for the source of the sound. Then looked again – a double-take as something caught his eyes. He could have sworn he just saw what looked like a shimmering monolayer of dark-grey insects flash across the pool and disappear through the far wall behind him. A groan sounded from a pile of rubble over to his left. He struggled towards it trying to fathom what had happened. He remembered the explosion. He recalled the troops, the threats, the fear.

He dug absently at the groaning heap of rocks and revealed Phlim, coughing and spluttering.

Where were the attacking troops?

The silence was almost as scary as the unbearable noise had been. Was this a game they were playing? A ploy to get in? To take them by surprise?

Phlim scratched his head, raising a halo of dust, looking around him in stunned silence.

Suddenly Practz stood and ran to where the door should have been and peered through the rough hole into the corridor. Wreckage, rubble and dust filled the passage, the results of two pounds of clay explosive. There were no bodies. No waiting troops ready in ambush. No sign in fact that anyone had been there at all. Except the footprints . . .

Phlim helped the technicians to their feet and staggered towards the jagged ex-doorway. He tried to take in the scene. Undoubtedly the attackers were nowhere around, unless they were extremely adept at disguising themselves as fragments of rubble and twisted door. Suddenly Phlim, too, saw the footprints. With surprise he took a sharp breath and collapsed in another fit of coughing. Through streaming eyes he stared at the mysterious patterns in the carpet of dust.

Twenty-four pairs of marks left by army issue footwear could be seen swarming towards the site of the explosion. They had stirred up the dust, heel crossing toe, a jagged line of disturbed dust crossing the prints like a scar where a misplaced foot had kicked a rock, gouging the dust to the stone floor. They had been in a hurry, rushing to surge through the hole in the wall and claim their prize.

But they never got there.

About two feet away from victory the footprints abruptly stopped. It looked as if the swarming band of troopers had just vanished.

Practz turned and looked at the wall behind him. The shimmering, he thought, could it be?

He daren't hope. It might be a bluff. He needed confirmation. The certain reassurance of cold hard facts.

In a flash he knew where to get that assurance. Forgetting his aching neck and parched, dust-filled throat he ran into the rubble-strewn corridor, turned left, ran out of the dust, plunging wildly on, flailing madly rather than running. He had to know the truth. Screeching to a halt outside a large oak door, his heart pounding, he slid back the small observation panel. Sick with apprehension he peered inside and almost collapsed with sheer overwhelming relief.

At the far end of the padded room, contained in a familiar dirty grey strait-jacket sat the wild, staring figure of Arathoostra, his icy eyes flashing cold fronts of annoyance at the face in the door.

'What you starin' at?' snapped the bearded figure. 'Where's my tea?'

Practz yelled with unfettered delight and relief and collapsed beneath a wave of sheer nervous exhaustion.

The small group of four youngsters stood on the edge of the valley and stared up at the droning wall of microscopic time flies as they hurtled towards them. The thrumming balloon continued to expand from the epicentre somewhere beneath the scrum of Cranachanians, filling the space between the ground and the sky, spreading to the far geographic and temporal horizons. There was no avoiding it, no escaping, no sidestepping its inexorable path. As if someone had knifed him in the heart with a four-foot icicle, Hogshead suddenly realised something.

If this was doing what he thought it was, then . . .

'Isn't it pretty?' said Dawn as the dark-grey sphere expanded.

'But what is it?' asked Firkin.

'The future . . .' said Hogshead. The other three stared at him. '. . . and it's about to start . . . now!'

As Hogshead spoke, tiny black specks began to appear on his shoulders and back, as if someone with black dandruff was headbanging next to him. He grabbed Courgette's hand as the time flies settled on all of them, clinging to their clothes, beating their wings with unshakable determination. Dawn swatted at them to no avail as in a moment she left the ground, lent wing by countless time flies. Hogshead wished he knew where Courgette would soon be. In the coming present would they meet again? Would she remember him? Would they have met in the first place? The logic of it tumbled around in his mind like a week's washing. The thrumming enveloped them, shimmering and flowing forward with unavoidable certainty. Hogshead gripped Courgette's wrist with his other hand as she was pulled away, tugged with the force of a thousand feathered tentacles, hauled upward with the weight of helium. It was irresistible, impossible to deny, as immutable as time itself. Courgette opened her mouth and screamed. No sound came out. In this timeless barrier between alternative futures frequency was meaningless.

Hogshead's fingers tightened around Courgette's leather bracelet as he struggled to pull her to him, fighting hopelessly against the combined might of the pre-ordained, the steely arms of utter certainty and the unavoidable, inexorable mattress of absolute inevitability.

The bracelet slipped over her wrist. Reflexively she caught at it, wrapping her fingers tight around it, realising the small leather ring was all that held them now. It cut into her fingers. She concentrated on the pain, aching for some reality. Hogshead struggled and flailed. The leather started to fray as it began to lose its battle against the forces of inevitability. Courgette stared into Hogshead's longing eyes, glistening in the turmoil. Their bodies tumbling now, held only by the disintegrating ring.

Suddenly, as it had to, it gave way, snapping in two, separating the two friends. There was no malice, no evil satisfaction at the sundering of the two. It was just something that had to happen.

In the thick, tumultuous thrumming Hogshead screamed an unheard scream as he watched Courgette spin away, carried on the wings of time, vanishing before his eyes, disappearing to who knows where?

In a small room, high in the roof of the west wing of Castell Rhyngill a small stone stopped spinning gently four feet above the table as the grey droning wall of the time-event horizon passed through. It dented the oak table that it landed on quite badly, but it would be a long time before anyone noticed.

High in a tall tower of the Imperial Palace Fortress of Cranachan a thin face sporting a black leather eyepatch peered out of the window waiting for the triumphant return of his King Grimzyn after the war with Rhyngill. He was certain it would be a victory. His spies in Rhyngill had kept him independently informed of all their troop movements. There was no way they could win. Or so he thought.

He watched intently, eager to be the first to know, straining his eye for a clue, a sign, anything.

A dark-grey cloud rose on the far horizon.

That's it! he thought. A cloud of dust kicked up by the troops returning. Or a pall of smoke rising from the burning bodies.

Fisk didn't notice the sudden shift in many of the clouds. Or the speed with which the 'cloud of dust' moved. He stared intently at ground level.

The buzzing wall raced towards the Palace.

He turned from the window, grabbed his telescope and began setting it up.

The sky shimmered, unnoticed by the Chief of Internal Affairs as he feverishly struggled with the tripod for the telescope. He peered through the eyepiece. He adjusted the focus ring and out of the fuzzy blur people swam into view. He saw the King, Frundle, Gudgeon and Khah Nij marching back towards him and . . .

Marching? Why weren't they astride their horses? Why the glum faces?

The grey translucent wall thrummed inexorably on. Correcting, altering and repositioning as it went.

He shifted the telescope slightly.

Two faces swam into focus.

Khardeen! Bateleur! Grinning victoriously!

Fisk swallowed hard and looked away. Shocked. He'd seen enough. Turning and running wildly, he dashed in a dizzying whirl down the spiral staircase in the tower as the shimmering time-event horizon buzzed through the Palace of Cranachan. Amending, revising. It washed through him as he raced into his quarters, feverishly flung a few of his most important belongings into a large bag, dashed to a large tapestry on the wall and disappeared into a small passage behind it. If he had forgotten anything he could always come back at a later date.

In a flash, completely unbeknown to him, his future had been reshaped almost beyond recognition. There would be no time spent in Rhyngill. No escape to Losa Llamas. No Frogs! All that power that wouldn't be his! Had he known, he would have been spitting with frustrated fury. Right now there were more important things to think about. They could be divided into two main categories. One: survival; and two: how in Cranachan could a poxy band of ill-disciplined reprobates calling themselves the Army of Rhyngill defeat the might of Cranachan?

In the fullness of time, he vowed, he would find out.

Whether he would believe the answer was a different matter.

In the meantime, as he locked the door behind him and crept away, he was immensely grateful that he, and only he, knew of the miles and miles of secret passages running through the Palace. Here he could wait, for years if he had to, eavesdropping at doors, spying on secret meetings, watching and listening for another chance at power.

He'd be waiting.

It was as if they were lying on the immortal leather couch of some cosmic chiropractor after a heavy session working off the chronological stresses and vertebral strains accumulated by the backbone of fate. There had been a moment of extreme pressure as the opposing thumbs of inevitability and the unavoidable fingers of karma had positioned themselves either side of fate's lumbar region; a whirlpool of bright lights as the pollexive digits had dug into the malleable flesh of fate and pushed towards the thoracic vertebrae of the immediate future; a ripple of acute rearrangement as the vertebral discs of destiny had slipped back into place, and now the feeling of utter relief and relaxation. The errors had been eradicated, the mistakes merely a thing of a distant past, the sequential solecisms in the language of time were gone. Everything was as it should be. A feeling of calm. Almost like floating for ever on a flat, tepid sea . . .

It didn't last that long.

Being in the right place at the right time means that all the laws of non-thaumaturgical physics apply. That includes gravity.

High in a valley in the Talpa Mountains in the year OG 1038 gravity was most definitely alive and kicking and liked everything to be where it should be. On the ground or, failing that, at least on its way there. Fast.

So, when three youngsters appeared quivering four feet above the ground, hovering in the instant before they were spotted by gravity's beady eye, they didn't stay there long.

Firkin, Hogshead and Dawn hit the ground at almost the same time raising a cloud of grey dust and a squeak of surprise from a small resident rodent.

A million-lumen flash of reality blasted into the darkness of their somnolent world. A loud and painfully sharp jolt of entirely unwelcome normality. One receives a very rude awakening when the fragile gentleness of blissful relaxation is shattered into a hundred thousand highly surprised fragments by a large continent in the small of one's back.

After the frenzied activity of the recent times it would have been a blessed relief to be able to lie immobile on solid ground and listen to the merry chirping of the birds, the rustling of leaves and recover from what would probably turn out to be three of the worst cases of met-lag in history. But . . .

No birds were chirping.

No leaves were rustling.

A waft of acrid smoke curled up from a smouldering chunk of wood and blew up Firkin's nose, making him cough. Another pale ghostly finger tickled the inside of Dawn's nose. She sneezed. Hogshead sat up and stared around him through a migraine of swirling confusion as met-lag began to set in. With mounting confusion and acute nausea he stared at their new surroundings.

The horizon wriggled with delight.

Black, naked trees shook long twiggy fingers.

The mountains he used to play in waved in psychedelic welcome.

Another veil of blue wood-smoke trundled across Hogshead's thrashing and rapidly unripening cornfield of view.

Through the kaleidoscopically undulating whirpool of optical nonsense a smouldering torch of charred fact plunged into Hogshead's swirling brain.

The numerous piles of smoking ash that surrounded them was all that remained of Middin.

If there is a place where the ashpans from the fires of Hell are emptied then it would probably look not too dissimilar to the way Middin looked right now.

Suddenly, it was too much for Hogshead. He turned pale-green as the wheels of sentience skipped on the points of disorder, the bogies of understanding leapt from the rails of cognisance smashing through sleepers and sending auric sparks in all directions. The engine of imagination toppled down the embankment of nonsense, pulling tender and carriages with it, blasting plumes of steam in explosive clouds as the pistons of perception ruptured . . .

In short, Hogshead's brain crashed.

A MIDSUMMER NIGHT'S GENE

Andrew Harman

At SPLICE OF LIFE PATENTABLE BIOSCIENCES LTD the excitement of discovery is rising by the minute. Professor Crickson has seen the future – and it tastes like chicken. The Prof can unite vegetarians and carnivores by implanting the genes of said flavour into those of corn. Chicken Fed Corn. It's bound to outstrip his previous culinary inventions: Boil-in-the-Bag Gazpacho, Microwavable Steak Tartare and Oven-Bake Sushi.

But someone – or something – has different ideas. As well as problems with a chicken rustler, the Professor finds vital pieces of equipment vanishing from his lab, and essential orders never arriving. Industrial espionage?

If only it were that simple.

When the local Chief Inspector's daughter is abducted by apair of very strange creatures, and mysterious strands of DNA begin appearing in the amniotic tanks, it would seem that the Truth has become mightily bored hanging around Out There . . .

Orbit titles available by post:

[ ] The Sorcerer's Appendix	Andrew Harman	£4.99
[ ] The Tome Tunnel	Andrew Harman	£4.99
[ ] 101 Damnations	Andrew Harman	£4.99
[ ] Fahrenheit 666	Andrew Harman	£4.99
[ ] The Scrying Game	Andrew Harman	£5.99
[ ] The Deity Dozen	Andrew Harman	£4.99
[ ] A Midsummer Night's Gene	Andrew Harman	£4.99

The prices shown above are correct at time of going to press, however the publishers reserve the right to increase prices on covers from those previously advertised, without further notice.

ORBIT

ORBIT BOOKS
Cash Sales Department, P.O. Box 11, Falmouth, Cornwall, TR10 9EN
Tel: +44 (0) 1326 372400, Fax: +44 (0) 1326 374888
Email: books@barni.avel.co.uk.

POST and PACKING:
Payments can be made as follows: cheque. postal order (payable to Orbit Books) or by credit cards. Do not send cash or currency.

U.K. Orders under £10	£1.50
U.K. Orders over £10	FREE OF CHARGE
E.E.C. & Overseas	25% of order value

Name (Block Letters) _____

Address _____

_____

Post/zip code: _____

[ ] Please keep me in touch with future Orbit publications

[ ] I enclose my remittance £ _____

[ ] I wish to pay by Visa/Access/Mastercard/Eurocard

| | | | | | | | | | | | | | | | |

Card Expiry Date

_____